When Walls Fall Down

When Walls Fall Down

An Adventure In Romance

C.F. McDaeid

Copyright © 2018 C.F. McDaeid

All rights reserved.

ISBN-13: 978-1-7905-7363-9

DEDICATION

To my wife for her unwavering support of myself. To B. for her willingness to read my words. To "The All Day & Night Ladies" of Berlin for taking the time to explain how things really are, and especially, to all of the good people of Ireland—for there are no better.

Chapter 1

Ireland

My name is Ciarán McKay, and like most Irishmen, I have a story to tell. I reside in the small village of Ballyamhras, just north of Dublin on the east coast of Ireland, and I have lived there all of my life. I should also tell you that I am not your typical Irishman. I am a wee bit above average in height, my hair is almost black, and I have brown eyes so dark, when I stare, it makes people squirm.

I suppose if there is any need to compare, my ma, Brighid, always said that I look a lot like Ernest Hemingway back in 1923. It was the year he lived in Paris with his wife Hadley, and before he grew that horrid mustache. I trust my ma would have known, since she was something of a writer herself and a big fan.

My ma and I'd been very close. She was a devoted, loving mother, and always taught by example. Sadly, I lost her to breast cancer in the fortieth year of her life. My da died the year before when I was at university, his lifeless body found face down between two small shops on the high street. The night had been heavy with rain and a shopkeeper arriving to open for the day, caught sight of his shoeless foot sticking out past the corner of the building. Rumor had it he'd literally drank himself to death. It was supposed that he'd stumbled into the alcove, and succumbing to his intoxication, died during the ensuing downpour. He and I never had much of a relationship. I kept it to myself that I was somewhat relieved that he no longer suffered from whatever had driven his anguish.

I returned home in 1988 and married my long time love, Isleen Byrne. Shortly after that, the Education Regents granted me a position as a teacher in our small school. At twenty-two years of age, I became the youngest of the educators. They'd been desperate for someone with the skills and they welcomed me with open arms.

Life just couldn't leave it alone, though. Isleen and I hadn't even been married a year when she was taken from me late in August. We'd been very much in love and courted for a long time before finally deciding to wed. She had a way about her that captivated me. There was a chemistry there like none I ever felt before. The only ginger haired lass in our village, she wore it in the style closely resembling that of Sinead O'Connor. She just went crazy one day in an act of protest and buzzed it to within a fingers thickness of her scalp.

Her mother had a fit, and the other womenfolk harassed her about it—but in a good-natured way. Isleen would raise her voice to them in a matter-of-fact fashion, "Don't like it long! Tis too much trouble and there just isn't time enough in a day." She was a non-conformist and terribly stubborn. Even so, she still had quite a following among the local lasses because of her charismatic manner.

I can still see her face with her alert green eyes and her cheeks littered with freckles. If she caught me staring, she would tease with that typical, 'WHAT?' look upon her face. Then pinching the end of my nose, she would run away in a manner that begged me to give chase. That was always the prelude to lovemaking. It could happen anywhere as long as we were alone—on the beach at night, in the long grass at the north end of town, or somewhere more private; like the abandoned lighthouse.

When the mood hit us, we would make that short walk north to the red and white tower. The beach ended there and the coastline rose up to a small cliff that projected out into the Irish Sea. Making our way to the top, we would sit out on the gallery that ran around the large glass lens. It gave us a spectacular view of the sun as it set behind the western hills, enhancing our romantic mood. When the brilliant, orange orb disappeared from sight, we would move around to the seaside of the tower. No one could see us there, and we would make love while the waves frolicked far below.

I proposed to her one evening as we stood upon a small cluster of gigantic stones amassed at the ocean's edge. It was the perfect spot for such activity, a favorite among lovers, and the lovelorn alike. The beach narrowed to nearly nothing at that point, fanning out again on the opposite side as it stretched north to the lighthouse. One could step out onto their broad, flat tops from the pavement that lay sandwiched between the lighthouse road and the short, grassy slope that curved down to the sand.

So, getting down on one knee and taking her hand, I looked up into her face. Her green eyes flashed and her lower lip quivered. After I asked, she got down on her knees and embraced me. Then came a slow, soft kiss—the kind that cements itself into your memory. Pulling back, she said in a level tone, "Why of course I'll marry you Ciarán McKay. What you thinking… I'm daft?" She giggled, but almost immediately her face went slack and her eyes brimmed with tears.

"Oh Ciarán…" she said, her voice quaking with emotion. The tears overflowed down her cheeks, magnifying her freckles and spotting her blouse.

"What is it, darling? Aren't you happy?"

"Of course I'm happy, you oaf. I just can't hardly believe it."

"Well, I…"

She didn't give me a chance to finish as she clamped my head in her hands. Her eyes grew large with mock seriousness and more tears spilled from their corners as she bellowed playfully into my face, "What took you so feking long, boy?" At that moment, a large wave crashed against the boulders, nearly soaking us to the skin. I remember we jumped up laughing. Standing fast, we held each other for the longest time, enveloped by the oceans salty breath.

There'd been a small ceremony at the village chapel, followed by a reception at Lafferty's pub. Everybody came, and the stout flowed. We agreed that there'd been more merriment that evening than ever before in the history of Ballyamhras. It left us totally exhausted, but feeling extremely optimistic about our future. The joy of that day lasted for weeks.

With the help of her folks, we purchased a small broken down cottage whose garden bordered the field of long grass where we made love for the first time. For a while, we were happy. Then in the midst of planning for our first child, she just up and died.

I had been at the school for the entire day. Upon arriving home, I discovered her lying face down on the floor. I rolled her over and shook her, calling out her name. Her lovely skin had gone grey, and she felt as cold as the sea. I called for help, but I knew she was gone. I sat there on the floor, rocking back and forth, sobbing, my arms wrapped around her limp body.

That's the way they found us when Captain Murphy of the fire brigade arrived, along with the ambulance service. They say that it took nearly twenty minutes of coaxing to convince me to hand her over. After that day, my whole world fell apart.

The loss of Isleen cast me into a bottomless pit of despair. She'd been a true friend and love. The grief was unbearable. The autopsy declared 'Ventricular Fibrillation due to Long QT Syndrome'. Her heart had gotten out of rhythm and she left this world lying alone on the cold, flat stones of our kitchen floor.

The school offered me time to mourn, but after careful pondering, I declined. My career had just gotten started. I didn't want to lose that too. So, putting on my happiest of faces, I dove into my work.

I soon became somewhat of a favorite among the young scholars there, much to the dismay of my older colleagues. A regular school day was always full of scrutiny along with a constant barrage of good-natured, but stern advice.

"Oh Ciarán, don't you get too close to the lads and lassies." or "Oh! You're a brave soul now aren't you McKay for putting yourself in the middle of that rabble!"

I would smile and nod, projecting a willingness to give their advice a wee bit of consideration. But most of the time, I let it roll off without a second thought. There were those who deserved my attention—and those who didn't. The former were few and far between. I strived to make that short list longer though, always hoping to add another special somebody. Anyone that could lift me up and free me from the dark abyss of grief.

***

Standing in the open doorway of the Secondary Ed. building with McDonough, the math teacher, we greeted students arriving for the first day of the 1989 school year. I addressed each one by name, getting the same in return and sometimes exchanging playful banter—much to McDonough's dismay. We were supposed to be counting heads, but I turned it into a jovial affair. The old fellow just wasn't up for it. So, as I tried to enjoy the atypical sunny morning, I had to suffer through the usual barrage of so called good advice.

"Keep your distance lad. Better to spare the spoiling, and rod the child with this lot," he said.

He seemed proud of his statement, grinning like he'd solved all the world's problems. I didn't want to appear disrespectful, so I turned away before rolling my eyes. I tried hard to hide my distain and ignore his absurd warning disguised as humor. I failed, a chuckle slipping from my lips.

Turning back to apologize for my impudence, he smiled and winked. I took this as a sign he thought I was amused at his wit. Better to let him harbor that thought than to reveal that it was his asininities that brought my mirth. People like McDonough, constantly tried to instill the belief that getting friendly with our scholars, or exposing human frailty, would cause a loss of respect. Bollocks is what I thought.

I expended a good part of my energy trying to create trust. Something I would rather do than struggle to bolster my status as an authority figure. I've always been of the opinion that creating any kind of wall between human beings would only bring an unsettling discontent. It seemed to me that young people are always under a constant barrage of scrutiny. So, they were inadvertently conditioned to project only what they wanted adults to see.

The constant underestimation of people their age has led them to believe that they can't do anything right. So, why bother? I believed as teachers, we needed to communicate that we valued what was important to them. It was the only way we would ever gain their trust.

Longing to be away from McDonough, I looked at my wristwatch to see how much more I would have to endure. At that moment, a lass with bright blonde hair came dashing in through the open front doors. She slipped on the dew damp marble, and the sound her backside made slamming into the hard surface made me wince. McDonough just snickered and walked away as I stepped over to help her up. I stuck out my hand, and she looked up into my face. Our eyes met, and I felt taken aback as 'This one's not Irish,' rolled through my head.

The natural, bright blond hair and the high cheekbones said it all. She had hooded eyes and a case of complete Heterochromia—one light blue, the other brown. I caught myself staring. With a flush of embarrassment, I refocused. She took my hand and I expressed my typical, diplomatic demeanor as I helped her to her feet.

"Are you ok, lass?"

"Ja," she said, looking hard into my face.

I had no idea what she saw there, but whatever it was, it caused her to lose the hold she had on her notebooks. Cascading to the floor, they lay scattered around our feet. We both bent to pick them up and promptly bumped heads. I stood up instantly, rubbing at my crown. She was now giggling and doing the same with one hand while trying to keep a grip on the largest of her binders with the other.

An old matchmaker myth came to mind, reminding me that, 'If a lad and lass bump heads, it's a sure sign that they'll become an item.' Not being much on superstition, I dismissed it as nonsense. She crouched to pick up the remaining books and glancing up at me, I could see she was flustered. Not knowing what to say, I grinned and transferred my clipboard to the other armpit.

Her focus seemed to be on my eyes and sporadic glances slowed her task. I found the situation annoying and wished she would hurry. She finally stood with the books balanced on her left arm and then had to go and heightened my annoyance by imparting that all too familiar phrase, "You have such very dark eyes."

Trying not to sound too sarcastic, I said, "I've noticed."

She then surprised me by sticking out her right hand and saying, "Anna Furtak, happy to meet you."

I got the feeling that she had practiced that line many times over, for it seemed well rehearsed. I imagined her practicing it in front of a mirror, checking her body language and modifying her facial expressions. Her use of the English language was good. But not so good that she could conceal her German accent.

This confirmed my belief that she came as a stranger to our village. I knew just about everyone in Ballyamhras, and it had been several years since I'd heard an accent like that within the parish boundaries. I took her hand and gave it a slight shake.

"I'm Mr. McKay, but you may call me Ciarán—if you wish."

"Karen?" She questioned. I flushed and jerked my hand free.

"NO! Ciarán! 'Kee-a-ran'… C-I-A-R-A-N."

Her face lit up, and she said, "Oh! Ciarán! Okay…"

"Brilliant! Now excuse me, I have to be off," I said with finality as the last of the students passed through the door.

I moved to go around her, but she wasn't going to let me. Sidestepping, she blocked my path. My annoyance changed to disbelief. She'd caught me off guard. It wasn't so much the boldness of her action, but the familiarity of it. Isleen had been quite fond of doing the same.

My mind flooded with memories and I fought to keep myself in the present.

"So… you are an instructor here?" she asked, sounding skeptical.

Her words brought me around and I said, "I am, why do you ask?"

"You don't look as if you're old enough. You look no older than I. Teachers are usually old. Are you having a joke with me or… are you actually an instructor?"

"I am! So, if you would be so kind?"

"Okay, I will take you on your word—for now."

She had me off balance. I found myself fighting to gain my feet, so to speak. Then she smiled this extraordinary smile. The effect it had on me was like one of those moments when you attempt to open a spring-loaded shade at the window. The lanyard accidently slips from your fingers, followed by that rattling snap as it hits the top. The light floods the room and everything becomes so clear. Despite my irritation—I liked her. Suppressing my reaction, I decided to sort my feelings later when alone.

I desperately searched for something to say, fearful I would stutter or my words would come out all mixed up. I couldn't pull my eyes from her face, and as her smile began to fade, I found myself wishing it wouldn't.

She moved to cradle her notebooks with both arms, hugging them to her chest. She rested her chin on their bindings and it seemed an action projected to finalize the moment. I gave her a fleeting smile and pushed my way past.

I had a schedule to keep, so there was no real time for socializing. My efforts to get away became moot though—because she followed.

I tried to walk faster, but she moved up beside me, trying to keep pace. Then as if our velocity served as a metronome, she started talking at about the same speed in which we were moving. I couldn't keep track of what she was telling me, so I stared straight ahead, my eyes fixed on my classroom door at the end of the hallway.

Reaching my destination, I stopped to bid her good day. That's where I caught the part about her being a Polish girl from Germany, who'd chosen to come to Ballyamhras as a foreign exchange student. I wanted to end the moment on a positive note, so I teased, requesting that she confirm whether she was Polish or German.

I studied her face and noticed the confusion there. Something had gotten lost in translation. Then that lovely smile came again as she grasped the humor. This was followed by what could only be described as a 'husky' laugh; not at all what one would expect from a person of her size. I cocked my head and looked her up and down. My inspection must have caused her embarrassment and she turned a lovely shade of red as she cast her eyes toward the floor.

It was an awkward moment. That few seconds when time stands still and you find yourself searching for some way to start it up again. I just wished her a good day and walked into my room. I had a class to teach and was already tardy.

It was a common thing for people in my village to host students from the continent. Being as close to Dublin as we were, we got the spill over, like many little towns around the outskirts. High school foreign exchange was big money, and ESE coordinators were a desperate lot.

Who now in Ballyahmras had opened their home to a young rover?

As I looked back at her through the small window in the door, I watched her place a pair of black plastic framed glasses upon her nose. Upon completing the task, she turned away and walking back down the corridor, she checked room numbers and peeked in windows.

Why such dowdy eyewear? Why did it seem like she was doing everything possible to conceal her femininity?

The way she wore her hair in a short pixie cut, no jewelry or makeup and lots of loose fitting 'boy-clothes' told me there was a story there. Making a mental note, I decided I would attempt to clear up the mystery the next time she cornered me for a chat.

***

After that day, it became known to me that she was a few months shy of her eighteenth birthday. More like seventeen going on thirty. She'd also raised quite a fuss about having to wear a school uniform, and suffered several scoldings for going barefoot during school hours. I soon discovered, by eavesdropping on my colleagues, she was allowed her transgressions only because they were all impressed with her higher than average IQ. I suspected she had charmed them.

I started seeing her just about everywhere I went. In the beginning, she spent a lot of time with her new mates. I would see them chasing each other up and down the high street, peeking in shop windows and being loud about things that should have best been kept personal.

On the warm days, I'd find them gathering at the large fountain in the square. I would stroll past on my way home, slowing my pace in order to overhear their conversations. Most often, her classmates would be overwhelming her with questions about life outside of small town Ireland. She became quite a sensation. Something fresh and different in a place where nothing much ever changed.

They could be seen sitting on the short granite wall around the pools edge, gossiping. Sometimes, without regard for their school uniform, they would wade and play in the knee-deep basin. They laughed, screamed, and chided each other, behaving like the child that they were fast leaving behind.

The first few times Anna saw me passing, she would jump up and move parallel with me, walking somewhat sideways as she fiddled with her school issued tie. Then putting on a Cheshire Cat grin, she would 'make eyes' at me. I itched for her to say something, anything at all. I would call out a "Hallo!" to break the moment, but she chose to remain mute.

Sometimes the others would tease her. On several occasions, I caught the word 'crush' being passed, but decided if it concerned me, it was nothing but a fleeting adolescent infatuation.

One day, on my way home late from a meeting, I passed Anna and the usual group of girls, at the fountain. She sat in the water fully clothed in her school uniform. When she noticed me, she stood up, the water running off her pleated skirt in torrents. She stepped out over the short wall and stood with her hands on her hips, rivulets forming a pool around her bare feet. Giving me that captivating smile, she cocked her head as if she was expecting me to make the first move. I have to admit, it made me nervous.

"Oh Mr. McKaaay! Look who's here!" Rachel Doyle meowed.

Shelagh Riley was right behind her with, "Ciarán! Oh Ciarán! Tis I, Anna, come to me! I want to kiss you all over."

Then making kissing noises, she jumped up and went to Anna, pretending to do just that. They tussled playfully as I continued on my way.

I thought it best to ignore them and make them think I was accepting their harassment as harmless banter. However, Anna's eyes haunted me. They weren't like the other girls. There was something there I couldn't sort. It left me perplexed.

After about a month, the newness wore off. I started to see her alone and the fountain was exchanged for our prominent set of boulders at the seashore.

She'd be sitting out there, looking east toward England, and I would have given a few punts to know what was going on inside her head.

I would call out to her as I passed. The first time I did, she jumped up, waving her hand like a mad woman. But as I continued on my task-induced trek, the hand would drop, leaving her to cross her arms in front of her chest as if rejected. Turning away, she would collapse in a huff onto her backside and bring her eyes back to the sea.

On one particularly cloudy day, I passed while she was in her lonely vigil. I was off to the school to retrieve a stack of papers that I'd forgotten. I was indulging in a brisk walk as I moved by. When she saw me, she stood, but only gave me a halfhearted wave.

I returned the gesture with a smile, but didn't stop. Her hands went into her trouser pockets and she cocked her head to the side. It appeared that she found it hard to believe that any business I had, could be more important than she.

The waves crashing against the rocks, the spray in the air, and her short, wind ruffled hair, all painted a melancholic picture. A feeling of despair took hold of me, but the reason for it was elusive.

Stopping to look back, it was Isleen I saw standing out there alone on those rocks. I gasped and quickly looked away, a feeling of panic rising in my chest. Picking up my pace, I tried desperately to push that picture out of my mind.

Chapter 2

"Death Leaves A Heartache No One Can Heal..."

Shortly after Isleen's funeral, I became the unhappy recipient of a case of what the doctor called 'Panic Disorder'. There would come these moments of terror when I felt like I might burst wide open. It wasn't a problem at home, but when out and about, the need to flee sometimes became overwhelming.

If at the pub or some shop, I could just be off and go for a rove. But at school, I couldn't. So, more often than not, I would sneak into the housekeeper's pantry to quiet myself, all the while hoping that ol' Meara wouldn't wander in for a mop or sponge. My doctor said that the condition should go away after a while and he suggested I take up exercise as a way to cope.

I made it part of my daily routine to walk along the beach just about every evening at sundown. I would stop and pick up a simple supper from Niamh's Chipper, and after exchanging pleasantries with ol' lady Niamh, I would head out to stroll along the surf until I finished my meal.

With supper complete, I would head back toward the pub with the thought of helping myself to a hot cup of tea and the company of my mates. Drink was out of the question at this point in my life because I was struggling to keep my woe from pushing me into alcoholism. Just being in the pub was temptation enough. Sadly, there was no other place to socialize in my village. So, since I no longer had immediate family, I took the risk.

It was on a Friday evening, early in September that I found myself walking out of the local Chipper. Pulling greasy fish and chips from the just as greasy newspaper, I scoffed them down as I did a slow walk to the seaside. I started my tramp in a southerly direction because I didn't want to have to look at the lighthouse with all its haunting memories; better to focus on the long wooden pier that lay in the opposite direction.

Small waves crashed and seabirds called as I strode along. The mist swirled about and the ragged clouds hung low. It was an oppressive mix of conditions, but nothing new for me. This was Ireland, and as an Irishman, my da had imposed upon me that, "An Irish man is always happy in his sadness." The philosophy of Dairmuid McKay. Something he would beat into me to make certain I didn't forget.

As I tossed a chip into the air for the gulls to snatch, I noticed someone off in the distance. It appeared to be a lad in an oversized, white Guernsey. He was launching himself into the air, jumping, spinning, and kicking. The movements were a mix of dance and gymnastics, a crazy ballet seemingly born of frustration.

I continued moving in that direction and soon discovered it wasn't a lad after all. Anna was in the middle of a Grand Jeté when she noticed me standing there. Losing her concentration, she fell onto her backside in the sand. Getting to her feet, she giggled, making a show of brushing the grit from her light grey jeans. She then apologized as if expecting to be chastised for indulging in something as normal as breathing.

"Hallo Anna!" I said with unexpected enthusiasm.

Walking to her, I noticed the tears on her cheeks. She saw that I had, and turned away, wiping at her face. It was an uncomfortable moment, so I attempted to put her at ease by saying, "Tis okay lass, you shouldn't fear your natural reaction to emotion. We all have these moments you know… and not one of us is to be spared. What's troubling you?"

Turning back, she rolled down the sleeves of the jumper and threw me a look. I couldn't tell if it was fear, anger, or irritation, I saw in her eyes. Perhaps all three. Her blond hair had grown dark from the wetness and lay plastered to her forehead. She brushed it out of her face as her purple scarf flapped out to tattle on the wind. Her expression softened, and cocking her head, she put her hands on her hips and said "Sooo…what are you doing?"

I could tell she was redirecting. She didn't want to discuss her issue. I countered by ignoring her question, and asking another.

"Would you like to stroll with me, Ms. Furtak?" I said with the haughty accent of the landed gentry. Wiping my nose with the greasy newspaper, I pushed it into my jacket pocket with a smirk.

She made a face of disapproval and replied, "Most certainly, Mr. McKay… or shall I call you Ciarán?"

She said this with her own version of a very German Englander, followed by a smile. I could tell she was relieved that I'd asked.

"Best you call me Mr. McKay in public, darling. We wouldn't want others to talk, you know."

"Most certainly… Ciarán... darling."

We laughed together, however, deep down, I grew concerned about doing anything that might perpetuate a more intimate relationship. I found myself torn between etiquette and compassion. The relief in her face told me it was the right thing, even if only for the moment. When she took my arm, I didn't resist. We continued in the direction I'd been going, our footprints fast being erased by the spirited sea, almost as if it wished to bolster our confidentiality.

I sought to keep the conversation going any way that I could, so I commented on whatever came to mind. The school, the teachers, the people of the village, the weather, and even the thickening mist. I mentioned how it lay on our clothes, making us shimmer like silver. She gave me that husky laugh, bringing to my attention that in Germany, 'mist' meant something entirely different. Something more foul, and could be found on the ground where cattle roamed.

Grinning at her, I realized she wasn't wearing her glasses. In the interest of perpetuating more discussion, I risked asking a question that might stir her ire.

"So… where are your glasses? Can you see without them?"

"I left them back at the house. I really don't need them unless I am reading. There is not much to read out here on the beach as you may well know."

I decided to push the issue, so I said, "Take no offense lass, but you look better without em. So… what's the story?"

"I have my reasons Mr. McKay, and I don't wish to share them right now," she said in a sassy manner.

"Come now lass, it can't be as complicated as you're making it, they're just spectacles."

"Well, okay, if you must know…" she said, her words trailing off in a gust of wind.

"Okay, give it to me lass, I can take it," I said with mock seriousness

"It's my mama."

"Your mama?"

"Yes, it was she who chose them. She thinks I am too attractive. So, she decided to buy me the ugliest pair she could find. The same for my hairstyle. Safer to look more like a boy than a girl… especially at a distance."

"Had me fooled. So… she made you cut your hair?"

"Ja, she is my mama, and it was her money. I had no control. I did as I was told."

I studied her face. Yes, there was an allure. The unusual eyes, skin as smooth as silk with that rosy hue. She had the so-called celestial nose, and eyebrows just dark enough to let you know she had them. Her lips weren't quite full, but her chin went well with the oval shape of her face.

"Sorry to hear it, however… your hair will grow back and you don't have to sport such hideous eyewear… if you don't wish." Trying to sound supportive, I am sure I came off obtuse.

"Yes… there is hope," she said with indifference, and her face told me she was thinking about it.

We'd gone only a short distance further when she surprised me by stopping suddenly and jerking me to a halt. Releasing my arm, she stepped over to face me, blocking my path, a move I remembered from the first day of school.

Standing about a forearms length away, she hugged herself and looked at me in a way that was more like looking into me. I could see there was a question waiting to be asked. I squirmed in anticipation, but was at a loss for words. She'd caught me off guard. Her eyes seemed to twinkle and a slight smile came to her lips.

"Ciarán… do you believe that there is a special someone for every person on this planet?"

"I don't know… maybe?" I said, as Isleen's face floated across my mind's eye.

I feared my response might have projected a reluctance to broach the subject. I didn't want that because I was starting to feel a kind of connection to Anna. Something akin to a metaphysical bond.

Standing silent in the growing darkness, we took each other in—the conversation on hold. Without thinking about it, I cupped her cheek affectionately with my right hand. Then feeling I was being too bold and fearing a negative reaction, I pulled it back. Yet the expression that came over her face was of pure gratitude.

"Sorry," I said, looking away up the beach. "That was just an impulse, I…"

"Then it was an honest action. A true feeling! You care for me… where no one else here seems too. It's like I am a… how do you say… a ghost or something. I mean… at first, everybody gave me much attention. But now, it is more like I am a problem."

I watched her bottom lip quiver as her eyes pled for understanding. Her cheerful demeanor melted away, and she sobbed out, "Ciarán… I am so lonely here."

She covered her mouth to halt another sob. Then burying her face in her hands she said, "Even when I am with people, I… I still feel so alone."

Her voice cracked at the end of her statement as she fought for self-control. I could only imagine my expression when she suddenly launched herself into my arms. Her hands met at the small of my back as she pressed her cheek to my chest. I heard a whimper escape her lips and then she wept openly, the tweed of my jacket soaking her tears.

We'd stopped just short of the pier, its massive bulk of creosoted wood presenting a dark shadow in the gloom. Worry crept in and I scanned the area for other souls who might be out. But unless someone was within ten meters of us, they wouldn't know who stood out here in the wet air. I couldn't find it in my heart to deny Anna a comforting embrace, though. It seemed the proper thing to do.

Laying my face on the top of her head, her short blonde hair tickled my nose. The fruity scent of her shampoo wafted in, and I felt the warmth that radiated from her body. Her fingers kneaded the fabric of my jacket as seconds turned to minutes. She would have to be the one to end the contact. I feared if I pulled away, she would take it as rejection.

When she loosened her grip, I figured she had all the comforting that she needed. I lifted my face from her hair, but then she squeezed me tighter. As she did, the breeze faltered, and I heard her say, "Endlich" in a way that seemed to finalize the moment.

"Sorry, what's that?"

"Nothing," she said, her voice thick with phlegm.

"Come now lass, just tell me."

"Honestly Ciarán, it was nothing," she said looking into my face and smiling through her tears.

She then looked left, where the sandy slope led up to the roadway and added, "I must go... my host mother wants me home before the old man gets in."

Releasing me, she stepped back and rubbed her eyes. Giving me the once over, I saw a look of satisfaction come into her face. Without another word, she took off running up the slope through the sparse, long grass, the bottoms of her bare feet, flashing sallow. She stopped at the top, and even though somewhat obscured by the mist, I could tell she threw me a kiss. I raised a hand to wave, but she melted away.

Alone again.

As I stood there wondering what she'd done with her shoes, a fishing boat sounded. Its far-away tone turned me around to see its lights blinking on the horizon. As I watched it moving through the gloaming, thoughts about my embrace with Anna gave way to thoughts of my ma.

I still remember her as a vibrant force in my life. She'd been my rock right up until the minute she left me. She loved to read and recite poetry, especially Yeats and my favorite, Mr. Seamus Heaney, himself. She loved books, every one of them a treasure. She could cite the stories within as well as the intimate details of the authors who wrote them. She also knew the old ways of the Seanachai. The storytellers of the time when she was young. Every village had one, and everyone as valuable as any library.

They carried the ancient tales in their heads, passing them along from generation to generation—not one word ever put to paper. It was the way of the Celts. Leaving no written record of anything, they doomed their way of life to be lost to history.

Now there weren't many of the Seanachai left. My grandda Ciarán would be the last in our family. The very person to instill the love of literature into my ma. The problem was—my da. He saw no sense in having more than the basic ability to read and write. Having been a Stonemason all his life, hard work was all he ever knew. When that kind of work all but vanished from the area, he often hired himself out to build or repair stone fences.

He never troubled my ma about her beliefs. He accepted it as being her way. But she could never talk to him about it. So, she saved it for me. With him, she always played the role of the obedient wife and that's all he cared about. He wanted the house clean, the laundry and dishes done and his dinner served on time. Diarmuid McKay was a true patriarch.

When they'd fight, it was more like a competitive discussion. If she bested him, which was most of the time, he would sigh, grab his flat cap, and walk out. He would make his way down to Lafferty's and upon returning, go straight to his bed. It was the same every time.

I despised having to tiptoe around the man. If I happened to be in his direct line of flight as he moved out the door, I would receive the brunt of the anger that brewed inside him. There would be verbal abuse, a slight shaking, or perhaps—a good slap. Anything to let me know where my place was in his little realm. He hoped I would follow in his footsteps and become the good laborer. When he sorted that I was going in a different direction at age twelve, things changed for us. I became more like the hired help than his son.

My ma watched out for me. When she sensed the bomb was ticking, she'd send me on some time consuming errand. Her orders were always the same: "Don't want you back, until you see your da making for the pub. Do you hear my words, Ciarán?" I'd nod with a convincing vigor and say, "I do, ma!" as I slipped out the back door. When I returned, she would keep me close until he was tucked away in their bed.

By the time I turned sixteen, I'd learned how to stay clear of him. A simple man has predictable behaviors. At eighteen, I was a head taller, and had given a few arse whippings of my own. The need to prove I was capable became moot. I went off to university and we soon existed in two separate worlds.

Standing there on the beach, I hunched my shoulders against the cold and shoved my hands into my pockets. A finger found my ma's Claddagh ring and slipped inside the band.

I'd been at her deathbed that terrible night when they told me she wouldn't see the sunrise. A few of the local women had gathered outside the door with Aine Nolan poking her head in on occasion. I remember my ma pulling the ring from her finger, and handing it to me, she said, "Keep this darling, it'll better suit you here than with me in the Otherworld. You can give it to someone that you come to love, just as much as you do me."

She appeared so serene during that moment of clarity. There was no hint of fear about what eternity might hold for her. I took the ring from her and said not a word; afraid I would break down. She would want me to stand strong and act as if her death came as an everyday occurrence. So, I did; up until the point where she drew her last breath. Then I did break. Falling to my knees, I sobbed into her blanket as Dr. Fitzpatrick declared that Brighid Ailsin McKay had taken her last breath.

I drew the Claddagh from my pocket and rolled it through my fingers for the millionth time. With that came a flood of memories of when my ma walked the green fields of Ireland, and danced with her wee baby boy on the beach at Ballyamhras.

A deep sadness pushed me toward weeping, but I fought it in spite of myself. I longed for relief from the perpetual sorrow brought by loss. What I wanted was someone with whom to share my life.

Was it time to start my search?

The breeze picked up and pushed the mist away, taking the thoughts of my ma with it. But Isleen followed in her place. The memory of when I tried to give her my ma's Claddagh came to me along with her words, "Sorry, but… no Ciarán. I'd like for us to have our own. Both of them forged from the very same bit of gold. I want them to be kin to each other—like we will soon be."

My feelings were hurt, so I pressed the matter. But she stood her ground. She then enlisted the help of her step da, Samuel, who placed an order for a set to be made and brought over from the west of Ireland. Now mine hangs from a wee ribbon over the top of our wedding portrait, and Isleen's went with her to the Otherworld.

Shoving the ring back into my pocket, I could feel it was going to be one of those nights. I would end up sitting at home, alone, ruminating for hours about Isleen and any unfinished business that existed between us. Hours filled with regret. Without a doubt, I would bring Anna into the mix, pondering the role she might play.

I noticed over the past few weeks an ever-growing awareness of the relief that Anna brought me. The chronic sadness that haunted me daily seemed to dissolve away when she was near. But it also brought an overwhelming sense of disloyalty. It was almost as if I was expecting Isleen to reappear at any minute as if she'd just been away on holiday.

The realization of how ridiculous that was, should have set me free. But I still floundered in a reservoir of anxiety that was dammed by a stack of tightly packed obstacles. My position as a professional educator, my standing in the community, social expectations, my loyalties, and the pursuit of trust—they all kept me treading water.

I craved a solution to break the cycle of anguish, but I wanted to do what was right—and cause no harm. I wanted to be Anna's friend. I wanted to be close to her so I could have more of what she brought—liberation from the pain.

A wave of irritation rose up in me. I paced back and forth in the surf, the ring cycling in and out of my pocket. When I'd decided I had enough of the beach with its darkening sky, I started back toward the village. As I walked, I planned, establishing goals for my evening and the days to follow. The first on my list—translating the word, 'Endlich'.

I knew a wee bit of German, but I didn't know that word, and the way she said it left me with such a strange sensation. Despite my unease, I felt like I was on the fringe of something fantastic. Yet I couldn't get myself to take the necessary next step.

Instead of socializing at the pub, I would go directly home. Once there, I would find my German/English dictionary and ease the ignorance that piggybacked my anguish.

As I walked along, the boat moved with me. Every once in a while it would make that forlorn noise as if to remind me I was alone and—lonely. The horizon, for a mere few seconds, sported a rose-colored meridian. Along with the smell of the sea, came another odor—ozone. Out of the corner of my right eye, I caught a shadow moving along behind me.

Spinning around and walking backwards, I spied the shape of a person in the mist. A spectral image vacillated in the dim light, just a stone's cast away.

The air seemed to thicken with electricity. My clothing snapped and sparked as I moved, and so did the patches of long grass at the edge of the beach. With each gust, the waving blades flickered and cracked. I felt as if I'd been submerged in an ocean of energy. With my eye on the shadow, I called out, "Anna?"

The positively charged air seemed to have an effect on the dead lighthouse and a shaft of light shot out to rotate just one time around. Its illumination passed over my mysterious companion and I felt the adrenaline flow in. My hair tried its damndest to raise my hat when I realized whoever they were, they were not standing on the sand, but instead, floated just above the breakers.

A loose peasant skirt flowed out and the white sleeveless blouse, too thin for the weather, radiated a surreal luminosity. Whatever it was, it smiled, showing some extraordinary white teeth in a pain filled simper. Above that, the eyes shone silver, like the moon on a cloudless night.

"Hallo Ciarán, my love."

It was Isleen.

I felt the cold as if I stood there naked. The breeze seemed to blow against me from all directions at once, and with it, the sensation of a million hands playing over my body.

Her arms opened and she cocked her head to one side as if to say, 'Come to me.' I turned away, intending to run—but I couldn't.

She seemed to have cast a spell that froze me to my spot. In a split second, I felt her at my back, cold lips at my ear. Her woeful voice came as if from across a vast space, "Keep me in your heart, Ciarán but… be free," she said, the last word trailing off to mingle with the haunting resonance of the distant trawler's horn.

I forced myself to look back where I thought she might be, but there was only her shade dissolving within the mist. A shiver ran through me and my paralysis broke. I stumbled into a run and finding my feet, I took off like a horse out of the gate at Galway. The closer I got to the village, the faster I went. Twenty meters short of our well-known cluster of boulders, I turned left and ran up a small set of concrete steps, placed for the ease of the older folks to access the beach.

Bounding up two at a time, I heard, "What's up with you, Ciarán?"

It was all I could do to keep from shrieking. Arlyn, the village watchmen, sat astride his bicycle just back from the top, a puzzled look upon his face.

"Mary and Joseph lad, you look like you've seen a ghost."

Out of breath and unable to find my words, I bent forward to ease the pain in my side. I was fighting off an impending panic attack, so I focused on how comical his massive bulk looked upon his bicycle. Then he said, "Did you see what I saw? The lighthouse… it… the lighthouse lit up for all of a wee second."

I stood up straight and glancing back to make sure I wasn't being followed, I watched the boat slip from view as the glowing band of rosy light settled to blue.

"You saw it too?" I said, "The lighthouse I mean? Uhhh… that's why I was running. I was out on the beach and saw it flash, but… you saw it too, hiagh? I am so glad. Thought I was going mad, I did."

He sat there in his homemade uniform, with his ill-fitting constable's cap, scrutinizing me. I wasn't concerned though. He was a pleasant enough fellow. An affable lad with a commitment to the community. Like me, he too was alone in the world.

He'd suffered the loss of his wife and son, fourteen or so years back. They'd been down Dublin way on a shopping excursion when an explosion ripped through the city center. It didn't kill them right off. They'd suffered in the hospital for a time, and then at home for a wee while longer before succumbing to their injuries. He'd been a baker at that time, and his bakery had been on the south end of the high street.

I'd been all of eight years old. I would stop in as I rambled home from school, lingering there to smell the fresh baked bread. If I loitered too long, he would send me on my way with a scone to gnaw and kind regards to my folks. He sold the shop soon after putting his loved ones in the ground, and moved his residence to the other side of town, just up from my place.

Descending into a grief-filled hole, he became the drunkest person I'd ever known. He could be seen staggering back and forth between the pub and home, a mere shadow of the man we once knew. Other times I heard him sobbing openly as he sat upon the boulders. At the pub, he would rage about the politics that cursed our island since the 1916 Easter Rising. An event he believed had, with indifference, kicked him into a well of misery. I empathized with him because I knew what it was like to be a walking wreck of a human after being struck down by loss.

As the story goes, one day he just snapped out of it. Showing up at the town hall, clean-shaven and dressed in a freshly pressed suit, he presented himself to the Lord Mayor. He'd gone there with a proposal. I am told, he expressed with good reason, how Ballyamhras should have someone watching over the village in the wee hours, and he was the man for the job.

Finding pity on him, Mayor Callaghan declared that he was creating a new position within the municipality for a village watchman, and commissioned Arlyn that very day. He would be the one to call out the Gardai, if things should go awry in the night. A callbox with a direct line to the Sergeant over in Lusk was installed on the wall outside the town hall, and a key given to Arlyn for safekeeping.

Sometimes upon departing Lafferty's late in the evening, I would spy him lingering in the middle of the street outside his old shop. I imagined that he'd been asking himself the unanswerable question, 'Why?'

"Well, I'm off!" he announced, snapping me out of my semi-trance. I stepped from his path and looking back over his shoulder, he said, "Could very well be vandals, you know. Would you be so kind, lad… if you don't see me back soon, go and gather some of the lads down at Lafferty's and send em my way?"

"No trouble a-tall Arlyn, will do." I said, trying to hide my lack of concern, knowing he would find nothing and no one.

"Unless, of course, you'd care to come along?"

I looked at him and seeing the age in his face, I felt a son's affection. I knew, as with any other night on this quiet expanse of seafront, he would find nothing but rocks, sand and maybe… a Merrow or two.

"Sorry Arlyn, my lad, I am off for home, have an early morning, you know. Have to be to the school by half seven."

At that moment, it felt as if someone had come up from behind and was straightening the collar of my jacket. Cold fingers seemed to caress my neck, sending another shiver up my spine. I kept my composure, but it was all I could do to avoid jumping out of my clothes.

Arlyn set the pedal on the bicycle and pushed off, saying, "Well, have a lovely evening lad, we can't have you late for school now, can we?"

Rolling away down the pavement that bordered the beach, he called back, "If you see my lamp go off, come quick, will you?"

"Certainly Arlyn, will do. And good luck to you."

The bicycle wobbled as he switched on the battery-powered lantern that hung from the handlebars. I watched him fade away into the mist, his light the only one to be seen out that way as he put some distance between us. I supposed he wouldn't want to be out there alone for too long. I imagined his large frame heaving back and forth, his legs pumping like mad to get himself out to the lighthouse and back in quick fashion. There was no real danger, but that didn't lessen the spookiness of it.

Pivoting back toward the beach, I feared I would see Isleen standing out there. But everything was as it should be. Turning back, I watched the pinpoint of light move as if Arlyn was off the cycle now and walking around the base of the tower. It soon swung high in the air as if he was waving the 'all clear.'

I stepped into the street and walked toward home as the speck of light moved back my way at a high rate of speed. When clear of the streetlamp, my walk turned into a run. I didn't stop until I was at my front door. Then stepping inside, I locked it. I stood there in the dark, scanning the room. I still didn't feel safe. But how can one hide from a spectre? I had to come to terms with this or I feared I would fall into lunacy.

Dashing around, I turned on all the lamps and drew the curtains. Thinking about a good cup hot tea, I panted my way into the kitchen to put on the kettle. Then sitting down at the table, I waited for the boil. My eyes fell on that single, empty chair across the table. Isleen's chair. Jumping up, I moved back into the parlor. I needed a distraction. I needed noise. I should have gone to the pub.

Then I remembered what had driven me home. “Endlich”. I started searching through the piles of books around my chair. I remembered I had an ancient copy of Köhlers German/English somewhere. Knocking over a pile, I found it. Grabbing it up with haste, I threw my arse into the seat.

As with a lot of German words, it had several meanings used in different context. But the one that fit the best was, ‘Finally’ like “Finally, she had me...” or “Finally, I gave in...” or…

Well, I suppose I would have to be completely blind to not notice how she’d acted in the past. The way she studied me when she thought I wasn’t paying attention. I’d been resisting any closer involvement because of Isleen—and for professional reasons. Now there was the moment on the beach with her shedding tears and then embracing me, followed by the odd appearance of the boat, and Isleen’s apparition.

I wasn’t much on the mystical. I didn’t give a lot of thought in my day to the Faerie world or any other world outside of my present reality. Yet there seemed to be something going on here that I couldn’t grasp. Something bigger than me. Like the cosmos had shifted ever so slightly in my favor. I’d a lot to sort out.

The kettle began its whistle and the sound of it unnerved me. I dashed into the kitchen to stop the noise and make my cup of tea. Returning to my chair, I remained there for the rest of the night, dozing fitfully, every light in the place, ablaze. I am sure anyone passing, would have thought I had a guest—and in a way—they would have been bang-on about that.

Chapter 3

"The Road Rises Up"

After that night on the beach, Anna and I spent a lot of time together. It seemed almost as if 'Endlich' had given her a green light, and the words spoken by Isleen's shade, had given slack to the tether that bound me.

Anna sought me out every day after school, and on Saturday. I would be walking down the street on my way to the post or the grocer, and as soon as I showed on the high street, she would come running. Arriving all out of breath, she'd cock her head and grin as if the greatest thing in the world had just occurred. Yet she'd only give me a simple, "Hallo" and would just stand, grinning.

It was almost as if she feared I might try to bolt and was sure to capture me before I could. She left it to me to come up with something to say though, and if I delayed, there would be minutes of awkward silence.

I truly enjoyed the companionship, but did my best to avoid appearing eager. I believe she saw right through me. More often than not, she would grab my hand and pull me down the street as if my errands were no longer of any importance. My time was hers. We would stroll about with no true destination in mind and she would chatter nonstop about all that had happened since the last time.

The older women of the village, for the lack of anything better to do, made it their business to know what transpired in their territory. So local gossip was created, exchanged, and revised. Heads would turn, come together, and words would pass in whispered tones. No one was free from it here. If you lived here, you would eventually be front-page news.

My turn had come around once again. The sequel to: 'The Death of Ciarán McKay's Wife' was being written, and in all probability, it would be titled: 'Ciarán McKay Becomes An Item Once Again.' As my relationship with Anna evolved, so did the blather.

During our conversations outside of school, I learned that Anna was a 'Wessi'. A German from West Berlin. She lived with her mother in the Spandau borough and had an undeniable love for the city. With her higher than average IQ, and her charismatic nature, there was never a dull moment. She was always telling tales of her life back in Berlin, her travels abroad, and the many hoops the ESE organization had made her jump through in order to become a Foreign Exchange Student. She harbored an insatiable love for politics, and hoped one day to work in government.

On clear, sun drenched days, we would buy ice cream and sit at the end of the pier watching the boats. She did most of the talking. Some days were good and, some were not. On the good ones, we would tease and mock. Joking about different things or discussing the ridiculousness of the world. On the bad days, I would sit in shock and dismay, as she shed tears, venting about the more horrific things that had taken place in her childhood.

There were accounts of ill treatment by her relatives, persecution by authority figures, or the general cruelty from people she had once thought friends. There came tales of abuse, drunkenness, and the terror that came in the night—something she wouldn't share beyond letting me know there was one.

She touched on the separation of her parents, her many anxieties, and a fear that her life might come to no good end. I suspected that Anna had a secret—one to which I would soon be privy.

I determined that her rants were usually triggered by some negative event that had happened either at school, or at the house where she was staying. A place I tried to get her to reveal, but with every attempt thwarted. She acted as if disclosing it might bring the sky down upon her head.

I would console her at the culmination of every rant, insisting that there were no absolutes in life, and that Justice remained a relative concept.

"I understand lass, I too have had a few terrible moments in my time."

"There is one that comes to mind," she confessed. "I heard about your wife from Shelagh."

I wasn't surprised. I supposed sooner or later she would find herself afloat on the sea of local gossip.

"So, what did you hear?" I asked soberly, and when my eyes looked for hers, she turned away to toy with a small hole in the knee of her jeans.

"That… you were married to a woman named Isleen, but she died of a heart attack… or something like that. I think it was around this time, last year, yes? And… even though you might be trying not to show it, I believe your heart is very broken."

I turned away to look at the lighthouse in the distance, an old familiar pain blossoming in my chest.

"More of a girl than a woman… but I don't want to talk about it."

"Why not? It might help? You can talk to me… you know you can."

Her tone was ardent, like helping me would give her purpose. Turning my face back, I saw her go from sitting with her legs dangling over the edge, to getting up on her hands and knees. She dropped her face and rammed my arm several times with the top of her head. It was a creative attempt to soften me up and it made me chuckle.

I feared she would topple over into the sea because we were perched right on the brink. But before I could voice my concern, she sat down with one leg stretched out behind me, the other tucked under her arse. Tilting her head backward, she squinted at me as if awaiting a response.

"Now… what was that all about?"

"Oh, nothing… spontaneity, I guess. So, come Ciarán… what do you say? Tell me all about it… please."

"No need," I declared. "I am past it now. It has been a long time. But I will tell you this much, Anna of Germany, you being here… helps a great deal—if you get my meaning?"

She gave me a look like she didn't believe it, but she stopped squinting and without another word, she turned and dropped her legs back over the edge of the pier. Then sidling up close, she took my hand and brought her attention back to the sea.

A pod of late season porpoise broke the surface heading south. Awestruck, she squeezed my hand with her left and pointed with her right. Then whooping, she raised her pointing hand straight up and made a militant fist as if to salute them.

I was still mulling over what she'd asked. The first part of what I'd told her was a lie. I was not over it. The second part was truth. But my intent was to take her off the subject. I'd accomplished that, thanks to the help of those supportive porpoises. I was almost willing to accept her offer of consultation and felt it was an even trade. She was quite mature for seventeen. I suspected she may even have parented her own parents, or at least, her mama.

At times life didn't seem fair, often stealing the innocence of childhood and pushing the young into a world that they were ill equipped to handle. I didn't fear Anna's reaction in learning things about me, but more of my emotional reaction once I did. I had a rule about shedding tears in public, and doing that in front of Anna was a hurdle I'd one day have to cross.

***

Weeks turned into months and we carried on as usual. At the school, prudence was in order. Fortunately, Anna understood this. If we were to remain close friends, discretion would be crucial. I would see her in the hallways, and in only one of my classes. History wasn't one of her required courses, but she chose it anyway. Transferring from one elective to another was permitted only once within the school year. So, she gave up her Irish Language class for Irish History. I suspected she did it just so she could torment me. She was bright enough to hold her own in any debate, and our exchanges always fired up the rest of the class, goading them into full-blown discussion. With Anna present, time flew.

The other students seemed to enjoy the subject more with her there, and I always felt in high favor because of it. They actually wanted to be in my classroom. It made me feel secure in my progressive philosophy. But in my heart, I believed if I'd been ten or twenty years older, it might have been different.

For the moment though, I'd a kinship with my pupils, and I considered myself more of a mentor then a teacher. Also, if there should ever come a serious falling out between me and anyone of my older colleagues, my relationship with Anna would most certainly fuel the fire. I had to tread softly if I wanted to maintain a happy balance.

December soon arrived and so did her birthday. She entered her eighteenth year—a stranger in a strange land. Officially responsible for herself, she was sure to let everyone know she'd now passed over the cusp of adolescence. No one could tell her what to do anymore. She merely compromised for the sake of harmony.

She asked me not to arrange a party or give her a gift. I resisted, conveying it wasn't proper for me, or anyone else, to ignore her special day. But I did as she asked. Her mates made a big deal of it though, and even when she tried not to show it, I could tell she liked the attention.

I tried to let the day pass without any thought about it, but I failed. I would gift her regardless of her request. I pondered for hours what it could be. Then in a moment of distraction, it came to me as I fumbled with my ma's ring.

Why not? Claddagh was supposed to be about friendship.

It seemed the prescribed next step in my life as if my ma had envisioned these future events before passing through the veil into the Otherworld. Isleen's denying of the ring, might well have been necessary for my ma's divination to be fulfilled. That was all speculation and I wasn't a big believer in Destiny. But certain events since Anna's arrival had me thinking I just might become one.

Did I care for Anna enough to bestow something so precious upon her? Perhaps.

Was there anything else driving me to make this commitment? If there was, it couldn't be sexual.

We'd joked about sex, yes, and there'd been insinuation, but only for the sake of humor. Besides, I believed that would ruin what we had. I just wanted to see her happy. To see her smile, to watch her eyes light up, or hear her laugh. I wanted to share things that smacked of joy, carefree moments that I felt fortunate to be a part of. Sexual activity seemed to be outside of that, and so very basic. I'd plenty of that with Isleen, and mostly toward the end of our relationship.

I wanted my life to be like it was as a wee lad—just roving with my mates, lads and lassies alike.

Maybe I just wanted to escape the adult world?

Being with Anna certainly helped me do just that. Her happiness while in my company was genuine, and she was fast filling a void. But there was a slight fear that gifting her the ring, could very well set us on a different path. It just felt right, though, and I sensed annoyance creeping at any indecision.

I would take the risk.

So, I had to sort out a way to present it to her and timing would be everything. Running a thin gold chain through the band, I stuck it in a spare ring box and wrapped it. Now I just had to wait for the right opportunity.

The next day after arriving home from the school, I hung my coat and set about preparing tea. Not five minutes later, there came a light tapping on the window of the back door. It increased in a whimsical fashion, telling me that someone knew 'Ravel's Bolero'. Peeking out of the curtain, it surprised me to see Anna spying on me through the glass. She gave me a shy wave and I opened the door.

"Hallo Anna, what's the story? You've never come around here before?"

She smiled, and forcing her way by, said, "I came through the meadow. I saw you walking home and I followed you."

I remained just inside the door, watching as she moved around my front parlor. She would stop, touch something, and then move on. The decor still hinted that a woman had once been present there. Everything as Isleen had left it. The scattered piles of books were the only exception. Walking around them, Anna came to the sideboard and examined all of my portraits.

"So this is her? Isleen?"

Picking up a framed photo of my wife wearing her wedding dress, Anna turned and gave me an inquisitive look. My wedding band pinged against the brass frame as it swung on its slim, black ribbon. The faerie-like intonation took me back to that moment when I stood on the beach with Isleen's apparition. Pushing it out of my mind, I said, "That would be herself."

"She was beautiful. Oh! She even had red hair, yes?"

I nodded, uncertain if I wanted to talk about that or not.

"A Nordic trait, not really Irish," she said, imitating me.

"That's correct. The Vikings brought that when they invaded us back in the Middle-Ages."

She put the picture back, but stood staring at it. "Yes, I remember the discussion in your class. You were quite energized with all that talk about Brian Boru." She laughed, but then mumbled, "I wish I was that pretty."

"I heard that! So… what makes you think you're not?"

She turned away from the sideboard and walked toward me. Stopping short of the archway that separated the rooms, she ended up next to my writing desk. Taking in the clutter on its top, she discovered her birthday gift. Running a fingertip over the colorful wrapping, she said in a flippant tone, "What makes you think I am?"

Crossing her eyes, she stuck her tongue out at me. I didn't know how to answer that, so my statement came as a cliché, "Eye of the beholder darling, eye of the beholder."

She giggled softly to herself. "So… what is this?" she asked, tapping a finger on the colorful paper wrapping the Claddagh's tiny box.

"That's yours."

"What do you mean? I didn't bring it." Picking it up, she gave it a shake.

"It's for your birthday. I'm aware you didn't want a gift, but I couldn't resist," I said and mimicked the face she had made.

She gave me a look of mock anger in response and pulled off the ribbon. Removing the paper, she exposed the red velvet box. Opening it, she withdrew the ring as the fine gold chain snaked out to swing freely. A squeak escaped her lips as she tried to control her excitement. She held it up in front of her face, the necklace hanging pendulous in her fingers. She studied the crowned heart clasped within the hands of friendship. Then her eyes looked past it, to me.

"So… you must really think I'm beautiful," She said, a slight quiver in her voice.

Putting it back into the box, she held it with both hands at her waist, just staring at it for the longest time. When she looked up, I noticed the wetness in her eyes. I started to comment, but that triggered her to declare, “I must go… I must go, now!” It was more like she was trying to convince herself, and breaking eye contact, she squeezed by to dash out the open door.

“But Anna, I wanted…”

Not letting me finish, she left the rear stoop at a fast walk. Entering the field, she halted and spun around, declaring with overwhelming sincerity, “Thank you Ciarán! Thank you so very much!” Removing the necklace from the box again, she caressed the ring in a loving fashion. I thought she’d changed her mind about departing, so I started out toward her.

“You’re welcome?” I said as I walked, still not understanding why she was acting the way she was. I wanted to be allowed to give her my carefully prepared explanation. Yet she turned away once again, moving at a faster pace. I quit trying to catch up and stopping, I watched her hasten away.

She paused under a large tree at the edge of the meadow; a place where Isleen and I’d spent many an hour in the early part of our relationship. I saw her hang the Claddagh around her neck and afterwards, he ran a finger over the bark of that huge oak. Then sprinting away, she disappeared down the path into the woods.

Isleen and I’d carved our names into that very tree. So, I decided to continue and have a look. I walked up to the ancient oak to see the familiar heart whittled deep into the wood. My name was just above Isleen’s at its center and someone had added, ‘+ Anna’ at the end of mine, inside a second, smaller heart. It brought a curiosity that gnawed at me.

With her birthday, there seemed to have come liberation. But also, some sadness. I wondered if she felt the same as I had when I was catapulted into adulthood, experiencing that reoccurring thought line, ‘Now, it’s all up to me’ coupled with the blossoming fear of the unknown. I returned to my cottage with a lot more to ponder.

The following day I met her coming out of the Post. An overwhelming happiness enveloped me and it made me giddy. I playfully teased her by trying to get a glimpse of the address on the envelopes in her hand. Sticking her tongue out in false disdain, she slipped them into the large patchwork bag she carried as a purse, laughingly declaring, "Not for you, Mr. McKay!" The Claddagh still hung from her neck; reminding me, I had a question that needed answering.

"So… lass, what was that all about at my cottage yesterday? You were off in a hurry if I remember correctly."

Her hand strayed to the ring and she rubbed it between two fingers. "I'm sorry, I didn't know how to act because of my emotions. If I had not gone away, I would have tried to do something stupid, like… kiss you."

"What would have been so stupid about that? What's a wee kiss on the cheek between friends?" I said, thinking about the old Irish custom of an embrace coupled with a simple kiss on the left cheek.

"Well, because… it wouldn't have been a wee kiss. Once I got started, I wouldn't have wanted to stop. Who knows where that could have taken us? I was thinking how it would not be fair to you."

"In what way?"

"I don't live here, Ciarán. I live in Germany. I must go back there soon. Do you understand?"

I nodded, but I didn't want to talk about that. I needed to stay in the now. I had my slice of sunshine and any thought about her leaving, caused that light to fade. I wanted to bolster the relationship, not dwell on its demise.

"I went out to the tree."

Flushing from the neck up, she looked away, saying, "And…?"

"And… I noticed your name next to mine."

"Does that trouble you?"

"Doesn't trouble me a-tall. Isleen will always have a place in my heart, but… there is room in there for others."

With that admission, I realized I had opened the door for a deeper accord. She could now pass through without hindrance. The next move would be hers. I watched her face soften and a smile braced her lips. She turned her back to me, and hugging her purse to her chest with both arms, she buried her chin in its fabric. I stepped up beside her, so I could see her face. She looked at me out of the corner of her eye and said, “Walk with me?”

We spent the rest of the afternoon together and it gave me a chance to explain about the Claddagh. After I finished, she seemed aggravated as if she might just give it back. But then rolling it between her fingers, she smiled in such a satisfied manner, I knew she never would.

Afterwards, her mood became brooding. She got lost in her thoughts like she might be trying to sort something. She wasn’t very good company. I could tell she still wanted to be with me though. It was the way she squeezed my hand and looked at me as we walked. We remained together until dark and she left me at the crossroads with even more questions than when we started.

Chapter 4

"Even The Loveliest Of Lads Have Enemies"

Winter soon turned to spring. March and April were warmer than usual and allowed us to spend more time together out of doors. It was almost as if we'd known each other for years instead of just months. I had to admit to myself that I grew more dependent on her with every day. Whenever thoughts of her upcoming departure popped into my head, I would push them back with a vengeance. However, at this point, no matter how tight I closed my eyes to it, there seemed a cloudbank swollen with rain just at the horizon. So, I was going to savor every moment.

Over the spring months, Anna seemed to grow and change right before my eyes, 'Filling out' as my ma used to say. When I thought she wasn't looking, I would give her the 'once over' noticing that her clothing had become a wee bit confining. It left me to wonder if it was normal for a person to round out that much, in such short time. I blamed it on the Full Irish Breakfast she was probably being confronted with in the mornings. But honestly, I didn't know what she ate.

Then came that wisp of fear, the kind that could bring on a panic attack. If she was changing in a physical way—would she change emotionally and have second thoughts about us? Would she return home to forget I ever existed? There had been no discussion about our relationship evolving into something more than what it was. I think she grasped that I would be happy either way. Yet she seemed torn.

Germany or Ireland?

Perhaps I needed to push my fear away and talk to her about life after Ireland. I'd no idea what she had planned. But talking about that was talking about—after. After she was gone. After our time was over. After… I chilled at the thought.

Early in the afternoon on the last day of May, I went for a ramble. Next to talking, walking was the best way for me to sort things out. It could lift my mood like nothing else. So heading south through the town, I stopped at Nolan's grocery on the high street to grab a cola. Aine Nolan was behind the register when I walked up to pay. Her husband, Michael, who would normally be standing there, was sick up the stairs.

"Ciarán darling! Are you out for a rove?"

"I am, Aine. The sun is out, and I wanted to take advantage of it. Something on your mind, lass?"

"There is… need to get some groceries out to ol' man Finn… was wondering if maybe you're heading out that way?"

"Cripes, Aine! You're a mind reader, you are. I am in fact."

She smiled, blushing, her ruddy, weatherworn face contrasting against her disheveled white hair.

"Lovely! So, if you're up for it… I, and Conor Finn, would be forever grateful."

"No trouble a-tall, Aine. Be more than happy to be of some service to you. I haven't forgotten that you were there for my ma during her last days."

Conor Finn was a shepherd. One of the remaining few that tended his flock in the old-fashioned way. So, even though his shack was on the Old Mill road, he spent most of his time with his animals out in the pasturelands by the Hackettstown Cottages.

Aine handed me a large, brown paper sack through an opening between the cash register and a display rack.

"Take these pratties and soda bread out there to his gaff, would you? And if he's not in, leave'm in the wooden box by the door."

"I'll see to it Aine," I said, taking the bag and giving her a wink.

She beamed, and reaching through, patted my hand. "Thank you lad, you are a lovely boy." Pulling a bag of potato crisps from a large wire basket, she handed them to me. "Have these for your trouble, something to nibble on while you're roving."

I took the groceries and set them on the worn boards of the floor, and after stuffing the crisps in a pocket, I opened the bottle of cola.

"Sooo! Ciarán McKay, I see you have yourself a new article."

That was Timmy O'Brian. He leaned in the doorway to a back room set aside for community. I could see his older brother, and two others back there. They were sitting at a table, playing checkers. It was pretty much all they did since they weren't allowed in Lafferty's. They had to do their drinking out of town—not something they were real happy about. Timmy had stepped over to the open door to look out, hoping to start some trouble.

The four of them were the local 'bin men' and were also tasked with collecting rubbish on the beach. They patrolled the sand from pier to lighthouse at low tide, picking up the trash and whatever else might have floated up in the night. As quasi-civil servants, they got paid just enough to keep them in food, drink and rent.

Not one of them of them had a wife, or at least—anymore. There was no way any sane woman who knew them, would consent to a relationship. Sean was a year older than me and was Timmy's big brother. The other two were, Donald and William Stuart, Scotsmen and identical twins at that. Their bushy hair, massive beards, and large gangly frames, made them stand out in a crowd. Somewhat shy by nature, they kept to themselves. The question on everybody's mind in the gossip circles was why they would want to spend so much of their free time with the village loudmouths. If they had separated from the O'Brian's in their off work hours, they would have been accepted back in the pub.

Sean and I had nothing to say to each other. I could see him through the doorframe, his eyes glued to the checkerboard. We hadn't spoken since his ex-wife Julia left him to return to Germany. It was I who had helped her make her escape from the abusive bastard. There had been a violent exchange between us at the pub when he learned of it. Therefore, he and his brother were barred from the towns' only drinking establishment—and they held me responsible.

I couldn't go on knowing there were days when Sean would beat Julia senseless. I got tired of seeing her with black eyes and bruises. So I'd been the one to arrange her passage back to Germany. The sole conspirator to see that she arrived at, and departed from the ferry port in one piece. This only served to fan the fires of acrimony between Sean and I. But that extended all the way back to our school days.

So, we became invisible to each other. Now this would have worked brilliantly except there was one small glitch—Timmy. He had a serious blurting problem. Discretion was not in his experience. Whenever Timmy was with him, and I happened on the scene, the veil would drop and I would magically appear to Sean through Timmy's instigation.

Timmy's inquiry was regarding Anna. He'd been rather bold about something that was not his business. Had it been anyone else, I would have accepted it as simple curiosity. However, it was Timmy. That in itself would be a good enough reason for an arse whipping. But I would not go that far this day, not in Aine's shop.

Before I could respond to his remark, Aine jumped in and growled, "You can just keep your pie hole shut, Mr. O'Brian, least, if you want to stay in my place with your brother and your mates."

He didn't have the sense to do that though. "So, you are having the lasses fight your battles for you, Mr. High and Mighty school teacher."

At this point Aine flew around the counter, and grabbing a large broom, she headed toward them. I watched the Stuarts spring to their feet and back up to the wall. Sean stayed where he was, but covered his head. Timmy dashed back inside and I could see him practically climbing the storage shelves to get away.

"SHUT IT!" she hissed.

"Aye, Mrs. Nolan." I heard the Stuart boys mumble with no distinction between them. Planting their arses back in the chairs, they went on with their game.

"You want to stay in my shop, you will abide by my wishes…, and I wish for you to—SHUT IT!"

I felt a great admiration for Aine. To see her standing there, holding that broom like a sword, and not taking any shite from the rabble.

She'd been addressing them all, but was looking straight at Timmy. When she received no response, she must have figured it was over. Sean uncovered his head and glared at me with his teeth bared. He was seething.

Aine gave me a sharp nod and I returned the same. After taking a long pull from my cola, I picked up the brown paper bag and walked out.

Looking back over my shoulder, I saw Timmy had left the room and was now at the window. He watched me cross the street, a scowl on his face. When he was sure I was looking, he bared his teeth and gave me the good ol', two fingers up gesture, flipping me off. Because my hands were full, I couldn't return the compliment. So, I stopped, turned, and throwing my arms out wide, I bowed and scraped in a sarcastic manner, my performance complete. Grinning as big as I could, I turned away and continued down the high street, hoping not to cross their paths again for a long time.

Chapter 5

"Who Gossips With You ~ Will Gossip Of You"

I strolled south, greeting and chatting with people on the way. Once I cleared the village, I picked up my pace. Finn's place sat a little ways down from the old mill, so I had a bit of distance to cover. Finishing the cola, I stuck the bottle in the sack. It would be difficult to eat crisps with only one hand free, so I decided to save them for later.

It felt good to have the suns warmth on my face. Other than the distant sounds of crashing waves, birdsong, and the breeze through the grass, it was quiet. After a kilometer or two, the shrubbery grew denser, encroaching on the byway. A short stonewall ran up from the west and where it found the crossroads, it turned south toward the mill. It ended at the canal, but they could have taken it all the way down to Dublin, being's there's no shortage of stones in Ireland. I suspected they grew tired of the dull task of wall construction and decided to entertain themselves by building a mill.

After about half an hour of steady walking, I came to the old Murray road, an ancient boreen that meandered its way east to the sea. Finn's gaff was on the left, just before one turned the corner onto that rarely used track.

It was a small, wooden framed shack, surrounded by a vine laden, decorative wire fence. Passing thru the gate, I expected to be met by

Spinner, the shepherd's collie dog. Finn had named him Spinner because he would spin around more times than necessary when herding the sheep. Running around the flock, he would stop, spin, and run on only to stop and spin again. On this day, there came no Spinner to greet me. So, I suspected there would be no Conner Finn either.

I walked up and knocked. When no one came, I peeked through the window. There was no one inside, only a small bed, a rocking chair by the coal stove in the corner, and a tiny dry sink with a tin bucket on the floor nearby. The rickety looking shelves that covered the back wall were filled with picture books, magazines, crockery, cups, and other assorted items. I wondered if ol' Finn ever considered the danger of the whole mess collapsing on him while he slept. It would most certainly crush him to death, leaving poor Spinner an orphan.

Opening the wooden box next to the step, I saw a note scrawled in pencil on the back of a label from a peach tin that read, 'Jus leev'um in the box wood ya!'

I chuckled to myself, thinking there was a good chance that ol' Finn never had much schooling. Not an uncommon thing in this locality. A good many of the people only went as far as their sixteenth year. Having learned to read, write and do a little arithmetic, they would soon take up a trade, most likely following in one of their folk's footsteps. I suspected ol' Finn had taken up sheep herding as soon as he was able, possibly inheriting his livestock from his da.

I let the sack fall inside the box, happy to be free from my burden. As an afterthought, I dropped the crisps in too, figuring he wouldn't mind a taste of the 'modern' once in a while. Closing the lid, I moved back up the paving stones of the short walkway. I realized I'd left the glass bottle in the bag. I would leave it. It would be a mystery. If I were to see him later, I could bring it up, and we could share a moment of good craic over the ambiguity of it. Besides, Finn could make use of it somehow.

I passed through the gate and stepping out on to the road, I looked in one direction and then the other. I wasn't sure if I'd had enough roving for one day, or if I should continue. Gleeful laughter floated to me from the bog across the way. Looking out over the stonewall on the other side of the road, I saw two figures trying to make their way through. They would stop and start, change direction, dash a short distance only to come to a halt again. It seemed they realized their choice of paths had been a mistake and had to re-navigate.

They'd been moving in my direction, and after circumventing the most difficult part of the peat, they were close enough for me to see it was Anna, accompanied by Carla Donnelly. Carla still wore her school uniform. Because the students complained incessantly about being burdened with a dress code, I thought it odd she would still sport her uniform on a Saturday.

The short green skirt with the white blouse and emerald blazer, were out of place here in the countryside. Her necktie hung askew, and even at this distance, I could see that her white knee socks were spotted with mud. When they arrived at the wall, they hailed me in unison.

"Hallo Mr. McKay!" they sang out and giggled. Anna crawled over the wall first and came to me, her red, high-top sneakers swinging from laces that wrapped her fingers.

"Hallo, Ciarán," she whispered.

"Hallo Anna," I whispered back, and then looked down at her muck-covered feet. Her jeans had been cut off at the knee. 'Deutschland!' was plastered across the chest of her black, sleeveless Tee shirt in large, orange and yellow letters.

"Oooh Mr. McKaaay!" Carla called out.

Looking up, I watched her swing her leg high in an exaggerated arc to cross the fence, exposing her knickers. Planting her arse atop the wall, she brought the other leg around, but remained sitting.

Her short skirt was now hiked up nearly to her waist, leaving nothing to the imagination. She tilted her head and gave me what she may have considered a flirtatious smile.

"Carla! You are such a slut!" Anna shouted in a playful manner.

"I am… aren't I terrible?"

A wicked giggle followed as she pushed off with her hands, launching herself out onto the road. Landing clumsily on her feet, her shoes clacked on the tarmac.

I'd once overheard some of the lads at the school conversing about Carla as they stood outside of my classroom. They were all in agreement she was something of an exhibitionist. They all said how they liked to follow her around, hoping she would give them a glimpse of the inappropriate. I'd poked my head out of the door just as they were laying odds on which one of them would have the best chance with her. When they saw me, Ruari Kearny was bold enough to ask if I thought the numbers were in his favor. I remember laughing at the comical manner in which he asked. Then ordering them into the classroom, I demanded they let poor Carla be.

Now she stood before me, her alabaster skin plastered with freckles. Her long brown, curly locks parted in the middle and hanging free. Green eyes glared through thick glasses and the odor that emanated, confirmed my concern—her school clothes had also served as her pajamas.

She moved to within an arm's length of me, and looking up into my face, she grinned, exposing her extra-large incisors.

"What's the story, Mr. McKay?" she said, her voice extra loud as she turned her head to grin at Anna. Then tilting it forward and looking at me out of the tops of her eyes, she whispered, "What you doing out here… you handsome man, you? Are you searching for a lover?"

Stepping back, she guffawed at the ground and slapping at her thighs, acted as if it was the funniest thing in the world. All I could think of was how much I wanted her to go away. I looked her up and down and then turned my face up to the sky as if to gauge the sun.

"Well, you know, Carla, I was out for a simple stroll in the countryside, hoping to avoid the eejits."

"So have you been able to?" She said, not laughing anymore. Looking back, I saw she glared at me now, twirling a strand of dark hair in her fingers.

"Uh, well… until now anyway." I said and imitating her, I slapped at my own thighs, laughing.

"And what is that supposed to mean, then?"

Stepping closer, she looked up into my face and there were daggers in her eyes. Anna stood silent. Out of the corner of my eye, I could see her watching our exchange, her sneakers swinging slowly back and forth.

"Miss Donnelly… it means, I was having a grand day until an interruption by some lass that started asking asinine questions of me."

"Arse-in-what questions? I'm sorry… I didn't quite catch it, Mr. McKay?"

She was fuming. She'd always been easy to setoff. Her face grew red and her eyes appeared even larger behind the heavy lenses.

"I am thinking you got the gist of it lass… appears that way, anyhow."

She looked at Anna, who shrugged.

"Let's be off Anna, seems we are not welcome here." Turning toward town, she raised her voice, "Come on lass, let's be off."

She gestured with her hand to follow, but Anna turned to me. We made eye contact and it was my turn to shrug.

"You go on, Carla. I have questions to ask Mr. McKay about a homework assignment from school."

Carla stopped and spun back to glare. Her hands went to her hips, and cocking her head, a "Uuugh" escaped her mouth. Her arms then shot straight down to her sides as she balled her fists. With eyes turning to slits, her lips puckered.

"Fine then, you can just stay here! But don't you call me… or try to spend time with me. We are not friends anymore, Anna Furtak! You can just go back to feking Germany or wherever you came from. Oh… and don't you never say another feking word to me. Got it, lass?"

With that came another, "Uuugh!" as she stomped off toward Ballyamhras. After several serious clomps, she stopped and said in a matter-of-fact fashion without looking back, "Oh… and by the way…"

Bending forward at the waist, she grabbed the hem of her skirt from behind and whipping it up to expose her knickers, she said, "Up your arse!" and letting go with an evil laugh, she hopped forward into an upright position and sprinted away. Anna looked at me, shrugged, and said, "I really didn't like her anyway."

"She's a troubled lass, that one. I am surprised that you are spending any time with her a-tall."

Anna looked down at the ground in mock shame and said, "Well, we aren't really friends… those are her words. I met her on the road and she suggested we go into the, ummm… boog? Bog? For the fun of it. I think it was a bad idea though."

We both looked down at her muddy feet with chunks of sludge still stuck between her toes. We laughed together as she shyly looked away toward the mill.

"So what's that up there?" she said, pointing.

"It's a mill, what did you think it was?" I said, teasing.

She looked hard at me and halfheartedly slapped at my shoulder, sticking out her tongue. Cocking a hip, she leaned on it with one hand and tilted her head to the side, all the while tapping a foot as if she was angry.

"We have no use for it anymore—tis abandoned now."

She put her back to me and shielding her eyes with a hand, she gazed in that direction. Then she startled me on purpose by quickly spinning back. Grabbing my hands and jumping in place, she exclaimed like a child would, "Ooooo! Ciarán, lets walk up there, I want to look at it."

"Ah shite, lass, you nearly had me messing in my trousers."

"Shite, indeed," she said, giving me a mischievous grin.

Calming myself, I glanced over my shoulder to see that Carla was now just a speck in the distance and not likely to give us any more trouble.

"Okay, so… let's be off," I said.

She gave a fake squeal of delight and taking my arm, we stepped off together.

Chapter 6

"When The Apple Is Ripe..."

We walked for a while without speaking. I was trying to think of something to say, something clever to break the silence, but she spoke first, saying, "It is so much nicer to be out here with you… than with that Carla. It feels… it just feels right."

She radiated a smile at me with a look of satisfaction. I grinned back and patted the hand of the arm still wrapped in mine.

"Tis my pleasure, lass."

Her eyes strayed to her feet, but mine remained on her face. She was bang-on about it feeling right. My thoughts strayed back to when we knocked heads that first day of school. Any two fools can bump heads, but that moment now felt fitting—the collision well worth it. As we walked, I felt again like that evening on the beach. Light and airy, free from any care. Anna was a remedy I seriously craved.

We soon arrived at the small, timbered tract that surrounded the mill. Standing under the canopy of leaves on the short bridge spanning the canal, we studied the mammoth wooden wheel.

"This is so cool." Anna said, a look of amazement on her face.

I had to agree. I recalled when the water had cascaded off it as it rolled, the great drive shaft rumbling and squeaking away in its races. It had been in my seventh year of life when that great wheel stopped turning. It seemed like such a powerful thing back then. But now, its moss-covered carcass lay mute.

I experienced a fleeting sense of melancholia along with a memory of me standing in this very spot, watching the wheel commit its final revolution. I remember the Millers exiting the big oaken doors, the last one out bequeathed with the task of chaining them shut. With lunch boxes in hand, they passed without me receiving a single acknowledgement. Their faces had been of stone, their eyes distant for reasons I didn't understand.

Anna startled me out of my reflection by blurting, "Do you think we could get it started again? Do you think we can make it go?"

I chuckled at the naivety of her question. I decided not to taunt her for it and said, "Not in this lifetime lass. At the least, its axel must be fairly rotted away by now."

She looked at me inquisitively, saying, "Rotted? I don't know that word. Rot in German means, 'red'."

"How about… decayed? The rod the wheel rides on has decomposed."

She just looked at me and I saw in her eyes that she still didn't get it. Losing interest, she dashed away to the end of the bridge without a word. Running down the narrow path to the stream in a reckless fashion, she gleefully expressed a "Wooo-woo!" Sitting down in the flora on the bank, she dropped her feet into the stream.

"Oooh! So nice!" I heard her say as I leaned over the bridge's railing above her head.

Her hair shone brightly in the sunlight that filtered through the leaves. It was longer now, and down there among the flowers, she reminded me of a wee pixie.

She soon grew still and appeared to be to be lost in thought. After a few minutes, I grew impatient. I decided to walk down to her, but she snapped out of it and smiled up at me. Pulling her feet from the water and inspecting them for any remaining sludge, she wiped it away. After slipping her shoes back on, she labored back up to the road. I turned as she walked past, pretending I wasn't there. Giving her a weak cough, she turned her face left, right, and up to the sky as if looking for the source of the noise. Then giggling, she looked back over her shoulder, throwing me a 'come hither' smile.

I followed, and we did a slow stroll back the way we'd come. She maintained a ten-step lead, acting as if I she were alone. Every once in a while, I caught her glancing at me out of the corner of her eye, a big smirk on her lips. It was a test to see who would be first to give in and break the silence.

A question popped into my mind as we played her little game. The urge to ask was great. I feared it may trigger her anger, though. But perhaps it was time.

"Anna?" I said with hesitation.

Stopping, she didn't look back and said to the air, "Yes?" while rolling the stem of a small purple flower in her fingers.

I too halted, leaving a short distance between us. After several seconds, she dropped her face, and turning her head to the right, looked at me with her one brown eye. I got the impression she was growing annoyed.

"Okay… if you could get on with it before I get old and die," she said and turning, she giggled. I maintained a sober look and her expression changed to worry. Still fearful of her reaction, I hesitated even more.

"WHAT IS IT?"

"Ah… so… why was it that your folks couldn't live together any longer?"

She let out a sigh and cast her eyes down. I could see they were darting back and forth as if she was trying to sort an answer. I continued walking and when I got to where she was standing, she fell in beside me and we moved back toward the village.

"It is difficult to talk about. I am not sure I can do it without getting emotional," she said and started pulling the petals off the flower one at a time.

“It might be good for you to tell somebody and… wouldn’t I be the most worthy of the lot? Least at this moment, anyway?”

“I suppose you are right. But I fear it may bring back some of the worst memories. I am sure to cry.”

It’s not like she hadn’t already gotten emotional in my presence, so it must be worse than I imagined. I got a sinking feeling that maybe I’d gone too far. I worried if she found the courage to tell me, the very act of doing so, might divide us. Yet there was also a chance it would do the opposite. That’s what I was hoping for.

“Okay, okay, I will tell you… but you must be kind. Because… you will be the first I have ever told. You must not share this with anyone.”

“It will be our secret, I promise.”

“Ok, let’s stop, I cannot talk about this while we are walking.”

She moved over to the hip high rock wall on our left, and finding a flat spot on the top, she crawled up. Pushing off her red high-tops with her toes, I watched them tumble into the small yellow flowers that filled the roadside ditch.

I climbed up on the wall beside her and taking off my hat, I closed my eyes and soaked in the warmth of the late afternoon sun. She’d grown quiet and I thought to prompt her. I took a deep breath and that was all it took to get her started. Her words came spilling out and she talked fast.

“One night… about five years ago, my father came home late from the Rathskeller, ummm… the pub? Yes, the pub...” She hesitated, throwing me a questioning smile before casting her eyes down and sighing.

“Go on, lass, its okay.”

“So… anyway, he had been there all afternoon. He was a lawyer back then, and every day seemed a bad day for him. I remember I was in our living room, sitting on the floor when he staggered in. My mama went to greet him and he started kissing her neck. She pushed him away and told him to go to bed because he was drunk.

He grabbed her and holding her arms, he forced himself on her. She motioned with her eyes for me to get out. So, I left them, going to my bedroom. I shut the door and undressed for sleep. That's when the fight started."

"So was it like a physical fight or… just words?"

"It was a… Ringen Wettbewerbs. A wrestling contest? I heard a noise like a dish or an ashtray being thrown against the wall. Then… tussling? Scuffling? And shouting… mostly about sex. There was running and the sound of furniture being pushed over. There was a loud crash, like glass being broken. I remember being so afraid, thinking he had tossed my mama out of a window."

She paused for a few seconds more, and after taking a deep breath, she continued, her voice growing frantic. "We had a glass tea table in the front room and I remember hoping it was what had been smashed. I was so terrified, thinking about my mama lying on the pavement below with blood, and leaving me alone with that crazy man."

Her hands had been fluttering about like two butterflies and I felt relief when she finally shoved them under her legs. Staring off across the roadway for several minutes, she gave a few false starts. Her lower lip quivered, and I knew she was on the verge of sobbing.

"This was the worst it had ever been," she said in a hoarse whisper. "I had just finished getting into my sleeping gown when the bastard kicked my door open. He stood there staring like a wild animal. My mama came up from behind and tried to keep him from coming in. That's when he said to her, 'If I can't have you, then I will have her.' That's when I screamed—and like I had never screamed before."

Anna's voice cracked and squeaked as she tried to keep her composure. She glanced over at me with a pain-filled expression, so I put my hand on her shoulder and said, "Go on, Anna, tis okay."

Tears spilled from her eyes and pulling her hands from beneath her legs, she covered her mouth as if to control the sobs. When she spoke again, her words were almost to faint to hear.

"He threw my mama to the floor and came inside slamming the door so hard it, ummm… jammed? Is that the word? Oh… anyway, it stuck and my mother couldn't get it open. I heard her outside threatening to kill him if he touched me. But her words didn't help. He came to me, grabbed the collar of my gown, and ripped it off with one pull. Then he pushed me down on the bed and he… he raped me."

Her statement ended in a sorrow-filled whimper. I shuddered, the bile rising in my throat. With a voice I hardly recognized, she turned her tear-filled eyes to me and said, "Oh Mein Gott, Ciarán… it was so terrible! He wouldn't stop pushing and pushing..."

Taking my hand with both of hers, she squeezed so tight I almost cried out from the pain.

"After a while, I… Oh Mein Gott! What is the word…? Ummm… I went unconscious? Yes… that is it, unconscious. When I woke up, I was under my linen, and my mama's tears were falling on my face. She couldn't stop saying how sorry she was. Her words sounded so sad… I can still hear them to this very day."

I didn't know what to say. Shock and anger had taken over. I knew there were men like that in the world, maybe even in my village. Who knew what might go on behind drawn curtains and bolted doors? I thought about Carla and a few others, wondering if maybe they'd been subject to such things.

I felt an urge to comfort Anna by taking her into my arms, but I was fearful how that may look from a distance. So I sat there like a fool, feeling guilty for just being male.

When her sobbing grew less, she sat up straight and taking her hands from mine, she pulled her Tee shirt up from the bottom to dab her eyes. She exposed more than I am sure she intended, so I turned away.

"Youuu fuckiiing bastaaard!" filled my ears and whipping my face back in shock, I prepared to bolt. But she was shaking her fist at the distant ocean as if her da were standing out there. Bringing her eyes to mine, I saw the anger and a fierceness I'd never seen before.

"I think if I were to see him today, Ciarán, I would try to kill him. He stole something from me… something I can never get back."

Her voice sounded gruff and frightening. Sobs racked her body again and her hands found their way back to her face. A lump rose in my throat. I swallowed hard, stammering out, "So, only your ma knows of this?" Her answer came barely audible through her hands, "Yes, and it must stay that way."

"You could not call the police?"

"No!"

Pulling her hands from her face, she made fists, pushing them between her thighs. Then as if on second thought, she pulled them out and held them against her chest. Bending forward at the waist, her face became a mottled mask of anguish. "The police would not believe us. He was very well connected, making it so nothing could be done. A Meister Der Illusion… he was always making it appear as if he were not at fault for his actions. If that didn't work… money would change hands and trespasses would quickly be forgotten."

"So, your mama did not get you therapy or anything like that? I mean… to help you cope with it?"

Here I was, the typical male, trying to solve the problem as if it was a simple matter. I feared I would aggravate her emotional state and leaned away, expecting a violent response. But she just looked at me like I was fool and said, "No… and he didn't stop there. Twice more he, uhhh… snuck? Sneaked? Oh! You know what I mean… into my room at night while my mama was sleeping… to have his way with me. The last time I fought so hard it woke her. She ran in and tried to pull him off. But he hit her and… knocked her up? Knocked her out? Oooo! I need to study my English! Okay, so she was made unconscious. He finished with me and left the apartment. After a few minutes, I crawled to the floor and shook my mama awake. She was okay, but she would have a… uh… bruise? She took me away that very night. We packed bags and went into an old pension across the Havel River in Spandau, Altstadt."

"Pension?"

She hesitated and then answered, "Yes, like a hotel or a hostelry?"

"Of course… sorry."

"The divorce came soon after, and he didn't challenge it. We secretly moved to a different apartment, but he found us anyway. When he would come around, she would call the police, pleading for them to take him away. They had no choice then, because she had made a writ against him."

Looking at me now, she rubbed at her eyes, her lower lip still trembling.

"I am so sorry, Anna, this should never have happened."

"Well, it did… but I believe I should try to let it be in the past again. There is nothing I can do about it. But… you should know, I do feel better for this moment. I have finally let it out. It has been so long buried inside of me. But like you said, it is like a burden has been lessened. So… now I understand I can expect you to be here for me, yes? Do you know what I am meaning?"

"I do. You have my word on it."

She leaned over and put the side of her head against my upper arm. After a deep sigh she said, "This life can be so hard… that is why good friends can be so very important, yes?"

"Indeed darling… indeed."

I thought back to my youth when I had some of the most trustworthy mates. Then how over time I lost them to distance, or death. I felt a compulsion to throw my arm around Anna's shoulders, so I did, and laying my cheek on the top of her head, I gave her a squeeze. Let the gossipers be damned! This was far too important for me to care what others might think.

Anna moved in closer and was quiet for all of a minute. Then in a low voice, she said with sincerity, "Will you be mine, Ciarán?"

"Your good friend?"

"Yes."

"Forever," slipped from my lips, followed by the realization I'd committed myself for a lifetime. But wasn't that what I wanted? I'd nothing to lose by it, and everything to gain.

She put an arm around my waist and we sat for the longest time, the wind whispering through the grass and toying with our hair. I'd left it up to her to decide where our relationship would go and she'd done just that. With my prompt, her confession had brought her to it. I now knew her deepest, darkest secret, but it would be safe with me. June would the crucial moment—Germany or Ireland.

I glanced over to see the most serene expression on her face. I sensed that she'd found some kind of peace. Her eyes moved to me, and she said, "We should head back before the sun is gone, yes?"

"If you wish," I said, a wee bit surprised that she'd pulled herself together so quickly.

I suspected she desired to lock away all the negative debris in some subconscious bin. The thought that she'd endured something beyond imagining, and was still soldiering on, filled me with admiration. I thought of the sanctity of childhood and the fact that there were those who were all too willing to trespass there, monsters feeding on the sacred fire of innocence. I made a vow to help Anna be happy for as long as I could.

Pulling her arm from my waist, she jumped from the wall. I watched her sit down on the ground to pull on her shoes—and I saw her as a child sitting among all the little yellow flowers. A wave of sadness came over me and I wanted to hold her like my ma used to hold me when life's troubles seemed too much. I wanted to somehow, convince Anna without words that everything was going to be okay.

Leaving her laces untied, she stood, and smiling at me, jerked her head toward the road. I came off the wall and we moved out to the tarmac together. Walking north in silence, she took my hand and playfully swung it back and forth as we ambled along. Every once in a while she would glance at me with a sheepish grin like she was uncertain if the action was appropriate. I would squeeze her hand or smile to reassure her.

"Are you okay?" she asked.

"I am good, but… tis you I am concerned about."

"I think I will be fine, Ciarán… as long as you are here for me."

Pulling her to me, I embraced her like I had wished to do back at the fence. She let go with a heavy sigh and seemed to melt in my arms. But it lasted no more than a minute, and retaking my hand, we continued.

The liquid call of the lark rolled across the waving grass. The sound of boats could be heard in the distance and the smell of the sea wafted to my nose. There was something about the end of a sunny afternoon that made me love Ireland. Even more so, the people in it. Now, there was Anna. I found myself equating her to this time of day, for she seemed to enhance the very beauty of it.

When we arrived at the crossroads, she came to a stop. The sun had fallen behind the hills with just the apex of the yellow orb peaking over their tops. She stood with her back to it, her hair aglow but her face cast in shadow. Unable to read her expression, I feared I might miss any message she may send with her eyes.

"I must go to my house now, it will be dark soon," she said with reluctance.

"Anna… if I may be so bold as to ask, who is your host family? I'm wondering if I might know them."

"If you don't already know, Ciarán, perhaps it would be best it stay that way. There is nothing to gain from knowing. I'll soon be done with them. They will no longer be a part of my life. We are not getting along very well and besides, they are kind of a private people. I am not to bring friends to their home… especially not one of my schoolteachers. That would most certainly bring hysterics, and not the funny kind."

I didn't press her even though I felt I should. This made the situation awkward, but I read the discomfort in her body language. So I shrugged as an act of surrender and left it alone—for the moment.

Anna backed away, her hand still clinging to mine. She kept her hold until the length of our arms played out. Then giving my fingers a quick squeeze, she let my hand slip from hers at the very second the sun fell from sight. The gloaming climbed the sky as her face came into view, disclosing her affection.

She gazed at me for a few seconds, sighed and turned away to skip down the road to the west. I watched her move from the tarmac to the stonewall. Jumping up, she walked along its top, her arms out for balance. Stopping, she turned and raised a hand high into the air.

"Tomorrow, yes?" she shouted.

Her words sounded strange as they dissolved in the air. I waved, and she turned to continue, disappearing from sight as the wall curved down the slope.

Why tomorrow? It would be Sunday and I hadn't ever seen her on that day. I assumed her host family restricted her because of religious beliefs and kept her close at hand.

I pondered it all as I hastened toward the village. I didn't want to be caught out by myself in the gloaming, taking the risk of meeting Isleen's shade on the road. As I entered the high street, I looked back one last time just to be sure I still traveled alone.

Chapter 7

"There Is No Need, Like The Lack Of A Friend"

Coming up on Lafferty's, I decided to go in and do a wee bit of detective work. I felt entitled to know who was housing Anna, and if I could find out without her having to say it, she wouldn't be to blame. So, I would question my mates and determine if anyone had any valuable information. I was taking a risk putting myself in the spotlight. But it might be good to get it out in the open and find out what everybody was thinking; but not saying.

Walking through the door, I was immediately enveloped by tobacco smoke, the odor of bodies in a small space, and the sour smell of stout. All these things filled my nose, confirming why Ireland was such a 'Pub Culture'. It was like coming home.

"God bless all in the house," I exclaimed in a jocular fashion.

"Dia Duit." was the resounding response. A greeting that meant, 'God be with you'. It too had been conveyed with humor. Mainly because, 'Keeping the Irish' was in debate. The topic had been tattooed on our gray matter and most everyone had grown sick of hearing the political, 'back and forth'. There was a good chance that schools would soon be teaching it again, and the language might make a comeback.

So, the usual mob at the pub would shout the greeting out in unison any time someone came in blessing the house in English. It was all for the sake of good craic. A few of the more solemn patrons just nodded and mumbled, "McKay," to acknowledge my presence.

"A round of pints for everyone," I shouted as I walked up to the bar.

"Oh! So you say," Samuel, the barkeep laughed out. "And with you being just a school teacher and all. Are you sure you can swing it, lad? That's twelve pints of the black stuff to start with—and you know it's not going to stop there."

"Start pouring em, Samuel, I've a few punts in my pocket."

He started filling the glasses. Those who were not already at the bar, gravitated that way; even the mumblers. Every time he handed someone a pint they would raise it to me in thanks as they moved back to their seat. So after all had been served and my arrival ceremony complete, I moved along the great mahogany bar to where Samuel stood. Leaning across, I mentioned my interest in Anna's host family. I knew he would announce it to the room once he sorted that he had no clue.

When he did, Old Huey, a Welshman twenty years in the village, piped up. His intoxication clear as he turned his ruddy face and said, "I've saynar lingerin' aboot the McGurks gaff."

The McGurks were a quiet, religious family that didn't mix in village business. They were peculiar, which made me wonder why they would even bother hosting a foreign exchange student. They had a daughter of their own, Mary. But she'd acquired a love interest at sixteen and ran off to London.

Brendan Brown, the Postmaster, let it leak that her folks never received any word from her even though the McGurks inquired at every opportunity. Once when I'd gone in to get my correspondence, someone questioned Mrs. McGurk about her daughter. She shrieked out in reply, "That one's dead to us!" Afterwards, she stomped out the front door in a fit of rage. So, there was what they wanted us to think—and then there was the truth.

They bought a great deal of fish from Huey. It was always at a greater price for them than those of us who traveled down to the dock, or to Nolan's. The McGurks' required that he deliver the catch to them personally. So I knew there was validity in what Huey said. Along with that, it had been toward their cottage that Anna had gone when leaving me at the crossroads.

Even though I'd gotten what I came for, I still felt compelled to harass him a wee bit, mostly because it was expected. If I failed to do that, it would appear I'd no time for him, or worse yet that he'd fallen into disfavor. So I said, "Is that so, Huey? Are you sure it was her? I know you to be full of shite most of the time. So… tell me true, lad."

Being of a good nature, Huey was just happy to have been accepted among the Irish. He fished with his boy Rees, always refusing any help offered to reduce the hardships that came with handling a small boat. Something of a braggart, he became a good source of information to the other hanger-on's at Lafferty's. He was always willing keep the gossip moving forward.

Sitting up to his full height on the stool and turning toward me, he crossed his heart and said, "Naw miztakin' her, McKay. There's noo-un around here that looks anythin' like that one! Shay sticks oot like a lobster inna net foola haddock! There's naw miztakin' dem eyes…"

Belching loudly, he raised his drink to me, drained it, and set the glass on the bar, asking for another. I nodded at Samuel and he topped it off with a perfect head of foam.

I had now opened the gate—an invitation to all those who had questions and commentary. Samuel handed me my usual cup of tea as I took my seat at the end of the bar and readied myself for the onslaught.

In the time it took to take a sip, Patrick Riley was first to address the matter, the 'burning question' so to speak. I'd no qualms about it being him, though. He was somewhat of a village leader and always the voice of reason. He was also a candidate for Lord Mayor. There was no doubt that he would win the election by more than a nose, and take over for Callaghan, who'd had his fill of local politics after fifteen years.

"So what's the story with you and that lass, McKay?"

Before I could give him any kind of answer, he added, "Would you care to refute any rumor's developing from the matter?"

I scanned the room, as it grew quiet. He turned his head, directing his unwavering gaze at me as he sipped his stout.

"Well, if it will take the burden off your minds and allow you to move on to something more productive in the way of gossip, I will tell you this much… tis simply the case of a lonely lass in need of a friend."

They all looked at each other except for Riley, who kept his eyes locked on me. "So, Ciarán, the real question on our minds is… are the two of you going to become an item?"

He rotated his whole body to face me like he meant business. Looking out of the tops of his eyes, he lowered his voice and said, "Are you making plans, laddy? Will there be an addition to our little village?"

I'd nothing to hide. Moreover, I knew his concern was benevolent. I felt confident he wanted to know in the case that—should he overhear anyone else passing the information along incorrectly, he could set them straight on the matter. I trusted him.

"The only plans I'm making Mr. Riley, and the rest of youse for that matter, is to see Anna through her stay. She's just a young lass, looking for an understanding soul to guide her."

That was true for the moment. Things change though, and June would be telling.

Riley opened his mouth to speak, but he was interrupted by the words, "And you would be the best man for that now, wouldn't you Ciarán?"

The statement echoed down the stairwell leading from the chambers above. An older woman entered the pub through the curtains at the far end of the bar. Her long graying hair, now tied back in a ponytail, still held traces of the reddish-blonde it once had been. There were still freckles apparent on her cheeks and her green eyes flashed when she spoke.

It was Isleen's ma, Clare.

She walked over and placing a hand on my shoulder, kissed me on my left cheek and said, "That wasn't rhetorical, lad. Answer the feking question."

"I am."

"Right you are lad! Right you are!" she said, looking around the room, glaring at the others, and daring anyone to refute her declaration.

Walking away, she picked up a rag off the bar and greeting the drinkers one by one, she collected glasses and wiped down tables. Looking back over her shoulder, she threw a wink at Samuel and me. They grinned at each other as he made a show of straightening up the bar top.

A well-respected woman about town, Clare had taken me under her wing after my ma had passed. She'd also helped to bring her only daughter and me together. I still remember how she'd clung to me at Isleen's funeral. It was all I could do to aid Samuel in keeping her vertical. She still grieved in silence. On her worst days, she would declare out of the blue, "No one should ever have to outlive their children." No doubt, she would be subject to a lifetime of despair.

Clare rivaled Riley in about everything that involved the village. At one time, they'd even been an item. They'd called if off after she had a night out with Samuel, and the rest is history. There were no hard feelings though. Riley, on a weekend holiday to Shannon, met a woman, who oddly enough, was named Shannon. After a short courtship, he married her and brought her back to the village. So now, everyone was happy with their arrangements. The focus had now fallen on me. I believed they wanted to see me happily married again, or at least, happily something.

By the end of the evening, all but the drunkest of the lot, had migrated to the bar. They stood two deep, tipping their pints, nodding and acknowledging each other. They all wanted to put their eyes on me as they listened to what I had to say. I revealed all I could, without delving into the more personal. I was fairly satisfied that I'd quelled their concerns with logic and reason. They all seemed satisfied when I bid them good night, every one of them nodding their heads at me, and each other.

Overall, I felt comfortable that they were familiar with my situation. I had no enemies among them. So it was not too difficult for them to understand that my intentions were good, even though a wee bit unprofessional. I felt I had a responsibility as a human being first and as a schoolteacher second. I didn't know what it would be like to be so far away from home and family. Yet I harbored no doubt that Anna did.

The exchange at the pub lessened the burden of concern and I felt a kind of peace as I walked toward home. That lasted all of perhaps, ten minutes.

Coming up on the fountain, I noticed four silent figures skulking in the dark, just out of the streetlamps reach. Two of them moved to sit down on a bench as I approached, and the others went to lean against the granite basin. The way they moved put me on edge. They weren't out for an evening stroll.

As I walked past, the two on the bench stood up and the adrenalin flowed in.

"Well, if it isn't Mr. High and Mighty," Timmy O'Brian said as he and Sean stepped up to block my path.

The two on the basin wall slide around to bring themselves into view, and I saw they were the Stuart brothers. They nodded at me, their body language saying they weren't a threat. But Sean stood with his arms crossed, his eyes glittering. Timmy lingered just behind him to his right, his malicious grin saying, 'Ha! Caught you."

Taking off my hat, I held the brim with both hands in a casual manner at my waist, the inside turned toward them. I'd chosen a loose fitting jacket for the day, so I didn't fear that it would bind me when it came down to exchanging blows. I couldn't take all four of them, but I sorted this dance was reserved for me and the O'Brian's. Timmy would be an easy mark, all bluster and no bite. Sean on the other hand, would be driven by rage—not approval.

Cocking his head, he said, "Been a while Ciarán. The last time if I remember correctly, you bested me. Tonight I'm going for a different outcome."

He sounded almost reasonable, like he just wanted to discuss the matter. I got the feeling he had been goaded into it.

"He is… going to kick your arse all over the high street, and I'm going to help," Timmy said.

"Ah… no you're not," Donald's voice came, deep and threatening.

That was the most I'd heard him say in years. He stepped toward Timmy, and William joined him.

"It's only proper for me to help my brother with this little issue, don't you think?" Timmy said to Donald.

"Not what we agreed. Sean settles it here, and it's done. If you make one move against Ciarán, Timmy, it's done. One way or another…"

"It's done," William said, finishing Donald's sentence.

"Tired of not being able to go into my own pub for a pint," Donald added.

Sean looked at them, and then at Timmy.

"Back off little brother, Ciarán and I are just going to have a wee chat."

"Ah, fek that," Timmy said, and stepping around his brother, he threw a right cross. Catching it in my cap, I dropped everything and jabbed Timmy in the nose. Falling onto his arse, he squealed, putting a hand to his face.

"Ah, little brother.... you are the eejit, aren't you."

Sean uncrossed his arms and I expected him to help his brother up, but instead, he threw the next punch. I ducked left, but he caught me in the ear. Going into a crouch, he said, "No one hits my brother—not even for a good reason. You just voided my peace negotiation, McKay."

Timmy jumped up, his nose bleeding. He fell in beside Sean, both of them squaring off. I watched Donald's arm came over Timmy's shoulder and under the opposite armpit. Pulling him back, Donald struggled to keep him out of arms reach of me. Sean looked at the Scotsman and said, "You let him go, big fellow… or you're next."

"Ah… no, Sean O'Brian. Did you really want to make this a war of brothers?" William said, and then putting Sean in a headlock, they gyrated around the wet pavement, both grunting in exertion.

I stepped back to watch them tussle. I thought perhaps to walk away, but Sean swept William off his feet and the big man fell hard, his head smacking the pavement. His bushy hair cushioned the blow; otherwise, he would have been down for the count. He lay there groaning and rubbing his head as Sean came back to me.

He danced around like he fancied himself a boxer. I turned as he circled me, waiting for him to throw the next punch. Timmy and Donald still wrestled, but the bigger man had him good.

"Okay, youse… I've seen enough."

It was Arlyn.

He walked toward us from the direction of the pub. Stopping just inside the streetlamps circle of light with hands on hips, he said, "Release that lad, Donald Stuart. This ends now. Sean, I seen you got a lick in on Ciarán, consider that to be your payback for whatever he did… or didn't do, a long time ago."

Donald released Timmy, and the smaller man, said, "You gobshite, Donald Stuart, what's the story, boyo?"

"Shut it, Timmy O'Brian. You're the gobshite, as far as I'm concerned. You and Sean don't live inside the village limits. If you want to be banned not only from Lafferty's, I'd quit now if I were you."

Arlyn eyes were doing some glittering of their own, and his voice sounded as I'd never heard it before.

"Why don't you shut it, old man," Timmy said as Sean stopped his shuffling moves and turned to Arlyn to say, "You can't keep us out of this town, mister wannabe Garda. Why don't you go bake some biscuits or something?"

"Oh, I certainly can keep you out. I'll see to it the Lord Mayor has you banned and you can do your business down in Swords. And of course, if you're barred from Ballyamhras, I'm thinking you can't be working here. So, give that some thought, will you?"

Sean steamed, glaring around at the lot of us. Turning back to me, he said, "You, McKay… I know you got that pretty little lass of yours, now. I'm thinking she's going to be off soon, and you'll have no one. How's that going to feel? Then you'll know just what it's like."

"I already know what it's like. But you didn't see me beating Isleen daily. She didn't leave me for the same reason Julia left you. That lass did it so she wouldn't end up in the same place—in the ground."

"Oh, such a shame, poor Mr. School Teacher lost his wife."

"That's enough, Timmy O'Brian," Arlyn said, bristling.

"I'm feeling like I want a little more of you, Ciarán McKay," Sean said.

He stepped in closer and his fists came up. Timmy came up beside him and did the same. That's when Arlyn stepped over and leaning forward, he put his lips within inches of Sean's ear, and said in a low, menacing tone, "Okay Sean O'Brian, let's just see how this goes between the four of us." Then leaning back, he sidled up to me and we waited for the O'Brian's to make their move.

"Make that the six of us," Donald said, and moving around from behind Sean and Timmy, he came and stood on my other side. William moved up beside Arlyn, still rubbing his head, and with a voice identical to Donald's, he said, "How's it look now for you, Sean? I'm thinking you might just be out of a job, hiagh? They're always hiring dishwashers down Dublin way. You might want to head on down."

Sean studied us, still trying to figure out a way to best me. He must have sorted that it was a lost cause.

"Just a bunch of maggots, you are," he said, and walking away, finished with, "I've had enough of this feking rubbish heap, anyway. Just remember McKay, I got the last lick in. So, you can go to hell."

Timmy followed after him, and turning to walk backwards, he flipped us off and said, "A bunch of maggots for sure, and you McKay… the worst of them."

Donald made a move like he might give chase, and Timmy took off at a run to catch up with his brother. Sean looked back after walking into the light of the next lamp and said, "Come along little brother," and then he flipped us off as well.

Donald turned to me and said, "So where you off to, Ciarán?"

"Home… had enough for one day. Want to put some ice on this ear. Sean's never been one to pull his punches."

"Are you sure you won't accompany the Stuart's and me, back to the pub?" Arlyn said. "I'm up for buying a round, what do you say, lad?"

"Ah… no, but thanks anyway. Maybe next time, hiagh?"

"Have it your way. At least… let us walk you to your gaff."

"Aye Ciarán, we could walk you as well, especially if it involves a pint," Donald said, with William adding, "I'm there with you, big brother. If you don't mind, Ciarán? I know we haven't said but a mere word to you over the past few years, but we still have plenty of life left to make up for it. If you'll give us a chance to do just that?"

“No problem, a-tall, William, I’d be happy to have you.”

With that, we all nodded in agreement, and they strolled with me as far as my front door. Then Arlyn led them away, yakking on about what he would have done if Sean had not backed down. Going inside, I realized I hadn’t even come close to a panic attack during the fray. It left me to wonder if I might be cured.

Chapter 8

"...Love Leaves A Memory No One Can Steal"

I did not see Anna the following day, or in school on Monday. The attendance record showed she was out ill. It was the last week of classes though, and many students skipped out to start their summer holidays early. Four more days went by as I watched my class dwindle to five of my most dedicated scholars; Anna not among them. I was a wee bit concerned.

Would she now avoid me out of shame?

On Friday afternoon, school dismissed early. I went down to the boulders to dangle my feet in the coolness of the sea and suffer in my rejection. I couldn't express my disquiet over Anna's absence because, once again, as a Irishman, I was expected to be happy in my sadness. For me, it was something more akin to what that fellow, Thoreau, said about, "Quiet desperation."

Perching myself upon a low shelf of rock at the seaside of the largest boulder, I removed my shoes and stockings. The ledge had eroded to be just long enough to accommodate four people, side by side, and deep enough, to lean back in comfort. Sitting with my feet in the water, only the top of my head showed to the street.

It was a mild sunny day and I took in the warmth of the granite, my flat cap draped across my footwear. I watched the Stuarts working the beach—without the help of the O'Brian's. Rumor had it Sean and Timmy had quit the village maintenance department. Their excuse: they could no longer work with Donald and William.

I waved to the two Scotsman who moved south toward the pier, pulling their light carts behind them, the chrome spokes of the bicycle-like wheels glittering as they rolled. They both raised a hand and then moved on. I dozed off, but soon awoke to someone saying, “Where have you been? I've not seen you for days.”

It was Anna projecting mock anger.

“Me? I’m thinking it might be herself who ought to come around more often.”

I remained motionless as I awaited her reply. I knew she was standing on the top of the boulder, looking down, but when she didn’t respond, I turned and smiled up at her. I’d a clear view up her short denim skirt, so I quickly brought my eyes back to the sea.

“What’s wrong, Ciarán? Don’t you want to talk me?” She said, sounding hurt.

“That’s not it a-tall lass, tis just… I can see up your skirt.”

“Oh Ciarán, it’s not like you haven’t seen it before,” she said and giggled.

“Perhaps, but it wouldn’t be proper for me to sit down here gawking at your pretty pink pants now, would it?”

Glancing back, I saw she’d stood fast, hands on hips. She moved her right foot forward about a step as if to help keep her balance, thus, exposing her undercarriage all the more.

“Oh Ciarán… you are such a puritan.”

Rolling my eyes, I focused on her face.

“Oh now lass … don’t start the name calling. Claim I’m a gentleman, if you must… but not a puritan. Come sit down by me, Anna. But don’t keep standing up there exposing your gee to the world.”

She hesitated, squinting at me as she mumbled, “Gee?” I chuckled, patting the surface beside me. She gave in and sliding carelessly down the stones face, she exposed even more. Then moving over next to me, she pressed in close, adjusting her short skirt as she did.

Her hip pressed into mine, so I attempted to move to the right, but she followed. I gave up trying to escape and glancing at her exposed thighs, I couldn't help but notice her flawless skin along with the slight tan she'd acquired. I forced myself to refocus on my feet as they soaked in the salty water. Conversation was in order, so I started to speak but she whispered, "Hush, no talking."

Her demeanor changed with the speed of flipping a switch. The jovial attitude she conveyed upon her arrival seemed to melt away. I found it odd, because the transformation was so abrupt. But she was experienced at putting on the 'Happy Face'. I expected that she had something important to tell me.

She put the side of her cheek against my upper arm, her right hand snaking around behind my back. I experienced a fleeting moment of concern. But then I relaxed, remembering we'd nothing to worry about now that our relationship was no longer a mystery. I turned my eyes back to the sea, but my thoughts remained on her perplexing behavior.

We sat for the longest time with the seabirds calling, and boat sounds echoing in the distance. With the smell of the ocean always in my nose, it was now underscored by the sweet scent of Anna's perfume. I stole a glance at her face only to find a tear now traced its way down her cheek. It caught me off guard. I'd not heard a sniffle or a whimper. As I turned my face to her, she looked at me and I saw the pain in her eyes.

Why such strong emotion?

I rubbed her back in an attempt to comfort her and my touch triggered a reaction. Throwing her other arm over my stomach, she moved her face to my chest and burst into tears. She sobbed so loudly that I became unnerved.

All I could do was endure and try to be supportive. I stroked her hair and whispered, "It will be okay, lass."

I don't think she believed a word of it. She seemed to be comforted by my soothing tone though, the sobs eventually subsiding to sniffles. Releasing her hold, she ran the palms of her hands up and down her thighs in a nervous manner.

"Tomorrow… I go home," she said and sighed. "My host family wants me on my way. They have had enough of me. Whatever they hoped would happen by having me there… simply didn't. The last five days have just been hell. We fought every day. The program was supposed to be for ten months, but even though I am ready to leave them… I am not ready to leave you. But my mama called last evening on the telephone. She wants me home. She was crying, begging me to come back to Berlin. So travel arrangements have been made, and my mama is now expecting me to arrive Tegel in the afternoon, tomorrow."

So that was it!

I was shocked. But I assumed too much. I never gave a great deal of consideration to her ma, or how she might influence Anna's decision. Now it was I who would be shedding tears. A feeling like I'd drank cold, liquid concrete filled my gut.

"I will miss you terribly," she said and sitting up straight, she rubbed her eyes.

At a loss for words, I sensed a panic attack coming on. I struggled to maintain my composure, yet I needed to say something. I couldn't just sit there like some kind of an eejit.

"I will miss you too," slipped from my lips, my voice cracking, as I feared it would. I wanted to beg her to stay longer and try to convince her that her ma could wait. But not weeping in public being my first rule, and not begging as my second, I kept my mouth shut.

An overwhelming feeling of great loss crept in and Anna wasn't even gone yet. It confirmed how much I'd come to rely on her presence. Tears stung my eyes, and I turned my face so she couldn't see them. I felt her move away and from the corner of my eye, I watched her stand up and brush the sand off the back of her skirt. I kept my face angled down and turned slightly away to the right, hoping she wouldn't notice my despair.

"Let's go walking, Ciarán, please? Just like we did before."

"Very well," I said as I pulled my feet from the sea.

Luckily, my shoes and stockings were on my right. I could be turned away from her as I put them on. When I stood up, I tried to mop at my eyes without her being aware. But no such luck. Grabbing my arm, she levered me around.

"Ciarán, you are crying… I have not ever seen you cry."

"Well, you know lass, I am only human. I too shed a wee tear once in a while." Chuckling, I tried to laugh it off.

"So… you will miss me. Oh Ciarán! This makes me so happy."

"And why wouldn't I… miss you, that is."

She didn't answer, but threw her arms around me and squeezed, twisting me back and forth. Then releasing her hold, she jumped up and down in place, clapping her hands, beaming.

"Shall we be off?" I asked. "Before you slip and fall into the sea?"

Without a word, she turned to the boulder to start her climb. I wanted to help, so I sandwiched her waist with my hands and gave her a lift. She raised a knee so her foot could find a hold, and the hem of her skirt climbed to bunch at her waist. This exposed pink silk knickers stretched taut across a firm backside—and only mere centimeters from my face.

Silkscreened there, in large, blue letters, was the word: LOVE.

Dropping my eyes and my hands, I refocused on her other foot. Interlocking my fingers, I allowed her to use it as a step and I gave her a boost. With my eyes averted, I started up, searching for hands holds like a blind man. I felt her grab my wrists, and she tried to tow me up, saying, "Let me help you, Ciarán." I brought my eyes up to her and smiled, thinking I was safe. But she now crouched above me, funneling my vision between her legs. Turning my head left, I felt my face grow hot.

When we finally stood together at the top, seconds passed in silence. She had her arm wrapped in mine, but I was looking south toward the pier as if there was something of great interest there. I felt her staring the whole time and when the heat left my face, I turned and gave her the, 'WHAT?' face. She giggled and said, "Don't you like my choice of lingerie? They're my favorite."

"Excuse me? Sorry?"

"I know you saw them."

"I've seen nothing, my eyes were clouded with tears. I… read nothing."

"Oh! You 'read' nothing? Hah!" she said and gave me a slight shake. A finger moved to wipe at my wet lashes and I playfully pushed it away. Taking a handkerchief from my pocket, I dabbed them dry.

A strong desire to spend all of our remaining hours together overcame me. Even though it was unsaid, I knew she felt the same. So, we strolled about the village at a leisurely pace, discussing things unrelated to her departure. We skipped our supper and took an expedition north as the afterglow faded from the horizon. The gloaming came, but I was with Anna, so I believed I had nothing to fear about what it may bring.

Turning back upon reaching the village limits of Skerries, we moved down to walk through the grassy fields that bordered the sea. Gaining the beach below Ballyamhras, we lingered there to play fully clothed in the breakers. Digging in the wet sand, we created ill-fated castles, subject to the whims of the surf. Then taking turns, we climbed atop the short, decapitated columns that once supported the old pier, and adopting hilarious poses while perched upon their tops, we laughed ourselves silly.

We grew tired of that and soon found ourselves sitting on the shore, snuggling in the dark of a two o'clock morning. The last of the lighted windows blinked out behind us, telling me the pub was closed. The drunk and weary had at last found their beds.

It was the epitome of romantic moments. I forgot all about who I was supposed to be, and the responsibilities that came with that particular role. Being with Anna took me back to my childhood and a time before death's shadow had darkened my doorway.

When we felt rested, we roamed back through the town square and found Arlyn sitting asleep on the bench at the fountain. Rousing, he opened one eye, mumbled a greeting, and dozed off again. I wished him a good morning, hoping he would forget he ever saw us, or perhaps, remember our meeting only as a dream.

From there, we turned to the west, making our way down a side street that I didn't frequent much. It soon transformed into a narrow highway that ran through a forested area before making its way up into the hills.

Upon arriving at the base of the slopes, we agreed to avoid the ceaseless gradients by turning back. As we walked, Anna chattered away about anything and everything. I listened, pondering all that she said. She expressed a great deal of optimism despite all her misgivings, and I adored her for that.

"Ciarán, do you think you would ever come to Berlin?" she asked, stealing a glance.

There it was. I sensed earlier that our discussion would go that way—it couldn't be avoided. I contemplated her question for a minute while looking up at the open swath of sky between the tops of the trees. A thin layer of cloud now veiled the moon, dimming the stars and darkening the byway.

"I don't know, why?"

"Why not? Could you not bear to leave your beloved Ireland?" she scoffed in a playful manner.

"Sorry darling, but I am not sure my umbilical cord will reach that far."

She giggled, and punching me lightly on the shoulder, said, "Would you please?" Then, wrapping my right arm in hers, she looked up into my face as we walked.

"I cannot make that kind of a promise, Anna. I have a life here, a job, and besides, I have never been to Germany."

Realizing how insecure that sounded, I regretted having said it. It was an evasive response, and without question—not what she wanted to hear. She sighed in disappointment and releasing my arm, she came around to face me. I had to stop so quickly, my shoes slid on the dew covered asphalt. Looking hard into my face, she proceeded to sandwich my waist between the palms of her hands, pleading, "Ciarán, I am begging you. Come to Berlin and… rescue me."

"Rescue you? You need to be rescued?"

"Ciarán! You are the only person in my life who has ever understood me. I cannot just let you go."

She moved in close, her hands sliding around to the small of my back as she pressed her breasts to my chest.

"So… I am the only one? There must have been others?" I said, trying to ignore the presence of her chest against mine.

"No Ciarán, there hasn't."

"Not even a boyfriend?"

"There have been boyfriends, yes… silly man! But young boys my age are foolish and do not understand love. Besides, I could never tell to them, what I have confessed to you. They would never have understood. I would be considered damaged. Kaput! Yes, it's true, I grew close to some of them. But I couldn't bring myself to continue our relationship. If they were to learn of my secret, it would be over in… how you say... a heartbeat, yes? Then there were the fights and arguments. They would always try to control me and I would get so angry. With you—it is not that way. You're a smart man, Ciarán and… you are kind. I am so happy for that, and there are other things, of course."

She finally stepped back, leaving me to breathe a quiet sigh of relief. A passion had risen in me and I needed a moment to calm myself. She remained in front of me though, and taking my wrists, she swung them in and out as if I were a squeezebox.

"There is also Jana… my mama. Always trying to influence me. Always interfering. Telling me it was in my best interest to end my relationships before they even got started. She didn't believe I could make good choices. Now there is this thing—this intuition. It is like a chemistry between you and me. I am so comfortable, like a… ummm… baby kangol… uhhh… kangaroo in its mama's bag… ummm… pouch? That's it! So, my decision is final. I don't want to lose that... or you."

"Why don't you just stay?"

"Oh I can't, Ciarán. My mama needs me. This is the first time she ever told me so. I cannot let it pass. It is my chance to show her I can be… what? Worthy? Valuable? So many things."

I felt torn. Was it logic and reason or, fear?

Pulling my hands from hers, I pushed the mist-laden hair away from her eyes. At that moment, the clouds scudded away and the moon broke through to illuminate her face.

"Ciarán, can't you see? I have been trying to tell you for a long time that… that I love you."

There it was.

The tone of her voice left no doubt that what she said was true, but it brought a memory of me and Isleen.

The morning of her passing, we stood embracing in the doorway just before I departed for the school. We kissed, and it was the last time I would ever hear her say, "I love you." Those words still echoed inside my head. Sometimes, even waking me from a sound sleep, my cheeks wet with tears. She was the only one, other than my ma, who'd ever said those three words to me.

But, what was love?

I'd always believed it to be the mix of joy and acceptance. If what I believed was true, then I would have to admit—I loved Anna as well.

I got lost in my thoughts and it must have been an awkward silence for her. She soon brought me out my reflective quandary with, "Do you love me, Ciarán?"

Her tone was fearful as if she expected rejection, but the words tumbled out of my lips without resistance, "Anna… darling, I believe there's nothing more certain in my life right now than the love I bear for you."

"Oh, thank you," she said and sighed in relief.

Tilting her head back, she startled me by bellowing into the sky, "Thank you, thank you, THANK YOU!"

She then embraced me so ferociously, it almost took me off my feet.

"Who you talking to up there, lass? Is there someone in the tree?" I said, laughing and nodding up toward the mammoth willow that canopied the roadway.

"Oh… you!" she said, realizing I was joking. Still clinging to my hand, she walked backwards, towing me along as she gazed into my face.

I continued to tease, saying, "Honestly lass, who were you talking to up in that tree?" Feigning more concern, I looked back over my shoulder several times.

"Such a comedian," she said and giggled.

Releasing my hand, she fell in beside me. The clouds had disappeared and the moon glow lit up the roadway. The stars were back, billions of them. They twinkled all the way to the horizon, now pregnant with the dawn. We still had about two kilometers to go before we would be back in the village. I wasn't in any hurry for our night to end. So, we kept our pace to that of a turtle race, and Anna fell to talking about all the things she would miss about Ireland. I only interjected when she couldn't find the proper English word to describe something.

As the sky lightened in the east, the radiance of the moon faded. Ballyahmras soon appeared before us, silhouetted against the horizon. I wished I'd brought a camera to capture the scene. But I didn't need a photograph to remind me of this moment with Anna. I felt the warmth of her soft hand in mine and it made me wish for more. It wasn't long before my bliss was fractured by the thought that—in a few hours, she would be gone.

A short time later, we found ourselves back on the high street, standing just outside the darkened windows of the pub. There wasn't another soul around except for several gulls searching the gutter for whatever mattered to gulls.

"I can't go on anymore Anna, I'm knackered."

"Oh… okay. We should rest then," she said, her face looking haggard in the early morning light.

She surprised me with an embrace, trapping my arms at my sides. This left my hands free, and they strayed to her hips. For the first time, I touched her in a way I had never before, nor ever thought I would. Feeling their muscular firmness, a familiar yearning came surging in. Tilting her head back, she gave me a look that said I had her consent.

"There is a secret I have been keeping, bend down here and let me tell you in your ear."

If there'd been more time to think about it, I would have sorted that there was no need for her to say it in my ear. A low conversational tone would have done the trick without waking the Lafferty's.

I did as she asked though, discovering that it wasn't my ear she wanted. Her lips met mine and even though unprepared, I didn't pull away. Closing my eyes, I let her breath fill my mouth. After about a minute, she pulled back, sighing. Opening my eyes, I looked into hers to see the intense fire that burned there.

"Come to Berlin, Ciarán," she begged softly. "Come to my city and make me happy. But please don't come down to Dublin airport to see me off today, I couldn't bear it."

Her eyes became moist and pleading. A pain rose in my chest, like the blade of a knife had pierced my heart.

"What? No! Anna… I need…"

"No! If you come, I may not leave, and there would be trouble," she said, her bottom lip quivering.

"How will I find you? Berlin is not a wee village, you know."

"So you will come!" she said, ignoring my question.

There was excitement in her voice and her eyes sparkled through their mist. Releasing me, she slid her hands under my arms to wrap them around my back, setting my hands free to embrace her. Putting her cheek to my chest and giving me another tight squeeze, she whispered, "Danke schön." Then she abruptly released her hold and sprinted away down the high street, saying, "I have to get back to the house, and it is very far. Besides… if I don't go now, I may not go at all. Goodbye Ciarán... come to me, soon! Please!"

At one point, she spun around long enough to walk backwards and wave like a mad woman. Her short denim skirt and light blue camisole soon faded into the distance along with those red high top sneakers.

She hadn't answered my question.

Now I had a dilemma. Short of chasing her down, I would not get an answer today. I could always go to the McGurks and ask for the information. I suspected they would have an address or a telephone number. Being that they were my fellow Irish, I was comfortable in the thought they would help me out.

I must have cut a pretty sad figure standing with the sun shining on me as it rested its arse upon the Irish Sea. My image in the pub window confirmed that thought.

My mind was a clutter. I didn't know what to think or do. There were too many things for my exhausted brain to sort out. I had a choice to make. I could drop everything, buy a ticket, and head for Germany, or fall back into the same old summer routine of a time before Anna.

The latter caused me some distress. So, I focused on the former. If I went to Berlin, my life would change drastically. I had to ask myself what a life with Anna would be like. Would she want to stay in Germany to live, marry and raise children? Would her mother interfere, or worse yet, cause me unwarranted trouble? My exhaustion made it too difficult to keep things straight. I needed sleep.

I tried to calm myself during the trek home, but nothing worked. I felt vulnerable to the world and I scolded myself inwardly for this weakness. I had survived the death of a wife, so I could, with certainty, survive this. It's not like I wouldn't have a chance to see Anna ever again. Unlike Isleen, she was still here on the face of the earth and still available for my embrace.

Upon returning to my cottage, I fell into bed fully clothed with only enough energy to remove my sodden shoes. I remained there for a good part of the day, sleeping fitfully. Post-funeral nightmares pushed me to the edge of consciousness, where they would dissolve away, allowing me to fall back into slumber until the next.

Faces drifted in and out of shadowy places, some familiar, some not. The ocean waves crashed against the rocks as they washed me into the swell, pulling me down. Then there was Isleen, standing on the green with a bouquet of small white flowers in her hand. Laughing, she turned and ran away from me, only to transform into a macabre skeleton that fell apart into a pile of bones. I stood helpless, watching the flowers float down onto the hideous thing that had once been my beautiful wife.

I startled awake, this time to sit upright in the bed and call out her name. The sun had made its way to the southwest corner of the cottage. It was already late afternoon. An oppressive melancholia lay over me like a heavy weight. Looking around the room, I saw the duvet was now on the floor. One muddy sock still clung onto my left foot, the other, hanging off the edge of the mattress. There were streaks of mud on the sheet, along with sand and the wet of the ocean. I lay propped up by my right arm, my left hand, resting on my pillow. I felt the wetness there and I assumed there had been tears.

Glancing at the clock, I saw it was half-four. I figured Anna must be back in Berlin by this point. I wished for a way to confirm she had arrived safely, but that only took me back to square one.

There came an overwhelming desire to get up and perform a normal act. Anything routine to make me feel like everything was all right with the world.

Shaving was normal.

So, in the haze of my after-sleep, into the bathroom I went. Losing all my clothing to the laundry hamper, I turned on the faucet to the claw-footed behemoth of a tub. While waiting for it to fill, I stood naked in front of the mirror, studying my face.

The memories crept in like a mob of boggarts seeking to pull me down. So I attempted to distract myself, and picking up my old safety razor, I went to changing the blade. My eyes fixed on the wafer thin piece of chromium steel and the thought that occurred was foreign to me. I shivered as a beguiling, faerie-like voice inside my head tried to convince me how easy it would be to end the pain. All I had to do was climb into the bath, lay back, and drag the keen edge of that blade up my arms. With the help of the hot water, I would simply drift off into the eternal sleep of the damned.

There came what felt like a slight shove from behind. Whenever I said something stupid around Isleen, she would give me a wee shove, saying, “Oh, you’re such an eejit, Ciarán McKay!”

Looking over my shoulder, I half expected her to be standing there. This triggered my ire, and I flung the razor hard into the lavatory. It bounced off the bottom and surprised me when it sailed over into the wastepaper bin.

“Good place for you,” I shouted as I climbed into the bath. “Maybe I’ll just grow a feking beard and surprise the shite out of everyone.”

I submerged to wet my hair and resurfacing, I lay with my head on the rim. A picture of me dead in cold bloody water, manifested in my mind.

A coward's way out.

I had never believed myself a coward, and up until this point, I always vowed that I would go out fighting.

Shivering again, despite the hot water, I found myself fretting to a degree that I'd not expected. I desperately wanted to hear Anna's voice, to touch her, and feel her touch me in return. Regret, for not having tried harder to keep her here, swelled like a balloon inside me.

Isleen's loss could not be helped. However, Anna's could. I'd been lackadaisical. I tried to convince myself that I had no clue the longing would run so deep. That didn't work. Anna was gone. I would not see her at the Post later today or playing in the fountain. The streets would be empty of her presence. Like some kind of horror movie, it all seemed so surreal.

Chapter 9

"The Road Falls Away"

Days flowed into weeks, and I lived my life in a bubble. I responded to inquiries as if a zombie, every day drifting into the next. Nothing seemed real, every action bordering on the mechanical. I was living my life as I had during the days following Isleen's funeral.

I found myself at home more often now that school was off. The whiskey bottle perched up on the top of Isleen's curio called my name in a faerie soft whisper. I tried to focus on other things, but to no avail. I could have simply walked over, picked it up and flung it out an open window. At least then, I could take a certain amount of joy in the shower of glass and malt as it shattered on the pavement.

But that would be too much like disposing of a set of crutches because you believed you would never break a leg. How could one foresee when one would be in need of something to lean on? I decided to just remove it from my sight and stashed it away in the least used kitchen cupboard. As an added measure, I stacked other items around it to hide the bottle from view.

In my daily rumination, I found I was growing tired of being the current topic at Lafferty's. Along with that, my daily walk on the beach was more of an annoyance than a comfort. Being out there alone always brought the temptation to walk out into the rushing waves and not turn back.

By mid-July, I was grievously missing Anna. It was a heavy sensation—an indescribable weight. Anna's face would appear in my mind either laughing or sporting that haunting look that came with her despair. The one that would tear at my guts every time and compel me to take her in my arms. She'd become a true friend and our relationship had become a sanctuary. Anna had transformed into a beacon of hope—the breaking dawn of my dark night.

More often than not, in the long, lonely hours after sunset, I would find myself wishing my ma were still alive. She was always good for advice, and always seemed to say the right thing. If she were with me now, I could confide in her without judgement. Yet wishing her back would have no positive outcome other than to reprocess the same old memories. I needed a solution, anything to end my cycling toxic thoughts, all bolstered by loneliness.

Then it came to me late one Sunday as I sat reflecting in my garden. The one person who could offer me some relief—but at a risk to her own piece of mind. I hadn't wanted to trouble her for that reason. But the time had arrived. I also feared that any mention of my weakness would trigger an explosive lecture. Knowing her as I did, it might be the best thing for me or—the very worst.

Putting on my jacket and grabbing my hat, I made my way to Lafferty's. Stopping outside, I looked in through the window. They weren't officially open on the seventh day of the week, but the door remained unlocked until around half nine at night. I still had about thirty minutes, so I slipped inside.

"What's the story, darling?" Clare said after stepping out of the stairwell. The dim lights cast their glow upon her hair as she laid a clipboard on a shelf next to some liquor bottles. I walked to the center of the bar and placing one foot on the brass rail, put my chin in my hand, resting my elbow on the varnished mahogany. I did my best to appear as forlorn as possible while nervously tracing the grain of the wood with a finger.

It got the results I expected. First the worried look, followed by her leaning across and kissing me on the cheek, and last, the laying of her hand upon mine to stop its motion.

"What's troubling you, Ciarán?"

When my eyes found hers, she gave me a look of genuine concern.

"I need your advice Clare. Or… at the least, an opinion."

"Well, I've never steered you wrong yet, have I lad?"

She smiled as she pulled two whiskey glasses from a rack and filled them with her best Irish. Sipping on one, she handed me the other.

"Ah Clare, you know I've sworn off drinking."

"Come now Ciarán, drink slow if you must, but share one with me. You know I'm best at sorting problems with a lovely glass of whiskey in my hand."

I didn't want to argue. I needed someone to help me regulate what I was feeling. Clare remained the only one available for the job. The last thing I wanted was to set her off.

"Okay lass, just half of that though, and add a wee bit of water to it will you?"

Clare smiled, dumped half of mine into hers and adding seltzer, said, "There you go, luv. Now, what's on your mind?"

"Well… tis Anna."

"The foreign lass?"

"Herself. It's that… she made a request of me before she was off."

"And what was that, then?"

To show her concern, she leaned in closer to my face. The smell of her perfume and the whiskey on her breath filled my nose. She tried for some serious eye contact, but I avoided it by averting my eyes.

"As you may know, we got kind of close. She was always seeking me out, and I didn't have it in my heart to turn her away. Then I learned she was just as good for me as I was for her. So… we spent a lot of time together."

Glancing up to catch her reaction, I quickly looked away from her searching eyes to focus on the stairwell. I noticed the curtain moved as if in a draft. Someone had opened the door at the top.

"Well lad, you didn't do a real good job of hiding that now, did you? What did you expect was going to happen… spending so much together?"

She emitted a husky giggle and continued, "Knowing you as we do Ciarán, the common belief here is that you were nothing but good for that lass."

'That's what I'm saying."

She patted my hand and gave me a look of reassurance.

"So that's a big part of my problem. Anna claims no one has ever been as good to her as I, and because of that, she couldn't help but… but fall in love with me."

I brought my eyes to her's and she shook her head, making a, "tsk-tsk," noise. She pondered my statement for a minute and said, "Not too hard for that to happen with you, Ciarán. I am quite aware that it didn't take Isleen long."

Standing up to her full height, Clare set her glass on the bar and gripped the edge of it with both hands. This told me she was preparing to say something that was going to hurt the both of us. Casting her eyes down, the words poured from her lips. "I remember herself running in that door and announcing it to the room. It was years ago after you spent the whole day together at the Samhain Festival. She was standing right where you're standing now, declaring, 'Mama, I'm going to marry that boy!' I remember as if it was yesterday. There she was, hands on hips, looking around as if daring anyone to challenge her decision."

Clare laughed, and reaching across the bar, slapped my shoulder in her mirth. It was the sign that her composure was swirling away like a basin of dishwater down the drain. I chuckled, and straightening up, I put my hands flat on the bar in preparation for my response.

She organized a stack of drink napkins with an index finger as her face softened and lower lip began to quiver. Her words sounded strained as she said, "My luv told me during supper that night that she would be with you for the rest of her life. So feking ironic… hiagh, Ciarán? She was bang-on about that."

Choking back a sob, she pressed a hand to her mouth. I didn't know what to say, so sliding my arse up onto a stool, I watched a single tear splash onto the bar top. She hurried to wipe it away with one of the napkins and gave me a pain-filled smile. More tears were welling up and I knew if they came—mine would soon follow. She turned and walked to the giant mirror behind the bar. Picking up a rag, she went to work dusting liquor bottles.

"You're all she talked about, day in and day out until you two became an item. Then she grew most secretive, making it her own business. Samuel and I didn't mind, it brought us relief to know it was our own Ciarán. Of course, you know very well how I helped it along."

She stopped wiping for a second as she studied me in the mirror.

"Isleen truly loved you, boy."

"As I did her Clare… as I did her."

I watched the light glint off the tears flowing down her face and my own lip started to tremble. I got that weird sensation in my nose, telling me my own waterworks were about to commence. Gulping a couple of times, I struggled to bring my emotions under control. I needed to finish what I'd come there to do, and not just sit there blubbering.

"Clare, I think… I think I have fallen for Anna."

I saw her eyes go wide for a second and pursing her lips, she said nothing.

"It's been driving me mad. I haven't been able to eat or sleep and I can hardly keep my thoughts straight."

She spun around as if angry. Wiping her eyes with the back of one hand, she shook a finger at me with the other.

"Ciarán McKay—you're a grown man now," she said in a loud, matter-of-fact way. "You have lived in Ireland all your life. You were born Irish, and you'll die Irish. Besides, there are plenty of young, available lassies here in the Lusk parish… and Baldongan for that matter. So let us keep to our own kind, hiagh boy? Let us… keep it in the family, so to speak."

I shifted on my stool as she stuck out her chest and planted her hands on her hips. Her reaction didn't surprise me. The odds she would choose to give me sound advice instead of a speech were not in my favor. I prepared for lecture mode.

"You know as well as I do, that Sean O'Brien brought a German back from one of his continental roving's. And how long did that last? Tell me Ciarán, how long? Gone after a year, back to Germany, back to her own."

I felt my ire rising and I lashed out, saying, "Ah cripes, Clare, Sean's an eejit. He's the worst of us. It wasn't Ireland that Julia ran away from—it was him. It didn't take long for her to learn about his true self."

Clare's eyes bulged, and she said, "He's an Irishman none the less, eejit or not, you should be considering that."

"No Clare, Irishman or not, he's a gobshite. An embarrassment to us all, and the rest of Ireland for that matter. That bastard should not be used as an example of how… we all should be."

I got down from the stool and stepping away from the bar, I got loud.

"Julia was a good woman, doing her best in a bad situation. When it got to where it was all she could endure, she did the smart thing and took herself out of the equation."

"Ciarán McKay, if I am not mistaken, you are raising your voice to me."

Looking down at the floor, I toned it down a bit, but continued. "Clare, I know you are still hurting over Isleen and… you probably always will be. No one should ever have to put their baby in the ground. I have to move on. I will always love Isleen, but I can't go on like this. Anna is a good person too… Irish or not. There is no good reason she couldn't be happy here with me. My path now seems clear. So maybe tis your blessing I'm truly seeking?"

Realizing what I said, I stopped. In the heat of my rant, I'd solved my own problem. Perhaps this was what I needed. Not so much taking Clare's advice, but knowing in the back of my mind that if I got into an exchange with her, I would get fired up and push myself into the proper frame of mind. It was like I was giving her my word, knowing well enough that my pride would not allow me to take it back.

"I'll be off now, Clare."

With that, I came around the bar. Embracing her with a kiss on her cheek, she whispered into my ear, "Don't forget who you are, lad."

Placing her hands on my shoulders, she kissed me back and stepping to arm's length said with a somber tone, "I am sure you will make the right decision, Ciarán. You have always been able to do that."

"Good evening to you Clare," I said as I turned back toward the stairwell.

"My best to Samuel," I announced loudly as the curtain blew open a crack and I watched a large, stocking covered foot being pulled back out of sight at the top. Samuel had been listening all along. I smirked at the thought as I headed toward the door.

Before pulling the latch, I turned one more time to Clare. She raised her glass to me, exclaiming, "Here's to you, Ciarán McKay, because we can't help but love you!"

"Slan," I said as if it might be the last time I would ever see her, and with that, I stepped out. Turning to my right, I walked to the corner of the building and stopped in the shadow. Leaning against the wall just shy of the window, I felt the need to catch my breath. There came a tremendous feeling of guilt for the way I'd reacted. I fought the urge to go back inside and tell her I was sorry.

Looking into the house through a dusty pane of glass, I watched Samuel enter the room. His grey hair was a bird's nest and his bushy eyebrows were apparent even in the dim light. He moved to Clare, his massive bulk towering over her. Placing a giant hand on her shoulder, he spoke. I didn't have to hear the words to know what he was telling her. Her face went into her hands, and her body was racked with sobs. He directed her to the base of the stairs and stopping there, watched her move up.

The sound of a sneeze drifted up the street. Turning, I focused my eyes and could just make out Arlyn in his usual spot. Leaning against a lamp pole across from his old bakery, he smoked a cigarette. He saw me despite the dark and waved. I put up a hesitant hand in response, wondering if he would make his way to me. But he remained where he stood—which was good. I needed a minute or two alone to ponder my situation.

I was torn. Clare was a good, loving woman, still haunted by the loss of her only child. Perhaps our exchange left her afraid that she might also be losing her adopted son. I could talk to the villagers all day long about the importance of being globally minded, but it would make no difference. Irish is Irish, and that's all. I would have to show Clare she was not losing a son—and might well be gaining another daughter. Maybe not an Irish one… but when love comes—it doesn't matter who you are or where you are from. I believed she could love Anna as much as she loved me. It was just a matter of time. A matter of trust.

Lost in thought, I brought my eyes back to the window to find Samuel staring at me, half hidden by the fancy burlap curtains. His large, square face was full of empathy, a look unaffected by his short grey beard and deep set, blue eyes. He'd come to lock up and caught me in my rumination.

As he turned to the door, I instinctively prepared to bolt as if I were a wee lad caught in some kind of mischief. But the door opened only a crack and I heard him softly say, "The best to you, Ciarán—and your lass, too." The door closed again with the heavy bolt clunking into its keeper. I watched as he pulled the curtains across the windows and his silhouette move away.

A fire of determination had been lit and I schemed. I would go to the McGurks in the morning and appeal to them for the information that would lead me to Anna. I didn't know them very well and only my da ever had anything to do with Aidan McGurk. So, I clung to the hope they would give up what I needed—and in a kindly manner.

Chapter 10

"Afflicted With An Itch ~ And No Nails To Scratch"

The next morning, I rose early. After eating a quick breakfast, I dressed in my best tweed jacket and flat cap. I supposed that it wouldn't matter much to anyone else, but dressing in my best, always boosted my confidence. My mind was abuzz with a hundred things at once, and upon stepping out of my front door, I realized how nervous I was. Telling myself over and over again that I had a grip on this, helped lessen the anxiety as I made my way toward the McGurks. All they could do was refuse. If they did, I had no other plan. It's not that I hadn't tried to come up with one. It was just, every time I tried to sort out a Plan B, I would draw a blank.

Any villager, who witnessed me passing by that morning and sorted I was a man on a mission—would have been bang-on about that. I was on a quest, and that is what it felt like. It gave me purpose, and with direction—came optimism.

I headed south toward the old mill and upon arriving at the crossroads, I turned west. Reaching the bottom of the slope, the stone fence gave way to hedgerow on both sides. From there, I had to endure a long, steady incline. Arriving at the top, I stopped to rest. The hedge ended there, granting me a clear view of the valley that spread out below me.

I looked down upon several small, white cottages, scattered about the valley. At that moment, the sun burst through a small break in the clouds, casting a bundle of rays upon the first cottage at the bottom of the slope. I couldn't help but smile thinking, Lugh, deity of the sun, was offering me direction. A positive sign, fortifying my belief I'd made the right decision.

The shadows of the clouds moved playfully across the valley as if begging for me to give chase. I whistled my own rendition of 'Rocky Road to Dublin' as I kicked a fist-sized stone that had worked its way out onto the road. Turning it into a one-sided football match, I worked my way down to the lane that led to the cottage in question.

When I arrived, I found a massive wooden gate blocking the drive. Just outside, to the right, someone had placed a small, weatherworn block of granite. 'MCGURK' had been carved into its face and the large, rough letters had been blackened with paint. No doubt, I had arrived.

I climbed the gate rather than try to open its massive bulk. I got a funny feeling it had been placed there more to keep people out than to hold the livestock in. It brought about a sense of foreboding, which caused my enthusiasm to melt away. Jumping down on the inside, I walked a few steps and stopped. Glancing back at the faded paint of the simple, but heavy framework, I had second thoughts about my plan.

As Anna had said, the McGurks were very private people. Also, Neila McGurk was considered just a wee bit off. I recalled an instance when I attempted to speak to her at Nolan's. She gave me a closed lip smile, casting her eyes to the floor. After an awkward minute, she bid me good day and hurried away. Aidan sat waiting outside of the door and rushed to her. Taking her arm, he helped her down the steps. Then throwing me a half-hearted wave, he clung to her arm as they moved down the high street.

Because they'd chosen to live such a great distance from the village, and possessed such a colossal gate, I expected a chilly welcome. Arriving at the well-stuccoed abode, I noticed the nose of their old, green Rover sedan poking out from behind the house. I'd seen it on occasion, rolling in a slow manner through the village with Neila McGurk hunkered down in the back seat, Aidan at the wheel. Not too many of the village folk drove cars. It was much easier to walk. I figured Neila preferred the protection of being sequestered behind glass and steel. At least that way, she wouldn't have to pass the time of day with anyone she met on the road. The presence of the Rover confirmed that they were at home.

Opening the gate in the small white picket fence, I stepped into the front garden. A banty rooster jumped up onto a corner post and flapping his wings in thunderous fashion, he crowed at me, announcing my presence. This brought a wee Irish terrier to the colossal picture window. He barked frantically, his front paws scratching at the large pane of glass as he danced left and then right, across the back of the sofa. Falling off at the end, he came back and started the process all over again.

I watched as small, pale hands appeared, and clutching the dog around its ribs, they pulled it away. Stepping up to the door, I barely got the chance to put my knuckles to wood, when it swung open, putting me face to face with Aidan McGurk.

"Dia duit er maidgen!" he sang out.

It was Irish for 'God be with you this morning.' I couldn't remember the standard response, so I said, "Same to you, Aidan."

"I believe you are Ciarán McKay? Diarmuid McKay's boy?"

I hesitated for an awkward moment and finding my words, I blurted out in a cheerful manner, "Right you are! Diarmuid was my da."

I wanted to put forth an enthusiastic appearance, but memories of my da were not pleasant, and I didn't want to dwell on the topic.

"Something of a cranky old prick, wasn't he?" Aidan said with a smirk.

"Aidan!" a woman's voice now, chastising the man.

I looked behind him into the room to see Neila standing in the door of what I believed to be the kitchen. She held the dog in her arms and even though it was no longer barking, there came a distinct growling. Taking off my hat, I nodded a hallo.

"Sorry, darling," her husband announced over his shoulder. Then leaning forward, he asked in a low tone, "He was, wasn't he?"

"Indeed, he was a cranky old bastard." Looking over his head, I smiled at Neila, adding, "Tis okay, Mrs. McGurk, it's the truth. My da was not a pleasant man to be with. He brought nothing but heartache to my ma."

She made a noise that sounded like, 'humph' and said, "Tis okay for you to call me Neila, we're not so formal around here."

Sidestepping through the doorway, she disappeared from sight. I heard a door creak open, followed by a rush of air that moved passed me. It brought kitchen smells with it as the dog started barking again, only this time, outside.

"Would you like to come in, lad?" Aidan asked.

"If you don't mind? I won't take much of your time."

He motioned me in, shutting the door. Neila appeared again and said in a gruff manner, "I suppose tea is in order, then?"

"I'm thinking a good stout would be… if it wasn't so early in the morning," Aidan said and laughed.

He motioned to a small table in the corner, by the kitchen door. I walked over and pulling out one of the two ancient wooden chairs, I sat where I could see into what was obviously Neila's domain. She'd returned to the stove and was putting the kettle on. Looking back at me, she scowled and moving to a tall narrow door, she went inside, pulling it shut behind her. Aidan sat down in front of me and glancing back over his shoulder, said, "Where'd that woman go?"

There came a muffled, "I'm in the pantry, you old fool."

Turning back and tilting his head forward, he snickered, "Ha! She be hiding from you lad. She's not much on company, you know."

"I'm not hiding, you ol…" but she didn't finish. The pantry door swung open, and she appeared with what I suspected to be the tea. I could see the redness in her cheeks. Her man was not making it easy for her.

I noticed she wore the standard 'older woman's wear' for Ireland. A one piece, print dress with an apron. She kept her hair up. In fact, it was pulled back so tight that it narrowed her eyes and brought a pinched look to her mouth. Everything about her seemed severe. Neila was the opposite of everything that my ma had been. I wondered if Aidan's wife had ever experienced a carefree moment in her life.

She then did the unexpected. Looking at Aidan, she made a face at him behind his back and threw me a nervous smile—just the way a child would.

This also cleared up the mystery why there was so much shyness. She had the crookedness teeth I'd ever seen. When she realized what she'd done, she clamped her lips shut and turned away.

"What can we do for you lad? You didn't come all the way out here for tea, I'm sure," Aidan said and chuckled.

Before I could answer, Neila's words came like a fusillade of bullets. "He's come about our girl, I just know it."

She walked up behind her husband carrying a tray with two ceramic cups, several spoons, and a glass bowl full of sugar. Aidan sat up straight in his chair and his face went from pleasant to stern.

"Is it true Ciarán, you come about our Anna?"

I felt shock at Neila's intuitiveness and I didn't respond right away.

"Was there a problem at the school?" he asked. "You know… she wasn't one for making trouble."

There came an uneasy moment of silence as they both stared at me. Aidan was squinting and Neila's eyes had gone wide, showing a hint of fear. If I didn't say something soon, things could go real bad, real quick. I imagined myself being chased out the front door by Neila, broom in hand, the dog's teeth locked onto my trouser cuff. Then there was Aidan coming along behind, swinging a blackthorn shillelagh and shouting encouragement.

"That's right, I've come for Anna's sake."

"Has something happened to her? Have you brought us bad news?" he asked.

"He has come for something else, Aidan," the woman said as she placed the tray on the table, her eyes locked on mine. Stepping back behind her husband, she rested her hands on his shoulders.

The tension was building. Neila's paranoid manner was pushing me toward panic. She stared unblinking as Aidan looked at me out of the bottom of his spectacles. He then gazed up into his wife's face and I saw something pass between them. Looking back, he said, "Is that true lad, you have come for something else?"

"Like I said, I've come for the sake of Anna. If you would be so kind… I was hoping I could get a telephone number, perhaps an address… anything that might help me get in touch with her."

Neila screeched out a response before her husband had the chance to answer.

"That lass has got enough trouble. She doesn't need you causing her any more, Mr. McKay."

It startled me, and I nearly let go of my bladder. Coming up out of my chair, I stared. Her response had been so bizarre that it left me unnerved. I should have departed right then. A little voice in the back of head was croaking, "Crazy! Crazy! Crazy!" like a frog in the mating season. Being the fool I was, I remained. It was as if my stubborn need had overridden reason and logic.

Her reaction also caused Aidan to wince. He slapped the table, causing the teacups to jump on the tray. In a loud, stern voice, he said, "Hush woman! Best not to go into hysterics." Then lowering his face back to me, his mouth set and grim, he said, "Neila's right,

Ciarán. That girl's got enough troubles. We wouldn't think too highly of you for bringing about anymore."

"Don't you hush me," Neila lashed out.

Taking a step back, she rubbed her hands together nervously. "I won't be helping you bring any trouble to Anna. I couldn't sleep at night knowing I had brought tribulation down on her young head."

"Aidan, Neila, please. I am just trying to keep a promise I made before she was off for Berlin."

There I was—begging—something I normally didn't do.

A hiss-like noise escaped Neila's lips, and baring her teeth, she pointed a trembling finger at me. Her face twitched and her right eye ticked.

"What could our Mary… Anna! What could our Anna want with the likes of you?"

Aidan placed his hand over her threatening finger and pulled it down. She jerked it away and with her eyes bulging, she moved just out of reach.

"Aidan! You know she was like a daughter to me. You know how I feel about that girl." I sensed that this was a lie, and Neila's theatrics were a tool of manipulation.

McGurk turned in his seat and looked at her, saying, "Calm down Neila. I am sure Ciarán means her no harm. He was her teacher, for Christ sake."

She backed further into the kitchen. Her voiced changed again and in a chillingly calm tone she said, "You will be getting no help from me, Mr. Ciarán McKay."

With that, she disappeared from view around the corner. Hinges squeaked and a door slammed. A stomping noise told me she was making her way up stairs. Above my head, floorboards creaked, followed by the unmistakable sound of bedsprings.

"I am going to have to bid you good day now, Ciarán," Aidan said, and standing up, he gestured toward the door.

"Please Aidan, can you talk to her? It's very important."

"Sorry lad, there's no budging that woman. Hasn't been the same since our Mary was off. She got quite used to having Anna around, but… even I have to admit that the poor lass had endured a great deal while living under my roof. Neila treated her as if she was Mary, herself. It was a mistake bringing Anna to Ireland. Neila is my wife, though. I have to stand by her, no matter what. Besides, even if she has Anna's address stashed away, I wouldn't have a clue where."

"Please Aidan, PLEASE! I made a promise. If Anna is as important to you as she is to me… Ahhh bollocks! You know damn well she would have left it with me if she could have. It's just… she was so excited about me coming to Berlin for a visit, and to meet her mother..."

His eyes widen at the mention of Berlin. He now knew my secret. I feared he'd let it slip to Huey, who would inform the entire village. I saw genuine concern in his face though, and there appeared to be sympathy in those eyes. So, maybe enough to keep this new bit of information to himself, but not enough to help me achieve my goal.

"Terribly sorry lad, I'll see you to the door."

I felt the tears coming as an intense anger built. I balled my fists, casting my eyes down as I followed Aidan to the door. Opening it, he stepped back to allow me to pass. I couldn't let him see me shed tears, or let the anger out. I was in a bad spot. They were the sole guardians of the thing I needed, and they would not relinquish. I stepped over the threshold and he patted me on the shoulder, saying, "Sorry, lad."

I stared back into his watery gray eyes. A tear rolled out onto my cheek, bringing me to wipe it away in a hasty manner. The action startled him, like he thought I was going to strike out and he jerked his head back. This was followed by a sympathetic expression and he looked away into the garden. I stepped out onto the porch and he shut the door. The latch set, and the bolt rattled into its keeper as if he feared I might attempt to force my way back in.

I walked out of the little gate and started up the lane toward the road. My fists ached from clenching. I forced myself to open them just to relieve the pain. Glancing back at the cottage, I noticed one of the flowered curtains in a small upstairs window fall back into place. I stomped up what remained of the drive and arriving at the gate, I raised my face to the sky and bellowed at the thickening clouds, "Damn it all to hell."

The terrier broke into a fit of barking. A moment later, a woman's voice calling, barely audible above the wind, "Come, Danny, come on in here."

Swinging around, I shook a fist at the cottage, roaring out, "And damn you all to hell, too."

Turning back to the gate, I leaned on the top rail with both hands and hung my head. I felt the heaviness of defeat nesting in the pit of my stomach. The thought of giving in, brought a cold, hollow sensation. A sob broke from my lips and I fought to control an overwhelming desire to fall to my knees. What was I going to do? With no address or telephone number, I would have to scour the entire Spandau district, or worse yet, all of Berlin. That would be an exhausting and time-consuming task. Yet if it came down to it, I would do just that. I wasn't going to give up or give in.

Obsession billowed within me. I would let it be the driving force in my quest. I was going to crusade for my cause and the sake of Anna. Before she'd come, I lived in a state of suspension, as I did now. It had been a static existence. I had felt no hope for a future in Ballyamhras. Every day had been the same, my waking hours overflowing with monotony. Then Anna ran in that door and by the simple act of slipping on the floor, we had come together. Aidan said it was a mistake to bring Anna to Ireland—I had to disagree.

Doing so, brought me glimmer of hope that evolved into a deluge of light. Every moment we spent together was another step up. I had experienced that old, familiar happiness from years before. I caught myself whistling while I was doing minor chores about the house. I started to notice small things again, like the flowers in the garden, or the hummingbird that came to the kitchen window. Joy had returned, and with it, an ever growing want to be part of the world again. All because of Anna. I had a stubborn need to hang on to that—to hang on to her.

I climbed over the gate and started back up the hill as an early summer storm brewed above my head. I felt foolish because I kept telling myself that the McGurks would support me because of our commonality. But their negative response had pushed me to the brink.

Perhaps that was a wee bit more of what I needed—like my talk with Clare.

My obsession roiled, causing Reason & Logic to flee. I would find Anna even if it killed me. If it did—at least the pain would end. I could always come back as a ghost and haunt the McGurks until they succumbed from fright.

The thought cheered me, but it wasn't realistic. I truly wished no harm to come to Aidan and Neila. I told myself that they were both only doing what they thought to be right. So, I still had some empathy. I focused on the fact that they may not have brought me an address or a phone number, but it was they who had brought me Anna. I could at least be grateful for that.

As I trudged up the roadway, I plotted. I could always rifle the records cabinet at the school and steal her file or, approach the guidance office with a made-up story. If I got caught trespassing, there would be trouble, and that would make my business their business. Besides, I did not think my conscience could cope with the dishonesty. I was resolute about fulfilling my promise to Anna, and I wasn't going to allow anyone to stand in my way.

I soon found myself on the old mill road as thunder drummed in the distance. My exasperation gave way to exhaustion, the events of the morning still cycling through my head. I wished I was already home, and as the village came into view, a soft rain began to fall.

Chapter 11

"Dublin's Rocky Road"

By August, I had a plan in place. I would spend every summer, from this point on, in Berlin. I would persevere until I found Anna, became disabled, or—met death. I would scour the city, ask questions, and use every resource possible. The need to set a departure date remained, and as much as I wanted to leave at once, it would be in my best interest to stay until the mid-year school holiday. I still hadn't received notice whether I was to remain for summer school or not, but I could easily circumvent that.

I spent a considerable amount of time in Dublin over the winter and well into spring. The bustle of the city and being with people that couldn't call me familiar, brought comfort. I desperately needed distraction if I wanted to hold out until the day I departed for the continent. So I decided I would focus on improving my teaching skills and try to bring something new into the classroom. Therefore, I ventured every weekend to the great library in the north of the city.

Walking what seemed like endless shelves, I would seek anything that might be related to Irish History. Bringing armloads of books back to the study table, I would bury myself in my work in order to create a lesson plan for the upcoming months. This helped to keep my melancholia at bay, and my mind off Anna.

By March of the following year, a new feeling had developed. I would have to describe it as a kind of uneasiness, almost as if something was pulling at me, something magnetic or electrical in nature. An unsettling agitation that wouldn't allow me to sit still for long. When it got to be too much, I would get up and walk around the reading room pretending to look at the bindings of books, venture into the stacks for more of the same, or loiter in the main hall at the drinking fountain.

I must have appeared as if daft and found myself thwarting the attempts of the library staff to render the assistance they thought I needed. I had to convince them there was nothing they could do, once even telling a young lad, "Unless you feel up to hitting me over the head with a Hurley stick to put me out of my misery..." He just grinned and walked away.

One person, who everyone called Maeve, quite fond of flouncy skirts and revealing blouses, would probably have taken me up on it. With her large hair, kilograms of makeup and mammoth hoop earrings—she was in my face constantly. I supposed she must have become frustrated with my presence. I tried to be understanding, but as the months passed, it grew worse. She took to making announcements from the checkout desk everytime I arrived, declaring to the room, "Oh look, if it isn't Mr. I-Can't-Stay-Put." I kept my growing dislike for her to myself, and hurried past to avoid saying anything I might regret later.

During those short excursions away from my table, I would often pass through the section where they kept the telephone books for the major cities of Europe. Their value never occurred to me until one day I was in their midst and took a tumble. It felt more as if I'd been tripped. I actually looked around, half-suspecting to see Isleen's apparition grinning from a shadowy cleft between stacks. It put me on my knees, and using the shelves as a means to gain my feet, the action put the telephone book bindings right in my face.

Perhaps, Berlin?

With a degree of excitement, I made my way to the B section, quietly praising Alphabetical Order. Expecting I would find it between Barcelona and Birmingham—I found nothing. The excitement leaked out and disappointment eked in. Fortunately, it was staunched by Isleen's voice within my head saying, "West Berlin, you eejit!"

I hurried down to the far end of the shelf and there it was. 'Das Telephonbuch-West Berlin'. I snatched it from its space and not anticipating its weight, I struggled to keep a grip on its sizable bulk. Searching the white pages for Furtak with a degree of urgency, I found a Gretchen and a Bercik, but no Jana. I repeated the action just to be sure, but ended with the same results. The flame of hope that had flared upon my discovery, now smoldered. I gave a heavy sigh as I slipped the book back into its slot. A hopelessness welled up, and with it, a horrid lethargy. Perhaps I'd become deluded, and my plan was nothing but an ill-fated endeavor. I fought the urge to sit down on the floor, put my face in my hands, and weep openly. Something I am sure Maeve would have found entertaining.

As I stood there sighing and rubbing at my eyes with one hand while leaning on the shelf with the other, Anna's plaintive voice came into my head.

"Don't let it go, Ciarán!"

It came so clear that I looked around to be sure she wasn't standing right there with me. Now I had two women inside my skull nagging at me, and I felt outnumbered.

"Hold fast laddy, hold fast," I told myself out loud and glancing up to see if anyone else had heard me, my eye caught the cover of another book across the aisle. 'GERMANY' in bold, yellow letters seemed to launch itself from the binding. With a surge of delight, I snatched it from the shelf, pulling several other volumes out with it. I left them to litter the floor as I studied the cover. 'Reiseführer für die Bundesrepublik Deutschland-A travel guide for the Republic of Germany'. The backdrop for the title was an aerial view of the

Victory Tower in the Tiergarten, including a shot of the Brandenburg Gate.

Unlike the phonebook, it was brand new and contained current information. Someone had been hasty in trying to perpetuate tourism in a country that may not be ready for it. Between its covers, there were maps of all the big cities, including, 'Das Neue Berlin and its boroughs: Spandau, Charlottenburg, Wilmersdorf and others. It gave a limited explanation for gaining access, acceptable accommodations and, within a large, red, multi pointed star on the back, the words, 'PLUS: WHAT NOT TO DO, WHILE VISITING BERLIN!'

I wasn't too worried about the latter. Germany was evolving because of Perestroika and Glasnost. The Wall was coming down piece by piece and reunification was still the topic on everybody's lips. Europe was in flux with the east reintroducing itself to the west. One could only speculate what changes would come with the fall of the Soviet Union, and the rise of the independent states.

"Berlin," I whispered, grinning.

Something about that name appealed to me. It seduced me, affecting me like a lover's soft caress. Anna's voice whispered in my head, "Yes—Berlin."

As I stood there between stacks of books, the clouds of doubt parted and the sun of relief shone down upon me. A powerful determination blossomed inside of me, erupting from my very core. The odds were not in my favor, but that didn't seem to matter anymore. For the sake of my piece of mind, I would take that leap of faith.

Time to go.

I carried the travel guide back to my chair, thinking I would sit down and give it a good looking over. But glancing up at the big clock above the doorway, I saw the lateness of the day; time to be getting back to Ballyamhras. I had to catch a bus and walk a short distance, so there was no time to linger. Sorting through the books that covered the tabletop, I separated mine from those of the libraries and stuffed them in my ruck.

Grabbing a strap, I hefted it up and made my way toward the main entry door. Upon reaching the checkout desk, I saw Maeve the Terrible, sitting there. She scrutinized me as I approached and popping her chewing gum several times, she acted as if she were being coerced into to putting down her copy of J.D. Bachmann's, 'My Love Abroad'.

"Anything to declare, Mr. Cant-Stay-Put?" she said in a snide manner.

"Not on this day, lass." I said and forced a smile, hoping to get through and be on my way.

I opened the spring loaded half door to pass by, but that's as far as I got. Her hand shot out and a finger pointed at my rucksack with her shouting, "How about that, there?"

Standing up, she leaned well out, over the colossal wooden counter top. Her flouncy, short red skirt made it inappropriate, and it caught the eyes of the two college age lads sorting magazines on the floor behind her. They turned and zeroed in on her backside, then looking at each other, they exchanged a wink.

I still faced the exit, thinking to myself that in a few short steps, I'd be free from her tyranny. But she extended her arm out as far as possible and her index finger danced in the air as if the action alone would bring whatever it was that she was pointing at, closer to her. Glancing down, I saw the top third of the Berlin book peeking out. The adrenaline flowed in as I realized I'd stuck the travel guide inside with my own books.

She laid herself out across the top of the counter, her black, scoop necked blouse, exposing sizable breasts that were barely contained by her lacey red bra. She now shrieked, "Mister! That book! Mister!"

I have to admit, I hated her at that moment. I looked around at the faces looking back, and the flush climbed my neck. Because the guide was a reference item, I knew they wouldn't loan it out. But I didn't want to lose it. So, as wrong as it was, I wasn't willing to give it up without a fray. She had pushed me into malice with her manner, and I felt I couldn't be held accountable for my actions.

"Mister! Let me have a look at that book or there is going to be trouble," she shrieked as if she knew it would make me look like the bad man that I wasn't.

The lads took their attention off her backside and put it on me. The bigger of the two stood up, and with one graceful leap, he came over the countertop behind me. He appeared well practiced. He seemed quite pleased with his achievement and threw me an evil grin.

I suspected he was showing off for Maeve, in hopes of winning her favor. At that point I felt willing to negotiate, but then he had to go and say, "Stop there, you feking bogger," and adding insult to injury, "Come on now, give it up, boyo."

I turned to face him and moving backwards, I pushed the little door open. A taut spring keep it tight up against the back of my legs, and I knew with one more step, I'd be free of it and the door would slam shut

Now I wouldn't normally let somebody call me a bogger or a boyo without acknowledging it with a solid right hook to the jaw. But I kept myself reigned in, the fist of my free hand still resting against my thigh. But his obstinacy got the better of him and coming at me, he reached out to grab the front of my shirt. So, I took that step, and sent the door his way.

He wasn't quick enough to avoid that and it struck him in the knees. The force of it caused him to bend forward with a grunt and slither down my side of the door, head first. This was followed by a somersault, causing him to land on his arse, his legs splayed out in front. He stayed there and putting his back against the door, he rubbed his knees and glared.

I felt pity for him. Here I was, a respected member of my community, stealing a library book. But I'd also become a bogger and a boyo. So I felt justified in exhibiting the traits of both. There was no turning back now; I was too far into it. So I spun around and hurried into the vestibule as he bellowed, "Where do you think you're off to?" and just before the door slammed shut, I shouted, "Berlin!"

Chapter 12

Germany

After making my way down Ebertstrasse, I stopped in front of the great Brandenburg Gate. A nervousness overcame me at the thought of making my way through. The other side had been a dictatorship only a few years before and I feared that the citizens of the old GDR might not be too accepting of foreigners just yet. The area around the gate was free of the concrete wall that once stood before it. Sections of it still remained in other places, and civilians chipped away at it in hopes to acquire their souvenirs before it disappeared entirely.

The year Anna came to Ballyamhras there'd been a Leonard Bernstein concert at the East Berlin Schauspielhaus on Christmas day. A celebration of liberty. In the last movement of the ninth symphony, Bernstein's soloists sang Schiller's "Ode to Freedom" and the people loved it. Reunification had come and Germany was whole again.

Upon arriving at the train station in the Spandau district, I started walking the streets of the old french borough, asking questions and showing a photo of Anna that I'd brought with me from Ireland. It was the only existing image of us together. Carla Donnelly had taken it on her new Polaroid Land camera, one of those modern items that produce the photo right there on the spot. She snuck up on us one evening as we sat together atop the boulders. It startled us, and Anna jumped up to give chase. Running to Carla, she demanded that she hand the image over. The other lass gave it up, but not without resistance, and a few choice words.

I visited many of the small businesses on the east bank of the Havel River, showing the photo and asking the merchants if they recalled having seen her. My hopes were all but dashed at a rundown imbiss at the Haselhorst U-Bahn stop. A tiny place called 'Jacob's'. At the serving window, I questioned a tall, slender, black fellow who I assumed was Jacob himself. He took one look at the photo and without answering my question, threatened me with bodily harm if I didn't go away. It had been a peculiar incident and as I hurried off to a safe distance, I wondered what might have triggered his explosive reaction.

After about four days, my lack of success had me thinking how asinine it was to search for Anna on foot with no clue where she might be. The thought crossed my mind that perhaps I should try a bicycle. Yet after a day of that, I returned my rental when I found I had to focus more on where I was going, rather than the people around me.

I rode the trains, walking from one end to the other, scrutinizing faces and trying to make myself noticeable. I lingered on street corners and sat on benches out in the public's view for many hours a day. I'd worked my way toward the Mitte at the center of the city and spent the night in a youth hostel, too tired to return to my hotel. Upon waking this morning, I reminded myself that it was time to cross over to what had once been East Berlin. I couldn't shake the confusion that accompanied my desire to search there. Anna lived in the Spandau district. Would she ever venture this far into the east of Berlin? Something told me she would. So, mustering all of my enthusiasm, I soldiered on.

Walking over to stand in the trees at the east end of the vast green area known as the Tiergarten, I studied the gate's massive columns and architrave, thinking how the photos had not done it justice. It was three times bigger than the Fusiliers Arch at Dublin's St. Stephens Green. It made me feel small.

I had no grounds for the fear that came over me, but I knew deep down inside it was the fight-or-flight reaction brought about by my Panic Disorder. Gone were all the foreboding symbols of repression. No one was trying to thwart anyone's attempt to pass through, and they did so at will. "Stop being such an eejit and just go, Ciarán!" said Isleen's voice inside my head.

A strange kind of excitement gripped me. My stomach rose up as if it wanted out. I battled the irrationality of the impending panic, leaving me to wish I could get a grip on what drove my malady. Forcing myself to take that first step, I headed for the opening between the two center columns.

I picked up my pace and it almost seemed as if someone was ushering me along, the pressure of a spectre like hand in the small of my back. I even looked over my shoulder to confirm that Isleen's shade hadn't accompanied me across the street.

I kept telling myself that I could do this, and then—I was through and on the other side. The action left me with a weird sense of accomplishment. Stopping on the plaza, I turned and looked up at a side of the monument I'd never seen before. I wanted to shout out to the Goddess of Triumph, perched upon the top, that I had done it.

I strolled across Pariser Platz and found myself so caught up in the moment, that I walked out into the traffic on Unter Den Linden. Realizing what I'd done, I did a fast but awkward gait back to the walk to avoid becoming a hood ornament. The patrons of a nearby sidewalk café had taken notice of me and as I scanned the crowd, faces turned away. I shrugged and reminded myself that I wanted to be noticed. I would just have to get used to a more extroverted-self as I searched.

I'd chosen to dress the way I always did back in Ireland, which—was certainly not German fashion. I wanted to make sure that Anna could pick me out of a crowd. I feared I would slip by unseen, but from the looks I was getting, I reckoned my plan was working.

I decided to travel as far as the Fernsehturm this day. It was that big television tower they built back in 1969; its presence seemingly a constant in every image of Berlin I'd ever seen. It rose up in the distance, projecting from the street as if it had pushed its way up through the tarmac from some subterranean cavern. Looking out the window of my room early yesterday morning, I saw the base obscured by fog. It made the platform at the top appear to hover above the city like a UFO.

Strolling toward it now, I marveled at its size. I had stopped looking where I was walking and collided with some tables and chairs outside a lively sidewalk café. I mumbled an apology to those effected and moved to the curb to walk around them. By the time I'd arrived on the other side, my embarrassment had reached the breaking point and I wanted to take flight. My face was flushed and there was a rushing noise in my ears. Yet that didn't stop me from hearing someone call my name.

I stopped to listen without turning, telling myself it's not every day, one hears the name, Ciarán, on the streets of a German city. It came again, but I found it difficult to turn back and face that mob of coffee drinkers.

Forcing myself, I rotated on my heels. Studying my audience, my face felt like it could fry an egg. After not seeing anyone I could call familiar, I decided to carry on.

That's when she stood up, right in the center of the throng.

My throat tightened and my head started to swim. I had trouble grasping what I was seeing. Then came the fear that I might pass out. Moving a few steps closer, I stopped and steadied myself on the back of an empty chair. Taking a deep breath, I smiled bigger than I thought possible.

She beamed back, showing that lovely smile—and time stood still. Then, like someone had pulled a plug, the anxiety that had been building inside of me, flowed out. The relief that followed was unbelievable. I vowed to never doubt the magic of that smile.

"Ciarán," she said again, as if she too had trouble accepting what she saw.

I watched my name roll off her glossy red lips as it spilled out into the air. I looked her up and down, thinking to myself how much she'd changed in a years' time. I could have easily passed her by on the street because the picture in my head, was not the woman who stood before me.

Her hair cascaded to her shoulders in curls. She had it parted in the middle and even at this distance, I could tell she wore a great deal of makeup. I was having a tough time believing it was she. But as Huey said, 'There's no mistaking them eyes'. She wore black, knee high boots with gray jeans and a short brown jacket over a frilly white blouse.

I noticed the purple scarf lying on the table and the memories flooded in as if a sluice gate opened in my head. It seemed I 'teetered' in my spot for a moment, almost as if the onslaught of memories had physically unbalanced me. I must have looked the fool as I stood there with, "I've found her!" snaking panoramic across my mind's eye. I wanted to howl it to the sky, but all that came out as I stared, was a muted, "Anna."

It brought a familiar glow to her eyes and I could tell she was resisting the urge to juggernaut through the maze of sidewalk furniture to throw herself into my arms. Turning her attention to her personal items, she gathered up her purple scarf, the old patchwork purse, and then bent over to pull a short black top hat from a chair.

I cocked my head and chuckled. I imagined her walking through a Flea Market and seeing it sitting boldly upon some tabletop, she snatched it up without a second thought. So very much like her.

With her hat in hand, she moved as fast as she could through the obstacle course that lay before her. Knocking over a chair, I heard her apologize to no one in particular. She never took her eyes off me, and some patrons actually cleared a path for her.

My smile could grow no wider and started to hurt from the strain. My happiness in seeing her brought an overpowering joy. I moved backward several steps to give her room and clearing the last table; she dropped the hat and leapt. Landing with her arms around my neck and her legs clamping my hips, I absorbed the brunt of the force, barely able to remain on my feet. Some of the patrons, satisfied with our performance, actually applauded before returning to their coffee and conversation.

She hugged me hard and made a gleeful noise that I cannot describe. I twisted back and forth at the waist, my face buried in her fragrant hair. After a moment, she lowered her feet to the ground but kept the embrace. Her chin rested on my shoulder, and I heard her softly weeping. My mind was abuzz with things I wanted to say, but—I didn't know where to start. After several minutes, she released me and stepping back, crouched to retrieve the hat.

"Sorry," she said as she turned her face up to me, her cheeks glistening with tears. "This is so unbelievable. You actually came to rescue me."

So yes, there I was, standing on a street in Berlin, and before me, the lovely ghost that had haunted me for what seemed like an eternity. But not a ghost anymore. She was real—flesh and blood—a beautiful young woman. Nineteen going on twenty, she was no longer the boyish lass that had once graced the halls of Ballyamhras Secondary. The tears welled up in my eyes and I turned away to hide them.

"Ciarán?" she said, coming around to face me.

Her compassionate visage blurred as the TV tower loomed up behind her. I wasn't able to speak. She embraced me again, and I closed my eyes, taking in the fragrance of her perfume.

She held me for the longest time and placing my arms around her, my hands caressed her back underneath the jacket. When she removed her head from my shoulder, I looked into her face. With tears lingering in my lashes, I had to open my eyes wider to see past them. She smiled at me and said, "Ciarán, please don't cry… I need to hear your voice—I need to hear you talk."

"Sorry, Anna," was all that came out, my voice trembling. Her hands moved to my waist, her fingers stroking the fabric of my shirt. Then she surprised me with a soft kiss on my lips, leaving some of her lipstick behind. She giggled and said, "Oops! Sorry," and dabbed at it with her scarf. Tilting her head to the side, she stopped the wiping, and after several seconds of scrutiny, gave me a slight shake in mock anger.

"Can you not speak? Please talk to me! It is so hard to believe that you are finally here… now my life will change."

Reaching up she removed my cap and pushed my hair out of my eyes. She then replaced it farther back on my head and I watched the smile leave her lips. In a more somber tone she lamented, "I was starting to believe it was a dying dream… and that I would die with it. But I have held on with every ounce of my strength and… here you are."

"I am so sorry, Anna. I must tell you though that I have thought of nothing and no one but you, since the day you left Ballyamhras. I came as soon as I could and have spent every waking hour for the last four days searching for you. When you departed Ireland, I was without a street address or telephone number for you. I pressed the McGurks for the information, but they gave me nothing. They believed they were protecting you from a roguish man with no good reason for pursuing you other than to cause you pain and heartache."

My voice cracked, and I looked away from her, focusing on the passing traffic. I wanted her to know what I'd endured, but I was doing a botched up job of it. Not knowing what else to say, I brought my face back to her and solemnly said, "Anna—you have become my reason for living."

Her tears came again and she pulled me close. Then almost as quick, she stepped back and said, "Let us get out of here."

"Are you sure? Maybe we could sit down for a cup of coffee or something?"

"No, I have had enough coffee for one day, let us walk. Where were you going?"

"I was off for the Fernsehturm."

"Well, let us go there… come!"

Putting on her hat, she took my hand and towed me up the sidewalk, giggling.

"Now that I have you, I am not going to let you go," she said, slowing her pace and falling in beside me.

I stared at the side of her face as we moved, my mind still buzzing with all the things I wanted to tell her. I saw her mascara was now running down her cheeks. She caught me looking and I smirked, pointing to my own eyes. She didn't get it, so I whispered, "Your mascara…" She scrounged through her purse and pulling out a small mirror, she studied her face.

"Scheisse," she hissed, and rubbed at her eyes with her free hand. Then after wiping that hand on her jeans, she put the mirror way and looking back at me, smiled and said, "Better now, yes? Oh… your hat is on crooked… you look silly."

Reaching up, I adjusted it, and looking at hers, she saw where my eyes had strayed.

"As you can see, I have one of my own now."

Tilting her head to the side, she made a movie star face, blinking her eyes rapidly. We both laughed, and I thought of how much she looked like a female Harpo Marx. It fit with her 'off the wall' manner and the occasional impulse to shock people by projecting eccentricity.

"The lass is a weird one!" I'd heard people say back home. Nonetheless, it gave me one more thing to love about her. She put me at ease, and the panicky feeling that had been sitting in my belly was now replaced with calm. My initial reaction to finding her had subsided, and the overwhelming emotion waned. The moment became epiphanal as the true weight of how much I loved this girl fell upon me. Not the desperation of dependency—just a deep sense of joy.

I stopped and turned her way. She halted in her tracks, acting startled. Taking off the hat, she held it with both hands as her eyes questioned.

"What is it?" she said in a timid manner.

"I just wanted you to know Anna that… that… I love you."

She blushed and said, "Yes, I know this, Ciarán. I can feel it. The way you touch me, the way you look at me. It's in your eyes and in your voice. I have no doubts."

I smiled, turning my face away as if something had caught my eye. Then my words simply poured out as I turned back.

"I've waited for this moment for what seems like an eternity. Please forgive me for falling apart back there. I felt quite dazed upon finding you. Kind of shocked, actually. You're such a lovely lass, and… I feel so much more than just lucky to have you."

I saw relief in her face. It was like she was happy that it wasn't bad news, and that someone loved her in a way that one should be loved.

She pivoted back and forth at her ankles and her cheeks went a rosy hue.

"Ich liebe dich auch, Ciarán… forever," She said and stepped up to me to play with a button on the front of my jacket.

"You must know, I hoped to return to Ireland, but it seemed I could never make enough money to pay for the train. So… I just waited. Waited for… how do you say…? Oh… it is in that story. Ummm… oh mein gott! I can't remember! For my… Oh! For my knight in shining armor, that's it!"

I felt myself flush. Knight in shining armor? I'd never thought of myself in that way. The Irish were not fond of knights of any kind, being they were Noblemen, or the landlord type. She was referring to the fairytale variety though, so I found that to be acceptable. Reaching down, I took the hand that was toying with my button and pressed the back of it to my cheek, saying, "I am sorry it has taken so long, and perhaps I didn't go about it the right way, but I am here now, and… that's all that matters."

The hand slipped behind my head and pulling it to her, soft lips came to mine, and they met no resistance. It turned into a long and sensual kiss, more passionate then any kiss I could ever remember in my life. It marked a turning point in our relationship, opening a door to a place we'd never been before.

Her lips were pressing just hard enough to keep the contact and when her tongue found mine, my knees buckled. My hands found the small of her back and I pulled her in tight to help stabilize my stance. Now both of her arms went around my neck as her hat tumbled to the ground. Her purse slid down to her elbow, jerking her arm, nearly causing us to break contact. But we held firm.

The pressure of her lips went from soft to hard as the kissing became more passionate. I slipped my fingers inside the waistband of her jeans at the back, and not meeting the resistance of any knickers, I moved them down to the silky, soft convex curve of her bottom. She almost collapsed. Hanging from my neck, she tried desperately to maintain the kiss. When she couldn't any longer, we parted, a soft moan escaping her mouth.

We gazed into each other's eyes as we straightened our clothing, allowing our skin to cool. She picked up her hat and putting it back on, she gave me a look that said, "Wasn't that lovely?" and wrapping her arm in mine, we continued toward the tower, glancing at each other on occasion as if we had a secret.

My aroused state diminished, but not enough so that the bulge in my trousers would go unnoticed. Buttoning my jacket, I attempted to hide it as I willed it to depart. I had not felt like this since early in my courtship with Isleen, and that brought a burgeoning concern.

I'd often worried that future liaisons with Anna might turn into something purely sexual. Our reunion now brought that fear in a way that could not be ignored. With Anna's eagerness to please, coupled with my long-term celibacy, there was a chance our relationship would spiral into an erotic picnic. I didn't want that. I wanted it to be what I'd had with Isleen. I wanted sex, yes, but I also wanted all that comes with a long-term association. The quiet, reflective moments together, the noisy and joy filled times with endless conversation and… oddly enough, the occasional heated discussion. I wanted to nurture her, and I wanted the same in return.

I studied her face as she chattered away about her days back in Ireland. Her voice was heavy with her accent, trading English for German and then back again and all of it punctuated with her husky laugh. I listened and nodded, getting the impression that this was the happiest she'd been in a long time. She wanted to show me all there was to see in Berlin, and seemed to know the history of everything, including the structure that now loomed above us.

We went inside and got aboard an elevator that seemed to travel at the speed of sound. At the top, we stood at the large windows of the observation deck that looked out over the city. A multitude of people filled the space, so she kept me close. Taking off the top hat, she stuck her left hand in the back pocket of my trousers and laid the side of her face against my upper arm.

Sometime later, the hand came out and the arm went around my waist. Glancing down, I saw her eyes were closed and her lips were moving like she was singing. With all the noise in the room, the words were inaudible. She caught me gazing and smiled, her cheeks going rosy.

"What are you doing?" I said.

"Nothing"

"Come now Anna, tell me."

She buried her face in the tweed of my jacket for a second, and then looking up into mine, she stood up on her toes and kissed me on the cheek.

"I was singing a little song, thinking how thankful I am for this moment. I cannot describe how I feel, it is all so unbelievable."

I brushed a loose curl from her face and ran a finger down the soft skin of her cheek. She cast her eyes to the floor for a few seconds and finally back to the large pane of tinted glass.

Looking past her, I saw two pre-teen girls standing close by. They watched us with great interest and when they realized I'd noticed them, they laughed and ran away through the crowd, looking back over their shoulders as they went.

Anna had spotted them too and said, "I was also very curious when I was that age. Someday they will understand what it is like to be me or, maybe I should say—us."

Pulling me close again, a sigh escaped her lips as she rocked herself and hummed her song.

We soon grew tired of the surging crowd, so departing the tower, we returned to the street. At her suggestion, we strolled over to the plaza at Gendarmemarkt to listen to the street musicians who gathered there. I sat on the mammoth stone steps of a museum and she lay with her head on my lap. Several of the songs she knew and sang along, her words soothing to my ear.

Without warning, she jumped up. I thought I heard her mumble something like, "I know that man," and rummaging through her bag, she pulled out some coins. Then running over to the young musician closest to us, she stopped long enough to say something to him as she dumped the coins into his violin case. He ended his tune in an abrupt fashion. Coming up off his seat, he set down his instrument and grabbed Anna's hand with both of his. I watched him nodding his head as they conversed, but I was too far away to hear their words.

Anna smiled, shrugged, and nodded in reply. Pulling her hand away, she pointed toward me. I stood up and moved down the steps. The man raised his hand in a cautious wave and hurrying back to his seat; he picked up his violin and broke in to what I knew to be a Vivaldi tune. I stopped at the bottom step and Anna met me there.

"What was that about?" I asked suspiciously.

She giggled and said. "He wanted to know if I was free for the evening, but don't worry… I told him that I was busy—for the rest of my life!"

With that, she took my hand, and led me away. As we walked, I realized the music had stopped. Glancing over my shoulder, I saw the musician was just sitting there, his eyes on us.

When he saw me looking, he bent his head low over his instrument and returned to his Vivaldi. I got a weird sensation about the moment, leaving me to wonder if he and Anna were more than just friends. It came to me that I was jealous for the first time with Anna. I needed to dismiss it, but I wasn't going to let it go until I asked her one question.

"Anna, who was that man?"

She smiled in an innocent way, "It is all good, Ciarán, he is with the Berlin Philharmoniker. How do you say… he plays the streets sometimes? Busker, is your word? Yes, that is it. Only in the summer when the symphony is locked? Ummm… closed? Do you understand?"

"Without a doubt." I said, teasing her now.

"Oh, good! We had a… uh… date? So… don't worry Ciarán, it was last year, and there was only one."

She chuckled and pulled me to her. I said nothing as a way to dismiss the subject, and we walked in silence. I could tell by her facial expression she was trying to sort something.

Climbing the steps to the S-Bahn platform, she held my hand with her left, but walked with her head cocked, an index finger at her lips. Her eyes were distant, telling me she wasn't 'with me' at the moment and minutes passed before she slipped her arm inside my jacket and around my back, indicating she had returned. We stopped at the yellow line near the edge of the large concrete deck and her other arm went around my stomach, her hands meeting at my side. She leaned against me as I rubbed her neck and shoulders. We watched the people, watch us. I sensed she had something to tell me, but didn't know how. I didn't want to press her though, and forgot about it as soon as the train arrived.

On board, she sat close and whispered stories into my ear that she'd made up about the other passengers. It was silly rhetoric about who they might be and what they did for work or, the logic behind their wardrobe choices. This caused us to burst out laughing on occasion, much to the dismay of our fellow riders. She went on about a man in a beige trench coat and alpine style hat. He wore dark sunglasses, and she said he must be a spy because he pretended to be sleeping. But she could see his eyes through the tops of his glasses and they were moving back and forth all of the time. Then there was the old woman, who must have put her stockings on in the dark, because her one blue sock contrasted with the brown one.

She then brought her attention to the nervous, skinny man sitting across the aisle from us. He couldn't keep his eyes off the backside of the tall lass who stood in front of him hanging on to a rail overhead. The curvaceous girl was chatting it up with her mates as she struggled to stay upright on her stiletto heels. Her tight, red knit dress kept riding up, and every time she attempted to return it to a more comfortable length, her eyes must have caught him gawking.

When he glanced our way, Anna, in bold fashion, raised her hands like claws, and hissed at him, baring her teeth. This embarrassed him and turning bright red, he jumped up and hurried to the far end of the car. We tried to stifle our mirth, but when our fellow passengers joined in, we let it out. The lass sat down in his place, and crossing her legs, smiled big at Anna and said, "Danke."

Our cavorting continued into the evening. The streets were coming alive with the local subculture. A few of the cafes converted to dance clubs, while others just closed down for the night. We made our way farther east, and after a while, found ourselves on Oranienburgerstrasse. Anna told me that she had an apartment nearby above one of the cafes, and that we should go there.

We walked north for another city block with Anna leading the way. There seemed to be haste in her stride and I felt surprise when she took a quick left and towed me in between two buildings. I stumbled over garbage bags, bottles, and stacks of newspapers. We went through a door and up a dingy flight of 'L' shaped stairs. Entering a hallway at the top, she unlocked the first door on our right with a key she'd taken from her bag. After stepping inside, she motioned for me to follow.

She closed the door as I stood looking around a single, large room. A small table sat in front of a double window on the far side, overlooking the street. A tiny kitchenette ran along the wall on the right, a string of cupboards hanging just above it. The WC at the end of the countertop in the corner closest to me was no bigger than what its name implies—a closet. To my left, behind the door, sat a tall, well-worn chest of drawers. The headboard of the bed was up against its side and at the footboard, a shallow armoire finished off the wall space. With no bath or shower present, I figured it must be located somewhere else on the floor.

Turning on a small, brass lamp atop the dresser, she threw herself onto the mattress with its tangle of linen. I walked to the window taking in the definite odor of female, and strangely enough, sex. The same odor had been evident in the hallway.

Turning back to give Anna a questioning look, I watched her rollover onto her back and point her feet in my direction.

"Help me Ciarán, please?"

"You mean with the boots?"

"Ja, mit meinen Stiefeln, bitte. They are too difficult for me," she said, her voice escalating into a coy whine.

I did so, but not without a struggle. Expecting to be hit in the face with the stink of feet, I was surprised when none came. I watched her as she pulled off her stockings, saying something in German that sounded like, "Forgive me." Afterwards, she sat on the edge of the bed and patted the mattress to bring me to her.

When I ignored her, she went to taking off more of her clothing. She flung her hat across the room to land on the counter in the kitchenette. Her jacket came off next, along with the scarf and they were tossed onto a pile of clothing that lay on the floor across the room. She cocked her head and smiling seductively, she patted again and said, "Please, come sit. Come rest."

I knew where this moment could lead, but I wanted to talk first. She seemed to want to hurry things along, letting nature take its course. I felt as if I was in a bubble and it took a minute for me to recognize the prelude to a panic attack. Sweat ran from my armpits, followed by a chill running up my spine. I started toward her, but changed my mind and turning, moved back to the window. The sweat popped out on my forehead, so taking off my hat, I dropped it on the table. It fell over a small silver jewelry box next to a large lamp with a beige colored shade.

I tried to stay focused, but drifted off in thought. A woman in a black evening dress called up a, "Hallooo!" as she passed, pulling me back to the now. We made eye contact and she grinned before disappearing into the cafe below. Loud music started to play downstairs as if cued by her entrance. I wondered how Anna could ever get any sleep in a place like this.

I became aware of a sudden flurry of activity behind me. As I turned, the small brass lamp atop the dresser went out. Anna now stood in the dark by the bed, the light from the street illuminating her naked body. As my eyes adjusted to the dark, I could see her clothing piled around her feet. With one hand on a cocked hip and the other behind her back, she tilted her head sideways and said, "Does this please you?"

I detected the nervousness in her voice and it served to bolster my escalating anxiety. Standing speechless, I stared. I thought how small she looked as the light shimmered off blond pubic hair. I looked for her eyes, but they were lost in the shadow. She whispered, "I would not do this, if I did not love you."

Walking toward me, her hands came up to grasp my lapels. Her almost perfect breasts begged me to fondle them with their areolas no bigger than an Irish half penny, their pea sized nipples standing erect.

"Let me help you off with this jacket," she said, her words soft and reassuring, but not like the Anna I thought I knew. The anxiety overflowed and it felt as if I'd fallen into a cold pool of water. Pulling away, I snatched my hat off the table, dragging the jewelry box with it. Crashing to the floor, the lid popped open and my ma's Claddagh fell out. We both looked at it—and time stood still. She tried to embrace me again and I stammered, "Sorry darling, sorry…" and pushing past her, I hurried across the room. In a blind panic now, I stumbled over her clothes and upon reaching the door, fumbled for the knob.

"Ciarán? Ciarán, are you okay?"

My throat tightened as I struggled to take a deep breath. Getting a firm grip on the knob and opening the door, I croaked out, "I love you Anna, but…"

I didn't want her to see me like this. So stumbling out, I fought the urge to slam the heavy wooden panel. A, "Ciarán, please…!" followed me out just before the latch clicked into its seat.

Standing just outside, my forehead against the door, I tried to calm myself.

"You eejit Ciarán McKay," I muttered. "What the fek are you doing?"

I had come unglued. I'd experienced quite a few panic attacks since my wife's funeral, but now this one had come at the worst possible moment. All brought on by the sight of a naked woman that was not Isleen, and like a fool, I'd run away. Now my pride, or something like it, would not allow me to go back in. But I needed some time to calm down, and I needed to do it without Anna being present.

Chapter 13

"Put Silk On A Goat, And Its Still A Goat"

I turned and did a clumsy shuffle to the top of the stairs. Making my way down, I grew dizzy and my vision blurred as I turned the corner. Grabbing the railing, I kept a firm grip to keep from tumbling down the rest of the way. Upon reaching the bottom, I heard a door open and Anna call my name. I stopped and stood silent. When the door shut, I continued. Anna must have thought I'd lost my mind, and that's how I felt. One minute, elated—the next, a vessel of despair. That's how panic disorder works. It had rendered me helpless and confused.

Stepping out onto the pavement at the base of the stairs, I stopped and took a couple of deep breaths. It cleared my head and my vision returned to normal. I had to be careful not to push myself into hyperventilation though. I consciously controlled my breathing as I stood in the gloom of the alcove and tried to put the pieces of the puzzle together.

My illusion had been shattered. I had formulated an expectation of this moment, but it had been limited to my experience with Anna back in Ireland. Lovemaking opened up a whole new frontier. That, coupled with being disloyal to Isleen, and everything happening so quickly, had caused me to lose control.

I needed something to help calm my nerves. I would take a risk and go for a pint. It had been a while since I shared whiskies with Clare, and I figured one glass of beer couldn't hurt. I moved down the pavement to the cafe and finding the door propped open, I walked up the three concrete steps and went inside. It was rather lively, and only a few people looked my way when I crossed the threshold. They were all too interested in each other to take too much notice of me. I pushed my way to the bar and the drink tender, a young, blond fellow with a peacock mullet, walked over.

"Give me a pint."

He looked perplexed and then said, "English?"

"Ah, no! Irish!"

"No! Do you want to speak English? You want a beer?" He said, giving me a wicked sneer.

I looked him square in the face, wondering why it was such a problem. By his appearance, I suspected he was trying to emulate Limahl of Kajagoogoo fame. The lead singer of that one 80's band that sang a song about being too shy.

I saw the annoyance in his face and then realized where I was. This was not Lafferty's, nor was it Ireland. I'd never been in a German club before and I now anticipated an education. I found myself distracted by his appearance and stood staring with curiosity. He glared back and realizing my impropriety, I said, "Oh, sorry, a Pils please, ummm... Eine Pils, bitte."

He nodded and turned around to face a large, waist high silver cooler. It sat on the floor beneath a massive mirror, surround by shelves and liquor bottles. Pulling out a bottle of pilsner, he stood for a few seconds, his reflection glaring from the mirror. It chilled me. Then picking up an opener, he came back. Popping the cap on the bottle, he set it down hard on the bar.

"Fünf Marks, bitte," he growled. I winced. Five marks was rather much.

"Five now," he said, shouting at me.

It caused me to jump. Anger and regret always came at the tail end of every panic attack and his actions topped off my ire. Reaching into my pocket, I pulled out what Marks I had and slapped five of them on the bar while giving him a look of defiance. His smirk came cold and mean. His extra-long canines made him look frighteningly bizarre, and I decided right then—I didn't like him.

Snatching up the bills, he put them into his pocket, and walked down to the other end. Stopping, he turned and leaned forward on the countertop to talk with someone who sat concealed by the mob of drinkers. I saw him jerk his thumb in my direction, and when we made eye contact, he looked away. I refocused on my bottle and taking a sip, tried to put it all out of my mind.

The beer tasted good. It had been a long time since I had a pilsner. It left me thinking I might let go of my caution and have a second. But that would be a bad idea. Getting soused in a strange place could only lead to no good. I had no friends here and the original idea had just been to calm myself so I could return to Anna with poise.

Scenes from the day flashed through my mind's eye. Anna's smiling face, the warmth of her hand in mine, and that extraordinary kiss. Then came the gleeful young girls in the tower, the musicians in the square, and that hilarious train ride. Anna was the one person who'd offered me the most hope for any kind of a future—and I'd just walked out on her. Even though I couldn't help myself, I felt I was acting the coward. I would finish this beer, go back upstairs, and present myself to her with an explanation of my condition.

I sensed a presence in my space. Turning to my right, she stood close enough for her body heat to start me cooking. The woman in the black evening dress, smiled and said, "Hallo, I'm called Giselle."

I took a moment to study her face before saying anything. Her eyes were the sharpest of blues and her long black hair, parted in the middle, gleamed in the dim light. Her face was a mixture of Teutonic and Turkic—a rather lovely combination.

"Hallo," I said with some caution. "So… Giselle? Like, G-E-E-S-A-L-A-H?"

"Well, close enough for English, ja. The 'G' is hard, like I wish you to be… very soon." She giggled and moved in closer.

"Sorry?"

"Nothing, bad joke. So I saw you upstairs in the window, ja?"

"You did."

"You were with Stacy, ja?" she said, her smile getting scary. I looked hard into her face, and her well-plucked eyebrows rose as if to hasten my response. I didn't know a Stacy, but I figured it was none of her business anyway, so I played along.

"You know this… Stacy?" I said, unable to keep the suspicion out of my voice.

"Ja, I know Stacy. Sometimes we are together."

"You are friends, then?"

"One may say we are. You are English, ja?"

"I am not! Do I sound feking English?"

With my ire still up, my irritation flowed out in my words. I was sure my response had been heard above the din and a few faces turned my way to confirm it. The smile fled her lips for a mere second as she detected my annoyance. But she flipped her hair and came right back, moving to press her body against mine. Her left hand rested on top of my shoulder with a finger from her right tracing the curve of my bicep through the wool of my jacket. I turned my face away and took a sip from my bottle.

"If you liked being with Stacy, I think you will like being with me…even more."

I turned back and saw her forehead was tilted toward me now, and she was looking at me out of the tops of her eyes. Her chin found its way to rest upon her left hand and her right moved to my side, above my hip. If she was after my wallet, she was far from it. I now carried it in my left, front trouser pocket after almost losing it to a sneak thief on the U-Bahn. But she confirmed my wallet was not her target as the hand moved to my stomach.

"And how are you better than Stacy?"

"If you were to come with me, you would see," she said in a singsong voice.

"I could also stay here, and just take your word for it."

Her fingertips now worked their way to just under my waistband and her lips progressed to my ear. The scent of jasmine was heavy on her and I realized how easy it would be to fall under her spell. She was a smooth one. Some five years back, I could have easily fallen victim to her charm. But now—there was Anna.

Anna!

I needed to get back up there. I hailed the bartender and he returned, bringing his malicious expressions with him. He glanced at Giselle as if for approval and then brought his sneer back to me.

"A drink for the lady," I said.

"Acht Marks," he demanded as his blond fringe fell into his eyes. Eight Marks? Feking gougers! I sorted I better get out of there before they bled me dry.

"Genau, Genau, Acht marks—Ich weiss!" I declared with contempt, letting him know I understood. Laying out ten Marks on the sticky surface next to my beer bottle, I said, "Keep the difference."

Picking up my pilsner, I turned to the woman, grinned and said, "Good night, Giselle... enjoy your drink."

Without waiting for a response, I walked out through the door and stopping on the pavement, I smirked at them through one of the large windows. Raising my bottle, I hollered, "Sláinte." They glared back as the barkeep mixed up Giselle's cocktail. The techno started and the rousing thump-thump took everyone to the miniscule dance floor, leaving Giselle alone at the bar.

"Gute nacht, English mann!" she yelled, the spite sizzling in her voice. Stomping her foot, she balled up her fists as she screeched out, “Scheisse!” followed by, “Eric! Give me my drink, you ass!” I chuckled to myself as I watched her climb up onto a stool and light a cigarette. Even at that distance, I could see she was seething.

Chapter 14

"When One Thing Becomes Two"

I strolled to the alcove, beer bottle in hand, not knowing what I was going to say to Anna. But I had some serious explaining to do. I would have to be honest and tell her all about my panic disorder. I was positive she would understand. I'd done my best to keep it from her in Ireland, with the upside being, I'd accomplished my task. The downside—it had manifested itself in the worst possible way.

I stopped in front of her door and after listening for a few seconds, I tapped with a knuckle on the peeling paint.

"Es ist noch nicht soweit," I heard Anna shout, telling whomever she thought it was that it was not time yet. She threw open the door and we locked eyes. The stern look that had been on her face, melted away and a single sob broke from her painted lips. Bringing a hand up, she covered them as if to stifle the next. She'd done up her hair, but the mascara had run with her tears. I suspected that she had wept the whole time I was away. She now wore a sparkling, azure dress, low cut at the front, with a single, wide strap angling across to her right shoulder. In her hand, she held a clutch purse of the same material.

My regret came as searing pain in my gut followed by a compulsion to get down on my knees. Deciding to save the groveling in case she rebuffed me, I said, "Anna, I'm terribly sorry… please forgive me."

She turned without speaking and walked to the window. The room was now lit by the lamp on the table, replacing the one atop the dresser. It bathed her in its glow as I watched her shoulders spasm and the purse fall to the floor. She than raised her arms from the elbow, balled her fists, and stomped her foot.

"Ooo!" she said, turning back.

Her fists dropped toward the floor and she held her arms as straight as Hurley sticks. "Ciarán, you drive me crazy," She screamed. "You cannot leave me to hang! I have waited too fucking long! Endless days of wishing and hoping that you would soon appear, always coping with this unbearable sadness at the end of the day when you didn't. Now, I find myself caught up in a life that will only take me to a bad end. A life I do not want! I am struggling to stay alive here as well as trying to put away enough money so that… so that someday I could come back to you. Ciarán, I am so tired of being afraid. On top of that, there was this terrible worry you might have found another woman and forgotten all about me. So yes, I know you had to wait almost a year to come, and that you have been desperately searching. But I have been suffering too. Do you think it was any easier for me?"

She gave a sigh that transformed into a sob and her face went into her hands. My first instinct was to go to her and take her in my arms. I shut the door and the click of the latch set her moving back across the floor, stomping as she came. Setting the beer on the dresser, I turned just in time to catch her arms, as she tried to pound my chest.

She got in a few light licks anyway, and collapsing into me, she buried her face in my shirt. I released her arms, and they fell limply to her sides as I struggled to keep us both upright. I lay my cheek on her hair as my own tears welled up, and I just let them come.

When the moment waned, she tilted her head back and we gazed into each other's moist eyes. She wiped at my cheeks in a tender manner, but then surprised me with a light slap.

Shaking her finger in my face, she said with conviction, "Don't you ever leave me again, Ciarán McKay."

I was stunned and started to protest, but she grabbed the front of my jacket with both hands and gave me a shake. Her actions were passive and mostly for show. She didn't really want to hurt me.

I thought it a good time to give her an explanation about the panic attack, but she came up on her toes and stifled my words with her lips. She knocked the hat from my head and peeled the jacket from my body. Falling to the bed, she pulled me with her, and the kiss became long and fervent, her tongue relentless.

Ten minutes must have passed before I pulled back to catch my breath. Rolling off her, we swung our legs up to lay on the bed in the way it was meant to be laid on. She slid to the wall and rolled up onto her right side, her cheek in her hand, her elbow buried in the pillow.

I can only describe what I saw in her face as relief. She didn't have to say it, I could tell all had been forgiven. I thought now was a good time to divulge, but she interrupted again with, "Maybe… no love making until you are more comfortable, yes?" She didn't wait for a response and moving forward into me, she curled up into a fetal position and put the crown of her head to the side of my chest.

"Don't leave me, Ciarán," she murmured.

She was shutting down. So, I said nothing. Her breathing deepened and I knew she'd found sleep. I suspected she'd grown exhausted from our busy day and now that I was back, she found the comfort she needed for slumber in order to rejuvenate. I went to removing my shoes, toeing the right off with the left. I hoped the noise it made hitting the floor would not wake her. However, it was not the shoe that roused her, but the knock on the door.

Seconds passed and she surprised me with a giggle. Tilting her head back, she looked sleepily into my face. Bringing a finger to her lips, she said, “Shhh!” and giggled again.

“Who could it be?” I whispered.

“Ummm… ein Mandant? A client? But he will just have to go with someone else; my work here is finished… forever.”

Her words were almost inaudible, and I narrowed my eyes in confusion. I wanted to ask her what she meant, but the knock came again, this time, louder.

“Hallo?” echoed in the hallway.

“Shall I see to it?” I asked.

“No, just be quiet, maybe he will go away.”

“I can’t… I want to see.”

Getting up off the bed, I kicked off the other shoe and padded to the door in my stocking feet.

“Okay, have it your way, but you may not like it,” she mumbled, and slid over by the wall to lay on her belly. Putting her chin in her hands, she rested on her elbows. She snickered, and it was my turn to put a finger to lips. Covering her mouth, she bent her legs up at the knees and kicked her feet back and forth in mirth. Her dress had ridden up, and now more than her legs were exposed. The soft roundness of her buttocks peeked out, distracting me from my task.

“Hallo?” came again, followed by pounding, the panel vibrating with every strike. Giving my full attention back to the intrusion, I unlocked the door and opened it a crack.

“What is it?”

He was a small man for all the noise he made. His short, salt and pepper hair was greased back and parted on the side. He sported a brown, ill-fitting leisure suit with a yellow shirt, its collar brought out to lay atop that of the jackets.

He wore black plastic framed glasses, and I smiled at the thought that he must have bought them at the same shop where Anna’s mama had gotten hers. In his hands, he held a small bouquet of flowers. He was going on a date.

Bringing my eyes down to his feet, I felt my irritation. He wore dirty, old white sneakers. One of my pet peeves—wearing tennis shoes with a suit.

"Ich suche Fräulein X-Stacy," he said, telling me of his search for Miss X-Stacy.

I replied in Irish, "Níl aon Miss X-Stacy anseo," telling him that there was no Miss X-Stacy here. He stared hard at me, and I could see the nervousness rising. He scrutinized a scrap of paper in his hand, looked up at the door number, and back at me.

"Sorry?" he said, trying English this time. I repeated it just as I said it before.

"I… don't understand," he retorted, pushing on the door, trying to peer around it. But I held firm, so he tried to peek through the crack at the hinge. But the door opened from the left when going out, so the bed was behind it. Unless he could get his head inside, he could not see Anna, who at this point, was giggling into her hands at the comedy that was unfolding.

My persistent denial of this X-Stacy's presence, and his ever-growing confusion, made her laugh even harder. The Irish words poured out of my mouth, telling him it was my room and there was no one else there, and that he'd better go away or there would be trouble. He didn't understand a word of it, and neither did Anna. It was the tone of my voice and my posturing that brought her suppressed amusement. I could barely keep a straight face myself, and I was sure he could see through the ruse. He glanced down at the scrap of paper again as if it had the answer to his question.

Finally giving me a look of disgust, he turned to the stairs and issued a string of profanity that would have made my da proud. He stomped away and I closed the door. Returning to the bed, I shared a laugh with Anna. Picking up my jacket, I flung it over one of the decorative corner posts as Anna rolled back, putting her bottom to the wall. Climbing in, I sat up with my back to the headboard, propped up by a pillow.

"Miss X-Stacy?" I questioned.

She giggled, "Yes, I had to have something for the street. I could not use my real name."

My head swam with confusion. There was something hidden here and I needed to know what.

"Anna, tell me please, what is going on here? Who was that man and how does this Giselle know you? Are you this Stacy she was talking about?"

Her eyes got large, and she put a hand to her mouth, then pulling it away just as quick, she said, "You met Giselle?"

"I have. While I was downstairs getting the beer. She said you are Stacy and she also tried to tempt me… but I wouldn't have it. She's clever, that one is."

Anna examined the fingernails on her left hand, and said, "I have a confession, Ciarán… Giselle is the reason why I am here on this street, in this room and working a job that will probably get me killed."

"Killed?"

"Yes, murdered. Here… let me tell you. It was about three months ago that my mama became angry with me over some little thing and… how do you say? Kicked me out? She had started to drink more when I was away in Ireland. After I returned, she acted as if she needed me here. But it was all false. She started to bring home a different man about every night, both of them usually too drunk to stand up. After a month, she told me I would have to get a job because I was becoming a… bürde? Burden? A week later she came home and asked if I had gotten work yet. When I told her that I hadn't, she… blew up? Went crazy? I am sure it was because she wasn't coping well with her own job and was under a lot of stress. I became angry and we had a big argument. Then she told me to get out."

Anguish came into Anna's voice, and I expected another ride on the emotional rollercoaster. Wanting to calm her, I said, "I am so sorry Anna. I wish I could have come sooner, but…"

"No!" she said, cutting me off, and sliding over, she put a finger to my lips to hush me. "It is not your fault, I don't blame you."

Her eyes brimmed with tears and for a few seconds there was only our breathing and the music from downstairs. Casting her eyes down, the words poured from her lips.

"It became a terrible night after I ran from that apartment. I rode the S Bahn from one station to another for a very long time. Soon I grew tired of riding trains, so I got off at the Lehrter Bahnhof… the City station? The main station? I went walking in the Tiergarten and soon came to the great Tor. Uhhh… the Brandenburg Gate. I wandered up to Friedrichstrasse and finally arrived here at the café. I stopped to rest at one of the tables outside about four in the morning. The dancing and drinking was coming to an end, and it was then that Giselle came out with that creep, Eric."

"Eric?"

"Yes, the Barkellner… Bartender!"

There was disgust in her voice now, and I knew exactly who she was talking about.

"I think I met him, can't say I liked him much."

"Yes, he is a bad man, but anyway… let me finish, please? So Giselle came over to me with questions. She wanted to know why I was here and alone on the sidewalk. She sent her boy away and sat down with me. She was charismatic and so charming. I couldn't help but fall under her spell."

"So… then…"

"So I explained to her what had happened. She made me think she cared, and even held my hand as I raged on about my mama. Giselle offered me this room, saying no one would bother me here and I could get some sleep. So, I accepted her offer. I was desperate.

She brought me up here and left me, saying to lock the door and stay for as long as I needed."

"Anna… you are telling me, you took a room from a total stranger? You did not suspect that she may want something in return?"

"Ciarán, please. I needed somebody, anybody. I was alone, and she was willing to help me, take me in, and give me shelter. She came back that afternoon and bought me lunch at the café. We talked about ourselves for a long time, and then she tempted me. She started with how I could make lots of money, have a private room of my own, and party every day. All I had to do was escort men. Even at one date a night, I could make a great deal of money."

She sniffed and sighed, still looking down. Reaching out, I cupped her cheek. She wrapped my hand in hers, kissed a fingertip, and squeezing it, lay it back on the bed. I watched as one lone tear traced its way to the corner of her mouth, but the tip of her tongue make short work of it.

Taking a deep breath, she rolled over onto her back and pushing herself up against me, she said, "Ciarán, as you know, I needed to get back to Ireland. I needed to get back to you. So I started escorting men. The first one was from Chicago in America. A nice guy at first, just a married man seeking an escape. It started out fine, but he offered to give me money for sex and I turned him down. He had taken me out to a nice restaurant in the Potsdamer Platz and afterwards, we caught a taxi back to the café. We danced for a while and drank wine, and he got close. I felt it was time to end the date and realized I didn't know how. I asked Giselle, who was there, how I should get rid of this man. She asked if there had been sex and I have to admit I was a little naïve about how this thing was supposed to work."

She stopped and glanced up to see if I was still listening. Running a finger under the shoulder strap of her dress, she made a face as if it was too tight and hurt her skin. She readjusted her position and continued with her story before I could ask any questions.

"So Giselle got angry when I told her I was not interested in sex with this man. She said it didn't matter if I were interested or not, and called me a stupid child. She asked me how I expected to have any money for myself. She made it clear at that moment that the escort fee he had paid was hers. The sex money was to be mine—if we had sex. This guaranteed her payment every time. But I would get nothing if there were no sex. She reminded me I owed her money for my room, food and some of the closes she bought me, like this dress."

She stopped to take a deep breath, and I became distracted by her use of 'closes' for 'clothes'. It wasn't just a Berlin thing though, it was a German thing. Something about the 'th' and 'es' together made it difficult for them. I supposed I could get used to it though. The Irish have trouble with the 'th' in any word, most of the time giving it a 'D' sound. I decided it was a discussion for another time.

"Ciarán?" Anna said, realizing she'd lost me.

"On with it lass, I am hearing you."

"Okay, so, it was five hundred American dollars she took from this man and said I should charge the same for the sex—if not more. She told me I was a classy dame and was well worth it. So, when I did start making money, she would take some of that too. Telling me I owed her, and there would be trouble if I didn't give it to her. She threatened me, saying I may find myself floating face down in the Spree if I didn't do as I was told. So… unless I started getting my brains fucked out nightly, I would never have any money."

Anna's choice of words had the affect I believed she had hoped to bring. I found my ire rising and thoughts raced through my head how I might get back at Giselle for duping her. For pulling her into a world where there was nowhere else to go, but down. Once the ball got rolling on this type of thing, it was hard to stop. I had to come up with some kind of plan. I felt I owed that to Anna.

"Anna, do you want your money back? I will make her give your money back."

She rolled over onto her side to face me and said, "No Ciarán, I don't want it back. The money has become unimportant now that you are here. Don't you see? I have worked maybe fifteen or twenty times since that first night. I numbed myself to the sex. There are no good memories. There was no pleasure in it. My only joy came from thinking about you, and the life we could have together. I would close my eyes and pretend it was you making love to me. It was the only way to cope with strange men, grunting and grinding on top of me. But sometimes they transformed into my father and it was all I could do to keep from freaking out. I avoided Giselle whenever possible. As long as she was receiving her fee for hooking me up, and two thirds of my sex money, she seemed content. She never asked if I was available, she just took the request and expected me to be ready. She also made sure I went to the clinic to be checked for disease and pregnancy. It is a good thing health care is free here or she would probably make me pay for that too. I have to buy my own condoms and they are not cheap. I could go on the pill, but that would not protect me from disease. I am so glad the nightmare is over."

She moved a hand to me and traced a finger down the seam of my sleeve. I watched it move up my arm and when I smiled at her, I saw her studying my face as if she was trying to sort out what I might be thinking.

"Is that all, or is there more?"

"No, there's more, like—eating was a problem and trying to keep myself in closes. Everything I had was worn out, so she started giving me things without asking if I wanted them. Then she would charge me for those as well. But I sensed you were coming, I could feel you. I believed it would not be long. I just needed to hold on, and you would be here soon. I am certain you know how I felt the moment I saw you walk by that cafe."

Moving her hand to my shirtfront, and undoing a button, she slipped it inside. She caressed my stomach in a circular motion and moving up my chest, she freed more buttons in the process. I felt the warmth of her hand as it stopped directly over my heart. Then looking up at me, she gave me a sheepish smile, almost like a child who'd been caught breaking the rules.

"I can feel your heart beating," she said, and taking my hand with her other, she placed it against her exposed cleavage.

"Feel that, Ciarán? Do you feel that? You know that my heart beats for you and only you. Please say you do?"

"Oh! So that is what a heart feels like when it's beating for me."

"Please Ciarán, be serious."

"Sorry…"

"Do you not want to make love to me now because I have been with other men? Please don't be angry at me for being a stupid girl."

"Why do you say that? You are not stupid, Anna. So, please don't say you are… and you'd been with others before we even met. How do I have any say? There was no commitment, but now that things have changed, there could be. Besides, I am only angry at predators like Giselle who prey on people when they are most vulnerable."

I felt that I needed to make some kind of a gesture to reassure her that I was ready, so moving my hand from her chest, I took the slider of the zipper that ran down from her armpit and pulled it to her waist. The dress fell open, exposing her left breast. Resting my hand on her hip, I watched her face for a reaction. She gave me an alluring look and taking that hand, she placed it on the alabaster mound.

"How does that feel?" she asked in a seductive manner.

"Lovely," I said, trying to sound confident even though my hand trembled. Feeling her heart quicken in her chest, I moved to trace a finger along the lower curve of her breast and then up to do the same with the areola. Sighing, her own hand strayed to caress the other, and closing her eyes, a slight moan escaped her mouth.

The anger that had built up inside me because of Giselle, melted away, replaced with yearning. Wanting a more comfortable position, I pulled my hand away and rolled onto my side to face her. Her eyes popped open and seeing what I was doing, she slid over to lay an arm across me, her forehead pressed to mine. She closed her eyes and we lay there just having a quiet moment.

My thoughts flew back to Ireland. I never thought at the time I would be where I was tonight. We'd been friends, confidants, and now, it was inevitable that we would soon be lovers. I wasn't new to this, but with Anna—it felt like I was.

Part of me was still trying to accept that she was a woman now and needed to be treated like one. I had to accept that I wouldn't be taking advantage of her if we progressed to a higher level of intimacy. We'd come to a turning point, and I had been overcome with a kind of helplessness. Something that had contributed to the panic. But with this new awareness, there came a great sense of relief.

I had a firmer toehold on the rocky cliff of my life and I was now ready to move up.

Chapter 15

"Bliss And A Bruise"

After a minute or so, Anna's lids fluttered open and slight smile came to her lips. This was followed by something I can only describe as a look of shyness.

"I love you, Anna."

"… and I, you," she whispered back. "Would you please make love to me now, Ciarán? I don't think I can wait much longer."

"My pleasure, darling," rolled out of my lips without hesitation, surprising me.

She moved quickly, and sitting up, she pulled the single strap off her shoulder. The dress cascaded to her stomach, exposing her other breast. Standing up on the bed, the garment fell to her feet, leaving her to grin down, wearing only a black, silk thong. She kicked the gown onto the floor, and straddling my legs, sat her lovely backside on my thighs. Her lips found mine, and as she stripped the shirt from my body, her tongue explored every part of my mouth. When she pulled away, she sat back on her haunches and removed the comb from the twist of hair at the back of her head. With one quick shake, her tresses fell to wreath her face.

"Are you ready for me?" she said with delicate hesitation, her voice so seductive that my response, "More than ever," was almost like a plea.

A confident smile played across her lips and there was voraciousness in her actions when she undid my belt and fly. After pulling my zipper down ever so slowly, she move to straddle my left leg and grabbing the waistband of my trousers, she slid herself down toward my feet, pulling them with her as she went. I could feel the softness of her vulva through the silk as it moved along my leg, and upon passing over my knee, she tilted her face to the ceiling and moaned. She did it again when she found my toes, and falling back against the footboard, she pulled off my trousers and flung them away.

Holding her feet just above the mattress, she peeled off her thong, her face framed by her legs as she gave me a look that said, "Don't worry, I'll be gentle." Then pulling my feet apart, she slid up between my knees. The palms of her hands moved up under my back and pressed against my shoulder blades as she kissed my chin and nose. Through the thin cotton of my drawers, my erection pressed hard against her supple belly. She kissed my neck a few times and then worked her way down my chest. Continuing past my belly button, she took the waistband of my drawers in her teeth and pulled them down to my thighs, exposing my now throbbing bud. Her eyes rolled up to meet mine and releasing the waistband, we shared a grin.

She came back up, dragging her breasts, and then her pubic bone over her new found friend. Pulling up a knee, she locked the waistband of my underwear in her toes and pushed them down to my ankles. Thinking it might be best if I helped, I flung them off with a foot. We watched them arc through the air toward the window and strike the lamp on the table. It fell over and the room went dark.

Now only the light from the street lit the room, creating a golden aura around Anna's head. We chuckled as she brought her face to mine. Placing my hands on the warm, smooth skin at the small of her back, our lips came together as she cocked her hips forward and then back to bring me inside her.

She gave a slight squeal, followed by a loud moan and a shudder. Her mouth moved back to my neck where she lightly bit moist skin over taught muscle. I returned the favor, nibbling slowly up to her ear. Her hips rose and fell in time with mine, and I breathed a quiet, "Anna," into her hair as we descended into blissful sensuality.

We made love for an hour without stopping, showing each other what we knew. We endeavored to bring each other to climax, but not to 'out do' each other. There was just a mutual desire to share. Anna was no amateur, and if I were to regret anything about her method, it would be what she'd been forced to endure in order to acquire it.

I expected reluctance because of her da's abuse. But if there had been any, I must have missed it. This brought a form of reassurance that she truly loved me.

There was also a vague awareness that I didn't sense my beloved wife around me anymore. Since her death, I'd constantly felt her presence as if she was just out of sight in the other room. Now as I lay here with the new love of my life, there came a blossoming clarity. In my mind's eye, Isleen walked away through a field of waving yellow flowers to disappear into the light of a radiant sunset. Instead of feeling sadness—I felt relief. It was as if Isleen had finally found her way into the Otherworld.

Anna and I lie naked on the sheets, I upon my back with my hands behind my head, and her, on her right side, one leg thrown over mine, her left arm and head on my chest.

"Are you good?" she panted, tilting her head back so she could see my face. I grinned and panted back, "Wunderbar."

She lay her head back down and whispered, "Yes, it was wonderful."

Running a finger up and down a small strip of hair just below my belly button, she came to an abrupt halt and said, "Ciarán, I am famished. I need food. I have not eaten since this morning."

Twisting my head around to read the clock on the dresser, I was unable to see its face in the dark.

"What's the time, anyway?"

Anna rolled away and reaching up, turned on the lamp. The light caused me to wince, and when my eyes focused, I saw it was just after two in the morning.

"Where will we get food at this hour? Do you have something stashed in your wee icebox over there?" I said, pointing to the grimy white, mini fridge stowed under the counter.

She laughed, "There is nothing in there but maybe… how do you call it? Lard?"

Sitting up, she put her back against the wall. Crossing her legs, she pulled the sheet over them. Curls of hair lay plastered against her forehead, and a slight shimmer of sweat was visible between her breasts.

"I have a Turkish friend, Zafer, who owns an imbiss. He promised me he would open up for me anytime of the day or night if I were hungry. He sleeps in the back of the shop, and all I have to do is knock on the door and he will come. I think he likes me. He is always telling me "Should you ever want to marry, I am your man!" But he is too old for me and perhaps he is, uh, just teasing? He treats me good though, better than most men do. So he is more like the father I never had."

"Are you sure he would open his doors at this hour?"

"No problem. I am pretty sure that he would leave his mattress if he heard my voice under his window."

She laughed, and I rolled to face her. Propping myself up on an elbow, I rubbed her knee through the sheet and teased, "Now tell me true lass, would he be a client by any chance?" She laughed again and threw her head back, bumping the wall. "Ow!" she said, rubbing the point of contact and adding, "No, no, Ciarán, he is just a lonely old man who lost his wife a long time ago."

She got a thoughtful look on her face and leaning forward, she kissed me on my forehead, “I suppose you know what that is like, yes?”

I returned the kiss to the tip of her nose and looking down, I toyed with a loose string on the linen. “I do know what that is like, but I have you now… and that makes all the difference in the world.”

She placed her hands flat on the mattress and gave me a shock, causing me to push back against the headboard when she rose up into a handstand, laughing. She then vaulted over me, the sheet falling away to expose her nakedness.

“Sooo… let’s go eat,” she sang out in midair.

I found myself speechless as she landed on the floor with the grace of a gymnast. She took her performance one-step further by standing with her legs straight and together, her arms projecting to the ceiling in a V. Then pushing herself up onto the balls of her feet, she bent slightly backwards and grinned up at the ceiling. Not knowing what else to do, I applauded and she threw kisses around the room to her pretend audience.

“I knew you would like that. When I was a little girl, I was a gymnast… I was fantastic,” she said with mock smugness.

She turned and moved away toward a pile of laundry in the corner. Getting up, I sat on the edge of the bed, watching her firm, round buttocks rise and fall as she moved. I thought myself a lucky man as I admired her physique. It would do her no harm to put on a few pounds, but I figured that would come in time. As far as I knew, she was healthy despite all she’d been through, and that’s what mattered.

“I stink,” she giggled, sniffing at an armpit. Then kneeling down, she rummaged through the clothing and pulled out a pair of blue jeans to put on.

“Ah well, you know it’s almost half two in the morning. Who’s going to be smelling you, but me?”

“Zafer. Zafer will smell me,” she said, her words muffled by the black T-shirt she was now pulling on over her head.

When her head popped through the collar, she blurted, “I smell like sex.”

Giving me a big grin, she raised and lowered her eyebrows several times before turning away to walk over to a narrow shelf above the sink. Examining a row of small bottles, she turned and added, “Good sex!” with an exaggerated wink. Picking up a small atomizer, she studied the label. Then spraying certain points on her body, she hummed a single note at each spot, progressing up the scale as she went from her crotch to her neck.

“You won’t have to worry what Zafer thinks after tonight, this may be the last time you will ever have to eat in an imbiss,” I said as I walked around putting on my clothes.

She was suddenly in my arms. I saw her eyes had grown moist and I presumed my statement had triggered another emotion.

“Are you sad again?”

“No Ciarán, I am happy. It is the happiest I have been in a long time. But I will miss my Berlin.”

I kissed the top of her head and the odor of roses invaded my nostrils. She released her hold and stepping back, wiped at her eyes before clapping her hands together, saying, “Button your shirt Ciarán, I’m hungry and want to go. We should go barefoot! I love to walk barefoot in Berlin, especially when it’s raining.”

“Sorry darling, it’s not raining and I’m not much on walking barefoot anywhere, well… except for maybe the beach back home.”

A lull came to the music downstairs and it lasted just long enough for me to pick up on a floorboard creaking outside the door. I saw the key hole go dark, and the adrenalin surged in. Glancing at Anna, I noticed she was not paying any attention as she focused on picking lint from her T-shirt.

“Did you hear that?” I whispered.

“Hear what? I heard nothing.”

Stepping to the door, I put my ear to the wood. Somebody stood just outside trying hard not to breathe. There came the smell of beer and bad cologne.

Anna said, “Ciarán, what is it?” but I ignored her.

Thinking her date had returned, I pulled the lock, but got only as far as to turn the knob. The door suddenly burst open as if kicked from the other side. It hit me in the forehead and I dropped like a sack of rocks. The last thing I heard was Anna screaming, “Nein Eric! Nein!” as my head bounced off the floor and I fell into darkness.

Chapter 16

"...Hard To Find, And Lucky To Have"

I'd somehow slipped from the pier and no matter how hard I tried to make my way back to the surface, an unknown force kept pulling me down. Struggling to hold my breath, I could feel the panic taking over. I twisted and turned, my legs kicking to no avail. Now there was a voice. Anna's voice. Through the murky water, her fragmented image stood above me on the dock. Reaching down, she called, "Come back, come back..." Not being able to hold my breath any longer, I opened my mouth and the sea rushed in.

Jolting awake, I spit water. My face was dripping wet, and I lay where I'd fallen. My head pounded, and there was a sharp pain in my left side. Someone must have kicked me. I'd been kicked before, so I'd had experience with that sort of thing.

But why was my face wet?

A musky, female odor rolled to my nose as I wiped the water from my eyes. Pushing myself up onto my elbows, I looked around. A woman crouched next to me, holding a clear glass with a trace of water in the bottom. Her burgundy colored miniskirt was now hiked up to her hips, making it clear that she wore nothing underneath. Quite aware my view was unobstructed, she only smiled and said, "Heissen sie?"

"Who am I? Who are you? I said, trying to bring her face into focus.

A blinding light flashed across my vision and my head thumped like a big bass drum. When the pounding lessened, my vision cleared. She had a round face and her black hair was styled into a super short bob, making everything very spherical.

Her sleeveless blouse was cowl necked, and extra folds of the collar hung loose upon her large chest. It was ridiculously bright gold. When she moved, it shimmered and flashed, making me wince.

"Sprechen Sie Deutsch?"

I didn't answer because sometimes there were two of her, and I struggled to maintain my focus, trying to decide which one was real.

"English?" She asked.

"Nah! Irish."

She cocked her head, "No, I mean, you speak English… maybe?"

"I speak English, and Irish, some German and even a wee bit of French," I growled.

"Fine. Super. I speak English too, but no Irish or French."

She giggled and stood up, setting the glass on top of the dresser next to the beer bottle. Towering over me now, her knee high black leather boots added a couple more centimeters to her height. Without them, she would have been even shorter than Anna. I could still see up her skirt and she did nothing to change that. She smiled wider now and said, "You like what you see? You may have it for a little price? A little price for… a little me."

"What? Ah… please! My head is splitting."

I gave her my best 'Give me a moment, will you!' look and she giggled. Reaching down with both hands, she said, "Let me help you stand."

Taking my hands, I could still feel the wetness from the glass and the many rings she wore on her fingers. Struggling to my feet, I almost collapsed, but she caught me by the shoulders and directed me to the bed. Sitting me on the edge, she sat down beside me.

"I am sorry I splash you. But I need to make you wake," she said, as I wiped the remaining moisture off my chin with a sleeve.

"It's okay lass and, uh… who are you by the way?"

Turning my face, I studied hers. She couldn't have been more than seventeen. She looked down at her lap in a submissive manner, avoiding eye contact. I noticed at the hairline on the back of her neck, a small, blue 'G' with a tiny star of the same color, next to it. She glanced up and caught me studying the tattoo. Putting a hand over it, she glanced away for a second, and then turning back, she blurted, "I am Friedericka, and in my work, they call me, 'Desiree'. But you may call me, Reeka."

She laughed, slapped her bare legs, and looking up, she grinned at me. But her eyes told me she was nervous and her manner was more bravado than confidence.

"Why are you in here?" I asked

"Oh…" she said and giggled in a long crescendo, cutting it off in an abrupt fashion. It made me wonder if Reeka was right in the head.

"I was walking from my room and I saw the door open. Anna does not leave her door open—ever. I wondered if she was okay, so I came in. Then I saw you on the floor. I thought you were tot, I mean… dead. But I saw you were just… how you say… passed out? Yes?"

She rotated toward me, and taking her hand from her neck, she put it on my back. Her other went to my knee and she ran it up and down my leg, coming ever closer to my crotch. Leaning in, she put her face in mine. Her lips came precariously close as her eyes sought favorable reaction. Then talking to me like a child, she said, "Were you drunk? You were drunk, weren't you?"

I took her hand and put it on her own leg. Removing the other from my back, I placed it on the bed. She made a loud purring noise and ran a finger inside the collar of my shirt. Pulling her face from mine, she brought her lips around to my ear and said in a seductive manner, "How are you called?"

"I am Ciarán, you may call me Ciarán," I said, with sarcasm.

I thought about it after, realizing I needed be nice to this girl. She was trying to help me and was an asset at the moment. I felt she couldn't be held responsible for most of her actions. They seemed to be the conditioned behaviors of a child. I felt Reeka could be easily manipulated, but I could see that she still struggled for some control, trying hard to project a degree of maturity.

Her eyes grew wide and she stifled a gasp with her hand. Her bright blue eyes got large, and pulling her hand away, she said, "Oh! You are Anna's Karen!" She threw her arms around me and putting the side of her face to mine, she started bouncing her arse up and down as if it was on fire.

"It is almost like I know you!" she said and releasing me, she put her hands together, bringing her thumbs to her lips, as if in prayer.

"It's Ciarán, not Karen."

"Oh, sorry! Spell for me, please."

"C-I-A-R-A-N… Kee-a-ran."

My head throbbed as I watched her eyes roll toward the ceiling, projecting deep thought.

"C-I-A-R-A-N. Ciarán—yes?"

"It is… fabulous work."

Her face became thoughtful for a few seconds, but then she whipped around to challenge me, saying, "Why are you here? What has happened? Where is Anna?"

I explained the events leading up to being laid out on the floor, and I watched the fear come into her face.

"Do you know Giselle? And why do you have a 'G' tattooed on your neck next to a star?"

Reeka looked at me like she didn't understand at first. I saw comprehension come into her eyes and she looked away, her hand going back to her neck.

"Because I am Giselle's. But—so is Anna."

Her voice faded to a whisper, but she perked up as if she'd forgotten something of great importance and said, "There are many of us here. We are Giselle's 'Ladies of the Night'. Isn't that what you call us?"

She started giggling but then cut it off as if she realized it wasn't called for. Putting a serious look on her face, she added, "Ladies of the night… so funny. We are ladies of the day also. We should be known as, 'The All Day and Night Ladies!' She burst out laughing, studying my face in the process like she was gauging my reaction.

Then she lost it completely and brayed like a donkey into my face. Realizing what she'd done, she clapped her hands to her mouth, embarrassed, leaving me convinced that Reeka might be nuts. I felt nothing but pity for her, though. I sorted this was why it was so easy for Giselle to manipulate her. Backed by a crew of hooligans, the procuress had quite a racket going. I wondered how many others were involved and thought about the man downstairs with the bad haircut and malicious glint in his eye. I was sure he was the 'Eric' that had kicked the door open, and had given me the boot.

He must have taken Anna somewhere—but where?

"Reeka, where would they have taken Anna?"

Before she could answer, footsteps pounded up the stairs. I wobbled to my feet and started for the door. I thought to close it, but Reeka grabbed me from behind. She wrapped her arms around me, her chest so tight against my back, I could feel her hardening nipples through the fabric. Standing on her toes, she looked over my shoulder and said, "No, no Ciarán, it is okay, it is only… how I can say… my date?"

A giant of man in a dark burgundy sport coat walked by, but did not look in our direction. After he passed, Reeka came around and peeked out the door. A heavy knock echoed down the hallway and she giggled. Turning back, she said, "It is only Adelric, he is a good man with much money. Tonight, I perform well. Then I will be a richer woman and… he will be a poorer man!" She purred and giggled, adding, "And he dresses to match mein Kleid… my skirt? You know Ciarán, English is very weird. It was so hard for me to learn."

She gave me a sad face and then grinned to let me know it was fake before she skipped back to me. Throwing her arms around my neck, she pulled my head down and kissed me hard on the mouth. Tasting mouthwash, I tried to pull back, but she stuck to me. I felt more embarrassed than angry. As ridiculous as it was, my impulse was to take a hold of her and shake her, so to bring her to her senses. I suspected that would do more harm than good.

When she let me go, she stepped back, looked me up and down as she wiped off her mouth, saying, "Oooo! Too bad you are Anna's, because you would be next, right after Adelric."

"Such a shame, oh well. Maybe in another life, hiagh?"

She looked confused for a few seconds as she tried to sort it, then gave up and said, "Good bye, Ciarán from Irland!" and turning away, she stuck out her backside and wiggled it at me while looking back over her shoulder, giggling. She pursed her lips and making a kissing noise disappeared out the door.

"Reeka! Stay!"

"Sorry Ciarán! Got to go… got a date," she called back, and then sang out, "Adelric!"

There came a deep masculine laugh, followed by, "Desiree! Wie Geht's?"

Poking my head out of the door, I saw the two of them disappear into what must be Reeka's room. They shut the door, so I closed Anna's and returned to the bed. Reeka's kiss had brought a dose of adrenalin and I was glad for that—just not how I got it. Pulling up my shirt, I looked at my ribs. A mammoth bruise was forming, but it appeared as if nothing was broken. My ire came up at the thought that Eric had put a boot to me, and I felt payback was in order. I would let vengeance empower me.

I sat, pondered, and planned. If I stayed too long, somebody might come back to finish me off. At some point, Anna would have to be returned to this room and they needed me out. They probably sorted that if they hurt me, they could scare me away. Then I would just leave Anna and get out of Berlin. If so, they'd underestimated Ciarán McKay.

A door opened and Reeka's voice resonated in the hallway. I stood up and opening Anna's door, I peeked out, and then opening it up all the way, I watched as she and Adelric came down the hall. She had wrapped her arm in his and when they saw me, he looked away.

"We are going on our date now," she said with a large gleeful grin.

"Please, Reeka, I need to ask you something."

Adelric looked up at the ceiling and then pretended to study movie and travel posters tacked to the opposite wall.

"Not now Ciarán, I am with my date," she said in a stern manner as she pulled him along. "We are going to the club. Maybe you would like to come there too… it is an exciting place. You might find what you're looking for." She gave me an exaggerated wink and giggled.

I watched them walk down the stairs, with Reeka calling back as they disappeared from view, "But be careful for a man called Karl! Er ist gefährlich! Uhhh… very dangerous!"

Going back into the room, I shut the door and locked it. I needed more time to think, but there wasn't any. Finding my shoes and socks, I put them on, and walking to the window, I studied the street. It was still dark and there wasn't a soul out there except for a large cat hiding among the cars as it prowled. I would need the darkness and the cars too, but I had to hurry. It would be dawn in a few hours, and I would lose a crucial element of my plan.

The table lamp was still lying on its side and as I righted it, my thoughts went back to that joyful moment when it had been knocked over. That's when I noticed a greeting card sized piece of paper that had been hidden by the lamps base.

I pulled it out and read a short menu from Zafer's Imbiss. It listed some of the foods he offered next to their prices, and at the bottom was a street address: 'Friedrichstrasse 111'.

Zafer was a friend to Anna, so perhaps he could be a friend to me. Tearing off the bottom of the card, I folded it and shoved it in my pocket. Preparing myself mentally to leave the room, I said aloud, "Panic disorder or not, those maggots are going to pay."

I decided it would be best if I didn't go dressed the way they would expect. Looking around I found the black T-shirt that Anna had put on before Eric showed up. I picked it up and seeing that the label showed it was unisex, I took off my shirt and pulled it on over my head. It was a wee bit tight at the waist, but the fit was acceptable. I'd lost some weight since I'd cut back on drinking and the usual bulge no longer showed.

Scanning the room, I looked over the assorted hats. One of them was a black knit beanie that I thought might work for me. Pulling it on, I winced when I ran the cuff over the bump on the back of my head. It fit okay as long as I kept it pulled down below my sore spot. That's when I noticed the sparkly blue dress on the floor, just visible beneath the jeans she had planned to wear to the imbiss.

So, what was she wearing now?

Looking around the room, I noticed the wee black number she'd kept separate from the rest was now missing from its fancy hanger. I gathered that: Anna's date must have found Giselle, complained about what had happened, and she had sent Eric to deal with it as soon as he could break free from the bar. He had come up, taken me out of commission, and pressing Anna to put on the dress, he then forced her downstairs to be with Mr. Leisure Suit.

Moving toward the door, I saw a pair of sunglasses lying on the dresser. I snatched them up and put them on. They were the type that were lightly tinted at the bottom of the lens, but gradually grew darker toward the top. I would have to walk with my head tilted back in order to see. I decided not to wear them until that crucial moment just before I entered the club. Hanging them from my collar, I grabbed the doorknob, but hesitated.

A picture formed in my head of me standing on the edge of a deep, dark wood, ill prepared to step into a world much darker than my own. But Anna was in there, and I needed to bring her out. She would be counting on me. I forced myself to open the door and another shot of adrenaline coursed in. The bile rose in my throat and swallowing hard to force it back, I moved out into the hallway.

Chapter 17

"To Be A Knight Without Shining Armor"

I closed the door and tiptoed down the corridor. Moving as quiet as I could down the stairs, I stopped at the bottom and studied the alcove through the window in the door. Seeing no one, I stole out onto the tiny, garbage-strewn niche, doing my best not to kick any cans or bottles. Peeking around the corner of the building and seeing it was clear, I hurried across the street to take up a position behind an older, black VW beetle. It gave me a direct view through the open door of the club and I stayed put to plan my next move.

The cafe had must have been a department store or grocery, at one time. One big advantage for me was that they had not removed the big plate glass display windows to opt for more privacy. Behind the large blue letters proclaiming, 'G's Star'–Clubrestaurant' colored lights flashed, and strobes created weird effects on the walls. Arms waved in the air, and people jumped up and down in time with the music.

I got a shock when a giant of a man came out and stood on the steps. Dressed in a black suit, the light gleamed off his large, shaven head. He scanned the street, so I dropped down to look through one of the VW's windows.

He soon disappeared inside, leaving me to focus on trying to get my heart rate to slow. Changing positions had improved my view, and I detected a shiny gold blouse moving around the dance floor. The distance was too great for me to be sure it was Reeka, but I would make odds on it.

I was now ready for action, but more afraid than I'd ever been in my life. Regardless, I decided to risk a frontal attack. I would just walk in the door and get lost in the crowd. If the big man came after me, it would be best to run. There was no way for me to take him in single combat, and the fear of Anna having to witness my demise, energized me even more.

Putting on the glasses, I did a fast walk across the street. Coming up the steps, I peeked around the doorjamb. Eric wasn't in sight, so ducking inside, I slid in behind a group of people and tried to blend in. The ones I bumped into looked me over, but only for a second. Breathing a sigh of relief, I moved to an open spot next to one of the big windows.

As the people gyrated around, they moved as a group back and forth across the floor. Girls jumped and bounced with their arms in the air, their male partners lurched about, ogling them in drunken stupor. At one point, when the mob moved toward the bar, I discovered Giselle sitting at a small table in a back corner.

Her chair had been strategically placed next the DJ's both, giving her the best view of the room. Her attention rested not on the action, but on a young woman sitting to her right. Her companion looked and dressed much like Giselle herself. Both of them were smoking and sipping from glasses of wine.

As I studied them, my heart leapt into my throat when I realized that the man in black was standing directly behind Giselle in the shadow. He had his arms crossed and was panning his head back and forth.

Without warning, he walked around the table and headed toward the door. I moved forward, pushing myself into a group of people that were all jumping to the beat, their arms waving above their heads.

Joining in, I kept a tall lass between me and the big fellow as he passed. The glasses and beanie would make identification difficult. So, even if he put his eyes on me, I suspected it wouldn't register. I assumed he'd never seen me before, and could only go from the description of those who had. Since I was dressed like a dozen other men in the place, I felt safe for the moment.

I waited for him to pass, noting his position every time I went airborne. I watched him perform the same action as before, and then coming back inside, he stopped at the bar and spoke to Eric. Pounding once on the counter, he pointed an accusing finger at the smaller man, but the bartender flipped his hair back and gave him a look of indifference. Karl was agitated about something and turning away, he shook his head as he waded back through the crowd. I stopped jumping, but kept my eye on him as I moved back to my original spot.

On the way to his post, he bumped into a young couple who'd been so busy with each other, they hadn't seen him coming. They stumbled out of his way, and when they did, a pair of dirty, white sneakers caught my eye. Mr. Leisure Suit.

He sat to the left of Giselle's girlfriend's, along the same wall. I zeroed in on him as I moved toward the stage, and that was when I saw Anna. She sat across the table to his right, and was barely visible in her black dress. It was the string of gleaming pearls around her neck that grabbed my attention. They were a distress beacon sent from the gloom.

The strobes were off now, but the colored lights flashed. Anna leaned forward to look toward Giselle and her blonde hair picked up the reds, blues, and greens. When she leaned back, Mr. Leisure Suit grabbed her arm, and said something in her ear. Getting to her feet, she walked to Giselle. Leaning down, she spoke to her boss, who violently shook her head no, and pointed for Anna to get back to her chair. That's when Mr. Leisure Suit jumped up and stomping over, began to protest.

Their voices rose above the din as an argument ensued. After a brief exchange, Giselle threw up her hands as if to say, "Do whatever you want." The man grabbed Anna's hand and jerked her toward the dance floor. When he turned his back to Giselle, she flipped him off and laughed about it with her girlfriend.

The music only stopped long enough for the DJ to change discs. It was one crazy techno tune rolling into another. An eerie Kraftwerk number boomed out of the speakers, and Mr. Leisure Suit reeled about the dance floor. Anna acted as if in a trance, her moves out of time with the music. The weird electronic sounds made the situation even more bizarre. It became evident that she wanted to escape, and my inability to offer a quick solution made it harder to remain cool.

I felt somebody grab my arm, and being wound up tighter than a spring, I spun around and drew back a fist. I was able to check myself though before cutting loose and smashing Reeka's cute little nose.

"Nein, Nein!" she shrieked, and reaching out, grabbed my forearms, yelling, "That is Karl behind Giselle. Be very careful, Ciarán. He is looking for someone, and I am afraid it may be you."

"I supposed that as well," I shouted back, glancing around the room to be sure I was still concealed by the people around me. Karl now leaned forward as Giselle spoke into his ear. She had a grip on his sleeve as if she'd pulled him to her. He laughed and standing upright, melted back into the shadow.

"I see Anna is being watched. Do you see? Giselle is trying to keep her close, ja?"

"Not for much longer if I can help it."

Looking back at Anna, I noticed she confined her activity to the corner of the dance floor nearest Giselle. I wrapped an arm around the small of Reeka's back and pulled her to me so I wouldn't have to yell. She took it as a come on, and her hand strayed to my backside. Putting my mouth to her ear, I said, "Reeka, I need for you to get Anna to this side of the room. Can you do that?"

"I know don't Ciarán… it could be bad for me."

She started kissing my neck and the level of her inebriation became apparent. I attempted to pull her hand from my backside and she gave it a quick pinch before giving it up. I grabbed her upper arms and held them, glaring at her out of the bottom of the glasses.

"Please Reeka, this is important," I scolded.

She didn't like being man-handled, and twisting out of my grip said, "Ok, I know what I can do. But you will owe me for this—if I live."

"Thanks, darling," I said, and patted her on the shoulder. She took that hand and placed it on her breast. Batting her eyes at me, she grinned. I jerked it away and cocked my head in aggravation.

"Someday we should come together, you and me… and Anna. I would not even ask for money from you."

She returned to the dance floor, doing a rhythmic little shuffle. Exaggerating the sway of her hips, she grinned back over her shoulder as if to say, "You like? Ja?"

I watched her return to her table and say something to Adelric. Grabbing him, she tried to pull him to the dance floor. He yanked his hand from hers and shook his head in disagreement. She jumped on him, straddling his lap with her skirt riding up as high as possible without becoming a belt. She clamped his head in both hands and planted a long passionate kiss on his lips. Then pulling her cowl neck down to expose her breasts, she pushed his face into her cleavage.

I was fearful that maybe Reeka wouldn't be able to pull it off. But when she removed Adelric's face from between her breasts and said something in his ear, he grinned and nodded with enthusiasm.

Fixing her blouse, she jumped off and towed him to the floor, sending a fleeting glance my way. The music changed to a song called, 'She Drives Me Crazy' and Reeka went into action, dancing Adelric closer to Anna with every move. When they arrived in her corner of the floor, Reeka worked her way in between Anna and Mr. Leisure Suit. The little man didn't notice at first because he was doing some extreme disco move that involved a spin. He bumped into Reeka, almost knocking her down. Obviously upset, he forced his way back to Anna.

She grinned and leaning around him, said something to Reeka. They both threw their heads back in a laugh and continued moving to the beat. Reeka took the risk of dancing in between them a second time and Mr. Leisure Suit put his hand on her shoulder as if to pull her out of the way. Adelric stopped his rhythmic swaying, and stomping over, gave the smaller man a shove.

The two men faced off and started exchanging words. Anna and Reeka moved out of their way, still dancing, but now toward me. Keeping an eye on Giselle, I saw her eyes were still on her girlfriend, and now, so were her hands. Karl stood absorbed in the girl-show, seemingly unaware of the ruckus unfolding on the dance floor.

Reeka maneuvered Anna to where she would be able to see me and said something into her ear. Anna snapped her face in my direction, but didn't see me at first. So whipping off the sunglasses, I gave her a big grin. Recognition crept into her face, and throwing her hands to her mouth, her eyes widened in surprise. She started to walk my way, but Reeka grabbed her arm and shook her head no. She then demonstrated to Anna a few slow dance moves and pointed in my direction without actually pointing at me. Anna followed her lead, and they slowly boogied my way.

Soon the two women were jumping up and down along with the others and every time Anna landed, she put herself two steps closer to me—and more distance between her and Mr. Leisure Suit. When I looked in his direction, I saw the eejit make the fatal mistake of poking Adelric in the chest.

Now's the time, lass.

Anna glanced back toward Giselle and must have thought the same. Without missing a beat, she jumped one last time and landed among the people loitering about the edge of the dance floor. She soon appeared on my side of that line of bodies and slamming into me, she hugged me so tight, I could barely draw a breath.

"Oh Ciarán, I was so afraid they had killed you."

I hugged her back, yelling, "Anna, there is no time. We must get out of here."

Unfortunately, the song ended half way through my statement, and the sound of my voice rose above the shouts of Adelric and his opponent. A rave tune blasted out of the speakers and the activity on the floor picked up again. I looked toward the bar and a bolt of fear shot through me. Eric had stopped serving drinks and was looking right at us.

He went to jumping up and down, waving to get someone's attention from the back. But Giselle was still engaged in her activity and Karl's focus was now on Adelric and Mr. Leisure Suit.

I grabbed Anna's hand and pulling her to the door, I said, "Time to go, darling."

I pushed through the people, trying to keep an eye on the bartender. I saw him launch a shot glass toward the back corner. It arced through the air and struck the wall above Karl, showering him with glass. Then several things happened all at one time.

Mr. Leisure Suit punched Adelric in the face, the dancers all surged away from the two in a huge wave of humanity, and Eric was coming over the bar with, of all things, a cricket bat. Reeka had been dancing parallel to our position, trying to keep her eyes on us. When she came to an open space, she grabbed Anna's arm.

"Du musst bleiben!" She yelled, telling us we had to stay, and looking back over her shoulder at Eric, she added, "Help me, they are getting away."

We had been deceived!

Tightening my grip on Anna, I pulled harder. It didn't make sense that Reeka would double-cross us. But I soon realized Reeka wasn't really pulling on Anna, it was more she just held Anna's wrist and allowed herself to be towed along. Then that terrible feeling of betrayal left me just as quick as it came as she threw me a wink and nodded toward the door.

Still holding Anna by the wrist, she swung herself around toward the bar. When she stood right in Eric's path, she let go, feigning as if she'd lost her grip. Falling backward, she gave a false squeal of fear.

I have to give Reeka credit, she put on a grand show. At the start, I thought her denser than a stack of peat, but she proved me wrong. She had it all sorted out.

As she tumbled to the floor, she kicked up, catching one of Eric's feet while he was still airborne. This flipped him backwards, causing his head to slam into the edge of the bar top. His body went limp as the cricket bat spun backwards, smashing the huge mirror and half a dozen liquor bottles. He flopped down on top of Reeka, and rolling out from underneath him, she shouted, "Beeil dich."

"Yes, hurry. We must hurry." I said, still pulling Anna toward the door.

She came with me, her face full of confusion as she tried to sort out what was happening. With no time for explanation, we arrived at our exit as the room erupted in chaos. Looking back one last time before exiting, I saw Adelric and Mr. Leisure Suit wrestling as Karl knocked people down, trying to get to us. I could not see Giselle, but I could hear her yelling Eric's name. She had no idea he was out cold and being trampled by the same mass of patrons that were now pushing us out of the door.

I threw my arm around Anna and pulled her in close, knocking the sunglasses off my face in the process. Having outlived their usefulness, I left them to the same fate as Eric. I worried about Reeka though. She may not have been able to get up off the floor in time to avoid the rush of bodies. But there was no time for us to check on her.

We jumped off the side of the steps to clear the door, but then had to work our way through the chairs and tables on the pavement.

Clearing the furniture, I looked back to see all the people jammed in the entryway. Occasionally one would pop out, so I knew it was just a matter of time before one of those people would be Karl.

"Giselle," Anna gasped as we moved past the last window.

Looking up, I saw her at the glass, pounding on it and shouting at us. She was stuck back in the corner of the room and couldn't get to the door. Sneering, I gave her a casual wave before we broke into a run. When we arrived at the street corner, Anna pulled me to the right, trying to force me to cross to the other side.

"We must go up this way; I know a place to hide," she said, yanking at my arm.

"Ah no, I have a plan. We must go straight down to Friedrichstrasse."

"Oh, scheisse! Okay."

We continued with our dash up Oranienburgerstrasse, fast running out of breath. Halfway through the next block, Anna snatched the beanie from my head.

"That's mine, and it's my favorite," she panted out

"Do you want the shirt too? Tis also yours," I huffed back.

"Yes, but you may keep it for now—I will take it off you later."

We both laughed, but the seriousness of our situation overshadowed the moment. I wondered if she could see the fear in my eyes. We were wheezing now, a sign we might not be able to keep up this pace all the way to the imbiss. I wanted to stop and take a breather, but that only increased our chances of getting caught.

"Where are we going, Ciarán? You do not know Berlin like I do. Where are you taking me?"

"Zafer's shop. We are going to Zafer's."

She found her second wind and moved ahead of me, calling back, "Follow me Ciarán, I know where he is at."

"Have it your way."

Glancing back every once in a while, I caught sight of a dark figure breaking out from between two buildings a block behind us.

Karl!

He must have been able to get through the kitchen and out the back door. Anna saw him too and shouted, "Ciarán, it is Karl."

"Tis lass… just keep going."

"We must hide. Come, let us go this way. I know a place," she said and dashing across the roadway, she ran up Auguststrasse.

"Anna, no," I said, but it was too late, she was already on her way.

She took a quick right just past the corner, and I followed her into a covered truck dock. "We can't stop here, Anna. We have to keep running."

She halted just inside and I ran into her. We grabbed each other to keep from falling and she grunted out, "Oh my side hurts so bad… mein gott."

"As does mine, darling, as does mine." I said, looking around for a place to hide.

The space was dark with only the light reflecting off a white building across the street to assist us. It also showed that if we had run any farther, we would have tumbled down a stairwell into a pit.

Anna ushered me to the wall on our right and down a narrow walkway that ran alongside that large, square, concrete hole. A spindly railing stood along its edge, offering us some safety. Positioning me behind a large, square duct coming down from the roof, she gave me a quick kiss.

"There is no time for this, darling."

"Stay here and be quiet," she hissed.

I didn't resist because I figured she had it sorted. I just wished she'd shared her plan with me. Using the railing to guide her back to the mouth of the pit, she turned and moved out of sight down the stairs. The massive opening stretched past me back into the dark. It smelled musty like a dank basement and I suspected it offered access to some service doors, situated below.

I could hear Anna rummaging around down there. After a minute or so, all went quiet except for my breathing and the sound of dripping water.

It seemed like an eternity before Karl finally showed. My ears detected him long before my eyes did. His stomping footfalls halted just outside. I peered through the crack behind the duct to see his sweaty face peeking around the archway that framed the entry. I stiffened, hoping he couldn't see me.

Glancing the other direction, I thought it might have been better to go all the way to the end, least that way I'd be out of sight in the murk. When I turned back, he stood brazenly in the open entrance, his massive bulk contrasted by the light colored wall across the street. Something that looked a lot like the black beanie hung from his fingers. Anna must have accidently dropped it just outside. I watched him toss it back into the gutter and taking a couple of steps inside, he stopped and turned an ear in our direction.

The way he stood there listening, sent chills up my spine. I was glad it was too dark for him to see. The large duct was a great advantage, but not for long if he kept coming. Walking painfully slow, he stopped at the opening to the stairwell and sniffed the air. He must have been debating whether to continue along the narrow quay, or go down into the pit.

"I can smell you little Stacy," he said in a low, singsong voice. "Your roses are not your friend, today."

There came the sound of an aluminum landing on the walkway to my right. It gave me a start, and I fought the urge to react.

Bollocks! What's that lass up to?

Karl crouched and moving toward me, held his hands out low in front like a wrestler. I prepared myself to jump on him when he got close enough, thinking maybe I could push him through the railing and into the pit. If I succeeded, I could only hope that he wouldn't fall on Anna.

He stopped just beside the duct, less than an arm's length away. Two more steps and he'd see me for sure.

Straightening up, he declared with a cynical harshness, "Your stink is in the air, Irland man… I will catch you."

He pulled something from a jacket pocket that gleamed silver. Holding it up, there came the unmistakable sound of steel on flint. A small shower of sparks fell down, casting a glow on his shoulder and the side of his face.

Shite! He has a cigarette lighter.

I had to take action or I would lose the element of surprise. Unfortunately, I was too late. He flicked it again and a small flame erupted. Time stood still as a flicker of light danced wickedly in the black eyes that found me, and as a predatory grin spread his lips, he said, "Hah! I have you Ir…"

That was all he got out. Something came swinging out of the dark and slammed into the side of his head. There was a 'thunk!' and he fell against the delicate railing. Seeing my chance, I grabbed the duct with both hands and swinging my legs up with feet together, I kicked out.

Catching him in the ribs, the air left his body with a whoosh. The railing, weakened by his initial impact, disintegrated at his second. With his arms wind milling, he went over. Disappearing from view, there followed a sickening thump as he hit the concrete steps below.

"Ahhh! Mein Bein ist gebrochen!" echoed forth from the dark void, followed by a string of profanity.

"Hah! He says his leg is broken. I think that should keep him for a while."

Moving out from behind the ductwork, I saw Anna standing there, a short length of 2x4 plank in her hands. Because he'd been so engrossed in grabbing me, he hadn't noticed her sneaking up behind him.

"Just in time, lass. I was starting to think my number was up."

Dropping the plank, she wiped her hands on her dress. Then looking over the side, she ripped the string of fake pearls from her neck and flung them into the pit, yelling, "Doof!"

Walking to me as if on a casual stroll, she took my hand and led me out of the passageway to the sound of Karl's angry shouts. Once back on the street, we broke into a slow jog. I sensed she wasn't in the mood to discuss what had just happened, but I sorted we would now have more time to talk about it.

Chapter 18

"Knocking Down The Wall"

My perspective on Anna was changing by the hour. She was not the person I'd first imagined she would be. But it had been based on what I had experienced prior. Back in Ireland, I'd been the mentor, something of a brother, or a father-figure. Now, we hadn't been together for one full day, and I was starting to realize that she was very much my equal. On top of that, she'd defended me against someone twice her size. The lass had courage, and she would fight for what she deemed hers. The bond between us was growing, creating a kind of balance that brought me hope.

I looked over at her as we hustled down the street, and in the brightening air, I could see the determination in her face. She noticed, and smiled tiredly. I gave her hand a squeeze and we picked up our pace.

Except for a few beggars and several passing cars, the streets were empty. We soon arrived at the intersection and looked to see Friedrichstrasse stretching south to the Spree River. The busier than average street, now lay dormant as if waiting for the onset of the daily bustle. Anna ushered me left along the shop fronts, and then stopping, pointed up.

The sign read 'Zafer's Turkish Delight' and underneath in smaller letters, 'Doener, Curry Wurst, and Tasty Kababs!'

A caricature of a balding, apron adorned fat man, grinned down at me. His arms crossed over a huge belly and a mammoth fork was clutched in one hand, a sausage impaled on its tines. I hoped he was as pleasant as the picture showed. We didn't need any more trouble than we already had.

Anna released my hand and beat on the metal gate drawn across the door. Grabbing the bars, she shook them, causing quite a clatter.

"Zafer! Zafer! Open up it is... Stacy! It is Stacy! Come open your door!"

I'd been scanning the street, and now looking back at her, I had to laugh.

"Stacy?"

In a near whisper she said, "He knows me as Stacy. You know, 'X-Stacy'? He does not know my real name. So, to Zafer, I am Stacy."

She made a face that said, 'Play along please, and don't call me Anna.' There came some movement inside, and seeing my reaction to it, she turned back to the gate.

"Zafer, hurry," she said, waving and pointing to the lock.

He finally got the door open, and I marveled at his likeness to the sign. Dressed in a white singlet and black trousers, his eyebrows were the bushiest I'd ever seen next to Samuel's. He smiled big at Anna as he hurried to unlock the gate, saying, "Frau Stacy! Is you OK? Is there trouble for you?"

The gate rattled open and he poked his head out. Giving me a hard look, he said to her in a low voice, "Who is this man?"

Anna pulled me closer and said, "Zafer, this is Ciarán. You remember when I told you about Ciarán?"

He looked me up and down, and reaching out with both of his hands, he bellowed, "Ah yes, Karen. Stacy has told me much about you."

He threw his arms around me, pulling me tight to his jiggling paunch and after kissing me on both cheeks, exclaimed, "Any friend of Stacy is a friend of me."

Pulling back, his hands moved to my upper arms. "Please come in Karen. You want to eat? Yes?" I will fix you food. Very good food."

"Uh… sorry, but it's, Ciarán, 'Kee-a-ran. C-I-…"

"Oooh, there is no time for this," Anna said, and pulling me out of his grip, pushed me through the door.

"Zafer, we must get inside," she said in an apologetic manner.

He looked perplexed. "What is wrong Frau Stacy, is someones after you?" Scanning the street, he backed inside the metal grill and pulling it shut, locked the huge padlock.

Anna and I walked into the dining area which resembled a wide hallway. We stopped and I looked around. The smell of Turkish food was thick in the air, and the place appeared spotless except for the white, grimy phone that hung on the wall at the far end of the counter. To the right of it, a large colorful curtain hung in a simple archway. Printed across it was what I knew to be the Dolmabahce Palace in Istanbul. I suspected Zafer's living space lay on the other side.

The fixtures were almost new, and even though the room was long and narrow, it was comfortable. There were several tables placed along the wall for stand-up dining, and seven stools sat at the counter to my left. In the corner behind me, just to the right of the front door, there were small chairs and tables stacked for use outside on the pavement. Bundled behind them, a bevy of large umbrellas wrapped by a piece of rope.

"Please Frau Stacy, tell me what is wrong?" he said, as he walked to us.

Anna took my arm in hers and wept out, "There are some bad men after us, please Zafer, may we hide here?"

Zafer made a face like he didn't understand. He placed the meaty fingers of a hand on her shoulder and said, "Please… again?"

She repeated it as he glanced from her, to me, and back again. Putting an index finger to his lip, he looked like he was trying to sort it out. Then he surprised us by snatching up her hand and pulling us toward the curtain.

"Come, we must go in here."

Anna kept a tight grip on my arm as we moved into the back room. The space was perhaps three long strides deep, but twice as wide as the dining area. Directly across from the entry, on the back wall, sat an ornamental chair. To its left, a sleeping pallet stretched out to the right hand corner with numerous pillows piled at its head. Beside them, along the right hand wall, sat a black, lacquered chest of drawers. Upon its top, sat a lamp much like Anna's, which illuminated several small Middle Eastern figurines spread across the surface.

Built into the wall on each side of the door, shelves held a few books along with what seemed to be all of Zafer's personal possessions. A lavatory with what had to be the smallest counter in the world, graced the wall to our left with a small mirror hanging just above it. A toilet sat in the opposite corner, cordoned off with a crimson curtain trimmed in gold. In the center of the room, stood a small, low table with a large ornamental Hookah perched upon its shiny top. Colorful cushions lay around it on a large oriental rug, suggesting the pipe wasn't there for just appearance sake. The whole place was painted in a warm nutmeg brown, a color that brought me a feeling of coziness.

Seeing some photos tacked to the wall around the mirror, I walked over to take a look. They showed a multitude of people, all Middle Eastern in appearance. There wasn't a smile among them except for a small boy in the lap of a woman. His grin was immense and on closer inspection, I could see it was Zafer.

"Please sit, Frau Stacy," Zafer said, pointing to the chair. Then tugging on my sleeve, he directed me toward one of the pillows on the floor and said, "Please Karen, rest."

"Thanks a million, but I'll stand," I said, looking down at him as he stood there smiling and rubbing his hands together. Anna sat down, and letting out a sigh of relief, slipped off her flats. Placing her toes on the rug, she curled and uncurled them against the tapestry of rough wool.

"I will get us some coffee," Zafer said.

Anna put the side of her head in her hand and propped it up on an elbow. "Yes, please Zafer," she said, her exhaustion apparent.

"Maybe hot tea, if you would be so kind?" I said.

"Most certainly, Karen. Some good, hot, Turkish tea."

Putting his palms together and bowing his head, he hopped back through the curtain before I could respond. I stood watching Anna's face as I rubbed my head, wishing the ache would go away.

"Are you OK, Ciarán?"

I nodded a yes and she stood up, directing me to the chair. I put myself in the seat and she sat down sideways on my lap, her legs draped over one of the large wooden arms. Laying her head against the front of my left shoulder, she said, "We can only stay for little while, and then we must get out of Berlin. Giselle will not forget about me too quickly. That woman is too stubborn."

"Is your passport good?"

"My passport is good, no need to worry about that."

"Brilliant, we can be off as soon as we finish at my hotel."

"Ciarán… my passport is at home, and of course, I also must say goodbye to my mama."

"Oh yes, forgot… I think I'm a little too tired to be having this chat."

"Yes," she said in agreement and kissing me on the lips, got up and walked to the sleeping pallet. Lying down on her side, she pulled up her knees and pillowed her head on her arm.

"I must sleep a little," she said, and sniffing the air, she chuckled. "I think maybe Zafer baths in garlic."

Chuckling to myself, I thought back to when his face had been in mine.

"I love you, Ciarán," she murmured, and after a few minutes, her breathing became deep and regular. I didn't want to sleep until I'd a plan in place, but my state of mind wasn't helping. I was counting on the tea to help me along, and grew impatient for Zafer's return.

Going back to my hotel and collecting all of my personal items was the first thing on my list. How we would get there, and then to Jana's apartment, remained a question. I wasn't sure what possessions Anna might want to bring along and hoped she still had some clothing stashed away somewhere. Otherwise, we'd have to go shopping and that would be an added risk. Everything she left back at the room above the club would be lost, including my cap and jacket. They'd been my favorites, and I felt a fleeting sense of sadness.

Zafer gave me a start when he burst through the curtain, a large, silver charger in his hands. It held a kettle accompanied by Turkish tea glasses, spoons and a clear glass bowl of sugar.

"Okay, I have hot…" he started to say and switching to a whisper, finished with, "She sleeps, no?"

I nodded and sat up, preparing to accept my tea. He placed the tray on the table next to the water pipe, and picking up the coffee pot, took it back to the galley kitchen. Returning, he sat on one of the pillows, putting his back to me.

Pouring dark liquid from a strange, double spouted teapot into a large clear glass, he said, "I have çay for you, Karen." Turning, he handed me the glass. In my eagerness, I took a drink and gasped, forgetting it would be hot.

"It is good for you, yes?" Zafer asked, his large bushy eyebrows rising as he looked over his shoulder.

"Brilliant, thanks a million," I said, trying to sound enthusiastic even though I'd burned my tongue.

"So you are from Ireland, yes?"

I nodded and smiled, "Ballyamhras, tis just north of Dublin on the coast."

After pouring his own tea, he rotated to face me. "Your family is there?"

I looked down into my glass, breaking eye contact. "Da and ma are gone, died years back, and I have no brothers or sisters."

Looking up, I watched him tilt his head back and look down his nose at me. "I am sorry to hear such sad news. I am from Istanbul," he said. "Now, I am in Berlin two years." Setting down his glass, he turned sideways and slid closer.

"When the wall came down, my brother-in-law brought me here. It is his building. My sister, Kutlay and he, live up the stairs. I stay down here and run this store. Someday I will buy it… that is correct, yes? 'Buy it'?"

I smiled as he tried to make me understand. "Buy it… that is correct, please go on."

"Oh good, yes, ah… okay. So, he is German, this Roderick Dietrich, and he took my sister as a bride. He met her while on holiday in Turkey and brought her back to this city. Here they married…" His voice drifted off and he cast his eyes down. "That seems so long ago."

"So they have no children?"

Bringing his eyes up, his face showed some distress.

"No… they have one. A girl, but she is trouble. Sometimes she comes here. I have no time for such a person. But I must give her food, and be nice to her. She sits outside with her men, smoking. She tries to make everyone think she is important, but… she is only famous inside her own head."

I smiled and chuckled at his humor. A low purring snore came from the corner. We both turned and looked at Anna. Her sleeping position exposed part of her backside and I glanced at Zafer to gauge his reaction. He chortled and rising to his feet, walked over to her. Pulling a light linen sheet up to her waist, he looked back at me.

"Poor little Stacy, she is so tired," he said with affection.

The sound of Karl's voice coming up out of that dark pit, now rang in my head. If Zafer seen what Anna had done to him, he would not think, "Poor little Stacy".

Zafer came back to his pillow and jerking his head toward Anna, said, "It was Giselle, my yeğen, ahhh… my niece, who brought Stacy to meet me, and to eat my pita bread."

"Giselle?"

He looked perplexed and his brow furrowed. We locked eyes, and he said in a shameful manner, "Yes, Giselle… she is my sister's child. You know Giselle?"

He sat down on his pillow and faced me. I glanced back toward Anna, happy that she slept peacefully. I felt compelled to tell Zafer all about our situation. He seemed like a reasonable man who had a sense of what was right. So, there could be no harm in it.

"Zafer… tis Giselle who is chasing us. Ann… I mean, Stacy, is not a friend to Giselle. Stacy works for Giselle."

His eyes grew large, and he shook his head.

"No, no, maybe you are mistaken, yes?"

Rising, I walked around him and placed my glass on the tray as I did. Then getting down on all fours, I crawled between the hookah table and the dresser to where Anna lay. She hadn't moved from her original position and I could see that her eyes were open a bit, the pupils darting back and forth. I could tell she was in REM sleep, so if I were careful, my activity would not wake her. I pulled her hair away from the back of her neck and she startled me by rolling her face to the thick pillow. That only made my task easier. Lightly brushing all her blond locks aside, I found what I was looking for.

Tattooed just above the hairline, visible beneath the darker roots, was a much lighter version of Reeka's tattoo. I motioned for Zafer to come and getting up, he moved to the bed to bend over me. I pointed to the blue G with its star. He stifled a gasp, putting a hand over his mouth. Anna rolled back and I pulled my hand away. Getting to my feet, I followed Zafer back across the room.

He stopped to pour himself another cup of çay, and I saw the worried expression. Making my way past, I moved to lean against the lavatory and caught my face in the mirror in the process. I hardly recognized it. I stood studying the two day old beard and the redness in my eyes. Zafer's reflection appeared next to mine as he stood facing my back. He took a drink from his cup and shook his head in disbelief. Turning to him, I leaned back against the sink, waiting for him to speak. He looked thoughtful for a moment and said, "This is what I am fearing. Giselle will destroy Stacy's life. She should not work for this devil of a woman."

Taking another sip, he added, "You must take Stacy from this place. Take her back to your home and give her a peaceful, happy life. I can tell you are a good man, Karen. You can give her that… this I know."

Reaching over, he placed a hand on my upper arm, and his eyes sought mine. "I came to Berlin after that horrible wall fell down, moving from a home I loved… but was not good for me. Now, I find peace here. But Stacy finds no peace even though this is her home. Now, like me, she must go to a different land in hoping to be happy."

He moved to stand beside me and look toward Anna. Then sliding his hand from my arm to my upper back, he patted me several times. "Now I must think of how I can be helping. But you, Karen… should sleep now."

He ushered me toward the pallet, and placing his tea glass on the silver tray, said, "Lay down with your tatlim and rest… you look terrible."

He chuckled and turning to the charger, took it and disappeared into the other room. I stopped to pick up Anna's shoes and pushing mine off with my toes, set them together beside the bed. Slipping in under the sheet, I lay down between her and the wall. Now facing her back, I lay my arm across her waist with care, fighting the urge to kiss the back of her neck.

She was dreaming again, and squirming slightly, she made a low squeal like a child receiving a gift. She then backed up against me and talking in her sleep, the words, “Mein Herz,” spilled from her lips in a low murmur.

My eyes grew heavy as I lay pondering everything that had happened. There came a familiar stirring in my loins as Anna’s backside pressed tight against my groin. I felt myself drifting away and it barely registered when Zafer re-entered the room. Pulling at the bookshelf just across from us, it hinged open like a door.

I could just make out part of a narrow stairway with sunlight coming from somewhere up above. He saw me watching and said, “I will be up the stairs for a while, my sister and her husband are in Denmark. So, I have the… ah yes… apartment, for myself.”

As he backed into the opening, he pulled on the shelves and before they closed, I heard him say, “I open the restaurant for lunch, but I will see that no one bothers you.”

I gave him an exhausted grin, then reaching down, I pulled the sheet to our shoulders and drifted off to the sound of Anna humming softly in her sleep.

Chapter 19

"Better A Coward For A Minute…"

Vacillating in and out of consciousness, I dreamed. One time I was running down a narrow path through a forest, a pack of wolves closing on me, their tongues lolling. Short yaps and barks filled the air and the second before they jumped on me, the scene changed to me standing on a beach, my arm around a woman who looked a lot like Anna—but talked like Isleen.

We stood gazing out toward the sunset, the small waves washing over our feet. The Anna/Isleen woman suddenly transformed into a small man, dressed in Middle Eastern garb. It was so real I could feel the coarse fabric of his tunic. I sensed he was a friend, and my arm around his waist brought me no discomfort. He looked away down the sand and spoke in a language I didn't understand. A fog rolled in, and he turned away to leave me standing alone. A dark shadow soon blocked my vison and I couldn't make out what it was, but I felt afraid.

Jerking awake, I lay listening. Angry voices filled the air, and I realized that there was an argument taking place. Still half-groggy with sleep, I couldn't remember right off where I was at. Then it came to me, and opening my eyes a crack, I found myself looking at the back of Anna's head. Lifting mine to scan the room over her mass of curls, I could just make out the ancient clock that sat sequestered between two large books on the rack. It read half four in the afternoon. The restaurant was open for business.

A bolt of fear shot through me when I realized it was Giselle's voice I was hearing. She was arguing with Zafer, who kept switching from English, to what must have been Turkish, and back again.

"Speak English, old man! I cannot understand you!"

"Do not speak so disrespectfully, girl," Zafer said with a hint of belligerence.

"I will ask you again, have you seen Stacy and that man she calls Ciarán?" Her tone was stone cold and a chill rolled up my spine.

"As I said before—no, no, NO! There is no Stacy, and there is no Karen in here today."

"Listen Zafer, you are a guest here in my father's house, so don't get to comfortable in your little illusion. I could end it all for you, and you will find yourself back on the streets of Istanbul with nothing."

"No! You listen to me, daughter of Roderick. I am here two years and will be here many more. You cannot fool me into thinking you have power over your father. I am here with his blessing, and I am knowing that he has forsaken you."

Pushing myself up with one arm, I leaned over Anna and covered her mouth. She came awake, her eyes wide and fearful. Whispering in her ear I said, "Stay quiet lass, we are in danger. Get up and come with me."

Now only Zafer was talking, still chastising his niece. I rolled over Anna onto the floor and standing up, I forced on my shoes. Then taking her hand, I pulled her to her feet, fearful that she would be too sleepy to act. But she came right awake and slipping on her flats, she moved to stand next to me. We both stood staring at the curtain as the volume of Zafer's voice increased. Anna put her lips to my ear and whispered, "What is wrong?"

Turning my face to hers, I mouthed the word, 'Giselle'. Her eyes got large, and she stifled a gasp. Giselle finally spoke, and I felt

Anna tense up, shirking away. Checking to make sure no gap showed in the curtain, I took Anna's arm and guided her to the bookrack.

There came a loud rattle of dishes, so taking advantage of the racket, I pulled on the shelves. They swung open to show the entrance to the stairs and Anna smiled at me in relief. There came a slight squeak from a hinge and I felt a surge of adrenalin as Anna froze. Tightening my grip on her arm, I pulled her inside, hoping Zafer's ruckus would mask our noise.

"Your Mama and Papa are away, so come back later when they are home. But do not stay and trouble me, Giselle. Now… I make myself a Cappuccino… you should go."

The sound of the raucous machine resounded through the rooms, and I pulled the bookshelf shut, confident any sounds we made would be cloaked by the coffee maker.

We found ourselves on a landing, in a small, musty space where two stairways met. One went up to a door with a decorative glass window, and the other, down into a dark place, which I assumed must be a cellar.

The cappuccino machine stopped and Giselle commanded, "Eric, come!" Heavy boots stomped into the restaurant and Zafer shouted, "You! You must get out! You are trouble and I do not want you here."

The response was in German and inaudible. A crash of dishes followed with Zafer's panicked declaration, "I will call the police if you do not go."

"Shut up, you old fool. Eric, look in the back, now."

Boots stomped again and curtain rings sang as they raced along the metal rod. Anna pushed close, her hand now on my arm. She stiffened and held her breath, as a shadow blocked the light that came in under the shelves. Frantically looking about, I hoped to find something to use as a weapon. But other than the bad smell and dust, there was nothing.

I thought about going up the stairs, but they were made of wood and I suspected they would creak. The ones going down on the other hand, were stone, and there was a greater chance we could move away from the door without alerting Eric.

Tiptoeing around Anna, I steered her toward the steps and nodded my head toward the cellar. I moved over to the brick wall and leaning against it for support, we worked our way down. Anna stayed close behind, her hands on my shoulders. There was a source of dim light coming from somewhere down there, and it helped us to navigate.

"There is a door behind the bookrack on the right. Check it, you doof," Giselle shouted.

"Stop! Get out of my room!" Zafer shouted, and more footsteps entered the sleeping area.

The sounds of a struggle followed, and the light that projected in under the bookshelf now danced macabrely on the wall in front of us. There was a great deal of grunting with an occasional howl of pain from both combatants. I heard Zafer wheeze out, "You get out of here. You may not go into my sister's house. You are not allowed."

"Schnauze," Eric bellowed, telling Zafer to shut up. There came a loud thump as if a body had fallen to the floor. Anna gasped in fear, and gripped my shoulders so tight it drove me to inhale with a hiss through gritted teeth. I too felt concern for Zafer, but we had to keep going. He fought to help us escape and going to his aid would only make his efforts in vain.

By the time we reached the bottom, my eyes had adjusted to the dark. So, peeling Anna's hands from my shoulders, I towed her around the corner into a large room. We bumped into an open door to our right and using it as a guide, we felt our way along it and into a storage pantry under the stairs. Anna moved around me and disappeared into the gloom. The bookshelf opened and as the light spilled down the stairwell, I quietly shut the door.

The smell of onions filled my nose and my foot hit something that rolled away, thumping into the wall. I froze, waiting for a reaction. When none came, I backed deeper into the closet. Bumping into Anna, she wrapped her arms around me from behind, putting the side of her face to my shoulder blades.

The wooden landing we'd been standing on, was now above our heads. I could hear somebody up there moving cautiously as dust and bits of debris fell on us. Eric crooned out in a wicked manner, "Hallooo, Junge Liebhaber."

He made it sound as if being young lovers was a bad thing, his tone confirming this was just a game of hide & seek to him. I didn't think it possible, but I loathed him even more for his indifference.

The wooden stairs leading up to the Dietrich apartment, creaked and groaned, making me grateful for my decision to avoid them. I suspect he'd studied the cellar stairs, and not liking the thought of coming down into the dark, he chose the alternative. Door hinges squeaked at the top, and footsteps faded away, leaving only the sound of our breathing.

Time stood still, and it seemed an eternity before he stomped back down. I awaited his arrival, imagining ways I could deal with him. The most logical was the tactic he used back at Anna's room. As soon as he unlatched the door to the pantry, I could kick it open with enough force to knock him to the floor, hoping the impact would stun him or even bring unconsciousness. We could then run back up the stairs and out the front door. I didn't think that Giselle was a physical threat since she wasn't big on doing her own dirty work.

The bookrack door slammed shut with Eric calling out, "Giselle! There is no one here but us!"

"Did you check everywhere? Did you look down in the cellar?"

"I looked."

Well, there was a good chance he looked down the stairs, but that was all. He sounded weary of the whole situation. I got the impression he wanted to be off. Giselle's persistence must have been annoying to him because I knew standing in the dark waiting for her to be satisfied, annoyed me.

"Oh Ciarán, will they ever go?" Anna whispered and sighed.

"Soon, darling, soon," I whispered back, my voice, sounding strange in the dark. I listened as Eric walked back through the dining room, moving toward the front door.

"Get the auto," Giselle ordered.

"Ja, ja," he said with just a hint of scorn.

I moved toward the door with Anna following, but my hopes of leaving the pantry were dashed when I heard light footsteps move into the sleeping room.

"Zafer, are you still alive? Ah yes, I see you still breathe," Giselle said, mockingly.

A bolt of fear shot through me as the squeak of the bookrack hinges filled my ears.

"Anna, if I find you were hiding here with that meddlesome Irishman, there will be much suffering for you and Zafer… not to mention your troublemaker boyfriend."

Anna let go with a light growl, followed by a barely audible whisper, "We will see who suffers."

After a moment of silence, Giselle moved back into the dining area. There came the unmistakable sound of ceramic dishes being smashed against the floor one at a time. This was followed by a massive crash as if she'd pushed over the entire rack.

All went quiet and minutes passed with only the sounds of the street filtering in. There was still no movement from Zafer and I became concerned. Opening the door, the ambient light from the larger room flooded in. Giselle also left the bookshelf open, making it easier for us to see. I stepped through the pantry door just as something darkened one of the tiny windows. I froze and Anna, who'd been moving past me, gasped and crouched down. Moving only my eyes, I saw a face pressed against the dirty glass.

Eric.

He remained for a few seconds, his hands shielding his eyes. Then standing up, he moved away.

"Stay here," I said.

"But Ciarán, I want to be with you."

"No, please stay and I will come back very soon."

"But… Ciarán," she protested.

"Please Anna, I am only going over to that window."

"Okay… go then."

Moving away from her, I turned to watch her sit down on a crate and give me a dismissive wave. Then putting her chin in her hands, she rested her elbows on her knees. I felt bad, but it didn't require the both of us.

Navigating my way through the boxes and barrels scattered about the floor, I crept to the wall, using the window to guide me. The sunlight streamed in to the left, so, I moved to the right to avoid highlighting my face when I peeked around the sash.

A dark blue, BMW E30 sedan stood just outside in the parking area. Giselle sat in the back with the window down, her arm hanging out, a cigarette dangling from her fingers. Eric leaned against the passenger side, glaring in my direction. I pulled back, flattening myself against the wall.

"Get in the car, you idiot, and drive me around. Then we will go back to the club."

"Scheisse! I am tired of this. Just let her go. You have other girls."

"Watch yourself little man, you don't tell me…"

A car door opened and slammed shut, drowning out the rest of her statement. There came the clicking of the transmission as he put it in gear. and tires squealed as he pulled away. I stole another look and saw them speed out of sight. The sound of the engine faded away, taking all the fear that had nested in my gut along with it.

Making my way back to Anna, she said, "Well, are they gone? I thought I heard a car?"

"You did, and they are… and we should be too."

"Where will we go now?" she said, standing up and brushing off her backside.

"To the hotel, I have to collect my things, and from there… I suppose your mama's?"

There came a rustling noise and Anna moved to me to clutch my arm.

"What was that?"

"Hold on," I said, and stepping over, I peeked up the stairwell.

The top of Zafer's head bobbed into sight, followed by a groan.

"Zafer!" I called out, and with Anna close behind, I took the steps two at a time. He was sitting on the bed when we arrived and was running a hand over the back of his head. He pulled it away, and I saw a trace of blood on his fingers. Staring at it, he grimaced, and looking up, held that hand out to show us.

"That prick pushed me hard down on floor! Where did he go? Has he gone?"

"They've gone," Anna said.

"For now, anyway," I added.

He stood up, wobbled, and sat back down.

"It would be better for you to sit for a while," Anna said, patting him on the shoulder. "He must have knocked you out, yes?"

"Yes, I tried to stop him going into my sister's house. I grab his arm, he grab me back, and swing me hard. I trip over the… how you say… mattress?"

"Yes, we understand and you must calm yourself. You are still bleeding from your head, and we must clean you," Anna said.

"I want to get up now."

We didn't argue, and taking his arms, we helped him to his feet. We walked him into the shop and sitting him on the first stool at the counter, we surveyed the damage. The small glass pastry cabinet lay smashed and the metal rack that had once sat upon the countertop, holding ceramic cups and saucers, now lay at the foot of a stool.

Pieces of crockery littered the space, all that remained of the cups Giselle had thrown with such force, that they had gouged the wood of the floor.

"Bu korkunç! Sorry… I speak my language...This is terrible. My best cups are ruined."

Anna found a clean white towel and soaking it in cold water from the faucet, came, and pressed it gingerly against the back of his head.

"I am sorry Zafer, they can be replaced—but you cannot," she said.

He smiled up at her, "Thank you Stacy, you are too kind to an old Turkish man who has no one."

She took his hand and said, "You can call me Anna, Stacy has gone away—forever."

Turning his face up to me, he said, "I know she is Anna. But… I know not if I should call her by a name she does not know that I know." We chuckled together as he pulled her head down with his free hand and kissed her cheek.

"This is proper, yes? It is okay?" he asked me with concern in his eyes.

Smiling at him and nodding, I lay my hand on his shoulder for confirmation. It was then I realized the door stood wide open and people were walking by, peering in. Now was not a good time for customers. I shut it, and turned the sign that read 'Wir haben geschlossen!' to the street, declaring that the shop would be closed for the remainder of the day.

Turning around, I picked of the metal rack and set it back on the countertop. With broken ceramic crunching underfoot, I collected anything that survived Giselle's wrath and set it next to the rack. The unmistakable sound of a BMW's diesel engine came to my ears. I thought of hiding, but went with my instincts instead and froze.

"Anna," I said with urgency.

As the car passed, I could see Giselle still seated in the back, both her and Eric, studying the shop. Anna startled and gasped, but Zafer said, “Do not worry,” and patted her arm. “They cannot see inside here from that far away with the lamps off. But I do see they have taken Roderick’s favorite auto. He will not like that. I am happy to tell you that he will be knowing very soon.”

Eric must have lifted the keys when he was upstairs. I assumed Giselle didn’t own a car. So, she was going to take advantage of her da in his absence. Anna looked over at me and said, “Giselle will regret that she took her papa’s auto. Roderick is an even bigger man than Karl, and a Tri-Athlete in his younger days.”

She smirked, and moving away from Zafer, leaned down to gaze out between the paper signs plastered all over the window. Chuckling, she added, “He will deal with Giselle when he returns. So… let us hope that is soon.”

I walked to her and we embraced. “We should go as soon as it is safe, yes? Will you be ok, Zafer? She said, looking past me to him. “Maybe you should go to the hospital?”

He slid off the stool and stood up. “No, I will be okay.” Taking the cloth from his head, he touched his wound with a fat index finger, and showing it to us, said, “You see, no blood.”

“Anna, we have to sort out how we’ll get to the hotel—and without too many eyes on us.” I said.

“Well Ciarán, I think we will have to walk. It might be best to stay off of the main streets though,”

“The hotel is too far for our feet. I am not so sure that is a good idea.”

I heard Zafer chuckle and turning, I watched him point a finger at the ceiling and say, “You will go by taxi. Go upstairs and down the… ahhh… the ladder for fire in the back. I will have taxi meet you there. I have friend that drives them. I will ask a favor, and he will not have to pay for his supper tonight.”

“Are you certain?” I asked.

“Yes, no problem, but you must not tell me where you go… then, if they hit me, I still cannot tell them.”

"Shall we?" Anna asked.

"We shall. I have a bad feeling about staying here much longer with Giselle poking about."

"So do I," she said. "Zafer, are the fire stairs hard to find?"

He moved to the opening at the end of the counter, and picking up the handset to the phone, dialed a number.

"No problem. Go upstairs, there will be a hallway leading to back of building. There is large window with no curtain. It is there—and how you say… you can't miss it!"

I thought about his command of the English language and decided to poke fun at him to lighten the mood.

"Well—I don't say that, but..."

They both smiled with Anna laughing nervously and chastising me with a loud, "Ciarán!"

"It is OK Sta… ahhh… Anna," Zafer said and started to chuckle, but had to cut it off to speak in Turkish to someone on the telephone. Anna walked to him as he hung up and embraced him with a kiss on his cheek.

Zafer looked at me and said, "Karen is trying to talk funny… so this way, his lady will smile and not be worried, yes?"

I let my grin grow bigger as he put an arm around Anna's waist, and she said, "Zafer, thank you so much for all you have done for us, but we must go. I am too nervous to stay."

"It is no trouble for me, you are good people, and now that your Karen is here in Berlin, he can take care of you."

"We can take care of each other… I think," she said, laying her head on his shoulder and winking at me.

He dropped his eyes toward the floor and grew quiet. I walked to where they stood and as I did, he looked up at me with moist eyes and said, "I am afraid I will never see you again. If you ever find yourself on my street, please come to me. We can have tea. I do not lose friends easily, so… it would bring me much happiness."

He beckoned me, and putting an arm around my shoulders, pulled us to him. He kissed our cheeks again and tried to speak, but his voice cracked. In a raspy whisper he said, "Take care of Anna, Karen… she is your treasure."

I watched as a tear rolled down Anna's cheek. So, before I started in myself, I said with enthusiasm, "Zafer, my friend, I think I can do that," and pulling Anna from his arm, we moved toward the backroom.

She slipped through the bookshelf door ahead of me and I stopped long enough to peer back through the open curtain. Zafer took up the bottom of his apron and used it to wipe his eyes. When he caught me looking, he stopped.

"Yes, Karen?"

"Sláinte, my friend."

He smiled big, and nodded, "Uzun Yaşam! Long life to you, my brother."

I gave him an exaggerated wink and backing into the opening, I pulled the bookshelf closed. When it seated in its jamb, Anna said, "Let us go, Ciarán. We need to get out of here," and taking my hand, we bounded up the stairs together.

Chapter 20

"A Good Retreat Is Better Than A Bad Stand"

Eric had failed to shut the door and we burst out into a corridor that ran along the entire front of the building on the second floor. We stopped to catch our breath as we viewed Friedrichstrasse through a long row of large windows.

In the same wall to left of the door we'd just came through, a round topped opening granted access to a narrow passageway. Peeking through the beaded curtain, I saw it ran to the back of the building and ended in what looked like a small sitting room.

"Must be it."

"Yes, I believe so," Anna said, pushing past me.

Her mood seemed to have improved because of our exchange with Zafer, and perhaps because we were now making progress toward our goal. But she seemed somewhat distant. I supposed that is how she coped with aggravation—one more thing for me to get used to.

I followed her down the passageway, but found myself distracted by the large, framed pictures that hung along the walls. The one that caught my eye was the Dietrich family portrait. It showed a giant of a man who I assumed to be Roderick. Teutonic and unsmiling, he sported a well-tailored, dark gray suit with pinstripes and the most unfeeling eyes. They were as cold as ice and sent an unanticipated chill up my spine.

He stood beside a petite woman in traditional Turkish garb, her skin, a lovely shade of bronze. There was a question in her pain-filled eyes, and I could only imagine how life must have been for her. Then there was Giselle—seated front and center and in the very chair Zafer had in his room. Her smile didn't reach her dark, contemptuous eyes.

Moving to the next, I found it contrasted the first. A large, faded 8x10 photo showed Giselle as a child. Adorned in a party dress, she stood in the sunlight on a well-manicured lawn. In that photo, her smile was genuine, her primary teeth showing their imperfections. In her arms, she held a kitten and a small ragdoll hung from a hand by its hair. It made me wonder what had happened in her younger life that had brought her to where she was now. I thought about Anna's relationship with her father and the tear-filled confession while sitting on that wall back in Ireland. As odd as it may seem, I felt a hint of pity for the woman who now wanted me dead.

"The taxi is here Ciarán, please, let us go."

I realized that Anna had continued into the sitting room and now called from the window. Hurrying to her as she threw up the large sash, I heard the counterweights rattle within the frame. She ducked through and I followed her, stepping out onto the grate of the fire escape balcony. The rusty metal creaked and groaned from our weight, leaving me to sort that no one used it much.

"Oh Ciarán… can this be ok? It is very old."

"Just go darling, and don't think about it," I said, closing the window.

She started down the open grill of the treads, one hand hooked in my belt and the other clutching the rod that served as a railing. I held on to the same, but with both hands sliding along the metal as we moved downward. The taxi waited just a short distance out from the building, grey exhaust lazily rolling out of the tailpipe.

I found myself relieved it was only one short flight of stairs from the top floor. It appeared as if there had once been a folding ladder attached to the bottom, but now the hinges hung twisted and broken on the edge of the last tread.

Upon reaching that point, Anna scowled at me. We would have to drop the last three meters. Sitting, Anna let her legs dangle, and with a gymnast's precision, she swung down, dropping lightly onto the pavement.

I wasn't as graceful. Turning around and getting on my knees, I grabbed the tread at the front, and letting my chest slide over it, I did my best to avoid the jagged metal. I was able to land on my feet beside her and she grabbed my arm as I stumbled backwards. We turned together toward the taxi as the driver's door swung open. An olive skinned lad stepped out and asked, "You are Stacy?"

"Ummm… yes, and this is Ciarán."

"Please, get in quickly, we must go," he said, his eyes resting on Anna a little too long for my comfort.

Walking around the ancient Trabant, he opened the passenger door, and folding the front seat forward, motioned for us to climb in.

I'd heard of this car. All models came with only two doors. It was an East Germany joke, and a poor choice for a taxi. I hesitated and thought to comment, but Anna beat me to it. Moving past me, she slid across the cracked vinyl seat, snickering out, "It's a Trabi."

"Tis," I said, squeezing in beside her.

"This car… it is so funny. I thought I would never ride in one."

I smiled at her and said nothing because I didn't want to offend the driver who was now climbing in.

"Hallo, I am Halim. I am friend of Zafer, I am also from Istanbul. That man, he says to me to take care of you. No problem. Where do we go?" Turning back to us, his eyes strayed to Anna's bare legs.

"To the Lietzenburger Arte Hotel, and please, try to be discreet about it," I said.

Glancing forward and then back to us, it seemed he couldn't keep his eyes off Anna.

"Sorry, what did you say? I don't understand that word… des… dis…"

"We don't want to be seen," Anna, blurted out.

At that, he released the clutch, causing the car to leap forward. It rocked to and fro as he wheeled the Trabi toward the exit. He kept looking back at us, talking, and gesturing with a hand. I feared for our safety, and we weren't even out of the parking area.

"Yes, Zafer tells me to be like hayalet. Ummm… ghost? Like ghost! So yes, no problem, I know this place where we go, I am there many times."

Halim, all of maybe nineteen, was a very nervous lad. Not just because of the situation, but more that he was just a high-strung kind of person. His fidgety manner kept me on edge. Yet even though he made me uncomfortable, I underestimated his ability as a driver. He showed a kind of intuition for getting around. The Trabi seemed to become part of him as he worked his way toward the Ku'damm.

Breezing in and out of alleyways, making short hops up busy streets, and cutting through parking lots, he made Anna squeal and squirm. Squeezing through a couple tight spots, I almost cried out myself, feeling embarrassment when we sailed through without incident. If anyone tried to follow, Halim would have proved himself to be a worthy getaway driver.

We arrived at the hotel sooner than anticipated and he drove us to a more secluded part of the car park. The taxi screeched to a halt and getting out, Halim flipped his seat forward and motioned with his arm as if he were a gameshow host presenting the hotel as a gift.

Anna struggled to get out and he stared unblinking, as if closing his eyes for even a second would make him miss the show. Losing her grip on the window frame, I caught her as she fell back against me. Her legs flew apart and I saw Halim's eyes go wide. It was like he'd never seen women's underwear before, or at least, ones that were actually on a woman.

Her second attempt was successful and she climbed out of the Trabi to stand beside him. I followed, not faring any better. Once I was out, he said, "Good luck to you, Herr Karen. You are Zafer's friend, so now… you are mine."

He grabbed my hand and went to pumping it up and down as he ogled Anna, a big grin on his face.

"Thanks a million, Halim," I said, wishing he would stop levering my arm as if he was expecting me to spout water. He then took Anna's hand in a courteous fashion and said, "Good luck to you, beautiful lady, and I want to say… you have some very nice panties."

She blushed and made a noise of false delight as if she was grateful he'd noticed. Turning her face as if to look at the hotel behind us, she rolled her eyes. Releasing my hand, Halim was back in the cab and shutting the door. He put the car in gear, but like he had an afterthought, he rolled down the window and said, "I know this Giselle, she is bad like rotten fruit. You must be careful."

"We know," Anna, and I said in unison.

He found it amusing and tossing his head back, he laughed.

"Goodbye Karen, goodbye Stacy. I go back to Zafer's now for my free lunch."

With that, he popped the clutch and the tires gave a short squeal before the engine bogged. Pumping the accelerator, he brought it back and the smoke from the tiny engine enveloped us, causing us to cough. We watched the car zoom away as the smoke cleared and Anna said, "There is a joke about Trabi that goes like this: Why was the Trabi made?"

Before I could make a guess, she answered, "It was a mistake… it was supposed to be a washing machine."

She laughed at her own joke and slapped her thighs. I chuckled more at her antics than the joke itself. She appeared pleased that I had, and I soon regretted it.

"What do you call a Trabi up the hill?" she asked and not allowing me an answer, she blurted out, "A miracle."

She laughed louder and longer at that. So I pressed my hand to the small of her back and directed her toward the side entrance of the hotel. I felt grateful her mood had gone from exasperation to general silliness, but I wasn't sure how much of that I could take.

As we hurried along, she asked, "What do you call ten Trabi up the hill?

"No clue."

"That must be where the factory is."

She laughed herself into a coughing fit at that, and I suddenly felt a need to be alone. However, there was no way I could leave her and go somewhere to sort my thoughts. I chalked it up to the importance of just getting used to her, and fell back on my tolerance skills.

Passing through the hotel door, I was glad I kept the key with me rather than dropping it at the front desk. We trudged up the stairs, Anna telling Trabi jokes all the way. She ran out when we arrived at the third floor, but then threatened to make up a few.

Reaching my limit, I said, "Please Anna, please. I've heard enough. I'll be dreaming of Trabi in my sleep if you don't stop."

"Okay, I am sorry. But I am very tired. Not like from working, because I have had some sleep… more like in my head. You know… mentally tired? So now I am a little crazy, yes?"

"Yes," I said, as I unlocked the door. Pushing it open, I half expected to find the room trashed, but I was just being paranoid. There could be no way Giselle and her minions would know where I'd established my base of operations. My appearance in Berlin was unexpected, like a bad storm I'd simply blown in and ruined their party.

Stepping inside, Anna glanced around and into the bathroom. "Nice enough, I guess. I have lived in Berlin all of my life, but never been inside this hotel."

Sitting down on the edge of the bed, she pulled off her shoes and lying back, stretched out and sighed. I realized that the room was tidy—not the way I'd left it. The bed had been made and the room freshened.

I'd even troubled myself to place the 'Nicht stören, bitte' sign on the door, telling people not to disturb me. But I hadn't noticed if it was still there on the way in. Pulling the door open, I confirmed its absence. Looking around, I didn't see it on the floor, inside or out. It must have blown off the knob, granting the housekeeper permission to enter. Closing the heavy panel, I threw the bolt.

Looking in the bath, I saw fresh towels and my toiletries were arranged in an orderly manner; something I would never do. There was also a scent in the air that was troubling me, but no matter how hard I tried, I couldn't place it.

My ruck was still on the table in the corner with shirts and trousers hanging out. Some personal documents, notebooks, and maps that I'd stacked on a chair also remained undisturbed. Checking the bag, I found nothing missing. Realizing that I was too 'out of sorts' to analyze rationally, I gave in to the illusion we were safe—at least for the moment.

"I need to change my closes, Ciarán. I am stinking."

I chuckled and smelling my armpits, thought the same of myself. I suspected Anna would not want her tee shirt back. Walking to the window, I pulled the curtain open far enough to view the street. Finding nothing out of the ordinary, I stood for a moment, lost in thought.

"Is everything okay?"

Anna's voice brought me out of my trance, and letting go of the curtain, I rotated on my heels.

"All's grand." I said as she stood and pulled the black dress off over her head.

"Yes, I am thinking everything looks fine from here," I added, as I watched the frock move up her body, first exposing her purple satin knickers, her flat stomach, her bare breasts and finally, her head. Her still buoyant locks bounced as they fell back into place. Dropping the dress onto the floor, she pushed it away with a toe.

Acknowledging my voyeurs stance, she struck a sexy pose, hands on hips. I expected a seductive statement to bring me to her, but all she said was, "I sleep now," and crawling into the bed, she pulled the duvet up to her chin.

Laying on her back, she murmured, "Mmmm, so good… Ciarán, come and keep me warm, the air in this room is so cold."

She didn't have to ask twice. Kicking off my shoes, I walked to the bed, shedding my clothes as I went. Going around to the opposite side, I slipped in. She rolled to face the window, and I moved over, putting my chest against her back. Wrapping her waist with my arm, I pulled her to me, bringing the warmth of her skin to mine. There could be no finer a moment in a person's life. I felt joy as if it had ridden the wave of Anna's body heat over to mingle with mine.

She soon drifted off, and finding that moment I needed, I mulled over the last two days. I never anticipated what was happening to us. I had a greater understanding of the meaning of 'Cat and Mouse' that was certain. We were trying to outsmart malicious minds, possibly psychotic ones—and we were unprepared for the fray. I believed when I found Anna, it would be, "Hallo, I love you, come back to Ireland with me." Not once did I consider I would be in a battle for her possession.

Giselle, and her lot, felt that they owned Anna—period. When she said I was to rescue her, I did not think she meant it in the literal sense. She seemed to be taking it better than I, though. Perhaps because she was accustomed to city life. As I lay reflecting, Anna's breathing deepened and there came a light purring snore.

Her hair lay in a manner that allowed me to see the 'G/Star' tattoo. It left me to wonder how many others in Giselle's troupe might sport the same mark, and if that maggot, Eric, had one as well. If he did, I imagined his must be enormous, considering how far he had his head up Giselle's arse.

For a brief second, the scent that filled my nose upon walking through the door came again. Perhaps a cleaning solution, or a hidden air freshener brought by the housekeeper. It troubled me because it was so familiar, and I couldn't put my finger on it. I quit trying to sort it and emptied my mind. Anna started to hum in her sleep, and like a lullaby, it relaxed me, bringing me to slumber.

Chapter 21

"Better Fifty Enemies Outside, Than One Within"

I found myself walking down an unfamiliar Berlin street. Stopping, my eyes fell upon a sign that said 'Flowers'. I stepped into the shop and an older, dark-haired woman with a large, floppy black hat greeted me. I moved over to a large box full of roses, and as I pulled one out, Zafer burst through a door in the back. Running toward me, he held his hands out as if to push me away. "Get out! You must go! It is not safe!" I backed up toward the door, dropping the rose. Hitting the tile at my feet, it shattered like fine ceramic. As it did, all the flower arrangements in the shop transformed into Jasmine, their vines crawling up and over everything.

The woman who met me coming in, now stood behind the counter and morphed into Giselle. The door behind me slammed shut by itself and there came the distinct sound of the bolt clicking home. The hair rose on the back of my neck as I watched Zafer sink to his knees and transform into a different man. Now dressed in a white steward's jacket, the smaller, skinner fellow apologized for his behavior. Giselle's wicked laughter filled the room and I felt fear. Jolting awake, I sat upright, the cover falling away.

Jasmine! That was it!

Somebody had been in this room wearing jasmine perfume. I blinked my eyes several times trying to focus and then slipping out from under the duvet, I pulled it back up to cover Anna. Padding across the room to the closet, I opened the small safe at the bottom. The contents were still intact. That included my passport, about two hundred Irish pounds, one hundred German marks, and about the same in British money. There was also a small black book for keeping notes and ticket stubs from the ferry crossings. Pulling everything out, I closed the safe.

Moving to my trousers, I stuffed everything into the pockets. Then folding them, I placed them on the sideboard next to the television. I needed more time to sort things, so I planted my arse in one of the two chairs by the table.

Watching Anna sleep, I concocted ways to get us out of Berlin. The clock radio said it was almost half-five in the morning; we'd slept for over nine hours.

Food would be necessary. I wondered if someone would be in the kitchen by now. We could only stay long enough to wash up and eat. If Giselle had been in this room, there was a good chance she would be back.

Anna stirred and appeared to be dreaming. She mumbled in her sleep and rolled over to face the opposite wall. Her legs started to move as if she was walking, and then rolling on to her back, she startled me with, "Mama! Papa is here… Nein Papa, nein..."

Her arms fought with some invisible foe under the covers. Then sitting upright in an abrupt manner, the duvet fell away to expose her breasts. Breathing hard she scanned the room, her hair in wild disarray. When she saw me in the chair, she let out a sigh of relief.

"Oh Ciarán, I was dreaming… it was horrible."

"I know. I'm sorry darling, what was…?"

Before I could finish, she rolled out of the bed, and did a fast walk to me. Crawling into my lap, her arms went around my neck, and she kissed me several times on my cheeks and lips. When she finished, she rested the side of her head on my shoulder, my face now in her hair. I could smell the hairspray and individual strands of gold stuck to my beard stubble. Her bare skin was warm and pleasant against mine, and it sadden me that I would have to end the moment.

"Anna, we cannot stay here."

Tipping her head back, she looked into my eyes. "Why not? We are safe here, yes?"

"Breath deep, is there something familiar to your nose?"

She sniffed, sniffed again deeper, and her eyes filled with fear.

"Oh my... it is jasmine. It is...Giselle!"

"Tis... and I fear she may have been in this room at some point."

Pulling her arms from around my neck, she brought her knees up and curled into a fetal position against my chest. I was grateful she was small, otherwise she wouldn't have fit, and it would have been terribly awkward.

"When will we ever be safe, Ciarán? When?"

Her voice crescendoed and trailed off into a whimper as a single tear ran out. Falling from her chin on to my chest, it created an odd sensation as it coursed down to catch in my belly button.

I just held her even though I had the overwhelming desire to get out of there. I wanted to go somewhere where I could relax without feeling threatened. It gnawed at me. I felt torn between what we must do to avoid another confrontation, and what I must do to comfort Anna. Yet I didn't want to come off apprehensive.

It was clear what she could do under pressure. She was quick to make decisions, used humor to cope mentally with fear, and had enough courage to take on a man twice her size. Nevertheless, she was still human. I realized at this point I would, in all probability, defend her to the death. If Giselle should win the day, and take Anna, it would be best if the procuress left me without a breath in my body. I could not live with the thought of Anna as Giselle's slave. If the miscreant should put me in a position where I had nothing left to lose, she might well be wise to understand that when a man has nothing left to lose, he becomes the most dangerous man in the world. I smiled to myself as the thought of my best mate, Girvin McCord, came to mind.

He was five years my senior, and someone I'd always looked up to. Some six years ago, we'd been in Lafferty's when a group of four Australian tourists staggered in for a pint. Samuel's da had been alive back then, and the pub was in his hands that day. I remember the look of concern on his face as the Aussie's lurched in through the door.

We didn't have too many outsiders show up in our village. But on occasion, they would—and there was always trouble. They'd been well past the point of drunk and comments had been made maligning the Irish. Girvin was the first to jump to his feet. None of our older lads would stand with him—so I did.

Australians are a hardy lot and I was having doubts that Girvin and I could win the day. He wasn't a big man that Girvin, no bigger than me anyway, and certainly not as big as the largest of their bunch. So, it was a giant of an Aussie who stepped forward. His weathered face and massive hands said it all. He laughed a deep, frightening laugh and threatened to clean the bar top with Girvin's face.

Turning, my mate smiled at me, and nodding toward the large fellow, said, "Big un, hiagh Ciarán!" Then turning back to the huge man, he said, "You know laddy, I may not know karate, but I know crazy."

It was a phrase he'd heard in a film once, and he used it a lot. On conclusion of the statement, the room seemed to explode. The big fellow lunged at Girvin, who promptly stepped aside, and using the momentum of the bigger man's motion, grabbed him and ran his head into a ceiling support, knocking him unconscious.

That left three. Girvin and I held our own for a while. The older patrons, standing along the wall, sipped their pints and I suspect, placed bets. When we were about to lose it all, old man Lafferty waded in with the Hurley stick he kept behind the bar. He mopped up the lot of them with a few well-placed licks, much to the dismay of those who'd wagered against us.

All bets were off then. So, we drug them out into the street, leaving them there with the advice it might be in their best interest to move on down to Dublin. Sadly, it wasn't but a year later that Girvin got so pished that he wandered off the end of the old pier and drown.

Now his voice rang in my head as if he was sitting across the room, "I may not know karate, but I know crazy!" I supposed that's where I was now because I didn't have a room full of men, or Girvin, to back me. So, crazy was in order.

"Ciarán, I am starving," Anna said, her voice breaking through my reflection induced fog. She'd tilted her head back again, her face now close to mine.

"We should shower. Better yet, you can shower, and I'll call down to the kitchen to see if I can get them to send something up."

Jumping off my lap, she faced me and said, "Will there be enough time?"

"It's early. I expect Giselle will be on her way to bed about now. So she probably has someone else on the lookout. She's the kind that would want to be present after they found us though. Whoever it is, they will have to make a phone call and keep us in sight until she can get here.

"Okay, then... I suppose I should get on with it, yes?"

Spinning around, she walked away, exaggerating the sway of her hips. Arriving at the bathroom door, she stopped and pulled down her knickers. Allowing them drop to her ankles, she stepped out of them, and putting her right hand on her hip and the other behind her head, she arched backwards. Smiling at me, she winked and mouthing my name, stepped out of sight through the bathroom door. The light came on, followed by the sound of the water raining down into the shower basin.

Now that my personal show was over, I stood to go to the telephone but faltered as pins and needles assaulted my legs. I stopped to rub at my thighs to stimulate the blood flow and Anna began humming her song. She'd droned the same tune in her sleep, and I tried to sort its title, but with no success. I made a mental note to ask her, and moving to the telephone, I dialed the front desk.

"Hallo, Rezeption?"

"Hallo, Meine Zimmernummer ist Drei hundert und elf…"

Before I could finish, he blurted out, "Ah! Hallo Herr McKay, you have returned, yes?" His response surprised me and I grew silent.

"Hallo?"

"Ahhh… yes, would it be possible to send up some grub, uh… breakfast? For two people, please?"

"Why of course, Herr McKay. They are in the kitchen now, preparing. What is it you wish?"

I went on to explain what I wanted and he hung up with the promise of having it up to us in an hour. Fair enough, I thought. Replacing the handset, I went into the bath. Standing in the doorway, I could hear Anna soaping her body behind the plastic curtain.

Stepping up to the mirror, I studied my face. I'd never seen myself so haggard. Even though I felt rested, the bags under my eyes said differently. I needed a shave and to brush my teeth, but it was the thought of a hot shower that lay foremost in my mind. My thought line was to wait until Anna finished, but that was my conditioning at work.

I finished with my teeth and quashing my bathroom etiquette, I whipped the curtain open in one quick motion. Anna squealed and placed her hands over her breasts and pubic area in mock fear. Her hair lay plastered to her head and rivulets of soapsuds ran down her body. Dropping my underwear to the floor, I exposed my flaccid member. She squealed again as it rose to attention and grabbing my hands, pulled me into the streaming water. Moving to the back of the shower, I pressed her against the tiled wall with a long hard kiss. Her hands moved to sandwich my face as her tongue started its exploration.

"Mmmm, toothpaste…" she murmured into my mouth.

I slid my hands down her back and under her bottom. Picking her up off the basin floor, she wrapped her legs around my waist. Her right hand left my face, and slipping down between our bodies, she found what she was looking for.

Guiding me inside, I felt her spasm, and groaning with pleasure, she closed her eyes, tilting her face to the ceiling. This exposed the front of her neck, and taking advantage of the opportunity, I grazed over the wet skin.

"Oh Mein Gott," she stuttered out, and tightening her embrace, she did all she could to hold on. I tried to avoid being loud, but it was difficult, and soon we were both making enough noise that anyone within earshot could have sorted our goal. I imagined us crashing through the wall into the adjoining room because my thrusts had grown so fervent. After our second and almost combined orgasms, it was time to stop. The food would arrive soon and besides, if we had any neighbors, they were sure to complain.

We'd been at it for forty-five minutes, and anticipating a knock on the door kept intruding on my passionate mood in the last five of those. Turning off the water, we stood cooling, our arms wrapped around each other with the side of Anna's face to my chest. I rested my chin on the top of her head as she caressed my backside.

"Oh Ciarán, that was so good. It has never been that way for me," she whispered.

She kissed my chest, her hand moving up to massage my back. The lovemaking, coupled with our meditative moment, had pushed me into a reflective mood. Memories of Isleen filled my head, and I found myself comparing the two. They had more in common than not, and I found I was savoring something I thought I'd lost. For

Anna, I believed it was the difference between sex with a stranger, and making love with someone who truly cared for you.

"Was it good for you, Ciarán?" she asked, looking up into my face. Losing my chin rest, jarred me back to the present. She moved her hands to sandwich my waist and her face grew inquisitive.

"Sorry, I was somewhere else." I said. "It was amazing darling—simply amazing. You have driven me speechless with your sexual prowess." We both laughed and as I brushed the wet hair from her forehead, I added, "We should get out and get dried before the food arrives."

Breaking her hold, I moved out of the basin and handed her a towel.

"You've already ordered food?" she asked, a look of surprise on her face.

"Don't you remember, I…"

"Ah! Of course, yes, what was I thinking? Sorry, I am still a little dazed. What if they had come while we were… how you say, ummm… in the throes of passion?"

Her words came in a playful manner and she formed an 'O' with her lips, making her eyes go wide as if alarmed.

"Then… they would have had to wait." I said, giving her back the same expression.

She sneered at me while wrapping the large towel around her body. Stepping out, she checked her face in the mirror. I moved over and leaned in beside her. Picking up my disposable razor, I shaved two days' worth of growth from my chin and cheeks.

"Do you have pinzette? Ummm… tweezers?" she asked. Looking at her, I wondered what it was she had to tweeze.

"In the bottom of the small black bag there," I said, pointing. She dug in, and brought them out. "Danke," she squeaked, imitating a cartoon mouse we both knew from television.

Giving me a, 'Sorry, I couldn't help it' look in the reflective glass, she went to work on her eyebrows.

Running the razor over the last of my stubble, I watched her various expressions. It felt good to be sharing what I considered to be a normal moment, and fell to hoping for many more.

After rinsing my face, I took advantage of aftershave and deodorant. Lightly slapping her on the rump, she growled at the disruption and threw me a look as I moved out to my rucksack. Pulling out a fresh pair of blue jeans, underwear and socks, I got dressed. I had one lightweight, long sleeved jumper remaining, a dark green number that may prove to be too much if the day grew hot. Yet because everything else was soiled, I'd no choice. As I pulled it on over my head, there came a knock on the door.

Assuming it must be the food, I went to answer, stopping just long enough in the bath entry to catch Anna using my deodorant. She became embarrassed, and blushing, threw me a shy smile. It was infectious, and I couldn't help but smile back. She seemed so content at that moment. I hoped the mood would last. I winked at her and pushed the door just short of closed.

As I peered through the viewing hole out into the hallway, I heard her say, "Now I smell just like you."

Opening the door, I was still grinning when I confronted the man on the other side. Stationing myself at the jamb, I kept him from entering. He was smaller than I and wore the white jacket of a hotel steward.

"Hallo mein Herr, Ich heiße Ferza, dein Essen." His German was poor, but most of the immigrants new to this country were still struggling with the language.

"Yes—my food—thanks a million."

"English?" he asked.

"Nah, Irish!"

"No, please, I mean, you speak English?"

Unsure why he was asking, I grimaced and searched his face. His eye twitched, and his nervous manner made me suspect he'd done something wrong—or was about to.

"Sorry, yes… I speak English."

"Oh, very good."

He tried to smile but failed miserably. I felt threatened by his presence, so I gave him a quick once-over. He was about thirty years old, appeared to be Middle Eastern, and looked somewhat familiar. His large, hooked nose and thin face gave him an evil appearance.

After handing me the tray, he looked hard into my face as if he was studying me. Seeming satisfied with his inspection, he took a step back, and crossed his hands at his waist. Realizing I should give him a gratuity for his trouble, I said, "Stay here. Bleib hier." He raised his eyebrows like he was surprised and sputtered out, "Okay, okay."

I walked to my soiled trousers still lying on the floor and setting the tray of food on the bed, I picked them up and pulled out some money.

I'd always believed that those who worked for a living deserved their gratuities. Being Irish, I felt strongly about the issue of people who held menial positions because they were considered no better than servants, or slaves. Unfortunately, in this case, I turned to find the man inside now, peeking through the gap of the bathroom door.

"Excuse me there…sorry, but I told you…"

He nearly jumped out of his shoes and turning to run, bounced off the back of the entry door. Letting out a somewhat strangled, "Sorry, sorry…" he found the opening, and scrambled out.

I heard him running down the hallway as I hurried across the room, and upon looking out to the left, I saw him disappear through the exit at the end.

Something caught my eye on the floor just outside the door, and picking it up, I turned it over to find it was a faded image of Anna and I back in Ireland—the one I'd been using in my search. I'd left it behind in my jacket pocket at the room above the club. Ferza must have dropped it in his escape.

How did he get it?

Stepping back inside, I closed the door and double locked it. Anna stuck her head out around the bathroom door and said, “Is there something wrong?”

I stuffed the photo into my back pocket so as not to alarm her. She’d lost the towel, so I suspected our intruder had gotten an eyeful. I decided not to bother her with that—her knowing would help nothing. It would only bring more cause for her to fret.

“No trouble a-tall darling, it’s just… our food has arrived. So... anytime now,”

She gave me a look like she didn’t believe there was no trouble and I felt a stab of unease.

“Excuse me for a moment,” she said flatly, and stepping back in, she closed the door in my face. I feared she saw through me and I was going to get an earful when she came out. But when I heard the toilet lid go up, followed by the unmistakable tinkle of water into the bowl, I sorted it. She was not ready to pee in front me just yet and the need came at a bad time.

Taking the food tray to the table, I pushed my rucksack onto the floor with an elbow and set it down. Pulling the two small chairs close, I sat in one of them.

Ferza troubled me. I sensed that we didn’t have as much time as I first thought. This man had come into my room when I told him not to, and there was the question of the photo. I was still mulling it over when Anna came out. She picked up her panties, sniffed at them, made a face, and tossed them into the trash bin.

“I won’t need those anymore.”

“Are you sure you want to give those up?”

Picking up her dress, she shook it out and pulled it on, not answering my question until she arrived at the table. “Yes, I am… they are stinking from our run. Besides, they were a gift from Giselle. So… they are now where she should be.”

She giggled at her own wit and changing the subject, said, “We should try to get to my mama’s today. I will need most of my closes from there, my passport and… Oh! Wunderbar! Food! I must eat!" and diving into the contents of the tray, she left me to chuckle at the thought that I had now become second to breakfast.

Chapter 22

"Don't Go Gentle..."

Too hungry for manners, she ate with her hands, stuffing sausage in her mouth like it was the last of it. There were different breads and meats, Camembert cheese, some kind of fruit that looked like mango, and a kettle of coffee, which she referred to as a 'can'. She tried to talk with her mouth full, but after spraying me with its contents, she gave up. I decided to start in, fearful that there would be nothing left for me. I also wanted to discuss our plan, so I hurriedly chewed and swallowed before I said, "So, we are going to have to make our way to Spandau, today?"

She swallowed hard and belched. "Yes, well... actually Haselhorst. It is in that district where I li... where I used to live."

Her face got thoughtful and then went slack. Her happy mood dissolved away, and she gulped, tears welling up in her eyes.

"What is it, darling?" I asked, sensing that the reality of leaving her longtime home had finally set in.

Wiping a hand on a napkin, she moved it to the back of mine, and looking into my eyes she said, "I am sorry, I am already homesick and I haven't even gone yet. Along with that, if we do make it out of Berlin, it will be much time before I see my mama again... and I know it will be longer than ten months. I feel I want to be right with her, do you know what I am meaning?"

Squeezing my fingers, she cast her eyes to the tabletop, and with a slight shrug, she tried to smile, as a single tear broke free to run down and hang at the end of her nose. Pulling her hand from mine, she wiped it away and poured herself a cup of coffee. She drank it slowly as her eyes moved around the room, avoiding mine. I suspected she feared if they made contact, she might lose all control.

"Don't worry Anna, for your sake I will see we get through this."

Finishing the coffee, she started to speak, but nothing came out. Her eyes seemed to focus on her cup and the seconds ticked away as she composed herself.

"I know you will, Mein Liebster… I know you will. I am not with you only because you are a handsome man… there are so many good things that pull me to this person called Ciarán." Raising her face, she looked at me out of the top of her eyes.

"I am not afraid that you will not be there for me, I fear that you will just not be. Then this power, this energy—this bond we have… will pull at me like a magnet for the rest of my life. There is no going back to where I was before. If I cannot be with you, Ciarán… I do not want to be at all."

Her eyes strayed over the table and suddenly her face lit up as she blurted, "Oh, I must have this Brötchen."

Putting down her cup, she picked up a bread roll from the tray and nibbled on its end as she turned to sit sideways in her chair. She went back to studying the room. I could tell she was trying to stay in the moment, searching for a more optimistic frame of mind. Her eyes came to me, only to dart away. I was at a loss for words. All I could think of was how much I loved her.

"I love you, Anna."

She stopped chewing and sat motionless, holding the bread with both hands. There came an unbearable silence and then she leapt from her chair. Slamming the bread down on the table, she came around to sit sideways in my lap. Throwing her arms around my neck and pushing her forehead against the side of my face, she sobbed. I held her, trying to come up with something to say that might sooth her. After about a minute, the tears came to a halt. She sniffed several times and raising her face to mine, kissed my forehead.

"I'm sorry. I did not think leaving Berlin and my mama would hurt me so bad."

"I know what that's like. I mean, with my ma gone and not being in my home."

She sighed and fiddled with my collar. I caught the scent of my deodorant on her, and wished she had the choice of something a wee bit more feminine. Perhaps lavender, rose, or even, jasmine.

That was it!

In my dream, Zafer had morphed into the man I now knew as Ferza. I trembled and Anna felt it. She tilted her head back to study my face and said, "Are you OK, Ciarán?"

I got to my feet, and she slid off my lap to stand beside me. My mind buzzed and my eyes lost their focus. In my head, the puzzle all came together.

Was I mentally spent or just stupid?

I turned to her, and she brought her hands to my face. Her expression was pleading. Her mouth moved and words were coming out, but I could no longer hear them. My impulsive response to Ferza's question: "English?" sealed our fate. He hadn't been looking through the crack in the door at Anna for his own pleasure; he was looking to confirm that the people in the room matched the ones in the photo. He'd seen me, and just needed to see if it was Anna in the bathroom.

I snapped out of my stupor when I saw the lever on the door, rotate toward the floor. Anna heard it, and with a sharp intake of breath, spun to face it. I pushed past her and she followed me across the room. Upon arriving, I could smell sweat, and looking through the peephole, I could just make out part of a shoulder, clad in white.

My ire rose, and I prepared for battle. With, "crazy, not karate!" running through my mind, I flung it open.

"You fekin..." was all I got out.

Anna yelped in surprise, and the little housekeeper that was trying to gain access, squealed in fear. Reeling back, she sat down hard on the carpet, her legs flying up to expose some rather colorful knickers. Dropping her keys, she covered her face with both hands, and cried out, "Nein, Bitte! Nein!" She went to blubbering as we stared at her in embarrassment.

"Shite. Terribly sorry. It's okay, please don't cry. I thought you were someone else." I said, and reaching down, took her arm and pulled her to her feet.

She babbled in German as she wrung her hands. Anna listened intently, then pushed a palm out toward her and said, "Stoppen, bitte." Then turning, Anna said, "She wants us to forgive her for not knocking on the door. She only wanted to check your room and did not know anyone had returned."

Looking her over, I noticed she was youngish, maybe eighteen years old. Her dark blonde hair was pulled back into a ponytail and her thin almond shaped eyes were such a light brown, they were almost amber. She wore a white bib apron over a short, gray uniform dress, white knee socks and scuffed, black shoes. I suspected Russian, or Ukrainian—another recent arrival to Berlin.

"Sprechen Sie Englisch?" I asked her.

"Nein, Herr McKay," she said, wiping her eyes.

She knew my name.

"Ask her how she knows my name."

Anna asked, but spoke much too fast for me to translate, and after several minutes of back and forth, she turned to me and said, "Her name is Angelina, she is just here from Smolensk. Ferza, the steward boy, tells her your name, and that you are his friend from Ireland. She tells me that yesterday in the morning, she came to clean your room, and when she was inside, Ferza came in while she makes your bed. He had with him a beautiful woman with long dark hair. Angelina asked him why he is in here, and he said he had a question for her but… he never asked it. While she hangs your towels, this woman walks around your room looking at things. Angelina told them to get out because they had no business there. The woman got angry and called her a little cow. Angelina tells me she is not a strong person, so starts to cry. She cannot make them leave the room. She says the woman looked inside your rucksack, but didn't take anything. Then the woman used profanity and stomped her foot. She pulled this Ferza outside and they left the room."

Angelina kept looking back and forth between us with an approval-seeking smile. Rubbing her hands together, she nodded her head whenever she heard her name mentioned.

"Ask her if the sign was on the door when she came to clean. The one that reads, Do Not Disturb."

There followed another short conversation with Anna's face showing no emotion. This contrasted Angelina, who talked like her life, or job, depended on giving us the right answers.

"She tells me that there was something strange. Yesterday she came by and saw the, ummm…Bitte nicht stören, ummm… the tag that tells us to not disturb, was on the door. So, she decided to clean the room across the hall instead. That was when Ferza passed her, taking food to somebody, and he would not say hallo to her. He acted like he was afraid. When she came out, the food tray was on the floor in front of door number 314. So, she finished cleaning the room and goes to move her… trolley? She now sees no more little sign. She thinks maybe you leave and remove it while she is in the toilet of the other people. So, she goes inside your room and that is when Ferza comes back with this woman."

Angelina was nodding more and more as she watched our exchange. Anna then spoke a few curt sentences directly to the housekeeper, who shrugged in return but then got excited and spoke quickly as if she'd remembered something else.

"Ciarán, she says when Ferza left with the woman, he stopped and picked up the food tray. Angelina says she could see that no food had been eaten. She believes maybe him… this Ferza… oh, how do you say it…? Er hat falsch gehandelt, uh… he was acting falsely. Like he needed an excuse to come up to this floor, so brought food."

"You mean like he was faking it? Like the food was not for anyone after all?"

"Yes! That is right. So, this girl checks 314, and finds no one is in there. She goes to reception and looks at the register book when no one was attending and sees that the room is not occupied."

It was becoming clear what was going on. We needed to get out of here and it had to be now. Reaching into my pocket, I took out the money I'd planned to give to Ferza, and handed it to Angelina.

"Warum, Herr McKay?" she said, asking why. Looking nervous again, she gave Anna a pleading look.

"Anna, tell her tis ok. Tis because she has been very helpful and besides that… I can tell she is a good person."

Anna expressed our gratitude, and in her excitement, Angelina embraced her. Then taking the money, she did the same with me. At that moment, Ferza came out of the stairwell at the far end of the hallway. Upon seeing us, he changed course and dashed back out of sight.

"Time to go, Anna. Thank you Angelina, uhhh… Vielen Dank."

I ushered Anna back inside, shutting the door. "Pack my kit, will you?" I said, but she was way ahead of me and was already stuffing my toilet items into the small vinyl case.

I grabbed my ruck and picking up my books from the floor, I pushed everything inside. Anna brought the small black bag to me, her brow now furrowed with worry. Taking it, I forced it into the sack and zipped it shut. I yearned for my jacket and flat cap, and frowned as I imagined Giselle happily burning them along with Anna's possessions.

I moved to the window and opening the curtain a crack, I looked down onto the street. Seeing nothing of concern, I closed it and turned to Anna, who was waiting by the bathroom door, biting her nails. The look of anguish in her eyes fired my temper.

"Don't worry darling, we'll get through this."

She came to me and we embraced. "Please hold me, just for a moment Ciarán, okay? Please?"

I did as she asked, and as much as I wanted the moment to last, my 'fight or flight' was up and wouldn't allow it.

"We must hurry Anna. I feel Giselle is already on her way. We might have to take a bus or a train. We cannot walk, and there is no time to call Halim."

Not five seconds later, we heard the screech of tires. Peeking out between the curtains again, I saw the blue BMW at the curb across the street with Eric at the wheel. Anna peered out, her head below mine.

"They are here," she said.

"They are… and we should be gone."

Ferza, in his white jacket, ran out from the building and pointed up toward our room. A man in a black suit came out onto the pavement after him. Shaking his fist at Ferza, he shouted something in German. I recognized him as the man who'd checked me in at the front desk and I suspected he was also the manager.

Anna said, "It sounds like the man in black tells Ferza he should return to the kitchen or just go home."

Giselle now stuck her head out of the window from the back seat and spoke to Ferza as he walked away. The steward stopped in the middle of the street and looking back gave her an agitated, "Okay!" That was when Eric got out of the car and followed. The man in black pushed Ferza inside and turning, yelled something at Eric. The bartender stopped and retreated to the car. Leaning with his back on the door, he defiantly crossed his arms as Giselle wagged a finger and appeared to be lecturing him.

"Let's get out of here," I said, and taking Anna's hand, I grabbed my ruck with the other. Opening the door a crack, I peeked out. Only Angelina and her trolley were between the back stairwell and us. We burst from the room and ran. Passing the housekeeper, she called out, "Goot look!" which I suspect was an attempt at "Good luck."

We burst through the stairwell door and took the stairs two at a time. Anna in her flats was doing a better job than I, and she moved ahead of me, swinging herself around every newel post we came to. The stairwell was the open type, so anyone coming up or going down could easily be seen and heard. Since I could only hear us, I figured we were safe for the moment.

Instead of exiting on the first floor into the lobby, we went down one more floor and through a door marked 'Keller-Nur Für Personal!' telling us that only employees were allowed. We entered a greasy hallway, lit with florescent lights and smelling of garbage.

Dirty trolley tracks streaked the grey paint of the floor and several black plastic bags of rubbish stood along one wall. It was the back corridor to the kitchen and gave access to the garbage bins and loading dock. I hoped for a service elevator or something, to take us outside.

Following the ribbons of filth left by the wheels of the garbage trollies, we navigated around racks of shelves and soon found ourselves at the end of the corridor. To our right there was a lift for the ease of freight delivery, and next to that, a short set of steps that would take us where we wanted to go.

We leapt up the metal treads, and breaking out through the door, we found ourselves in a large enclosure, surrounded by a shoulder high brick wall. There was a roof suspended above us on pillars, leaving a gap that allowed a view to the surrounding area.

The pavement was much greasier than the hallway, and bits of paper and other debris floated around in the air, propelled by the exhaust from the kitchen ventilators. There was row of small maintenance vehicles on our left, and two gargantuan metal garbage bins sitting on our right, creating an aisle that led to just what we were looking for—a gate out.

We made for it, and as we did, Ferza surprised us by jumping out from between the two containers. He must have expected our departure through the back and posted himself to wait. He blocked the route that would take us to freedom, and in his hands—a broomstick minus the brush. I stepped in front of Anna as another dose of adrenalin rushed in. Letting the rucksack slide off my shoulders, I assumed Anna must have caught it because I didn't hear it hit the ground.

Rolling up my sleeves, I advanced on Ferza. His eyes grew wild with fear and he held the stick like an American baseball player holds a bat.

"You must stay," he screamed. "You must stay for Giselle or I will strike you."

His head pivoted back and forth, as if he was expecting help. But his manner didn't convey confidence, and I did not falter in my stride.

He made good with his warning, and I ducked, sidestepping the broomstick as it whistled passed my head. He hadn't counted on the slippery pavement, and his feet flew out from underneath him. With his arms gyrating, the stick flew from his hands and spun across the space. Striking the back of a garden cart, it reversed its spin and landed on the ground about the same time he did. It rolled past me and I heard Anna say, "I have it."

Ferza somehow avoided smacking his head on the ground, and now lay on his back trying to catch his breath. I was on him in an instant, and making a fist with one hand, I grabbed the front of his jacket and picked him up off the ground with the other. He didn't fight, he just dangled as he held his hands out to protect his face.

I shook my fist at him, but decided against punching him. Instead, I let go of his frock. His head did bounce off the pavement this time, but as if unfazed, he scrambled to his knees. He kneeled now, keeping his eyes down.

"Please, forgive me, please, I no fight. It is Giselle, please, it is Giselle!"

From behind me, there came some semblance of a war cry. Ferza threw up his hands to cover his head, screaming, "No, please! No," as Anna flew past me, the stick poised to strike. I grabbed her around the waist as she went by and said, "No Anna, he is done. We don't hit people who are down."

When she stopped struggling against my arm, I released my hold and we stood looking into each other's faces. I could see the fury in her eyes and whipping her hair back, she turned her gaze to Ferza and said, "Well… maybe you don't, Ciarán McKay."

With that, she smacked Ferza in the jaw with an upward stroke of the broom handle. There was a sickening 'thwack' and he tumbled forward, apparently unconscious. Dropping her weapon, she bent over him and shouted, "You don't try to hit us with a stick. We have done nothing to you."

He lay motionless, his white jacket no longer so. With my eyes wide in amazement, I stared at her in disbelief.

"Anna," I said, as if I was her da scolding her for some inappropriate act.

She brushed off her dress and looked around nonchalantly as if she was indifferent to my complaint. A few seconds passed before she looked into my eyes and said coolly, "We should go before the others come."

Shocked as I was, I couldn't help but chuckle.

"This is the second time you have wacked a man with a stick you know?"

Putting her hands on her hips, she cocked her head to the side and said, "Well, Ciarán, I have had all I can take. If you have taught me anything Irishman, it's that you don't take shit from anyone."

I laughed now and leaned down to feel Ferza's neck. There was still a strong pulse, so at least she hadn't killed him. A large angry looking welt was forming on his jaw though, so at the least, he would have something to show Giselle to prove he'd tried.

"Come Ciarán, let us go and see my mama."

"Very well," I said, and shaking my head, I chuckled at the absurdity of it all.

We walked through the gate and moved up the short alley. Crossing Fasanenstrasse, we took care to make sure no one could see us from the street at the front of the hotel. Upon arriving at the opposite side, Anna directed me into the front door of what appeared be a health clinic.

Hurrying through, we exited out the rear without question from the occupants. Finding ourselves in a 'green area', we moved north toward the busy Ku'damm, hoping to get lost in the crowd.

Now shielded by buildings on both sides, we could move through the park-like landscape without being seen. We strolled along until we found that it curved back to the street, narrowing to a gated passageway between buildings. Stopping short of the pavement, we moved to hide along a wall, behind a line of shrubs.

"What now, lass?"

"In here," she said, and pulled open a door in the wall where she leaned. It was the back entrance to a restaurant and inside, kitchen help moved back and forth in a hurried manner.

"Are you sure?"

"It's okay. If we move quickly, we can get through just like the clinic. It is almost second breakfast and they will be busy."

She stepped inside and motioned for me to follow. I entered with some reluctance, and we slipped through the kitchen without incident, the staff ignoring us until we entered the dining room.

We were doing a fast walk to the front door when the host glanced up from her podium and gave us a hard look. She turned and tapped the shoulder of a man in an ill-fitting grey suit that was organizing menus. He looked at us, and leaving his task, followed at a distance. We picked up our pace, and arriving at our exit, squeezed our way through an incoming group of people. Having to attend to their new arrivals, they lost interest in us.

We stepped out into a wave of pedestrians going in both directions. Negotiating our way through, we stopped to stand within a row of small trees, benches, and trash bins at the curbside.

"Where to now?"

"The underground," she sang out, following it with that husky laugh.

"How far is that?" I said, looking around and not seeing any signage.

Her face told me she was toying with me and wanted to make me guess. When I didn't, she sighed, rolled her eyes and said, "Not far at all."

Grabbing my hand, she pointed with her other at a waist high, decorative railing, shaped like a horseshoe. It sat on a long concrete island in the middle of the street. Because I was looking at it from the side, I couldn't see the sign.

"You see, U Bahn. We will take the U9 to the Zoo."

Giggling, she squeezed my hand and when the traffic cleared, she towed me across to the entrance where we moved down the dimly lit stairs into the underground.

Chapter 23

"Don't Give Cherries To Pigs..."

Arriving at the platform, we found it overflowing with travelers and it was easy to get lost in the crowd. Keeping an eye on Anna, I watched her continuously scanning the area; her head rotating back and forth like a hawk in search of its prey. We sought familiar faces, people who might know her, or worse yet, someone who might know Giselle.

"Oh shite! Eric!" I said, seeing him head our way through the crowd.

"Where? I don't see him?"

"Over there, coming our way," I pointed.

"What? Ahhh... that's not Eric. Ciarán, you scared me."

"It's not? Oh, sorry..."

Relief flooded in as the Eric doppelganger embraced another man, kissed him, and headed for the exit. I was hallucinating bad guys now, growing more anxious by the minute. I feared a panic attack right there on the platform. The initial safety I felt from being enveloped by the crowd dissolved away. Then Anna startled me by grabbing my arm and nearly shouting in my ear, "Ciarán, take off the ruck and carry it in front. There are too many people in here."

She was right, it was way too convenient for pickpockets while it hung on my back. I was going to have to hold it or set it on the floor though, wearing it in front was too awkward. She helped me slip it off, and I let it hang from my hands by its straps. Closing my eyes, I attempted to control my breathing. I would just have to let Anna do the guarding while we waited.

The situation reminded me of that children's story about the Country Mouse and the City Mouse. I smiled to myself and Anna noticed. "What are you doing? What are you smiling about? You look silly with your eyes shut, keep them open. I don't want you to fall onto the tracks or something worse."

"I am trying to calm myself."

"Relax, I will take care of you. Okay? I know what I am doing."

"But that's… what I was doing?"

"Okay, shut up now." She said and smiled, patting me on the back to let me know she wasn't serious.

It was her show now. In fact, she'd taken control the moment she'd wacked Ferza. It was as if taking him out made her feel on top of the situation. That was two down and two to go, as far as I knew. I wouldn't argue or resist her direction for the time being, especially if there were sticks and boards lying about.

The noise of the arriving train filled the station. When the car halted and the doors slid open, we pushed our way in and grabbing an overhead rail, I threw her a nervous smile. But she didn't see it because she now hung by a hand from a strap, her other arm dangling, her gaze fixed on the floor. She appeared exasperated and sighed loud enough for me to hear.

A few minutes passed and looking up, she said, "I'll be so glad when this shit is over, we can only hope there will be enough room on the next train. It is a bad time of day to ride the U Bahn."

The passengers closest to us looked at her and then at each other, grinning. I suspected they agreed. Shoppers, elderly folk, business people, and many teenagers filled the car. It made everything claustrophobic. I was glad it was a short hop to our next destination.

Once we got away from the Ku'damm, the loads would be lighter, and I wouldn't have to feel so much like a sardine. I turned my attention to the advertisements above the windows, reading each one under my breath in German to put my mind on something else.

Arriving at the Zoological Garden, Anna stood up straight and leaning toward me, said, "I need to make a telephone call."

"Going to call your mama?"

"Yes, but I also want to check on Zafer and find out if anything has happened that we should know about."

The train stopped and the doors slide open. We dashed out and walking up a wide set of stairs, we discovered a bank of pay telephones along the right hand wall at the top. They'd been placed just out of the flow of human traffic, so one could stand there without being run over by the ebb and flow of human bodies. The problem was, it didn't allow us to be out of sight. So, stopping there to make a phone call, posed a wee bit of a risk.

"Do you have some, ummm…? Münzen? Uhhh… coins or something?" she said, sounding irritated.

Reaching into my pocket, I pulled out a fistful and let the entire mess fall into her cupped hands. She moved over to a phone and dumped the coins onto the metal shelf at the front. Dialing the number, she deposited several into the slot and waited. A smile soon came to her lips and she said, "Zafer, ist Anna! Wie Geht's? Ummm… how are you? No, no, they have not caught us yet."

She nodded and affirmed different things. After about a minute she sang out a "Tschüss!" and hung up.

"Well, what did he say?"

"He says that his head is better and that Giselle has finally stopped driving around his place. This does not surprise me though, since they were at the hotel… and are stupid enough to probably still be there. So, nothing has changed. I will call my mama now."

She hesitated and stood looking at the phone, her fingers hovering over the handset.

"Is everything okay, lass?"

She gave me a sheepish look and shrugged. Turning back to the telephone, she went to pushing the coins around with a fingertip. They made a scratching noise on the metal shelf, which only helped increase my annoyance. She started lining them up in rows, confirming procrastination was in play.

"Anna?"

Turning, she said in an apologetic manner, "Ciarán, it has been a very long time. My mama may not even want to talk to me."

I pushed a displaced curl out of her face and said, "Make the call, lass. All she can do is hang up on you. Even if she does, we still need to go there to get your passport and such."

My statement got no response, so I added in a jocular manner, "We might even have to kick down the door if she is not home."

She gave me a worried look. I grinned as big as possible so she would see that it was all for a laugh. She ignored it and casting her eyes downward, she said, "I have to stop being afraid of her. My life has been hell because of it. I think it is time to show her I'm no longer a child."

"That's the spirit, darling. Better to try, than to just wish. Shall we get on with it?"

She didn't react and continued to hesitate. I took my eyes off the crowd and bent down to look in her face, giving her my complete attention. She wavered for another couple of seconds and when I drew a breath to speak, she punched in the number. Dropping in the required amount of coinage, she waited for someone to answer.

It seemed like an eternity before she said, "Mama? It's Anna, mama."

The tears came and switching to German, she talked so fast I lost my place. I stopped trying to translate and just listened to the tone of her voice. There came a degree of desperation, followed by pleading. It then became frantic and finally insistent before she stopped talking and just listened. After a few minutes, Anna started talking again and there seemed to be some kind of reconciliation.

It appeared as if she and Jana were battling to see who would control the situation. There was nothing I could do, so I rubbed Anna's back to reassure her I was there, and turned my attention back to the room.

I scanned the entry hall, looking for any familiar face. Glancing over Anna's head, I saw a woman come up the stairs and walk straight toward us. Her dark eyes were unblinking as she zeroed in. Her choice of clothing comprised a short, tight red skirt, black leggings, and knee high black boots. She wore a short brown jacket with a large fur collar, something totally out of place for the season. Her black knit top was transparent and revealing. She looked like someone who'd dressed in a hurry and without choice—almost as if summoned at the last minute.

She strode toward us along the phone bank and I got a sneaking suspicion that I knew her from somewhere. Fear rose up in me as her pace became brisk. I could tell she was trying to eavesdrop on Anna's conversation.

"Okay Mama, okay… Bis später," Anna said, ending her telephone call. She hung up the handset, just as the woman stopped and said, "Stacy?"

Anna spun to face her. "Zen!" she said with spurious delight.

Electricity filled the air and the hair on my arms came to attention. Anna moved to put her back to me, and looking over her shoulder, I studied Zen. I remembered her. She was the other woman at the club. The one that Giselle had been fondling.

The handles of two, nearly full, KaDeWe bags hung looped over each wrist. Letting them slide to her elbows, she embraced Anna. It was halfhearted; like when people kiss 'at' each other, rather than actually touch lips. Anna stepped to my right and moving in close, she pulled my arm over her shoulders. This left me face to face with

Zen. We locked eyes and her irritation at Anna's maneuver was apparent.

"Why are you here, Stacy?" she asked, feigning as if she didn't know the situation.

I recognized the ploy and played along. Before Anna could respond to the first question, Zen said, "Why is it you are dressed this way? This black dress is for evening, yes?"

Anna chuckled and said, "Out late partying, haven't had a chance to change."

Zen gave a dry laugh and said, "I can understand that."

They laughed together for a few seconds, but the situation only grew more awkward. "And who is this?" she said, and held out her hand, limp wristed, as if I should kiss it. Clasping her fingertips, I gave a shallow nod and let them drop.

"This is Günter, he was my friend for the night. We are on our way to Zur Letzten."

Again, they laughed together, but it was derisive. Zen took a half step toward me and dropping her chin, she looked at me out of the top of her eyes as if deciding it was time to get down to business.

"Wie geht es dir, Günter?" she said, testing my German.

"Mir geht es gut, Danke!" I answered, giving her my best fake smile.

Anna wrapped an arm around my waist, putting her other hand on my chest. It was an action that clearly said, 'Don't touch—this one's mine.' She sneered at Zen and gave her an evil glare. Zen's cold eyes flitted back and forth between the two of us. I got the impression she was trying to decide what she should do, or worse yet, trying to keep us occupied while Giselle closed in for the kill. I subtly scanned the room for other threats, but detected none.

"Well, we should go now, we have a lunch," Anna said, and pulling my arm from her shoulder, she took my hand.

Zen set her bags down on the floor and stepped right up to Anna. Glaring down, she moved to clamp Anna's hips in her hands, and burying her face in blond curls, she whispered something that didn't make it to my ears. I clenched my teeth in preparation to intervene as I watched Zen crouch slightly in order to run the fingers of her right hand up and down Anna's thigh. The third time the hand came up, it took the hem of the black dress with it, and cupping Anna's left buttock, Zen said, "Ooooo... no panties! I could just eat you alive. Sooo… watch your hinter, sweet girl."

The last part came as a growl and giving Anna's derriere a quick slap, she turned to me. Rolling her lips back in a snarl, her eyes smoldered. I fought the urge to punch her in the nose, and maybe just hard enough to break it. That way she would have to go around with one of those nose casts for weeks after.

Zen's lips fell loose again, and just like it had never happened, she said, "Tschüss," and picking up her bags, she walked away.

I watched her go, and she glanced over her shoulder several times as if expecting us to pursue. She had a tough time navigating the stairs in her high-heeled boots and I hoped she would trip and fall.

She soon disappeared, only to reappear on the opposite side, going up. I watched her stumble in her urgency and I couldn't help but grin. Turning to Anna, I saw she was seething, her fists balled tight.

"Ooooo! I hate that bitch," she said.

I picked up the ruck and she surprised me by grabbing my hand and towing me toward the doors. "Ciarán, we must go. We must get out of here."

"But the train?"

She didn't reply and we exited the building on the Tiergarten side. Crossing the parking area and the surrounding plaza, we hastened into the trees. Finding a bench along a walkway, we sat down. From there, we had a good view of the station through the sparse shrubbery. Without taking my eyes from the entrance, I said, "What was that all about? Who is this Zen person?"

Anna jumped up, and throwing her hands into the air, she paced back and forth.

"Zen-Sation! Stupid bitch from Kreuzberg. She was supposed to be one of Giselle's girls, but instead, they turned into lovers. So… she became privileged."

Sitting down hard, she planted her elbows on her knees and put her face in her hands, covering her eyes.

"Scheisse! Why do I even give a fuck?"

"Giselle is lesbian?" I said, realizing too late, how stupid that sounded.

Opening the fingers on one hand, she looked at me with her brown eye. "No. She goes both ways. That woman is purely opportunist. She would never limit herself to any one thing or way of being."

Taking her hands from her face and sitting straight backed, she turned to me.

"That woman is like that lizard... is that correct? Lizard?"

I nodded and she continued.

"Yes, the... ummm... sha-mil-yoon."

"Chameleon," I corrected.

"Yes, yes, that's it. She changes colors constantly. She cannot be trusted."

Her elbows went back to her knees and her chin to her hands. Studying the pebbles at her feet, she went to pushing them around with the toe of her shoe.

"So, Zen was there that night at the club when we made our escape?"

"That is right, and I am positive at this very moment, they are discussing what happened at our meeting and are making plans on how they will capture us."

She leapt to her feet again, even more agitated. Then walking across the path, she pulled a branch aside to peer toward the station.

Getting up, I walked over to her and put my arms around her waist from behind. She sighed and leaned against me.

"Ciarán, I am so tired. Tired of all this running around like we are the criminals. Tired of..."

I quit listening when I saw blue BMW enter the parking area.

"Well, they have arrived," I said.

"Yes, so they have."

The car stopped on our side of the lot and Zen opened the back door to step out. Before she could, a small green and white police car rolled into the entrance and cruised past.

"Polizei," I heard Anna mutter, as Zen was yanked back in and the door pulled shut.

The BMW kept moving forward as the police parked their car a short distance away in the shade of the trees. Getting out, the two officers leaned against the front grill of the Volkswagen and lit cigarettes. Giselle's car made a quick U-turn and exited onto the street. Taking a right, it moved out of sight up Hardenburgstrasse.

"Tis time Anna, let's be off. I'm sure Giselle will want to stay away from the guard, so… would you agree now is the time to go back and catch that train?"

She put on her smiley face and said with enthusiasm, "I do."

I took her hand, and we strolled out of the hedgerow like two lovers. I could feel the eyes of the police upon us, so I gave them a friendly smile. One of them wolf-whistled at Anna, so she threw a grin their way and waggled a hand. They both waved back and one turned, saying something to the other. Then laughing loudly, they went back to smoking.

We picked up our pace as we moved across the now baking tarmac. Going inside, we read the schedule board and Anna turned to me with a look of dismay and said, "Ciarán, we've missed the train."

"Shite! What now? Is there another train on the way?"

Frustrated, I looked around at the people and glared at the ones who happened to be facing our way. I was in a 'fight picking' mood, so in order to avoid making our situation any worse, I closed my eyes and tried to think positive.

"The next S-Bahn is to Bismarckstrasse. We will go there, and get the underground to Haselhorst," Anna said.

Taking a deep breath, I opened my eyes and said, "Okay, so… where do we go to get on board?"

"Follow me."

I did and we did a fast walk up a flight of concrete stairs to another platform. The sound of the next inbound filled the station, and she sang out, "We are there," and grabbing my arm, she laughed in a glee-filled manner as if the whole day had been salvaged by the simple arrival of a train on schedule.

My tension dissolved away as it pulled to the platform. The doors opened, and we pushed our way in even before the passengers could disembark. They voiced their dislike for our behavior, but it didn't matter. We would soon be gone, and I was sure they would not want to linger to chastise us for our rudeness.

We found a vacant bench seat on the station side of the train. I sat down with my back to the end panel and stretched my left leg out along the seat with my right dangling off. Anna sat between my thighs, and leaning back against my chest, she pulled her knees up.

We both looked out the window as the doors slid shut and the train started to move. Anna gave me start when she abruptly dropped her knees and crossed one leg over the other. A voyeuristic teen boy had changed sides and came over to sit at my feet, repositioning himself for a better view up Anna's dress. We both scowled, and he turned away way, striking up a conversation with his mates.

Glancing back out the window, the adrenaline surged in upon seeing Eric standing at the top of the stairs. This time it was the real Eric, and he was inspecting the train cars as they went by. When I was sure he saw us, I waved and grinned.

This caught Anna's attention, and looking his way, she raised the middle finger on her left hand and held it against the glass. He'd been carrying a small duffle, and slamming it down hard on the concrete floor, he shook his fist at us.

A large, rough looking man in a short black leather jacket had been coming up the stairs and tripped over the duffle. An argument ensued and Eric grabbed the man by his jacket front. Giving him a shake, Eric then pushed him backwards toward the edge of the platform. The man did a wee bit of pushing of his own, and just as we were turning out of sight, I saw him grab Eric by the hair and give it a pull.

Chapter 24

"There Is No Need Like The Lack Of A Friend"

We rode to all the way to Bismarckstrasse with Anna's back to my chest. Her face, reflected in the window, showed her eyes closed with her lips soft and loose. I wished I could relax, but I was still coping with the adrenaline dump from seeing Eric. I felt grateful that Giselle and her mob were not hardened criminals. They could have killed me and dumped my body after they took Anna—but they didn't. Besides that, I'd seen no weapons other than a cricket bat. They could have shown guns and it would have been a whole different game.

I suspected Giselle's da, Roderick, was a more serious type. I was glad it wasn't he who was after us. In the portrait back at the rooms above the imbiss, his eyes were cold, the look on his face, chilling. This reinforced my supposition he might be involved in some criminal business of his own. I imagined Giselle's mother obediently standing by, subject to his every whim, and doing as commanded with no resistance. Giselle and her lot seemed to be no more than a subspecies of the criminal world. But I was still fearful of the outcome if they caught us. I suspected if we pushed back too hard, things would get worse. I had to prepare for the showdown I sensed was coming, by forcing myself into the proper frame of mind to deal with it.

The train soon pulled into the station, and I patted Anna's leg to rouse her. She had dozed off, and jumping up, she looked around and said, "We are there?"

"We are... but now we must get to the U-Bahn platform," I groaned out, feeling stiff from the ride.

She grabbed my hand and dragged me from the bench.

"Sorry," she said as I scrambled to find my feet. She brought my hand to her mouth and kissed my knuckles in an apologetic manner, but then jerked me forward as the doors hummed open.

As much as I didn't like all the jerking, I suppressed my annoyance and let her lead me down the stairs. The clock above the timetable told us we'd about two minutes to wait. We stopped between two large columns, trying to stay out of sight as a train pulled in going the opposite direction. Coming to a stop, the passengers piled out, and among them, a group of teenagers wearing red tee shirts. They trailed after a woman and a man with clipboards, who were chatting with each other but seemed indifferent to the gaggle that followed. One girl passed close to Anna with a large leather purse slung over her shoulder. A black bandana hung from an open zipper and Anna's hand darted out, grabbing the silky cloth. It slid out with no resistance, and the original owner continued without noticing.

"I need it more than her right now. I just hope it wasn't a gift... I would feel bad."

She folded it into a triangle, and placing it over her head, tied it under her hair at the back. It looked odd coupled with the evening dress, but at a distance, her bright blonde hair would be less noticeable and harder to pick out of a crowd. This gave me an idea and reaching into a pocket on my ruck, I pulled out my sunglasses. They were 'unisex' and I purchased them days before on Stuttgarter Platz in Charlottenburg. I handed them to Anna who made a face as she took them from me.

"Not my style... but let us see."

Pulling them out of the packaging, she put them on. “Lovely,” I said, as she studied herself in the reflective housing of the train map. “Ah no, too much, I don’t like them.” She handed them back, and I placed them upon my own nose before tossing the packaging in the bin.

The train soon arrived and we climbed aboard. We were the only ones in our car who had to stand on the way to Haselhorst and clinging to my strap, I felt exposed. The ride was uneventful though, and upon entering the Spandau district, I felt safer. We were a good distance from the Mitte now, and well out of Giselle’s territory.

Anna moved in close and said, “We need to watch for inspectors, if they catch us without a karte… uhhh… a ticket, we will have a different kind of trouble.”

I searched for an official person in uniform, but saw no one. “I don’t see anyone that looks like an inspector so… we are safe for the moment?”

She stood on her tiptoes so she could lower her voice even more, and said, “You won’t know they are here, until they have captured you… unless, they should catch someone next to you. They look and dress like everyone else.”

I did not think I could handle any more trouble, and this information only served to bring more worry. I was also hungry and seriously hoping Anna’s mother would allow us in, give us food, and offer a bed for the night.

“In Kürze erreichen wir den Bahnhof, Haselhorst. Dieser Zug hält, Ausstieg links,” a recorded message warbled out from the speakers, telling us we’d arrived, the train was stopping, and we were to exit left.

“Finally! This is where we get off, Ciarán.”

Putting an arm around my middle, she directed me to the exit. The train came to a halt, but the door didn’t open right away. Anna prodded the ‘OPEN’ button with her free hand, and the panels begrudgingly separated.

Stepping out onto the platform, we both got a start when a large man resembling Karl, appeared before us. With a quick intake of breath, Anna pulled me back and we stood gaping in disbelief. He stared back, his expression unchanging. Then saying something in what sounded like Russian, he pushed past us.

We scurried out of the train car and looking back over my shoulder, I watched him glare at us and say, "Idiot Fritz…"

"Sorry? What's that?" I said to him as the doors slid shut.

"He told us to get out of his way."

"Oh, so you speak Russian now do you?"

She grinned at me, and pulling the glasses from my face, she said, "No, but my mama does. When I was a child, she would say to me in Russian: Anna, get out of my way!" Giggling, she put the glasses back on my nose and then pinched the end of it.

Straightening them up, I asked, "So… what's with the 'Fritz' thing?"

"Don't worry about it Ciarán, be happy he thought you are German," she said, and towed me up a long, narrow stairway with so many right turns, I lost count.

When we arrived at the top, I found myself under a small metal canopy. Stopping for a few seconds, I looked around as Anna let go of my hand and walked away. I'd been there before. Thinking about having been this close to her mama's place was disheartening. But I pushed the thought away, drawing solace from the fact that I had persevered.

"We have to walk about a kilometer. Do you want a cola, or something to eat?" she asked, pointing to a small shack-like building.

Doing a double take, I recognized the Liberian's place where I'd asked questions and received threats for my trouble. Not wishing for a repeat, I said, "Uhhh… thanks darling—no. I'd rather have me a plate of peat out of McKinnon's bog back home."

"Okay… well, we can keep going then," she said, and taking my hand, we continued, passing close by the imbiss. As we did, a small group of people walked away after making their dubious purchases. This left a skinny man with long, greasy brown hair, seated on one of the two stools. He had a week's worth of beard growth on his face and his large nose bent a few degrees to the left as if it had been broken. His untucked work shirt was too large for him, and his faded blue jeans were covered in grime. He studied us intently, and when he realized I was looking, he turned his attention back to the beer bottle in his hand.

Glancing over my shoulder after crossing the street, I watched as the owner came forth from the inside. He said something to Mr. Greasy Hair, who brought his eyes back to us. The black man reached down and bringing up an old rotary style telephone, he set it on the plank serving as a counter. Mr. Greasy Hair removed what looked like a small piece of paper from his shirt pocket, and pushing the handset off, he dialed a number.

"Anna, I think we may have trouble."

"Why is that, Ciarán?"

When she looked at me, I jerked my head toward the imbiss. Glancing back, she sighed and scrunched up her face. "Scheisse. Let us walk faster," she said with aggravation. "I know the dark man owns the imbiss, he is from Liberia. But I don't know the other. I have never seen him around this neighborhood before. But I have been away for a while."

We hurried along the tree-lined streets of the borough, walking past many block long, multistoried buildings, each one identical to the next.

"What are these places?"

"Apartments for the laborers, ummm… the people who work at the factory across the Havel."

"Your ma lives close by, then?"

"Ja, but very far up that way at the end," she said, pointing.

My eyes kept straying behind me, expecting any moment to see the 'car of doom' come into sight. But the street remained clear. Anna seemed more concerned about reuniting with her mother than with whoever might be coming up behind us. We held hands as we hurried up the pavement. Her palm was sweating, and she kept looking at me as if she had something she wanted to say.

"What's on your mind, lass?" I said without looking at her. Out of the corner of my eye, I saw her look away and a chuckle escaped her mouth.

"Whatever do you mean?"

"You have something to say, I can tell."

Now I turned my face to her, and she squeezed my hand. "Ciarán, I am so nervous about seeing my mama. It has been such a long time and I am afraid how she will treat you. Part of the reason we argued was because I kept talking about Ciarán McKay. She said I should forget about you and pressed me to meet some nice German man, or perhaps someone with money who lived in Berlin. But not a person from a different country."

Just like that night back in Lafferty's, when Clare tried to influence me to do the same. It wasn't just Ireland where people felt this way. It seemed all the world feared some severe consequence for becoming intimate with a person outside of your own culture. There was supposed to be some logic in, 'Sticking to your own kind.' As I mulled it over, Anna asked, "What is wrong, Ciarán?"

"Why?"

"You are shaking your head like there was something troubling you."

I was not aware that I had. But looking at her, I knew there was no way I could let that narrow-minded way of thinking stand in our way.

"It was nothing... well, not true… sorry. I was thinking about somebody else who believed the same."

"Who was that? Somebody back in Ireland?" she said, looking even more worried. "It doesn't matter, tis in the past now. Besides, it would never bring me to feel any differently about you."

She started to say something, but thought better of it. Moving in close, she wrapped my left arm with her right and leaned against me as we walked. After a short distance, she took my hand again and moving it to her lips, she kissed it. It was becoming a regular thing, this hand kissing. I was not used to being held in such high regard, but I supposed I could get used to it.

We halted at the next corner, and as I was stepping into the narrow side street to cross, she grabbed my jumper and pulled me back. Throwing her a look of confusion, she gave me a halfhearted smile, her embarrassment clear. She pointed a finger down that narrow street and said, "That building down there, you see it? That is where we are going, the one with the roof colored, uh... red?"

I noticed the street ended in a 'T' intersection. Beyond that, another long building—except it, and the one on each side, shared red clay tile roofs instead of the typical brown. They had three floors instead four and appeared to have been built before the others. Their entries had elaborate front stoops instead of plain concrete slabs. There were slim ionic columns supporting small roofs, and decorative lattice enclosed the sides, offering support to tangles of English Ivy.

"The one at the end of the stras… street. Is where we… she lives... oh scheisse! I am so stressed," she said and embraced me, burying her face in the gap between my left arm and my chest. I hugged her and said, "It will be ok, Anna. It has to be done, so… let's be off and end this. Keep in mind, darling, I will be standing beside you the whole time."

She seemed to have forgotten all about Giselle and the consequences of capture. The thing is, she only had to fear a beating, a life of prostitution, and possible drug addiction. I had to worry about extermination. Now I was soon to meet the woman who raised

Anna from an infant, and I wondered how Jana could be scarier than the criminals who stalked us.

I felt prepared to meet the other significant person in Anna's life, and was happy that I would soon be able to decide for myself, what kind of a person she was. Not that I didn't believe Anna—I just needed the satisfaction of seeing with my own eyes.

Anna rotated in my embrace and faced toward the building where her mama lived. Pulling my arms tighter around her, she said, "I can't remember how many times I stood on this very corner, looking at my home… so very afraid to go there. The dark would soon drive me from the street, still holding onto a serious hope it would be the one night I had been afraid for no reason."

I kissed the top of her head and dropping my face down beside hers, I looked in the same direction and said, "Let us make tonight that night Anna. Leave your fear on this corner and go there knowing that nothing inside that apartment can hurt you."

She turned her face to me and we kissed.

"Just in case…" she mumbled.

I frowned as I watched her tears well up, and I said, "Just in case… what?"

"Just in case I am never allowed this moment again."

"Darling, let us go and get this over with. We have been too long in one place. We have to get off the street."

A strangled, "Okay," broke from her quivering lips, and she moved out of my hold. Stepping off the curb, she hesitated. It was my turn to tow her along, and taking her hand, I pulled her toward the building.

Arriving at the copper colored entry door, we found it secure and requiring a key. There was a call box, but Anna was reluctant to use it. The door soon opened though as an elderly woman exited holding a large shoulder bag. She must have recognized Anna because she smiled and said, "Hallo." But when she looked at me, her brow furrowed.

She held the door long enough for Anna, but stepped away afterwards to let it close on me. I turned to comment, but she hobbled away, mumbling something unintelligible. Anna hadn't noticed because her back was to us, so I let it pass, making a mental note to be more cautious around old German women holding doors. We moved into the entry hall and exchanged glances. Anna put on her 'stone face', trying to appear strong.

"Which way now?" I asked, still irritated about being attacked with the door.

"To the second floor," she whispered as if she didn't want to be detected, even though the sound of our feet were heavy on the thin carpet of the open stairwell. She gripped my hand with such intensity I thought she would crush it. Arriving at the top, we had to turn right to exit the landing. We now stood at the center of a corridor, facing four red doors evenly spaced along the far wall with their brass hardware gleaming in the dim light of the ceiling lamps.

"This is it," she said, pointing to the one in front of us. "Number 202—this number is stamped into my brain… I will never forget it."

I got that weird sensation of being watched as a tiny ray of light shot out of the viewing hole. I could see a shadow moving back and forth through the crack under the door. Whoever was on the other side was waiting for us to knock. Anna must have noticed as well and changed her grip on my hand, interlacing her fingers in mine.

We stepped to the door and with her free hand, she rapped hard with a knuckle. Someone pulled the latch and Anna slid over to the knob side of the door, pushing me behind her as she did. Holding my hand at her back now, I waited, looking over her shoulder. It was as if she was preparing to defend me.

Her behavior could have easily triggered a panic attack, so I calmed myself with the knowledge that it was simply the fear of the unknown. There was no real danger here for me. Anna would just have to cope with whatever demons had survived her childhood, and I needed to be in the proper state of mind to catch her if she fell.

Chapter 25

"When Mistrust Comes In – Love Goes Out"

The red metal panel swung open, revealing a woman about forty something years of age. She stood as tall as Anna, her light brown hair cut into a bob. Her face, an older version of Anna's, left no doubt it was her mama. Her eyes were green though, and her mouth appeared to be set in a permanent scowl. Anna pulled the bandana from her head and realizing I still sported the sunglasses, I took them off.

The woman startled me when she burst through the doorway and breaking into tears, took her daughter in a tight embrace.

"Oh Anna, meine Anna…"

"Guten Tag, Mama," Anna croaked out as if unable to take a breath.

I let go of her hand and stepped back, watching them hug and cry together, feeling like an intruder. After several minutes, I grew annoyed, wishing for an introduction. My hand strayed into my pocket looking for the Claddagh that wasn't there. With that option no longer available, I rubbed the small of Anna's back to give me something to do.

They soon separated, and the woman spoke in a language I did not know. She grabbed Anna's hand and pulled her inside. Taking a hard look at me, she said, "Proszę!" and motioned me in.

I didn't understand her word, but I knew hand signals, and it was not, "Go away." Before I could follow her instruction though, Anna grabbed my sleeve and drew me into what looked like the living room. The woman closed the door and peeked through the viewing hole as if checking for pursuers. Turning to face us, she rubbed her hands nervously on her thighs. She dressed in the fashion of a teenager, wearing tight, low cut blue jeans, and a pink, short-sleeved knit blouse with a scoop neck.

Her red 'push up' bra was visible, supporting a full bosom. The bottom of the shirt didn't quite meet her trousers and exposed her belly button. She wore several rings on her fingers, a gold necklace, and large delicate hoops at her ears. She smiled at us with the stained teeth of a chronic smoker, and I caught a whiff of coffee as she forced a heavy sigh.

"Mama, this is Ciarán. Ciarán, this is my mama, Jana."

Jana's hand darted out and took mine. I gave it a quick shake and let it go, watching as she pulled it back to hook a thumb in her waistband.

"Karen?" she said with an inquisitive expression.

"No mama, 'Kee-a-ran', C-I-A-R-AN." Anna said as Jana focused on her lips. "You remember mama, I told you before."

Anna sighed and looked down in disappointment. Her hands went to her hips, and she tapped a toe as if irritated.

"It's okay, not important," I said.

Jana was now squinting at me as if trying to understand my words, my accent not helping much. The language barrier would be an issue, and I didn't want to make it worse by arguing semantics.

Jana flew forward, words pouring from her mouth as she threw her arms around her daughter a second time. Pulling her face from Anna's shoulder, she kissed her on the lips and the tears came again. After a minute, she released her daughter and turning her face to me, smiled apologetically.

She hastened into the middle of the room and directed us to a cream-colored sectional along the back wall underneath a large, long window. We sat together at a glass tea table, Anna sandwiched between us. Her eyes never left her daughter's face as they conversed in German and what I sorted must be Polish. They talked for the longest time, Jana's right hand patting Anna's knee, the left one fluttering about. I heard my name mentioned more than once and each time, I could see Jana's eyes dart my way. Otherwise, I just sat and listened, feeling invisible.

Since I was not part of the conversation, I focused on the decor. There was a narrow archway in the far corner of the wall to my left, and I could see that it opened into a corridor. I suspected it led to the bedchambers and bath. In the far corner on the right, another archway showed a tiny kitchen. A small breakfast table sat in the living room to the openings left, and just passed it on my immediate right, a second, larger archway.

Through it, I could see a small, sunny room with a set of sliding glass doors on the outside wall, granting access to a balcony.

It was the library. Floor to ceiling shelves, overflowing with hardbound books, covered two of the walls. A small Fainting Couch, placed diagonally at the center, offered just enough room to squeeze past to grab a book. For dreary days or nighttime reading, a pole lamp stood at its head.

Jana also had a love for plants, because they were everywhere. Every corner held a large urn of exotic vegetation along with smaller pots placed upon tables and shelves. Portraits covered the walls, and for every small plant that sat upon a horizontal surface, there was a framed picture to go with it. They were mostly of Anna, seemingly arranged to chronicle the stages of her life.

I looked for an image of a man that could be her da, but I didn't find one. It only made sense that the person, whom Anna referred to as 'Der Böggel Mann', would not be adorning the walls of her mother's home.

Jana decorated in what I considered the modern German style—an overabundance of colors that clashed. One wall shade rivaled the other. The fabric of the chairs assaulted my eyes, and of course, none of the damaged items went unnoticed. A lower corner on the television's housing was broken open, revealing plastic gussets. There was the cracked leg on an end table, mended with wire and yellow glue, and the lack of glass in many of the portrait frames, a testimony to violence.

I imagined Anna as a child playing on the floor of this room with an ominous shadow hovering over her. An evil presence that cared nothing for the sanctity of innocence, or the sensitive nature of a child. It had been concerned only with itself, and in satiating its own twisted desires. Taking what it wanted, it left pain and suffering in its wake. Happiness had not lived here.

"Ciarán? Earth to Ciarán?"

"What? Oh… sorry. I was somewhere else. Yes, what is it?" I said, realizing the conversation had stopped and they were both staring at me.

"Herbata?" Jana said.

"Tea? She wants to know if you want tea."

I could see in her eyes I should answer yes and stammered out, "I'd be wanting that! Uh… ja, bitte."

Her mother stood up and moved across the room. We watched her walk toward the kitchen, her backside struggling to break free of its denim bonds. I met Anna's eyes, and she grinned at me, stifling a snicker. Jana's blue jeans were too small for her, and no matter how much she pulled and yanked at the waistband, she couldn't keep them from working their way down.

In her attempt to keep things covered, she accidentally hooked a finger in the waistband of her knickers and pulled them into view. Realizing that she'd exposed the lacey red fabric, she looked back over her shoulder at me, her expression more approval seeking than contrite. I turned away giving my attention to a nearby flower arrangement. When I looked back, Jana had disappeared into the kitchen where dishes rattled and cupboard doors squeaked open and banged shut.

"I hate it when she dresses like a teenager," Anna whispered.

"I suspect tis not easy to get old, she is just trying to keep her youth."

Jana, with a look of curiosity, popped in and out of the kitchen doorway as if she was trying to catch bits of our discussion. About the fifth time she stuck her head out, she said something in Polish and Anna translated.

"She wants to know if we would like cakes… ummm… biscuits?"

I didn't want to appear desperate, but I was famished. "Yes," I said, trying not to appear desperate as I nodded and grinned.

Jana smiled back, but didn't return to her task right away and stood for a minute, staring at me, a cardboard tube of Bahlsen biscuits in her hand. I got a weird feeling and looked at Anna, who threw a frown her mother's way and motioned with her head for Jana to get back to work.

Jana disappeared from sight and Anna hissed out a, "Oh Mein Gott."

"What is it now, lass?"

"Oh nothing, I will tell you later," she said, as Jana reentered the room carrying a tray with a kettle, cups, and biscuits. Setting it on the table, she returned to her seat, and they resumed their conversation.

I dived into the biscuits and consumed about a third of them before realizing I was making a pig of myself. I noticed the conversation had lulled and looking up at the two women, they grinned and giggled at me.

"Sorry, I'm starving."

Anna grinned and wiped what must have been crumbs from my chin. Jana raised her well-plucked eyebrows and said. “Czy miałeś swój obiad?”

“My mama wants to know if we’ve had our lunch.”

Turning back to Jana, she told her in German we’d not eaten since breakfast. Jana looked out of the window as if to gage the height of the sun. Turning back, she said in broken English, “I will make… soon.”

A surprised expression crossed Anna’s face. “Mama! You speak English.” Jana blushed and said, “Ein bisschen… ummm… ja, a little.”

We laughed together at this, and I felt we’d broken through a barrier. I also suspected that Anna was now fearful her mother had grasped the content of our conversation while she was in preparing the tea.

They kept on talking though, speaking in Polish as Jana asked question after question. I drank tea, ate biscuits, and watched their faces. Sometimes their tone got serious. Jana would occasionally gasp, “O Boże!” Then Anna’s voice would become insistent, as if begging her to be more sympathetic. Jana’s hand came forth in a motherly fashion and patted Anna on the knee. But then she cocked her head and lectured. Anna’s lip quivered, and the tears returned. She took her mama’s hand and amidst all the Polish, I heard ‘Ireland’.

Now it was Jana’s turn for tears, and she gave Anna a pained filled look. Switching to German, she said, “Nein, gehe nicht! Bleibe bitte in Berlin” she said, telling Anna to please stay in Berlin.

“Nein, nein, Ich gehe.” Anna said in a stern manner, telling her that the decision was final and she was going.

She let go of Jana’s hand and finding mine, held it instead. I put down my cup and placed my other hand on top of hers. Jana stared at them and her eyes glazed. She was looking, but not seeing.

"Hier ist es für mich zu gefährlich, ich muss gehen," Anna said, confirming the danger if she were to remain in Berlin. Not getting a response, she raised her voice and said, "Mama."

Jana snapped out of her trance and in a distant voice said, "Es gibt Gefahren?" She now questioned us about the threat. Anna nodded in a frantic manner and said, "Ja mama, ja."

The conversation went back to Polish and became heated. Anna took her hand from mine and leaning forward, grabbed her mama's upper arms with both hands. She held on as Jana attempted to pull away. Her tone became passionate, and I heard, 'Giselle'. Upon the mention of Roderick, fear came into Jana's face. The talk stopped in an abrupt fashion. Anna tilted her head and said, "Es tut mir leid, Mama… I am sorry."

Releasing her mother's arms, her hand came back to me. Jana tried to smile and as she did, more tears coursed down. Leaning forward she cupped Anna's face in her hands and gazed into it, communicating only with her eyes. When she let go, she stood and looked out of the window in a nervous manner. She must have realized the danger in having the drapery open after dark and pulling the cord, she lowered the blinds. Moving into the library, she shut the curtain in front of the balcony door, but pulled it open a crack and peered out for a minute. Coming back into the room, she stopped and looked at us, rubbing her hands up and down her thighs for the twentieth time.

"Mittegessen?" she said with a sad look.

Anna gave me a halfhearted smile and answered, "Yes, we could eat."

Jana moved back into the kitchen a second time. The ceiling light came on, and I heard the clicking of the knobs as she turned on the stove.

"Come with me," Anna said, and taking my hand, we moved through the narrow archway on the left. I glanced back at Jana, who was absorbed in her task and didn't bother to look our way. She'd gone to weeping, and I felt pity for her.

Anna turned on a ceiling lamp as we moved down a windowless, 'L' shaped corridor. Before taking a left down the shorter leg, we moved by a closed door on our right which I assumed was the bathroom. Just past the corner on the same wall, we approached another door, and tacked to its face, a white plastic nameplate. There were smiling flowers, bees and butterflies, scattered around 'ANNA' in large, pink letters. It didn't escape my attention that the doorknob had been smashed at one time and now hung loosely in its rosette.

Anna struggled to open it, and as I waited, I scrutinized another door at the end of the corridor. Jana's room. The woodwork showed signs of repair around the latch and heavy scuffmarks covered the bottom half of the panel.

After Anna got her door open, we went inside. It was a small, well-lit room, the décor more suitable for a young teen. Anna slammed the door and flung herself into my arms. We stood for a minute with only the sound of our breathing, and when she tilted her head back to look up into my face, we touched lips. She gave me a quick squeeze and turned away to open an armoire standing along the wall behind her. Pulling open a drawer at the bottom, she said, "This is my room as you can see. Everything is as it was, when I went away. I think my mama has touched nothing."

Looking around, I saw many posters of rock bands tacked to the walls. There were two medium sized bookcases full of books, a small television, and a stereo. There was a writing desk with pigeonholes at the back, coupled with an armless swivel chair, the only one in the room. A full-length mirror, cracked across the bottom half, hung on the back of the door. There was no real bed to speak of, just a linen cluttered mattress on the floor against the far wall. I cleared my throat and pointed.

She turned and her smile dissolved away as if my action brought an unwanted memory. “The bed was broke a long time ago. The mattress is good enough.”

She forced that husky laugh and said as an afterthought, “It doesn’t matter though… does it? After tonight, it can all go into den Müll… ummm… into the garbage.”

She turned back to her task, indicating that the subject was closed. Reaching into the drawer, she pulled out knickers, a matching bra and stockings.

After laying them on the desk, she tried to pull the dress off over her head. She had a difficult time of it, so I grabbed the hem and helped, her blonde curls bouncing as the garment came clear. She dropped it on the floor, and standing before me naked, I felt she was the epitome of beauty. I no longer had the fears and doubts that caused me to panic on the first day of our reunion. I now craved her.

She turned to take her lingerie from the desk and I focused on the small of her back and the curve of her bottom. Moving against her, I placed the palms of my hands flat against her warm belly. With my groin pressed tight against her backside, my passion flared. Dropping the blue bikini panties back on the desk, she flipped her hair aside as an invitation to kiss her neck. As I did, she sighed and said in a low seductive voice, “Do you wish to make love to me, Herr McKay?”

“I do, Miss Furtak.”

She rotated within my embrace, dragging her firm breasts across my chest. I watched her erect nipples go from a rosy red, to light pink, and back again. When I dropped my face to hers, she kissed me hard on the lips, the bulge in my trousers, now tight against her belly. Slipping a hand down between us, she rubbed slowly up and down. Then coming to an abrupt halt and breaking the embrace, said, “Sorry, I tease… we cannot make love now, not while my mama is awake.”

"Oh, what a shame… and with me in this state." I whimpered with mock disappointment.

She patted my erection through the denim and leaning down, consoled it like a child.

"So sorry, maybe soon, yes?" she said and kissing a fingertip, she touched it to my fly.

Coming back up, our eyes met and we gave each other a "Oh, well" kind of smile. She reached around behind and ran a hand over the desktop searching for the knickers. Finding them, she fought to keep her balance as she pulled them on. I could see they were a wee bit tight, and I suspected they were from a time before Ireland. She snapped the waistband with a finger and patted her stomach, chuckling as she did. Pivoting, she picked up the matching bra, and put it on. It too, was tight, and her breasts fought to escape, top and bottom. It was all too stimulating for me, and I turned away. Strolling about the room, I feigned an interest in all her memorabilia, trying to will my rock hard member back to a flaccid state.

When I arrived at the large window, I pulled back the faded orange curtain and studied the view. Anna's room was at the front of the building, and looking to the right, I could see the roadway ended about two blocks away at a park-like area. It bordered a wide canal coming off the Havel, with a large factory building looming up on the opposite shore. Peering the other direction, I could make out Gartenfelderstrasse in the distance and the place where we'd disembarked from the train.

Anna's activity caught my attention, and looking back, I saw she was now hopping around, trying to put a foot into a pair of black jeans as she bumped into things. I rushed to her aid and let her lean on me while she pulled them up.

"Thank you, my lover."

It surprised me to hear that come from someone else's mouth. Only Isleen ever used that phrase.

"Where did that come from?"

"What are you meaning?"

"I want to know why you said that."

She finished her task, and taking a step away, turned, and looked at me, perplexed.

"I don't know... it just popped into my head. Why? You don't like it?"

I smiled and moving to her, kissed her forehead. "Tis fine... just something Isleen used to say."

"So... you won't mind if I say it now?"

I stood there looking down into her face, her eyes wide open and questioning. I stroked her hair, thinking to myself what a lucky lad I was to have her.

"Tis okay, anytime you wish, just... not in front of your mama. I don't want her to know."

It took a few seconds for her to grasp the humor. She laughed and moved to the chair to put on her stockings. Afterwards, she took the light blue camisole shirt out of the armoire. It was the same one she'd been wearing the morning she left me standing alone on the high street of Ballyahmras.

"Are you remembering?" she said, a slight smile on her lips.

"I am," is all I said.

It seemed so long ago, and that we were such different people then. So much had happened since that day. Life seemed to be an out of control rollercoaster, with us barely hanging on. But Ireland was still insight—all we had to do was holdfast.

She pulled the shirt on and when her dressing was complete, she sat in the chair and pulled open the bottom drawer of the desk. Lifting out a small metal box, she flipped opened the lid. Inside there was a German passport, a mini travel guide and a roll of money wrapped with a rubber band. Taking them out, she laid them on the desk.

"I have a small amount of money here so I can help pay for my passage back to Ireland. That way, the burden is not all yours. I have kept it in this schuleblade… ummm… this drawer? Yes, drawer… for many years. I suppose if I will be in Ireland, I should practice good English, yes?"

"Or good Irish," I said and shrugged, "You're doing just fine lass… just fine." Reaching out, I caressed her cheek with a fingertip. "We should get that money changed to pounds, though. So… we might have to make a special stop."

"We can do it at the Stadtbahnhof, there is a, uh… kiosk? So, no problem. It should take only take a few minutes," she said and standing, stuffed the passport with the money into her pocket.

I could smell food cooking now. An exotic, spicy aroma filled the room and my mouth watered. "Let us go have food," she said and patted my arse as she stepped around me.

Jerking open the door, she motioned for me to exit. We returned to the living room and found Jana placing several steaming platters on the small table. After setting the last plate, she pointed to me and one of the chairs, "You sit," she said as she made her way back into the kitchen.

Pulling it out and wiping dust from the seat, I sat down. Anna sat down next to me, and as soon as we were settled, her mother leaned out of the door, and said, "Esst! Uhhh… eat!"

Anna growled at her in disapproval and passed me a small tray of something that looked like dumplings. "Pierogi," she whispered, "Very good. I love it." Taking some, I held the plate for her while she helped herself. Jana came out, sat down across from me, and ladled something else onto my plate. Anna leaned over and said into my ear, "Bigos—not so good." Jana made a face at her, sticking out her tongue, and looking back to me, she smirked.

"Silly girl, this one is," she said.

"You see, my mama has learned many new words in English. When I went away—she knew none of these."

Jana grinned and made a wee bow with her head. I gave her a thumbs-up and returned to my meal. They soon started another round of question and answer, leaving me to wish for silence as I ate. Focusing on the cuisine, I thought how different it was from what I was used to.

I presumed what sat before me were leftovers from an earlier meal. But I was too hungry to care. Jana was a good cook, and I hoped Anna would be too. Then, she could teach me. I now found myself anticipating something different on the menu back in Ireland. Something that wasn't fish & chips, or Irish Fry.

In the midst of savoring my meal, I felt what I thought was Anna's toe tracing a line down my shin. There was a lull in the discussion, and when I looked at her, I saw her attempting to spear a Pierogi with a fork. I grew uneasy and turned to make eye contact with Jana. She gave me a shy smile, batted her eyes, and the toe went away.

Scowling at her, I pulled my leg closer to my chair. I put my attention back on my plate and prepared for what may come next. Jana adjusted herself in her seat as if to give herself a longer reach and the toe returned, this time closer to my crotch. I looked back at Anna, who now gazed at me with a, 'What's the matter?' kind of expression. She didn't recognize the look of discomfort that I was trying to project, and giving me something of a seductive smile, brought her own foot into play.

At some point, the wandering toes made contact and everything came to an abrupt halt. Utensils clanked down on ceramic plates, and the two women locked eyes. Jana leaned back in her chair and Anna shot to her feet, knocking hers over backwards.

"Mutter! Was machst du?" she yelled, leaning on the edge of the table with both hands. The guilty party started to say something, but thought better of it. Caught in the act with no excuse, Jana would now have to weather the storm.

There was a heated exchange in Polish and Jana dropped her face down in submission. Anna continued to browbeat, and her mama still said nothing. When she couldn't take any more of what Anna was dishing out, she stood and took an empty platter into the kitchen.

Anna mumbled something to herself, and reaching over, wrenched the fork out of my hand. She helped me to my feet without regard to my protests and led me to her room. We stepped inside and she forced the door shut. I was still hungry and wanted to finish my food, but the look on Anna's face said, 'Shut your pie hole'.

"I am so sorry about that. She cannot help herself," she said, and leaning forward, put the side of her face against my chest, her hands going to the small of my back.

"Tis okay lass, I understand. She probably hasn't had a man for some time, hiagh?"

"Yes, but she may not have mine," she said with a growl.

Releasing me, she walked over and faced the door. After a few seconds of silence and a long intake of breath, she looked back, her eyes on fire.

"Stay here until I come to you," she ordered, and after a pause, she finished with, "No matter what you hear."

Exiting, she slammed the door, leaving me wishing for my food. I sat down in the chair and listened intently. The discussion started out low and grew louder with every statement. It never turned into a shouting match, but remained a loud, fast moving conversation. I sat contemplating a poster for a band called, Golden Earring, as the dialog between the two women came to an immediate halt.

Someone stomped down the hall, and then Anna burst in. Turning, she put one hand on the doorframe, the other on the knob, and leaning back out into the corridor, shouted "Gute Nacht!" Which sounded more like, "I hope you die in your sleep."

Banging the door shut, she spun around and threw herself onto the mattress. She ignored me as she lay on her stomach, chin in hands with elbows planted in the single pillow. She sulked for a few minutes before rolling over with her back against the wall.

"Come to me, Ciarán," she said, reaching out her hand.

Pushing the chair back to the desk, I stood and kicked off my shoes. Falling onto the sheets, I lay on my back with my hands behind my head. I wished for a pillow too, but I would wait until she cooled off before I asked.

Glancing over at her face, I saw the vulnerable child that she had become. No doubt, Jana had been pushing her buttons during their exchange, triggering old guilt. Anna placed her hand on my upper arm and I took it as an invitation to open dialogue.

"What did you say to your ma?"

She sniffed, and I noticed the moistness in her eyes as she said, "I told her to keep her hands off of you. That my love for you is serious, and it would be bad for her if she interfered."

"Anything else?"

"She did not like it. So in trying to hurt my feelings, she said she would like just one night with you to change my mind about Ciarán McKay. She believes she can show me you are just another untrustworthy man who follows his penis in trying to manipulate me. Now that she is very angry at me… she will try even harder. It is more like we are sisters, then mother and daughter. It seems we are always competing for something."

There came an odd kind of discomfort at being the point of contention between two women. Something I'd never experienced before. Anna must have seen it in my face because she cocked her head and gave me a curious look. Sliding her hand up to my head, she stroked my hair.

"I think she will not get her way because… I know you, Ciarán. I know how much you care about me. It makes me so very sad though that I have been away for so long, and still nothing has changed. She loves me, this I know… but has no idea how to show it properly. So, I cannot be with her. We will stay the night and will go away in the morning as we planned."

She slid against me and throwing her right arm over my stomach, she put her forehead against the side of my chest. I tried to fathom how hard this was for her. I equated it to my relationship with my da. There were issues between us that—unless he returned from the grave—would never be resolved. The weight of unfinished business lay heavy on my shoulders and now the only thing that gave me relief was being with Anna.

She brought me stability and a sense of balance. We worked well together. It was almost like that whole Identical Twin thing where I would start a sentence and she would finish it, saying exactly what I intended. If I were performing a task, she seemed to know how to help without taking over. She would give me credit for a job well done, compelling me to do the same. I felt so at ease when it was just the two of us. We fit together like pieces of a puzzle, and I liked who I was when with her. I didn't want to lose this thing we had, and I would do whatever was necessary to keep it. The offer of sex from someone else would never turn me away from Anna.

Jana was not a good parent. Yet back in Ireland, I saw many positive things about Anna that only a mother could have taught. She had a sense of what was right and took the proper action when necessary. As a negotiator, she had the ability to recognize the value of other people's ideas.

I also believed many of her mother's bad behaviors were a form of negative reinforcement. Teaching Anna how not to be. The approval seeking behavior, so apparent at the start of our relationship, now seemed to have waned to an acceptable level. The last few days had shown that her eagerness to please only existed with me, and mostly during intimate moments. She'd given me a degree of control over her life, and I knew the importance of respecting that. This was the trust that bound us.

She soon dozed off and her breathing grew heavy. I lay in the dark, listening to the clock on the desk tick away and voices from a talk show on the TV. The noise from the living room stopped and bare feet slapped into the hallway. A door shut and water ran for some time. Jana was showering.

The faucets squeaked off, and after about ten minutes, the toilet flushed and the door opened. Footsteps came slowly and stopped just outside. Jana didn't try to quiet her breathing, and the sound of it sent a chill up my spine. I was relieved when she moved away and her door opened and closed.

The wall between the rooms must have been parchment thin because I could hear the obvious sounds of bedsprings, a drawer opening, and a rummaging noise. Now there came a low buzzing accompanied by moaning. Realizing it could be only one thing, I covered my ears, trying to force myself into sleep. When that didn't work, I decided to go to the bath, hoping she would have completed her activity before my return. Standing, I padded across the room as Anna stirred and rolled to face the wall.

Chapter 26

"Tis For Her Own Good That The Cat Purrs"

I tried to open the door with as little noise as possible, but it took a great deal of force to loosen it from the jamb. Upon closing it, the doorknob rattled, causing me to cringe. Leaving it, I hurried to the bathroom and bolted its door to avoid any unwanted guests. Standing there in the dark, I just listened. After about a minute of not hearing any movement in the hallway, I turned on the light.

Waiting for my eyes to adjust, I pulled off my jumper to study my body in the mirror. I cursed Eric for the large purple and green bruise on my ribs. Would I avenge myself if I got the chance? No doubt, I hated the man for all the misery he'd caused.

Stepping to the toilet, I dropped my jeans, and directed a stream of urine into the bowl, all the while imagining Eric's face at the bottom. Grinning at the thought, I said to myself, "Pish on you Eric, and the rest of your lot."

I realized then, I was what my ma used to call, 'Over-tired', fretting about trivial things already past. When I finished, there came a reluctance to flush and make even more noise that would announce my business. Taking the risk, I pushed the lever and closed the lid. Pulling up my drawers, I stepped out of my trousers, my socks coming off with them. Grabbing everything, I rolled them all together in a ball. On my way out, I caught my face in the mirror.

My eyes were even more bloodshot than before. The stress was getting to me. We had to get out of here. I needed to be back in my own country. I needed Ireland.

Exiting the room, I forgot the light and stepping back, I flipped the switch. The door to Jana's room swung open at the same time and she appeared in the opening, back lit by a lamp somewhere in the room. It was as if she'd been waiting to ensnare me. I knew at that moment what a mouse must feel like when trapped with the cat poised for the kill.

She was dressed in a short, red, transparent gown, barely long enough to cover her backside. She wore nothing underneath. A mound of dark pubic hair was evident along with large brown nipples on sizable breasts. She leaned against the doorframe, her left hand high on the jamb. Tilting her face down, she looked at me out of the tops of her eyes, displaying a frightening, 'I want you!' grin. Shaking her wet hair back, she expressed something between a moan and a sigh, as her right hand rubbed a slow circle over her belly. I expected her to start purring at any moment and I shivered, wondering how I would get out of this one.

I decided to go back inside the bathroom, but Anna's door swung open, and she burst out. Now dressed in her own short, gauzy gown, the transparent white fabric showed that she was braless—but still sported her knickers. Walking to me, she took my hand and jerked me inside.

As she shut the door, she muttered loudly, "Hündin."

If I'd ever called my mother a bitch, there would have been a sound thrashing, no matter what my age. Yet my mother would never have behaved in a way to deserve it.

Rolling the chair back over to the desk, Anna turned away from me with arms crossed. I could see she was trying to calm herself, so I remained silent. She must have gotten up when I'd gone to the toilet, and disrobing, donned her nightgown. Anticipating her mother's reaction to me leaving the room, she had taken up a position by the door to sit watch.

I dropped my clothing on the floor and stood waiting for whatever may follow. She turned, and hooking a finger in the elastic band of my underwear, hauled me to the mattress. Falling backward, she pulled me with her. Her actions led me to believe that lovemaking would soon follow. Instead, she kissed me, pushed me off, and pulling up the top sheet, she rolled to face the wall.

"Sleep," she commanded. "My mother—pleasuring herself in her bed—has left me in no mood for sex. I am positive that we would have made much less noise together, then she does by herself. She wants you to know what she is doing. So… she tries to tempt you by being loud."

That was all she had to say. Sliding over to her, I put my chest up against her back, my left hand on her hip. She took it and pulled my arm around her waist. It was clear that she wanted the reassurance of knowing I would not leave her. So, I didn't resist. However, I wished she would at least relax her grip.

"You can relax now darling, I'm not going anywhere, except with you—back to Ireland."

She loosened her hold and murmured, "I am just so tired."

After a while, her breathing grew steady, and she snored that light purring snore of hers. I found it odd that she could just drift off like that.

It took much longer for me to find sleep. The light from outside invaded the room through the curtain, turning everything an eerie shade of orange. But it surprised me that a city of three million people could be so quiet. I strained to hear any noise that came from the street but there was only the ticking of the alarm clock—and Jana.

I lay awake, analyzing everything that had happened since we arrived. I concluded that it was a good thing for Anna to have removed herself from Jana's territory. Especially if this was the type of thing she'd been experiencing. There was no question that she knew how intimate Anna and I were. So, her attempts at seducing me were rather brazen, a near total disregard for Anna's feelings.

Closing my eyes, I visualized us back in my cottage in Ballyamhras and in the comfort of my bed. This calmed me, and as I drifted off to sleep, there came a realization that I was homesick for the first time in my life.

I soon fell to dreaming. The kind where I knew that I was, but couldn't do anything about it. I jerked awake to Anna rising from the bed, pulling the sheet off me as she went. Rolling onto my back, I watched her walk off the end of the mattress and face into the corner. Through sleep-filled eyes, I saw the clock read 2:43. Turning back, I found Anna swaying as if music played in her head. Fear formed in my gut and I said as quiet as I could, "Anna, darling?" I got no response.

"Are you okay, girl?" Still no answer.

Moving her right hand to the wall, she tried to grab onto something that wasn't there. Being unsuccessful, she dropped her arms to her sides and hung her head with a heavy sigh. After a moment, she jerked it up and in a low, pleading voice, said, "Mama? Mama, kommt Papa? Ich muss mich verstecken."

She was asking her mama if her da was coming, and telling her that she must hide. The room grew quiet again and I wanted to get out of the bed and go to her. But I knew she walked in her sleep. So, I supposed that would be the wrong thing to do.

"Okay, Okay," she said with another sigh as if defeated, and grabbing the hem of her gown, she pulled it off over her head. Letting it drop to the floor, she slid her knickers down to her knees and putting her hands high on the wall, she dropped her face toward the floor. A whimper escaped her mouth, and I fought to remain where I was, my nose numbing as my tears welled.

Her pelvis thrust forward as if violently forced from behind. She squealed in pain, and my tears rolled out hot onto my cheeks. I started to get to my feet, but she stopped, stood erect and after pulling her knickers up, she returned to the mattress.

When she arrived, I hissed, “Are you awake, lass? Anna darling, are you awake, girl?”

She stood as if catatonic at the foot of the bed, staring toward the window. In the glow of the outside lamp, I could see her eyes were open, but they weren’t seeing. Her Heterochromia enhanced the bizarreness of it all as her one blue eye shone more than her brown. It unsettled me, and I shuddered. After a moment, she got down on her knees and crawled back into bed, laying as she had before.

A glass prism hanging by a string near the window, rotated once around, casting a spectrum of colored light across her bare back. Feeling the chill of the room, I drew the bedclothes over us as she started to hum. I heard the same elusive tune at the hotel. It started out low, and increased in volume until it reached normal conversational tone.

After a few minutes, it subsided. I decided to bring it to her attention after waking. I lay there sorting different ways I could approach her on it without causing too much discomfort. I decided to be direct and deal with whatever came. Happy with my decision, I changed my focus to more pleasant memories and fell back into slumber.

Chapter 27

"The Longest Road Out, Is The Shortest Road Home"

A rustling noise brought me awake and I opened my eyes. Assaulted by the light, I closed them again and just lay listening. A drawer opened and shut, followed by the bang of the cupboard. I rolled to face the wall, my hand reaching for Anna. There was only empty space and I finally sorted that she was the one making all the noise.

Rolling back, I forced my eyelids open, shocked to find her now sitting next to me, cross-legged on the floor. She studied me over the top of a dirty, red rucksack perched in her lap. Her hair was wet, and she'd taken the time to apply light make-up.

"Hallo my lover..." she said, a glee-filled smile on her face.

"Good morning darling... what's the story?"

"We should be on our way, yes? Time to move on to my new life?"

I sat up and leaning across the bag, we kissed and I tasted her strawberry lip-gloss.

"Allow me to at least get dressed, will you? And... maybe we should have a breakfast?"

She scowled at me. "I don't want to look at my mama for too long and eating breakfast here... means I will have to. I have packed my ruck with all of my closes and I am ready to go."

"Where's your coat for winter? You will need one, you know."

She smiled and said, "To take it… would be too much. I will buy one in Ireland. You do have them there, if I remember correctly?"

I attempted to tousle her hair and she ducked back. "Don't! I have just washed it. It is in order now… so do not mess it."

I got to my feet and walked past her to my clothing. She seemed to be in a good mood and I had second thoughts about saying anything regarding her nighttime activity.

I pulled on my socks and trousers, and slipping my jumper on over my head, I stepped to the window. Opening the curtains all the way, I saw there wasn't a cloud in the sky. It would be a good day for travel and excitement grew in me as the prospect of returning home seemed more of a reality.

Hearing Anna get up, I looked over my shoulder to see her move to the chair and sit down. Realizing I was watching, she smiled in a sheepish manner, her hair now in her eyes.

"I almost forgot something," she said, pulling a shabby looking pocketbook from a pigeonhole at the back of the desk. Opening it up, she removed several photos, mostly the wallet-sized version. Laying them out on the desktop, she arranged them into rows.

Turning back to the window, I scanned the neighborhood. It seemed rather tranquil. People walked by on the street and I assumed they were all starting their morning routine as I tracked a man riding by on his bicycle. He passed a young woman, who was strolling up the block toward the busy boulevard. He called out to her, and she gave him a short wave. Walking on, she didn't get very far before being startled by something on her right.

That was when Mr. Greasy Hair appeared, stepping out of the shrubbery between two buildings. He now wore a black duster and carried what looked like a knit cap in his hand. I could see he was trying to talk to the young woman, but she wasn't interested and hurried away. Her rejection seemed to agitate him, and stepping up to the pavement, he peered in my direction.

I stepped back, a familiar knot forming under my breastbone. I wanted to say something to Anna, but I chose to keep it to myself. She didn't need to know just yet. Nothing would happen to us while we were inside. If I could get a little food in me and allow Anna to say her goodbye, I would tell her outside on the stairs.

I turned to see a vacant look on her face. In her trance-like state, she stared toward a poster showing 'The Bangles', an all-girl band from the early eighties. That's when a short verse slipped from her lips and realizing it was the 'mystery tune', I saw my chance to make the unknown, become known.

"Anna?" I said, but she didn't react.

Walking over, I crouched down in front of her. She still held the pocketbook in one hand and a photo in the other. Even though I was right in her face, it took a few seconds for her to realize it.

"Oh!" she said, and the pocketbook slipped from her fingers to bounce off the carpet. Looking embarrassed, she said, "Sorry, what?"

"You were out of it. Where were you off to?"

She frowned at the photo in her other hand, an image of her standing at the curb in front of Tegel airport, appearing as she did the first time I met her. She gave me a look of confusion as if she couldn't remember why she held it. Breaking into a grin, she said, "Sorry, I day dreamed."

"It was more like a trance or something, and you sang a song."

"Oh, did I?" she said, looking everywhere but at me.

"You did. You've also been humming it in your sleep."

I was getting irritated. I couldn't tell if she was being coy or not. She cupped my cheek as if she was aware, and sought to calm me.

"So… did it sound like this?" she asked, and proceeded to hum a few bars.

"It did. Please tell me the title before I go mad."

She laughed and stood up, forcing me to duck walk backwards a few steps. Moving to the bed, I sat down on the mattress and waited.

After setting the photo on the desk, she spun the chair around and sat on it backwards. Resting her chin on the top of her hands at the back, she beamed at me. I sorted that she was now ready to explain, but she bent, picked up the pocketbook, and tossed it across the room. It hit the wall and bounced into the rubbish bin.

Her activity was impulsive and unnecessary. She was procrastinating. So, I knew she was embarrassed. Bringing her attention back to me, she grinned, blushed and confirmed it when she said, “Sorry, this is embarrassing for me. This song… it is called, ‘Eternal Flame’, a song from the Bangles. I first heard it on the ummm… plane? The day I flew home from Ireland. I had cried all the way back to Germany, I was so sad. When I was able to translate the words, I related to it. It comforted me because I missed you so much. Anyway, I kind of got, uh… hooked, or… attached? Maybe… obsessed! That’s it! I memorized the words, and now sometimes… it just comes out. If what you say is true, and it is even coming in my sleep, then…”

She stopped talking and took a deep breath. I felt my agitation subside, and started to say something to fill the silence, but she spoke again.

“So it has become our song. I know that sounds silly, because it is so much like little girl’s behavior. So naïve. I found much comfort in it, though. Every day was an emotional one after my return. I think my friends must have gotten so sick of hearing about my wonderful year in Ireland.”

Another question was buzzing in my head like a mad hornet, but she started in again, and I squirmed with impatience.

“Now… I am thinking about the McGurks. I live for a year in their house and they treat you this way, even though it was my wish for them to help you come to me. They did not really care about my feelings. I asked them to give you my address so you could find me, and as you know, they denied you… even though they promised me.

They thought they knew what was best for me, and they were so wrong."

"Tis all in the past now darling, we can let it go. Now that the song mystery is cleared up… I have one more concern."

"There is more? Oh no, what now?"

"I don't know the best way to say it, so I will just say it… you were sleepwalking this morning and…"

She gasped and closed her eyes, "Oh Mein Gott… this is terrible, yes? I know that I did that in the past, but…" Opening her eyes, she gave me a pain filled look and finished with, "So, I walked this night?" Dropping her face in shame, I watched the red creep up her neck.

I explained to her what I'd seen. She looked up at me, her eyes now brimming with tears. "I do not think I have done this thing for a long time. It is because I am back in this place. Too many memories… none of them good." A tear rolled down and dripped onto her shirt.

"Please… I must apologize. Ciarán, I think I have made you afraid of me. I am…"

She didn't finish and looked away as she choked back a sob. Her statement shocked me. I wasn't so much afraid for myself as I was for her.

"Afraid? No Anna, don't trouble yourself with that."

Rising from the mattress, I put my hands under her arms and lifted her to her feet. She pushed the chair to the side with her foot and I wrapped my arms around her, whispering in her ear, "Don't be afraid for me, lass. This is what comes of a life with a man like your da. There is no need to ask for my forgiveness. We'll sort it out together, okay?"

I held her until I felt she'd had enough. Kissing the top of her head, I stepped back to watch her wipe at her eyes.

"Thank you. You are so kind to me. I think it will take some time to get used to someone being so nice to me… instead of exploding like a bomb and trying to punish me."

She picked up the stack of photos and walking to her ruck, she stuffed them into one of its pockets. I moved back to the window. Our stalker was nowhere in sight. I wanted to believe he'd given up, but it wasn't likely. Anna picked up her bag and moved to leave the room.

"Everything is okay out there, yes?"

I nodded and gave her a halfhearted grin. She tugged opened the door and we walked out. Her mother's room was open, so I expected to meet Jana in the living room. Exiting the hallway, I smelled coffee. Jana stood in the kitchen and upon seeing us, came out to put the kettle on the table.

"Morgan," she said, her tone glum.

"Morgan," Anna replied with indifference.

Dropping her ruck next to mine by the front door, she went to the table and sat down. "Guten Morgan," I said to Jana, who gave me no more than a glance as she returned to the kitchen. Anna poured a cup of coffee and pulled a bread roll from the plate. Cutting it open, she spread butter on the inside. I sat down across from her and pouring my tea, studied the array of food platters.

There were several different kinds of cold deli meats, a stack of bread rolls, and some cheese next to a pile of ancient looking sausages. I pointed them out to Anna and she snickered, rolling her eyes. Helping myself to a bread roll, I sliced it open and folded some meat inside.

Jana said something in Polish from the kitchen and Anna answered. Translating for me, she said, "My mama wants to know if we will leave soon. I told her—very soon."

It grew quiet in the kitchen and Jana burst out, wringing her hands and sobbing. She started to wail half way across the room. Running into the bathroom, she slammed the door. I glanced at Anna's "Oh, well!" expression, and looking past her, I saw the clock said it was half ten. Gulping down my food, I winced as the unchewed contents plowed down my esophagus.

"Anna, tis late. I didn't realize the time. We've slept too long."

With an annoying degree of nonchalance, she dunked her bread in her coffee and before she ate the last of it, said, "You mean—you have slept too long—Ciarán McKay. I had already stood up, cleaned myself, and was waiting."

I didn't want to make it an issue because we'd not agreed on a wake up time. She finished her coffee and standing, brushed the crumbs off as she walked to the rucksacks. Sitting down on the carpet, she pulled on her red high-tops. I finished my food and pushing back my chair, I went to the window and looked out into the courtyard.

Surrounded on all four sides by buildings, it had a decorative archway at every corner to allow access. Through the southwestern most opening, I could see the street and a small, clear plastic shelter used for a bus stop. There was movement inside and focusing, I could just make out our watcher standing behind graffiti-covered windows.

So, he had now crossed the street and taken up a position where he could view the window where I stood. I froze, hoping I was far enough away from the glass to avoid detection. I heard Anna call to her mama, so I turned and moved away. Going to where she was, I picked up my bag. She called out again in aggravation, and being so close, it startled me. I realized that seeing Mr. Greasy Hair, coupled with knowing we were going outside, had escalated my anxiety.

The door to the bath opened and Jana came sniveling into the living room. She stopped and stood rubbing her hands together as she looked back and forth between us. Her face was red from crying, and her nose ran as she tried to wipe it with a tissue. Anna walked to her and they embraced. Jana sobbed uncontrollably as she tried to pull Anna closer. I stood there, feeling like a voyeur.

Turning my focus to my shoes, I forced them on without untying them. I heard Anna sigh and I looked back to see her pry her mama's hands loose, and keeping a hold on them so Jana couldn't grab her, she kissed her mama on the cheek.

"Tschüss mama, Ich liebe dich," she said, saying goodbye and telling her that she loved her. Her mother said in broken English, "Please… come when it… when you are safe."

Jana surprised us by pushing past her daughter and stretching her arms out to me. I felt bad for her, and prepared for an embrace. But Anna stepped between us.

"Nein! Just a shake of hand."

Putting one arm around her mother's shoulders, she forced Jana's left hand down and grabbing her right, extended it out toward me.

"Anna, I think it will be…"

"No!" she said, an unusual sternness in her voice.

Grabbing my hand now, she brought it to Jana's.

"But Anna, she may be my mother by law, someday." Anna glared at me, her eyes stone cold. "Yes, and when that is… then you may. But not today, Ciarán."

Taking Jana's hand, I said as kindly as I could, "Ich wünsche dir alles Gute," telling her, I wished her the best. She seemed to understand and smiling at me for a second, she turned her face back to her daughter.

Anna grabbed our arms and pulled our hands apart. Then she picked up her ruck with one hand, and swinging the door open with the other, we made eye contact. She nodded toward the opening, but the abruptness of her action startled me and I froze. I'd been harboring a gnawing fear that Giselle and her thugs would be waiting in the corridor, just outside. But it was empty. So—we were still safe; for the time being.

Chapter 28

"If You Dig A Grave For Others…"

Anna grabbed me and towed me out as she went. "Danke schön!" I called back. Jana let the door close by itself and the last thing I saw were her hands going to her face. The latch clicked and as we stepped to the stairs, Jana began to wail. The hair stood up on the back of my neck. Startled, I grabbed Anna's arm, feeling her goosebumps rise.

"Quickly, Ciarán, we must get out before I… we must go, before I change my mind about her."

"Anna, there is something I must tell you before we go outside of this building."

"No, don't try to tell me what…"

"Anna!"

She stopped in the middle of the stairs and spun around. "What now, Ciarán? Can it not wait?" She was rubbing her hands together and when she realized I'd noticed, she stuck them in her trouser pockets.

"It cannot! I must talk about it—now!"

My tone was patriarchal, so of course, she chose to ignore it. Turning, she walked down to the bottom of the steps, slipping on her rucksack as she went. I did the same and hurried after her. Fearful she might walk out before I could warn her of the danger, I hooked a finger through a carabiner ring attached to her ruck and jerked her to a halt.

Her head fell back, and she growled at the ceiling. I released the ring, and stepping around in front of her, tried to make eye contact. She brought her face down, but kept her arms crossed, her eyes closed. Her mother's mournful noise continued and with tears leaking out, Anna sobbed once and said, "Please Ciarán, we must go out, I cannot stand to listen any longer."

"Then you must listen to me first," I said, grabbing her upper arms.

I looked hard into her face, trying to will her eyes open. When they did, I saw a profound sadness, and dropped my hands.

"Anna… they are waiting for us outside."

Her face changed from sad to fearful, and she wiped the wetness from her cheeks.

"Outside? Now?" Her panic filled tone echoed in the hallway and her eyes strayed toward the exit.

"I thought we would make it. I tried to make myself believe they would let us go."

She fell forward into my arms, burying her face in my chest.

"I'm sorry darling, but there is no time for this. We must steel ourselves and think of a solution. Perhaps there is a back door we can use?"

She groaned and pulled away without looking at my face. "This way," she said as she walked fast toward the other end of the hallway. I hurried after her, but she came to a halt and declared, "Scheisse! This just can't be happening."

Looking over her shoulder, my brain acknowledged the chain with the huge padlock, securing the back exit. There would be no escape that way. I anticipated a panic attack, but none came. Instead, I seemed to bypass the anxiety phase, and moved right into warrior mode. A good fight just might be in order.

I wasn't afraid of Mr. Greasy Hair or Eric. I believed I could take either of them—as long as there were no guns involved.

I grabbed Anna's hand and pulled her with me toward the front entrance.

"What will we do now, Ciarán?"

I didn't answer right away and she said, "Talk to me. I need to know what you are planning."

Arriving at the front door, I spun back and said, "We will fight them. We will find you another stick, and you can do to them, what you did to Karl."

A look of disbelief crossed her face and she said, "Ciarán, this is serious, they will murder us."

"No, they will murder me. They cannot kill their prize. You're too valuable to them. They might hurt you a wee bit, but they won't kill you."

I was growing angrier with every passing second, and a kind of a fever was taking hold. Rational thought had abandoned me, but I was okay with that. There would be no reasoning now. My primitive instincts were taking over, and I welcomed them. Releasing Anna's hand, I turned and scanned the street through the small window in the door. I was hoping to catch sight of our foe, but the angle was wrong.

"Ciarán please… We could just go back into my mama's and wait until dark."

"Anna, I've had enough. I am going out. I would like you to be with me, but if you wish, you can go back up the stairs. Your decision, darling… whatever you want."

I felt the coolness of the brass handle in my grip and I opened the door. Stepping out, I peered through the lattice. The man's legs were visible through the side of the clear plastic booth, his upper body hidden by the large route map plastered to its side. I moved down to the pavement and stopped, facing in his direction. He did the same.

We glared at each other over the length of one long building. A 'showdown' scene from a film called 'Once Upon a Time in the West' rolled across my mind's eyes. It was a three-hour long spaghetti western starring Charles Bronson and Henry Fonda. It had been one of my favorites.

Did real gunslingers felt as I did, dry mouthed, the bile rising into their throats and hands shaking as adrenalin coursed through their bodies? I needed to focus on my task, so I put it out all of my head and prepared to get physical. I had a case of tunnel vision and didn't notice Anna stepping up, to stand beside me.

"Is that him, Ciarán? Is that the man?" she said, startling me.

"Tis him, darling," I answered, trying to keep my voice calm.

I turned and putting a hand on the small of her back, I directed her across the narrow street to the corner. I wanted to test him, and when he did the same, we stopped. His goal was clear, he would block our path and keep us from going up to Gartenfelderstrasse. I wondered what he would do if we ran down the street to our right—I didn't have to wonder for long.

There came a squealing of tires and looking that way, we watched the blue BMW whip out from the curb. Anna grabbed my sleeve and blurted out, "Ciarán! It's Giselle… run!" With no time to think, I went with her as she turned and sprinted away, leading me to believe she was making for the apartment's front door. But she passed it by and continued north toward the canal. Glancing back, I saw Mr. Greasy Hair was in pursuit.

Fleeing was not supposed to be an option. We'd been running too much, and I wanted to face them and give them what they had coming. As we dashed away toward the end of the block, I looked for possible weapons, anything to swing fast and hard at an unprotected head.

There came a screech of tires and I looked again to see Mr. Greasy Hair bouncing off the grill of the BMW, as it rocked to a stop. It would have been hilarious, had the situation not been so dire.

I had to smile to myself though. Maybe this was why I couldn't take these people too seriously. The word, 'Losers' came to mind, and I chuckled out loud.

"What is it, Ciarán?" Anna asked as she huffed.

"They ran over the long haired man… I think by accident."

We both looked back to see Eric was out of the car now and dragging Giselle's spy from the street. Leaving him on the lawn, unmoving, Eric returned to the car. The unexpected accident would give us more time to decide our path. We picked up our pace and coming to the corner, we passed over the street into the park.

There was a narrow drive that ran down a short slope into the green area and curving right, it went for about three hundred meters past flowerbeds, benches, and small, ornamental trees, before it bent back to the roadway at the far end. A wide strip of grass bordered it on the canal side with a beach like area. There were small boats pulled up onto the sand, and a vacant snack shop.

"Can we hide in the trees?" Anna said, her huffing having changed to wheezing.

She was in pain. That made me wonder how I must have looked to her because she was in much better shape.

"We can, but not for long," I panted out.

Hurrying down the macadam of the drive, we broke left, and pushed our way into a wooded area. Hiding behind tree trunks, we stopped to catch our breath. The rattle of the BMW's diesel engine reached my ears and looking through the foliage, the dented grill came into sight at the intersection. They seemed to have lost track of us and were probably arguing about which direction they should move.

"Ciarán, there are boats… We could take a boat. Maybe we could lose them by sailing out into the Havel."

That same idea had been bouncing around inside my head. Yet I didn't think there was enough time to untie it and set the oars—if there were any oars.

"They'll catch sight of us if we move out of the trees. There's nothing to hide us between here and there."

"Jump in and swim… maybe?" she said.

"Too difficult. The current runs against us and we would have to swim upstream. Please… give me a minute to think. If we wait, perhaps they'll drive away," I said, still watching the car.

"Oooh, scheisse! It's the boats then," she said and broke into a run.

"Anna, no," I yelled, but it was too late, she was already on her way.

Her rucksack bounced as she sprinted out onto the roadway. She knew I would chase her if she ran, and having no choice, I went after her.

The hope I felt as the BMW started to make a left turn, dissolved away when it jerked to a stop. The engine raced and the rear tires spun and smoked. It swung back toward us and sped into the entrance, sliding around the curve as it rocketed our way.

I didn't notice that Anna had slowed, and I plowed into her, knocking her down. I watched in horror as she slid on her stomach in the loose rock. Bending over to help her up, she rolled onto her side, cursing and grabbing at her left knee.

The car slid to a halt a short distance away, peppering us with pea sized gravel. Anna sat up as I crouched beside her. Through the windshield, I saw Giselle sitting in the back seat, barking orders at Eric. She was pointing in our direction, but he just sat there studying us, the sun glinting off his dark glasses.

"Get up Anna, you must get up."

It was more of a plea then a command and I attempted to lift her up at the armpits. "No Ciarán, there is too much pain."

Blood was seeping from a large tear in the knee of her jeans and it was hard to tell how much damage there was.

Everything seemed to go into slow motion. The seconds ticked by like hours with Giselle's voice never ending. Eric's mouth moved, but I couldn't hear his words. His right hand left the wheel and soon reappeared with the cricket bat. Anna was weeping, but her face remained a mottled, mask of anger.

"What are we going to do Ciarán? He has that stick."

"I suppose now there will be a wee fight?"

The sound of more car engines filled my ears. A taxi pulled to the intersection, followed by a black Mercedes limousine. They stopped as if waiting for someone, and then the limo whipped around the taxi and roared into the park. Bouncing down the slope, it careened around the curve and halted centimeters shy of Giselle's bumper. The back door swung open and a very large, angry man climbed out.

"Oooh… it now gets worse. It is Roderick. We are all dead," Anna said.

Eric opened his door and got out, bat in hand. The larger man called out as if he were greeting a friend.

"Hey, Strichjunge."

There was a hint of evil glee in that deep voice, and he was not hiding the contempt he held for the barkeep. He strode right up to Eric, who now turned toward him and raised the bat, his action more as a defense than anything else. It didn't help. The big German, with the reflexes of a cat, snatched Eric's bat away with one hand and punched him in the stomach with the other.

I heard Giselle's scream as the blow lifted Eric off the ground. He fell into a heap and then tried to get to his feet, but without success. Roderick broke the handle portion of the bat off over his knee and tossed the pieces onto the lawn across the drive.

To help Eric realize how precious life was, Roderick picked him up by his shirtfront and punched him hard in the jaw. The ham-fisted blow sent Eric the way of his coveted stick. Landing on the grass, he sprawled out with a groan.

"Dussel," the big man said, and throwing his head back, he laughed loud and deep. It was as if the almost lifeless body collapsing on the ground was the most hilarious thing he'd ever seen.

He turned and looked at us, his eyes narrowing. Anna shuddered as I wrapped my arms around her shoulders. We waited for what was to come, but his attention was fleeting as he moved around to the side of the car where Giselle sat. She scrambled to get to the lock and there came a, 'Thunk!' as she set it.

She wasn't quick enough to get to the front door though, and grabbing the handle, Roderick flung it open. His actions were deliberate, cold-blooded and calculating. When he got the back door open, she screamed again, and we both winced as he jerked her out by her arm. She shot like a rocket through the opening and landed sprawling on the gravel.

"Nein Papa… Bitte Papa, bitte, please, no, please…"

"Oh? English now, ja? Okay then, hear my words bitch. You do not, take, MY AUTO!" he roared at the crown of her head as she got up onto her hands and knees, sobbing.

He grabbed her collar with one hand, and her decorative belt with the other, picking her up off the ground. Her arms flailed as he carried her to the limo, shouting, "Simon!" The driver jumped out and ran around the car to open the back door. Roderick flung her in and there came the unmistakable 'clonk' of her head hitting the window on the opposite side. He slammed the door shut and putting his head next to the drivers, he said something indiscernible. The chauffeur, without a second of delay, double-timed it back to his seat, and even before the door could have latched, the Mercedes backed away at a high rate of speed.

Had it not been for the noise of the moving car, I am sure we could have heard the obscenities Giselle was flinging the drivers way. The car soon crunched to a stop, and turning right, sped up the short incline, disappearing from sight. We were now left to the mercy of Roderick, our demise to be witnessed only by whoever drove the taxi parked back near the entrance.

The big man brushed off his suit and walked to the front of the blue sedan. Bending down, he examined the dent in the grill.

"Scheisse! Ich werde dich töten." he said with a hiss, saying he would kill her. Standing up, he turned our way and studied us. I was sure he was trying to decide if we were a threat. I got that 'trapped mouse' feeling again and I felt Anna's heart pounding through her back.

But instead of moving our way, he strolled to the driver side door and standing behind it, said, "Ihr solltet jetzt gehen, solange ihr noch könnt."

He raised his eyebrows as he exposed his perfect teeth, and imparting a wicked laugh, he squeezed into his car. Closing the door, he put it in gear and after rolling by us, he hit the gas, showering us with pea sized rocks and dust.

He exited at the other end of the park and as he drove by on the main road, he gave us a short blast on the horn as if sending a friendly goodbye. His humor was thinly veiled, and I knew it was based in cruelty and contempt. He was the kind of man who shook your hand with the right and stabbed you with the left. A typical, successful sociopath. This also explained Giselle's character with the utmost certainty, and again, I pitied her mother.

"He told us to go away while we are able," Anna said.

"No trouble a-tall. It's just what we are trying to do."

A wave of relief washed over me. Happy that we were still alive and that it was over. The only thing that stood between the train station and us—was how to get there. Anna didn't seem to realize that we were safe; unless she knew something I didn't. I sorted she would come around as soon as the shock wore off. I gave her a quick squeeze, and she closed her eyes, laying her head against me.

There came the crunch of wheels rolling slowly over the loose stone. Looking up, I saw the taxi moving our way. Anna raised her head when she felt me tense up. The vehicle looked familiar. The very second I recognized it as a Trabi, it came to a halt and a smiling Halim burst from the driver's seat.

"Hallo my Karen! Hallo my Stacy! You need ride? I have ride for you."

"Halim! Oh, I am so happy it is you," Anna said.

"Hallo, laddy, good to see you."

He screwed up his face and said, "Laddy? What is laddy? This is a good thing, yes?"

Anna tried to stand, so I helped her up. As I did, the skinny Turkish boy tilted the seat forward to allow us into the back. Walking over, he realized Anna's condition.

"Oh! You have a wound Frau Stacy, how did this happen?"

"Please call me Anna… that other person is gone now."

I glanced at Halim's face, watching his eyes move down Anna's form. I didn't like that he always looked at Anna like she was fresh meat, but there was a good chance he'd never been with a woman. So, I would go easy on him. Now was not the time to discuss it, he was an asset and we needed him. I supposed he was harmless enough, and I was confident he would do the right thing.

"Anna, we will carry you to the car."

"No, no, Ciarán, it is okay."

"No argument lass, you are hurt. Halim, please help."

We formed a cradle with our arms and lifted her from the ground. Carrying her to the car, I focused on Halim's face. His eyes moved to her bosom, and then traveled down to where her shirt had separated from her trousers, exposing her belly. He looked up and saw we both had eyes on him. He grinned with embarrassment, and jerking his head toward the car, said, "We are almost there."

We had difficulty getting her into the back seat, and after a few choice words, I got her laid out with her head against the window. Pulling the front seat back into place, I walked to where Eric lay, leaving Halim to get the rucksacks.

Giselle's punk was still breathing, and I noticed a small bare patch on the top of his head. The result of his altercation at the bahnhof. I looked for other wounds that would tell me he'd been bested that day at the Zoo station. I noticed his earring was missing and the lobe torn open. Blood covered the side of his jaw and his mascara was a mess.

The moment of truth had arrived—the opportunity to give him the boot and leave him with a little something to remind him of the time he messed with Ciarán McKay. I didn't feel right about it though, so I let it go. Roderick had doled out plenty, and leaving him to fend for himself, would be revenge enough.

"Eric! Are you feeling it lad?" I yelled, without response.

I prodded him with a toe and he moaned. This brought to mind that there was a wee bit of a mystery to solve. Crouching down, and keeping vigilant in the case I had to jump back, I picked up a small stick. Putting it to the back of his neck, I pushed away his dusty hair, exposing a blue 'G' and star at the hairline. Disappointment came when I saw it was small like everybody else's.

"Is he living, Karen? Does he breathe?" Halim shouted as he slammed the lid to the Trabi boot. Walking back to the car, I answered, "He'll live, but let's get out of here before he wakes up."

I slid into the front seat and Halim followed, both doors slamming at the same time. Anna groaned, and I looked back. She'd rolled down the window and lain her head on the sill. Throwing an arm over her eyes, a loud sigh escaped her lips.

"Go easy Halim and no fast driving."

"No problem. But Karen… where do we go?"

I thought for a minute, "Perhaps, back to Jana's?"

Anna pulled her arm from her face. "No! We are done there. Go to Zafer's," she commanded gruffly. "Besides, it is close to the bahnhof. That is where we are going anyway, yes?"

"I think that would be a mistake, darling. That would put us back in Giselle territory and I am done with that business."

"Ciarán, I want to change my jeans, and fix my knee. That is the best place, so… do not argue, please."

"It is okay," Halim interjected. "Roderick is sending Giselle off to her homeland. My homeland! She goes to Turkey. Zafer tells me Kutlay, Giselle's mother, is visiting family and wishes for her daughter to be there. So, Roderick makes her to go. He goes to Amsterdam after, for his own business. My friend, Zafer, has been allowed to use the rooms up the stairs. He is very happy about this, and tells me I may stay, also."

"Very well, but will they be off before we arrive?"

"I think they go to airport right away. To Tegel, to get a flight quickly. I do not think Giselle will be happy. I think it was her papa who packed her bag, and there is no time for her to put on makeup."

He laughed, and forced the stick shift forward, the gears gnashing. We moved out of the park, the car jerking and bouncing.

"Oh, sorry," he said and shifting into the correct gear, the vehicle's motion smoothed out.

"Halim, please," Anna bellowed. I glanced back and saw her scowling as she picked at the tear in her trouser knee.

"How is it?" I asked.

"It is OK, it is only the skin… I just want to be out of this Trabi. So, let us go."

Halim looked back at her, "You do not like my auto, Frau Stacy?" he asked, sounding hurt.

"I am sorry Halim, it is too small, and like I told you, you can call me Anna."

"So you are Anna now? Okay, I call you Anna," he said, his voice, almost inaudible as he turned his attention back to the street.

"… and you can call me Ciarán… not Karen."

"Oh! So you are not Karen now?" he said, looking confused and screwing up his face in the usual way.

"And I never was. Tis Kee-a-ran. C-I-A-R-A-N."

He smiled and pointed an index finger at the ceiling, “Ah! I see now, ‘Ciarán’. Okay, I see mistake.”

“By the way Anna…” I said, “What is Strichjunge? Roderick called Eric, Strichjunge."

Halim giggled as Anna said, “It is like ‘Rent Boy’ or ‘Whore Boy’. Eric sometimes had to work like me. So, if someone would come into the club who was interested in him, they could tell Giselle, and she would make a deal so he would have his own date.”

I shivered at the thought.

Chapter 29

"Patience Can Conquer Destiny…"

It was a quiet ride back to 111 Friedrichstrasse. Halim did his best to drive without jostling Anna. But because of his overzealous nature, he failed miserably. She soon removed her head from the window to keep from getting her brains bashed out on the frame. Pulling her knees up, she slid down to lay fully upon the seat.

The streets became familiar, and upon recognizing certain landmarks, I said to Halim, "Slowdown, go past the imbiss and let me take a look."

"Yes, okay Kar… Ciarán! You look for Roderick or Giselle, yes?"

Anna lifted her head and scanned the area. With tiredness in her voice she said, "Yes please, Halim, we need to be sure." Laying back down, she smiled and kissed at me. Then turning her face to the seatback, she mumbled, "I have such a headache. I need a bed… and some kind Irishman to rub my back?"

She rotated her head just enough to gaze at me out of the corner of her eye, and I said, "Well, you know darling, I would like that too."

"You need a kind Irishman to rub your back, too? We are short on those around here. Perhaps… Halim?"

Hearing his name, he said, “Sorry, what is that? What do you say?”

“Tis nothing. Anna is having some fun with us.” I said, as he looked in the mirror and grinned at her.

Passing the shop, I saw the door was open, and Zafer was doing business as usual.

“Turn onto Oranienburgerstrasse and go down toward the club.”

Halim nodded and sped up. Scanning the car park and other areas as we passed, I searched for the BMW.

“Halim, where does Roderick park his cars, when he is at home?”

“I do not know this. Maybe we ask Zafer?”

“It might be best if you park the taxi and we walk to Zafer’s when we get back around?”

“Yes, no problem. I will do this for my new friends.”

He was excited now, and it seemed the prospect of danger brought a much-needed change for him. A definite break from the humdrum life of driving a taxi.

“Okay, so Halim, take us up to the club, but turn right just before we get there.”

“No problem Ciarán, but are you sure you want to go to that place?”

“Just get close, I’ll stay low. Anna, we are driving by the club, so stay down.”

“I can do that… but I don’t think I can get much lower than I already am—unless I get down on the floor,” she said and snickered despite her pain.

As we approached, I leaned forward and studied the building. There was no activity, and the street was vacant of cars. But I got a start when I caught sight of someone sitting on the front steps, smoking.

“Turn right! Here, Halim, here!”

He wheeled the Trabi around the corner. I started to duck down, but before I did, I recognized Reeka as the subject of our concern. Halim waved, and she waved back in a frantic manner.

"What is wrong Ciarán?" Anna asked with worry in her voice.

"Nothing darling, Reeka was sitting out on the club steps is all."

"Oh, poor Reeka. I am wondering how she is."

"That girl looked good… very good," Halim said.

We rolled around the next corner and moved back toward Friedrichstrasse. I'd a much clearer view of the parking area behind the imbiss now, and saw no vehicles I could call familiar.

"I believe we are safe for the moment, Anna."

"Yes, good, but please… get me out of this car."

I glanced at Halim as he gazed at Anna in the rear view mirror. He made a face, sighed, and said, "Soon I drive Mercedes or BMW, like Roderick. You and Anna will come and drive with Halim, and I will see you happy in my car, yes?"

Anna didn't acknowledge his statement, and I sensed that she felt bad about what she'd said. I laid my hand on his shoulder as he stopped for the busy street.

"Thanks a million Halim… for all you have done for us."

He looked over at me, grinned, and clasped my upper arm for a few seconds, giving it a squeeze.

"I think we could be like brothers, you and me. You are good man, Ciarán."

Returning his hand to the wheel, he chugged around the corner and pulled to the curb, saying, "I will turn it off. Sometimes it try to leave without me."

Turning off the key, he released the clutch too soon. The car leapt forward and stopped with a jerk. Agitated, Anna snarled out a, "Scheisse."

Before she could chastise the young Turk, he exited the vehicle. Jogging to the imbiss, he disappeared inside. I waited, watching with my eyes glued to the shop entrance. He soon reappeared, this time with Zafer at his side. They both waved, and the older man motioned for us to come.

"Anna, they are saying come in."

I exited my door and leaning the seat forward, she attempted to climb out.

"You okay, darling? Need help?"

"No, I am okay. I am happy to get out of this small space."

She still struggled to get completely free of the Trabi. I saw the tear in her jeans was much larger now, but the scrape no longer bled. I sorted, a quick cleanup, a bandage, and a fresh pair of trousers and then off for the bahnhof.

"Here, let me help you, lass."

"No, I am ok. The pain is all in my head now," she said, managing a smile.

I wanted to joke about that, but thought better of it. Closing the door, we walked toward the imbiss.

"Anna! Ciarán! So happy to put my eyes on you again," Zafer said.

Standing on the walk now, he wiped his hands on his apron. When we got to him, he took Anna in an embrace, and without a word, she hugged him back. I glanced at Halim's face and saw the envy there. Releasing Anna, Zafer did the same with me, except he kissed both of my cheeks.

Stepping up into the doorway, I counted five men sitting on stools. They had no food or drink, so I suspected they'd come by to chat and pass the time of day. They resembled Zafer in appearance and were all about his age. I presumed they were his mates. He confirmed that when he said, "Okay, my friends, I close for a while. Come back in an hour, yes?"

They looked at him and then at each other with confusion on their faces. Talking fast amongst themselves in Turkish, they rose in unison and squeezed out the entryway as one. Talking with their hands as much as their mouths, they moved out onto the walk. Zafer moved to shut the doors, but Halim remained outside, one foot still on the pavement, the other on the bottom step. He looked like he wasn't sure if he should stay or go, and I could see the child in his face.

"Halim, come in. What are you doing? You think you are not welcome? Come in! Come in! I must close this door."

He smiled shyly at Zafer and hurried inside. The old man shut the door and turned, focusing on Anna.

"Come, your wound needs care."

He beckoned her with his hand and moved to push the curtain open at the back. We followed him through and watched him step to the cabinet above the lavatory. Turning to pull the drape, I watched Halim move to the counter and sit down on the stool closest to the door.

Zafer directed Anna to the single chair, and handing me a small box containing bandages, gauze, and a topical antiseptic, he said, "Take care of your woman, Ciarán. You know how to do this, yes?"

"I do," I said as I caught Anna's eyes closing, only to pop back open as she tried to stay awake.

"Very good," he said, and leaning in, he whispered, "She is very tired, yes?"

I grinned and he moved out, leaving the curtain open. I soon heard the water faucet, followed by the clanking of dishes and the low drone of conversation between him and Halim.

Crouching in front of Anna, I poked at the injury with a damp piece of gauze. She winced, and it was clear either she would have to remove the jeans or I would have to make the hole bigger than it was. She bent forward, and in a low voice, said with aggravation, "Just rip them Ciarán, they will become Kurze hosen, uuuh… shorts, very soon."

Leaning back, she looked up toward the ceiling and closed her eyes. I tore the pant leg open and finished swabbing. Once clean, I dabbed on some ointment, and put a large, adhesive backed bandage over the scrape.

"Ciarán, I want us to be on our way. I feel I cannot stay here. I need to look on a different landscape," she said, as if speaking to the ceiling.

"Very well, darling. But I have questions that need answering. So, let me talk with Zafer a wee bit, and then we'll say our goodbyes."

After tidying up our first-aid debris, we took ourselves back out into the dining room. Anna sat down on the stool at the opposite end of the counter from Halim, who was now drinking a coffee with a ridiculous grin on his face. Zafer's focus was on cleaning Demliks, those Turkish teapots with the double flumes. The one he held was a large ceramic elephant with a smaller elephant on its back, their noses acting as spouts, their tails, as handles. It had been the focus of their humor before we'd returned.

Zafer was facing the sink, making elephant like noises as he walked the Demlik through the air. He was so caught up in his performance that he hadn't noticed our arrival. Turning, he smiled sheepishly, his face turning a dark red. He brought his focus back to the sink, and I heard a low chuckle as he returned to his task.

I couldn't help but grin, as I moved up behind Anna and rubbed her shoulders. Her head lolled from side to side and letting out a wee moan, she caught Halim's attention. His smiling face changed to something akin to arousal as he tried to keep his focus on his cup.

"Halim," I shouted in a playful manner, and he almost jumped out of his skin.

"Yes, my friend?" he stuttered back, looking like a boy caught with his hand in the biscuit tin.

"I have to ask… how did Roderick know where to find Giselle and his car?"

He looked at Zafer and said, "You should ask that man. It was his plan to destroy that girl." Laughing, he pointed at Zafer, who glanced back at us and winked.

"It was not my idea to destroy the girl—only to destroy her business. After you left my place this last time, I decide that woman will cause no more misery to my friends, or me. So, when Roderick returns, he asks me, 'Zafer, where is my auto? Where is my BMW?' and I say to him, 'Oh, Roderick my friend, I think your lovely daughter has borrowed it for her pleasure riding.' So, he gets angry and tells me, 'Ask around Zafer, find out where she has taken it.' Then Stacy… I mean Anna, calls me from the bahnhof, do you remember?"

Anna nodded, and I leaned over the top of her head to look at her face. Her eyes were wide open now as she listened to his story, and she kissed at me before I pulled back.

"So, I know she is going to her mama's and then this Giselle calls my phone this morning and asks if Stacy is here. I tell her no. So, she says to me that her friend… Zen? I think it is…"

Anna blurted, "Yes, it was Zen that had a talk with us at the bahnhof. She must have known I was speaking with my mama."

"Yes! So, my niece tells me that Zen tells her, where it is, you had gone. So, Giselle is driving out to Spandau to collect you. A few minutes go by, and then this boy… this Halim! He comes for his morning Kahve, and while he is here, he talks about Anna and Ciarán."

I could see Halim was blushing. He saw I was aware and turned away like there was something of interest outside the window.

Zafer chuckled and continued. "So, he tells me he recognizes Anna from one year ago. This is before he breaks his first taxi."

Halim spun around on his stool and facing us, threw up his arms, saying, "It was Škoda 105. It was beautiful auto, and I did not break it! There was accident. A drunken man runs into me." Dropping his arms, he shook his head in disgust and sighed out, "That car, I love."

"So, anyway, this boy here…" Zafer said, and reaching over his new pastry shelf, tousled the younger man's hair. "He tells me he knows where Anna's home is because there are four times—maybe five, that he takes her and the mother home with his taxi. He confesses that he is loving this beautiful, bright haired girl." Zafer laughed and pointed at Anna, giving her an exaggerated wink.

Halim, now redder than before, jumped down from his stool and said, "Your rucksacks, they are still in my taxi, I get them." With that, he dashed from the imbiss, leaving the door wide open. Zafer laughed again, "He is, how you say… embarrassed, yes? So, Ciarán, Anna, I get this idea. I go up the stairs and find Roderick with Kutlay, in their kitchen. I tell them that their daughter calls me to say hello. She tells me she goes to Spandau and… oh, by the way, I have a boy in my shop who knows where she is going. So, Roderick he jumps up, and calls to his man, Simon, who is in his little room. He tells him to get the car and bring it to the front. Roderick comes with me down, and I show him Halim, who already knows my plan. My brother-by-law gives him one hundred marks and says to take him to his daughter—and his BMW."

Halim still had not returned, and I worried that in his humiliation, he'd taken off with our rucksacks. Zafer must have been thinking the same thing, and looking toward the open door, he mumbled, "Where is that boy?"

Dropping his towel in the sink, he walked over and looked out.

"Halim," he yelled out, and in his native tongue, said something, which the only word I knew was, 'rucksacks'.

Zafer returned, and as he walked behind the counter, he said, "Halim is talking to a girl. I think we know her."

I felt the fear creeping in, and I about came out of my own skin when Halim startled us by running in. He stopped to catch his breath and said, "Sorry, my friends, I get busy talking and forget."

Dumping the bags by our feet, we watched him back-up to his stool and slide on. I tensed and felt Anna do the same as a shadow fell across the open door, and with it came the scent of jasmine.

Chapter 30

"A Long Life, And Death In Ireland"

Reeka stepped in and with the meekness of a mouse, said, "Hallo." Anna and I'd been holding our breath. When we saw who it was, we let it out at the same time and shouted, "Reeka!"

Anna jumped up and ran to her. Slamming into each other, they embraced. The taller lass made eye contact with me over the top of Anna's head and grinned. Her hair was even shorter now and dyed blond. Instead of the bob, she now had a spikey pixie cut with all the tips dyed black. It exposed a small cut at the hairline in front, and a faint bruise showed on her cheek.

"Anna, where have you been? I was so afraid I would never see you alive again." Putting her face in Anna's, she smiled affectionately.

"Reeka, you have changed your hair, and what has happened to your face? Has someone struck you?"

"Oh, it is nothing. Eric was a little mad with me that night you ran away. He thinks I help you. I am now afraid he will come to me for more," she said, and looking around the room, smiled at everyone in a nervous fashion.

"You will not have to worry about that anymore," Anna said.

"Why is that? What has happened?"

Anna grabbed her hand and said, “I think Eric will not be hitting anyone for a long time. Besides that, we do not have jobs anymore.”

“Why do I have no job?” Reeka asked as she moved to sit down on the stool next to Halim, looking confused. She was dressed almost entirely in black with a long sleeved turtleneck over a miniskirt. She sported dark gray knee high boots and her jewelry was faded gold. Dropping her trendy, but worn shoulder bag on the floor, she rubbed at her cheek.

“Giselle is off to Turkey and may not be back for a long time,” I said.

“This is terrible… I will have no money.”

Spinning around toward the counter, Reeka put her elbows on the top and her cheeks in her hands. She flinched when she put too much pressure on the bruised area. Zafer poured a glass of sparkling water from a bottle and set it in front of her.

“Danke Zafer, you are too kind.” Sighing, she stared down into the bubbling liquid.

“You are welcome, and do not worry about a place to live, your room is owned by Roderick. It will be much time before he puts you out. I would find a new home before Giselle comes back, though. She may try to make you her slave again. Also, there is no reason you cannot keep all of your good customers for your own business.”

He placed the empty bottle on the lower prep counter and added, “You may now keep all of your money for yourself, yes?”

Reeka didn’t react, but I could tell she was thinking over her options. Anna, who’d been standing behind her, rubbed her friends back and said, “Reeka, you are free now, don’t you see? You may go where ever you want.”

Anna’s tone was soothing, and I saw the other lass close her eyes as if savoring the attention. A few minutes passed and Reeka crossed her arms on the counter in front of her glass. Raising her face with her eyes still closed, she said to the air, “I don’t know if I want to be free… maybe I cannot be free because it is better for me not to be.”

Anna wrapped her arms around her friend from behind, and tipping her head back to meet Anna's, she turned her face to me and said, "Besides, I do not have a Ciarán to come and rescue me."

I glanced at Zafer, who'd been looking at her in a thoughtful manner. He seemed confused and there was pity in his face. He must have felt me staring and his eyes met mine. Shrugging, he raised his bushy eyebrows. I expected words of wisdom, but none came. Anna leaned in and kissing Reeka on her uninjured cheek, she said, "I'm sorry," and walked back to me.

Since I'd taken her place on the stool, she turned and fell back into me, pulling my arms around her waist. Halim, who'd been sitting quietly at the end of the counter, was gazing with affection at Reeka. I saw him sniff at her and I almost snickered.

"Reeka, if I may be so bold, why do you now have the scent of Giselle?"

"Oh! You don't like it? I found the bottle in the club toilet. So, I thought I would take it. Giselle has many perfumes, and I wanted to try this one. She will not miss it."

"That smell will always remind me of Giselle, no matter where I go," Anna said.

"I am sorry, I did not believe I would meet anyone today who would know it."

"It's okay lass. I would rather remember Reeka when it finds my nose—not that other vile person."

"Agreed," Anna said, with Reeka looking our way and throwing us a grateful smile.

I laid the side of my head on the top of Anna's, looking toward Zafer, who was switching on a stereo cassette player. What sounded like traditional Middle-Eastern music poured out of the speaker and looking back toward Halim, I watched his head bob along with the beat.

"Anna, what has happened to your knee?" Reeka blurted.

Anna ran a finger over the bandage and looking back, said, "Oh, I fell, uh… I was running and Ciarán, uhhh… ran into me."

Reeka's face lit up as if she found pleasure in Anna's words and I questioned the logic of her response.

"Oh, I just remember… I have something for you," she said and I realized the expression was for something unrelated as she picked up her bag and reached inside.

She pulled out a familiar little box and held it perched on her palm in front of her face. Then smiling even bigger, her eyes opened wide, and she looked past it to us. Climbing down off the stool, she came over and presented it to Anna who squealed with delight. Taking the box, she opened it to show the Claddagh ring with its gold chain.

"Ciarán, Reeka has brought my ring. She has brought my Claddagh. Oh Reeka, I love you."

Kissing Reeka's cheek again, the other lass just blushed and returned to her seat.

"I think no one has ever loved me before," she said, her voice sounding sad.

"Thanks a million, Reeka," I said, giving her a wink.

"I must change my jeans now, Ciarán," Anna said, as she fixed the tiny chain around her neck. Then putting the box in her ruck, she lifted it up off the floor and went into the back room.

She whipped the curtain closed tight at the center, and I heard the drapery rings at the toilet sing, as they rode along the metal rod. Halim had zeroed in on Anna's departure, and slipping down from the stool, walked toward the back.

"Zafer, I need to make phone call. I use your phone for only one minute, okay?"

Suspicion rose in me, and glancing back, I saw the large gap where the curtain met the side of the doorway. When Anna slid it closed at the center, it had opened where it met the wall. Standing at the telephone would give the caller, a clear view to the toilet area, and that curtain sported a gap as well.

Halim seemed a helpless victim to his hormones. So, when he came abreast of me, I grabbed his arm.

"Halim," I said in a loud and stern manner.

He was so focused on his goal that I startled him out of his task induced daze, and stopping, he said, "Yes, Ciarán, what is it?" Still not looking at me, his gaze remained fixed on the gap in the curtain. He even tilted his head as if to get a better view.

I would not be too hard on him because of his interest in Anna. However, I was growing tired of it and felt compelled to redirect. Standing, I turned him back in the direction he'd come from, and like an obedient child, he did not resist. Putting my arm around his shoulder, he looked at me, his eyes asking, 'What is going on?' I took him to Reeka and said, "Halim, you know Reeka, right?"

"Yes, why?"

Reeka had been sipping on her water and running a finger back and forth across her cut. When I said her name, she stopped and looked around at us, her eyes showing concern.

"Huh?"

Halim looked at her and then me. "Yes Ciarán, I know this girl. We talk sometimes. It is strange that you ask me this."

Reeka smiled in a seductive way. "Yes, I know this boy," she said and rotated around to face us.

Opening her knees wide, she made us aware she still had not found her knickers. Halim's disposition changed instantly. He did nothing to hide his amazement as his eyes locked onto her undercarriage. She was not a proud lass, and it made me wonder how long she'd been in the business because she was so young.

"I would like for the two of you to become friends."

"But Ciarán, we are friends," Halim said, with Reeka giggling.

"Better friends, Halim—better friends," I said, and chuckling, directed him back to his stool.

"Talk to Reeka, lad. Let her know you are interested in the person that she is. Perhaps the two of you can work toward a more serious relationship."

Reeka's grin was just shy of wicked. She rotated further around to face him, a knee contacting his. I saw him tremble and gulp. I sorted what I believed in the beginning to be true. He'd yet to experience his first time.

Zafer stopped pulling bags of coffee from a large box and was now watching. "Oh Ciarán, you are such a matchmaker, no?"

He laughed loud and long as Anna came through the curtain.

"What is happening here?" she asked.

Zafer stopped laughing and said, "Your man is trying to matchmake these two young people." Bending back inside, he let go with another laugh that echoed inside the box.

"Ciarán is that true, you are trying to bring Halim to Reeka?" Anna said with mock concern.

She came to me and dropping her bag, draped her left arm around my neck. Halim blushed now and hung his head, portraying the vulnerable little boy. This behavior seemed to appeal to Reeka, and she ran a fingertip down one of his arms.

"Ciarán, can we be on our way now? I am ready to go."

Reeka took her attention away from Halim and put it on us.

"Anna, where do you go? My only friend is going away?"

"Oh Reeka, please, you know I must go to Ireland. I am sorry, but it is time. You now have a friend in Halim. I can see it. You will become good friends with this young man."

There was a calm sincerity in her voice, and Reeka's eyes soon brimmed with tears. She climbed down off her stool and moved to us. Anna came around in front of me and they embraced, their tears mingling. An idea came into my head and reaching into my pocket; I pulled out two hundred German marks. Reeka had complained that she had no money, and I'd promised that I would pay her back somehow for helping us escape.

After a minute or so, she pulled back so she could look into Anna's face and through her tears, she said, "Please, Anna, when you marry your man, call to me to come. Do not forget your friend Friedericka Stoltz, okay, please? I will want to see you again."

Releasing Anna, she came, and we embraced. She tried to kiss my lips, but I turned my head and all she got was my cheek. I kissed her's back, trying to avoid the bruise and finding her hand, I slipped the money into it. She tried to avoid taking it, but I held fast.

"What is this for?" she whispered in my ear.

"Tis a gift from Anna and me. Do you remember that night at the club? You said that I will owe you. Do you remember? Well, this is how we will repay you for your trouble. A gift. If it'd not been for you, we may never have escaped." I kissed her cheek again and added, "Thanks a million for being such a good friend to us. Now, maybe you should take this young fella out for lunch… or, something?"

I let her go, and she stepped back, her eyes questioning. Then like a light bulb had come on inside her head, she smiled so hard it made her eyes slant up at the corners.

"Oh! I understand. I am getting it. Yes, thank you so much."

She spun and going to Halim, took his hand and dragged him from his seat. He looked bewildered, but went with her. He stopped at just before exiting and pulling loose from Reeka, he came back.

"Anna, Ciarán, you go now?" he asked.

I smiled, looked at him, and said, "We do Halim."

Grabbing me by my upper arms, he gave them a light squeeze, and pulling me in, did the cheek-kissing thing. Stepping back, he shook my hand in a vigorous manner and said, "Thank you my brother, someday, we meet again." Turning to Zafer, he said something in Turkish, and Zafer responded in kind.

Walking to Anna, he opened his arms. Her first reaction was to grab his hands as if to hold him back.

"Please Anna, may I just… take you… embrace you? Yes, embrace you, one time?" he said, pleading.

"Okay, this one time," she said, rolling her eyes.

He took her into his arms and kissed her cheek. She was quick to peel his hands away as they migrated down her spine toward her backside.

"Okay, Halim that is enough. Thank you for all you have done for me… me and Ciarán."

He stepped back, but remained staring, as if he wanted to get in one last look. Reeka came and grabbed his hand, leading him outside.

"Tschüss," she said, and blew us a kiss.

"Goodbye, Reeka, goodbye, Halim." we called out together as they moved out of sight.

Anna picked up our bags and handing mine to me, she said, "Ciarán, it is also time for us to go to the bahnhof."

Zafer set down the trays he'd been washing, and coming around the counter, he wrapped his meaty arms around the both of us at the same time, and squeezed. Kissing Anna's cheek, he stepped back and took my right hand.

"Goodbye again my friends. I wish you great happiness."

He had trouble keeping his composure, and he hurried away to move behind the counter. He went to putting two of everything in the way of his Turkish cuisine inside a brown paper sack, followed by a large bottle of sparkling water. Handing it to us over the counter, he said, "You will need to eat. Have the döner sandwiches first, for they will be bad soonest."

A tear escaped from the corner of his eye as I took the bag, and he turned away, pulling up his apron to wipe his eyes.

"Go now, please, I do not want your eyes on me at this moment."

I looked at Anna who shrugged and took my hand.

"We should go, Ciarán... good bye Zafer," she said. He nodded his head several times but didn't turn back.

"Goodbye my friend." I added. He nodded again as a sob broke from his lips. Doing a fast walk into the sleeping room, he slipped out of sight through the curtain.

Anna led me out onto the steps, and setting the lock, I closed the door to give him a few moments of privacy.

A thin layer of overcast now darkened the day, but that didn't seem to dampen Anna's mood. She hummed as we strolled south toward Johannisstrasse. We soon passed the group of old men, who were returning to the imbiss.

They were having a lively discussion as they walked along. One of them quite animated, his hands fluttering about as he talked. All went quiet and their eyes locked on us as we moved by. I turned and saw they were still looking, so I waved. One of them raised a hand, and smiled, but the man next to him pulled his hand down and frowned. The guilty party just looked back at him and shrugged. Throwing an arm over his mates shoulder, they continued down the pavement.

We stopped to watch for a moment and when they arrived at the shop door and found it locked, a heated discussion ensued. Some walked in circles, throwing up their arms, while a couple others knocked on the windows, calling out to Zafer.

Laughing at the spectacle, we resumed our trek toward our destination. When we arrived at the corner where we were to turn west toward the station, Anna surprised me by releasing my hand and sprinting across the street.

"Come with me, Ciarán," she said, waving for me to follow as she trotted toward the Spree River bridge.

"What is it, lass?" I said. "This is where you turn to get the train… or am I mistaken?"

"There is something I wish to do first. Please Ciarán, I cannot leave Berlin without doing this one thing."

She was in such high spirits, I didn't want to do or say anything that might change that. So, I followed, and upon reaching her, I didn't resist as she playfully pushed me along the pavement that ran the length of the bridge.

"Slow down lass, no need to push."

"Sorry, I am desperate to do this. I have wanted too for so long and told myself that the day I returned to Ireland, would be that day."

Not knowing her secret, I was at a loss for words. She quit pushing and hurried by to stop at the apex of the bridge. When I arrived, she was standing, gazing at the water over the decorative railing. The breeze ruffled our hair as boats passed under our feet. People walked by in lively conversation, a few turning their heads to give us a look.

When the pavement cleared for a moment, Anna dropped her rucksack, kneeled down, and unzipped a pocket. Taking out those black plastic framed glasses, she stood, beaming at me, and then turning back to the railing, she launched them high into the air. I watched them arc through the sky and when they splashed into the muddy water, she shouted out, "Auf Wiedersehen altes Leben."

I knew this to mean, 'Good bye, old life' and I had to chuckle. An act of defiance. An action that symbolized that she was severing her bond to a life she no longer needed. She gazed at me, radiating a confidence that told me she believed in her heart that this was a sure thing.

Yet, there are no absolutes in life. I knew after an unpredictable amount of time, she would want to return. There would come a day when our bond would be tested. Homesickness would come knocking, and she would long for her homeland. You can take the girl out of Germany, but you can't take Germany out of the girl.

Grabbing the bags and throwing an arm around each other, we strolled, nonchalantly, back to the end of the bridge.

"Can we walk to the bahnhof," she asked. "It will be my last walk through Berlin before I go. Okay? We will be on the train for such a long time... please?"

"No trouble a-tall lass, tis not that far, anyway. Besides, tis not like I have anywhere else to go."

"I love you, Ciarán," she said in a way that made my heart expand within my chest.

"And I, you," I replied without hesitation.

Pulling her arm from my waist, she took my hand and swung it happily back and forth. We were soon meandering along the river. The sun emerged and the clouds retreated.

Its light pushed a well-defined line of shadow eastward across Berlin, illuminating the city as it passed. The Neo-Renaissance facade of the Lehrter Bahnhof soon appeared in the distance, basking in the glow. I felt a sudden pang of sadness with the realization that my time prowling this city was at an end. I didn't know, with any certainty, how soon I may come back—if ever.

"Are you okay Ciarán? Your face looks, ummm... funny?"

Anna's statement broke me out of my musing, and looking at her, I took in the sparkle of her eyes and felt the warmth of her hand. I smiled and said, "Ich bin gut, meine Liebe, Ich bin gut," confirming that I was fine. There came a thought as I looked into her joy-filled face and I wondered to myself: Who had actually rescued whom?

ABOUT THE AUTHOR

C.F. McDaeid is a full time fiction writer and poet who came with his family to the Midwest of the United States during his childhood years. While he grew up in the rolling hills that form the western banks of the Mississippi River, his interests in people, places, and genres are cosmopolitan in scope. His love for writing and telling stories come second only to family, followed by music, dogs, and nature. He has backpacked Ireland, Scotland, England, and the European continent to experience other cultures, as well as to make friends all over the world.

Made in the USA
Lexington, KY
12 May 2019